I0721781

SUICIDE STRAP

M.G. MARZEN

WORKBOOK PRESS LLC
187 E Warm Springs Rd,
Suite B285, Las Vegas, NV 89119, USA

Website: https://workbookpress.com/
Hotline: 1-888-818-4856
Email: admin@workbookpress.com

Ordering Information:
Quantity sales. Special discounts are available on quantity purchases by corporations, associations, and others. For details, contact the publisher at the address above.

ISBN-13:   978-1-954753-16-7 (Paperback Version)
                978-1-954753-17-4 (Digital Version)

REV. DATE: 12.02.2021

TABLE OF CONTENTS

07	Chapter 1
13	Chapter 2
17	Chapter 3
23	Chapter 4
27	Chapter 5
31	Chapter 6
34	Chapter 7
60	Chapter 8
78	Chapter 9
85	Chapter 10
96	Chapter 11
103	Chapter 12
111	Chapter 13
119	Chapter 14
122	Chapter 15
131	Chapter 16
135	Chapter 17
142	Chapter 18
147	Chapter 19
151	Chapter 20
162	Chapter 21
170	Chapter 22
175	Chapter 23
189	Chapter 24
203	Chapter 25
216	Chapter 26
228	Chapter 27
234	Chapter 28
241	Chapter 29
251	Chapter 30
257	Chapter 31
262	Chapter 32
272	Chapter 33

CHAPTER 1

He didn't believe it. He was actually cleaning Jennifer's pool naked as a jaybird. He meant it as a joke when she asked him to clean her pool. "Only if I can do it naked," was Mick's reply.

So here he was. He didn't believe he actually had the nerve to be scooping leaves out of the pool in all his freedom. Mick had already set up the automatic skimmer. It was traversing back and forth along the bottom of the pool. It was a beautiful day for this anyway—bright sun with a slight breeze.

Perspiration was forming on his arms and heat was building on his shoulder, which made him think to put on some sun block lotion. Better put some on his stand-out white butt cheeks too, he thought. How would he be able to sit down if he got sunburned there? Normally, he wouldn't be doing this in the buff, but the security fence was high enough to hide any unwanted viewers.

Mickey Swift was a well-built man, a handsome man, six feet tall, 200 pounds, full head of slightly graying hair, and ten years Jennifer's senior. Usually more reserved, he figured why not let all the inhibitions fly? He was starting to feel more comfortable about his nakedness. Let it all hang out, he thought, grinning to himself. Either his naturally excessive testosterone level or testiness wanted to find out what was going on. What did he have to lose?

Jennifer's home was a custom-built tri-level. The inside was decorated with an artist's flair. Pastel wall colorings: shown brightly with the light pouring through the sky light in the cathedral ceiling. The art deco furnishings in the living room showed off her style. The family room had the only couch, complete with fireplace, TV, and a jukebox. Her bedroom was complemented with a whirlpool bath.

Mick had been at the house many times before, sometimes socially, sometimes for maintenance work. It seemed to Mick that he just inherited the maintenance work when Jennifer bought the Golden Door Lounge, as Mick was doing the maintenance work for one of the old owners, Joe Segal.

Jennifer and Mick rebuilt everything when she took over: replaced the tile and the countertops, put new sinks and faucets in the restrooms, razed the bandstand and constructed it anew. They painted this and that, replaced the old ceiling tiles, repaired the heating and air-conditioning, and added new electric service. She really kept Mick busy there for awhile. All first class. Spared no expense. She turned that dark, dank bar into a posh, trendy lounge.

That was Jennifer's style. She was a self-made professional. Her other job required business suits by day, but when she dressed for the night out— wow! Her jet black hair showed off her pearly white smile like nothing else. Throw in a body that kills, and you really had something special. She was kind and generous, loved to party and have a good time. No wonder she was so popular. Just the type of woman Mick had always dreamed of having for his own. Except (!) for the rumor that she was gay.

That would explain why she had no boyfriend. Maybe she was a switch-hitter. Mick questioned himself, Why did she kiss me at her Christmas party? Why is she always so nice to me? Was that the reason Mick dared to clean the pool naked, to test the waters and find out what she really felt? Mick was not an exhibitionist by nature. Even though the sun felt good to him, his nerves were a bit on edge, gawking about from time to time to check and see if anyone was looking in, seeing him acting like a fool. Did Mick want to show the lighter side of himself? Did he appear too straight-laced and somber to attract her? Was this a test? So many questions, no answers. Mick's mind was racing with thoughts while he was methodically netting the leaves and debris out of the pool. Mick's mind distracted him so; it took his mind off his nakedness. Until, out of the corner of his eye, he saw Jennifer watching him out of the kitchen window.

He successfully ignored her gaze but he couldn't ignore the tingle and twitch in his groin, as he felt himself slowly starting to swell. Oh! No, not that it would be too embarrassing, but he couldn't walk around with a boner. Mick instantly felt his face start to blush. He always knew she would be coming out to sunbathe. Busted! Not actually, but for a minute he felt like a teenager going through puberty. Mick kept dipping the net in the pool, and the blush from his face dissipated with his riser. He grinned a sigh of relief.

Then he heard the patio doors slide open. Jennifer was standing on the threshold, pausing.

Mick could no longer ignore her gaze. "Hi," he said, looking at her. Then he had to turn as a mischievous smirk crept across his face. His groin started to grow again too. Oh no! Not this again! That's it. He threw the net aside and dove into the pool. Ah! Instant relief as the cold water surrounded his body, robbing it of the heat.

As Mick swam about cooling his jets, Jennifer made her way out to her lounge chair on the patio deck to sun herself. Mick swam to the edge of the pool where he had his trunks and towel within reach. He always had an emergency plan. If someone came by unannounced, he could dive in the pool and retrieve his trunks on the side. But now he was free of her gaze. Mick just climbed out of the pool and slipped his trunks on. Jennifer was stretched out on her lounge chair sunning, while Mick was thinking he's got to have rocks in his head for pulling such a stunt. And why was he so attracted to her in the first place? After all, if she really was gay, for sure they would have nothing in common.

She hadn't said a word to him yet, since she let him in that morning. Was she mad at him? Was she angry with him? Mick couldn't help thinking these things as he put away all pool cleaning equipment. She looked indifferent as she lay there sunning.

Finished with his work, Mick finally approached her on the patio deck. Before he said anything, she sat up with her business face on. "Would you like a beer?"

Mick said, "Sure."

"Well, help yourself. You know where they're at."

Just like that, as if his previous nakedness meant nothing. He did warn her, after all, but she acted as if it was nothing—completely indifferent. He turned to go to the kitchen and retrieve a beer, paused, and thought to ask, "Would you like one, too?"

She replied, "I'll have a diet cola, thank you."

Mick returned and sat on the picnic table bench near her, handed Jen the can of soda and said, "I should have asked you if you wanted some ice in a glass."

"No," she replied. "This will do, thanks. Mick, I do have more projects for you." She went on, "I need my laundry room painted and new shelves installed."

Mick said, "No problem. Can I do it naked?" He laughed with a grin. Pushing his luck, he thought.

"I really don't care how you do it, as long as the job gets done. What's with you anyway? Are you on a naked kick or something?"

"No," Mick answered. "I was just kidding. I guarantee you I would never paint naked anyway. Paint naked ladies, yes. But never paint naked. Too much splatter. Imagine how hard it would be to get cleaned up."

"Well," she said, "thanks for putting your swim suit back on. Heather is coming over. We're lovers, you know, and she would probably throw a fit if she saw you naked."

There it was, matter-of-factly speaking. Mick was disappointed, but not surprised. He popped the tab on his beer and gulped some down. Feeling a little flabbergasted, Mick would have loved to have been Heather's lover, too. What a waste of women. Feeling a little queer himself now, he couldn't figure out how he fit in here. Just to ease his uneasiness, he quickly changed the subject and said, "Beautiful day out here."

"Yes, it is," she said. "Look, Mick, let me explain something to you, so you don't get the wrong idea. I was raped once when I was only fifteen..."

She wasn't really raped, but she had been using that excuse for so long now to explain her sexuality, that she acted almost like she believed it was true.

"...so I have a hard time enjoying men, sexually speaking, so I also had a hard time when I was briefly married. I only did that because I thought if I had a baby, I would change. I was a little confused at the time. That was a long time ago, but I still miss being a mother. I've had my eye on you for awhile now, and I was wondering how you might feel about adoption?"

Mick's eyes popped open as he raised his brows in shock. Strangest thing anyone had ever asked him. Jennifer noticed the off-guard look on his face and interrupted before Mick could, or would, answer.

"Would you like another beer?" Her glorious smile returned to her inviting face.

"Sure." Mick tilted his head back and inhaled the rest of his first can of beer. This time Jennifer rose and went to the kitchen.

This left Mick perplexed. What was she driving at? He wondered. What an unusual day's conversation. Before he could gather all his thoughts, she returned.

"Here you go, Mick," she said as she handed him the beer. She settled back in her lounge chair. "Let's see now, where was I? You know I feel a little chatty today. Somehow you make me feel at ease. If you let me, I will talk your ear off. You will keep this conversation between us, won't you?"

"Of course I will, " Mick said.

"I thought so. I do like to keep my privacy. You were married once, weren't you?"

"Yeah."

"Well, can you tell me about it, Mick?"

"It was a shotgun marriage. I was only seventeen when I knocked her up. That's the kind of thing that happens when the little head does the thinking."

A sly smile sprouted across Jen's face. Mick could barely see her closed eyes through her sunglasses.

"Anyway," Mick continued, "it's hard on any relationship when one feels trapped, but I did the best I could. I think it was the financial pressures that did me in—as well as everything else. I've been divorced over fifteen years now, but I did my duty and got my children through college. Aside from the loneliness, I guess I enjoy my freedom. No more hassles or pressures. Is that what you want to know?"

"Yes."

As she lay on the lounge chair soaking up the sun's rays, Mick looked at her stillness, wondering if she was in some kind of trance, or, like a patient on a psychiatrist's couch. She hardly drank any of her soda, but Mick had worked up a thirst. He was almost finished with his second beer.

She started, "I have a proposition for you, Mick. I like your work and your company. If you think you can handle a Platonic relationship, I could offer you a position at the Golden Door, say, as an assistant manager. You will be well compensated, and a good-looking man like you should have no problem finding women to suit your needs."

Taken back a bit, Mick stammered his reply, "Ah, ah, sounds good to me, but I don't have any experience at it, or at least… ah… ah…"

Don't blow this opportunity, Mick thought. "Well, I was a soda jerk when I was a teenager." "Don't worry about it. I'll teach you everything you need to know. Most of all, I need honesty. Someone is ripping me off over there, and I need to find out who. I don't have the time… with my other job. You understand what I mean, Mick?"

"Yes, I do."

Talk about matter-of-factly speaking, her lips were the only parts of her body that moved during the whole conversation. She continued, "I've ordered security cameras. I would like you to install them for me. They should be delivered sometime this week. Can you handle that, Mick?"

"You bet."

Heather appeared at the patio doors.

"We're here!" she clamored as she bounded down the patio steps to the pool, stripping her top off and hopping out of her shorts on the way. Her bikini revealed a luscious body, but, before Mick could fully appreciate the view, she dove in the pool and started swimming laps.

Debbie and Jackie followed more casually. They were all waitresses from the Golden Door. Mick crushed his can in hand as a signal to break off the conversation, and he got up to retrieve another beer.

Mick knew all the girls—a really fun group, with Heather being the most outlandish. Never had he witnessed anyone with so much energy. Her moniker at the bar was "Ping-Pong" for the way she bounced back and forth behind the bar, serving her customers. If she would wear leotards back there, she could pass for an aerobic fitness instructor. Debbie and Jackie were both divorced mothers—really nice people, hard working, loved their jobs. Jennifer rose to join them at the poolside table and chairs.

Mick returned with beer in hand. He stayed on the deck; half leaning on the railing, watching Heather swim her laps. The women were chatting. Mick started to feel out of sorts, but he still had some questions for Jennifer. Maybe it would be best if he just left, and talked to her later.

Finishing his beer, he moseyed down to where the women were. They were talking about things at work, so Mick just excused himself and said, "Jen, I'm going to leave now, and I was wondering what time you wanted me to start."

She paused to think, so Mick added, "Monday?"

"Yes, that will be fine. Eight A.M. sharp."

Mick smiled at the girls and said, "How's it going?"

"Fine," they replied in unison. Mick gathered the rest of his clothes and towel, then left.

As soon as Mick left, Heather was out of the pool asking Jennifer, "Is he going to do it?"

"I don't know yet. I didn't get that far with him, but I believe I could talk him into anything. You should have been here this morning. He was cleaning the pool in the nude."

"Nooooo, you're kidding!" Heather quipped.

"No, really. He's got a nice-looking ass, too!"

They all laughed giddily.

CHAPTER 2

The phone rang at the police station. It was Mayor Quibly asking for the chief, Jake Weasley. "Jake," the mayor bellowed, "I just got off the phone with the state's attorney. He told me the City of Griffith was awarded a grant. We need this money—with the mills going bankrupt and all. I expect a shortfall in revenues this year. I want you to instruct your men to start writing citations for seatbelt infractions. Also notify them that the D.U.I. limits were lowered from .10 to .08. I want you to concentrate on the thru-traffic on Ridge Road and by that dyke bar down there… I've been getting too many complaints about those fuckin' faggots. Naturally, use your discretion with the locals. I'll send you the proper notices as soon as I can. Got it, Jake?"

"Yes, sir!"

Click! The phone went dead.

"Sheeeee-it!" Jake murmured. He told the mayor before that he had his informants in tight in the joint, keeping an eye on things for him, and that it's a sports bar not a fag joint. What in hell's tarnation is up the mayor's ass now? How can he be getting complaints? Never had any before when he was half-owner of the bar. Then it was different. "Give 'em a ride home in the squad car if they're too drunk to drive," he used to say.

"Marilyn!" Jake called out to his dispatcher. "Make a note to all officers. Meeting tomorrow. Topic: seatbelt violations. And D.U.I. limits were lowered to .08. Thank you. That is all."

Griffith is an iron workers' town, middle class, neat and tidy, with scattered Cape Cod and ranch houses, businesses throughout, industrial tracts, rural farms, and still plenty of room to grow. Mayor John Quibly was a regular Boss Hog, rotundly built, flashy smile, and sticking his fingers in every pie he could find.

Chief Jake Weasley had always been a cop, ever since he graduated high school. He rose through the ranks fast. He had the right political connections. Besides, at 6-foot, 4-inches and 250 pounds, nobody messed with Big Jake—an iron man in an iron-man's town.

Mick was already drinking coffee when Jennifer walked in the bar— 8:00 A.M. on the dime. She didn't say anything, just kept walking through the kitchen to the office. Betty, the cook, was slinging eggs and pancakes. Jackie was tending bar. Customers were scattered throughout.

Mick was contemplating ordering breakfast as he waited for Jen's instructions. Jackie came over with a fresh pot of coffee and refilled Mick's cup.

"Are you going to order anything this morning?" she asked.

"Yeah. You talked me into it. Two scrambled, double bacon, and grilled onions with the hashbrowns."

She took out her pen and pad and started to write. "What kind of toast—white, rye, or whole wheat?"

"Rye," Mick said.

Mick was sipping his coffee and watching the morning news when Jim the painter came in and sat down next to him. Regulars get auto-service. Jackie knew exactly what he wanted. Jim likes his coffee piping hot, so she just poured him a cup, put it in the microwave and nuked it, calling in to the kitchen, "Gimme a 'painter's omelet'" (which is a veggie omelet with green peppers, onions, mushrooms, and cheese).

Jim and Mick exchanged good-morning pleasantries, and then Jim inquired, "What's new in the news? Same ole' same ole'—more kids killing kids and more politicians getting busted for swindling public funds?"

Mick interjected, "Did you get that light for the church yet?" Mick offered to install it free of charge. He didn't do that often, but it was for the church, after all.

"No," Jim said. "They haven't made up their mind what type they want."

Mick's breakfast came first. He scooped up the scrambled eggs and put them between the rye toast and ate it sandwich-style. He peppered his eggs and ate them, saving the bacon for last. Neat and orderly, one thing at a time is the way he always ate. When Jim finished his breakfast, he left his money on the bar and was off with a "see ya's!"

Jennifer finally came out. She was probably counting last night's receipts, Mick thought. She was wearing a dark blue pinstripe business suit. Her dark hair had a wet, slick look to it, all pulled back into a ponytail. The bar lighting made it shimmer like a satin sheet. Her dark red lipstick had a sheen to it, too. "Looking good enough to eat" crept into Mick's head.

"Good morning," she said.

"Hi," Mick replied.

The breakfast crowd was winding down, allowing Jackie to come over without being called.

"Jackie," Jen said, "show Mick the ropes—how to count the drawers, change the barrels, inventory, stock… everything. And, Mick, if you could check the beer coolers? There was a note on my desk about excess water or something. Now, Mick, I want you to learn the operation from Jackie in the mornings, but I need you to watch the operation at night—something like eight-to-noon and then ten-to-close all week. Here's an advance on your salary that I'll talk to you about later when I have more time."

She laid out 200 dollars on the counter and said, "Everything clear?"

Mick and Jackie nodded yes.

"Well, I've got to run. Bye." She spun on her heels and was gone.

Jackie said, "Finish your coffee, Mick. I'll be right with you."

Mick saw two guys at the other end of the bar, flagging her. Mick picked up the TV remote and switched to the stock market report station.

Blast it anyway, another "down" day. What's wrong with this market anyway? He questioned himself. At least he could get some solace from watching Maria, his dream lover, and there was probably a couple million others dreaming of her, too.

Jackie came back as Mick was finishing his coffee.

"Where do you want to start?" he queried.

"Well, let's start with the banks. Everybody starts with fifty dollars in their drawer—one ten, four fives, ten ones, and a roll of quarters. I only use two registers on days. They use all three at night. You know where the liquor room is. Once a month I count all the bottles and log it in this notebook. The beer driver comes twice a week, and I log everything in this notebook. Wait a minute."

The guys were flagging her for more beer. This time Jackie also gave them ten dollars worth of Crisscross pull-tabs. She rang up the drinks on the register and slipped the money for the pull-tabs into a slot in the Formica countertop for a container underneath.

Jackie was a good-looking woman, even if a little plump. She was well-proportioned, like mothers sometimes are. Mick had danced with her before at the Golden Door. It was one of those nights, either a Friday or Saturday, when the live bands play. Mick often came to the bar as a customer just to hear the bands play. If it wasn't for the age difference, Mick would have hit on her. It was a weird feeling that stopped him. But if she would have hit on him, he would have been all for it.

Jackie came back to the counter where Mick was standing, and was going to explain to him how the pull-tabs when… "Yahoo!" was hollered out by one of the patrons. When Mick looked, the two guys were "high fiving" each other.

"Looks like they got a winner," Mick said.

She turned around and went back to cash their winning ticket.

Mick never played the pull-tabs. Odds were against you, he knew. Not that he didn't like to gamble; because he did. Jackie excused herself as she squeezed by Mick. She had to go back to the office to get the money to pay off a one-hundred-dollar winner, as there wasn't enough money in the till yet to pay out that much.

While she was doing that, Mick went over to the beer cooler and checked on the excess water complaint. Sure enough: standing water in the bottom of the cooler. The evaporator drain appeared to be clogged. As soon as Jackie came back, he planned on getting his tools from the trunk of his car and make the repair.

Jackie came back with the money, paid off the guys; they guzzled down their beers and left. She showed Mick the winning ticket, tore it up, and threw it into the garbage can. Mick thought nothing of it until Jackie said, "Boy, those guys are lucky. They seem to win a lot."

The morning rush was over and the bar was now empty—just Mick, Jackie, and Betty. While Mick was repairing the drain, Jackie and Betty were conversing in the corner. They were laughing heartily about something. Mick wanted to finish the drain job before the lunch crowd and the regulars started pouring in. Such was the business at the Golden Door.

CHAPTER 3

Monday night was pool tournament night. Mick thought to sign up, even if that meant starting his shift early. If he paced his drinking right, he knew he could last until closing time. Besides, if Jennifer came in after work, he had some questions for her.

Jack was running the pool tournament. He was a big man—sometimes bartender and sometimes bouncer. Straight Eight Ball was the game: winners' and losers' brackets, double elimination. Everybody knew the rules, but Jack read them anyway.

When it was Mick's turn to play, he quickly lost. Rusty, he thought, or was it distraction? He was partly watching Ken, a regular customer and a construction contractor by trade, who was playing Crisscross. Mick had watched him play before as a casual observer, but never in any official capacity. Ken would buy twenty dollars worth at a crack, and then sit there ripping those pull-tabs off like nobody's business. *Rip-rip-rip!* He would stack all the losers in a neat little pile. When he got a winner, he would push it off to the side. Most of his winners were of the two- to five-dollar variety, and he would just cash them in for more tickets. *Rip-rip-rip! Over and over.* Hardly taking a break to have a drink.

He kept piling up the losing tickets until the waitress would come over with a wastebasket and literally use her whole arm to swoop the losing tickets into the basket she held with her other hand under the edge of the bar. Mick thought his hands would be tired after opening a hundred or so, but Ken used his wrists more than his fingers. Ken held the cards in such a way as to break the back first, exposing the four tabs, then pinch the tabs between three fingers and the heel of his thumb, twist his wrists, and all four tabs would open. Only if the card was a winner would he finish ripping the tabs all the way off, indicating he had a winner. *One-two*—as quick as that he had the tabs open. In an hour he must go through five hundred, easy.

Mick had seen other people play video poker machines like they're in some kind of trance. He could never figure out how anyone could sit in front of those machines, hours on end, shoving their money down a bottomless pit. Well, he thought, like the saying goes, "It takes all kinds to make a world."

While Mick was waiting to play his next game of pool, he deliberately positioned himself next to Ken and put his empty beer on the bar, looking for a refill.

Mick said to Ken, "How's it going?"

"Oh, it's going all right. Been better. Hit for a couple of hundred last night." He looked away and continued. *Rip-rip-rip!*

Other people played Crisscross to usually five or ten dollars' worth, play off any winners, and then quit if they didn't hit anything big. Mick wondered how Ken could afford his habit. He got another beer and went back to the pool tournament.

This time, in the losers' bracket, Mick got the feel of his stroke back and mowed through the less qualified players. Watching the bar from the far corner, he saw nothing unusual from his vantage point. Business was brisk. Heather and Debbie were running back and forth as usual. The speed queens, Mick thought and grinned to himself.

Mick then had to play in the winners' bracket, and he had to play the same guy that beat him the first time. Pat was his name—a little guy, but a good shot. Mick lost the coin flip and had to rack the balls. That's all he had to do because Pat ran the rack from the break.

Mick was disappointed he didn't finish in the money, but he knew there would be other nights when he would clean up. Mick used to be a pool hustler in his youth, and with a little practice he knew he would be back to his old professional self.

Mick went back to the bar, sat down, and got himself another beer. His eyes had a lot to do. They were dancing about between the cash registers, the tournament, and the customers. The TVs were muted on the sports channel. He watched until the replays were reruns. The pool tournament was still going on, Pat was still winning, the jukebox was playing, girls were dancing on the stage. Don, a.k.a. "The Donald" (because he looked like the "Trumpster") and otherwise known as the night manager, started to restock the beer cooler, and Ken finally quit playing Crisscross.

Pat won the pool tournament and was looking for a "money" game. Jack paid the winners their prize money, and then sat down at the bar next to Mick.

"Pat's a real good player," Mick said.

"Aw, he ain't the best that comes in here. He just got lucky tonight," Jack replied.

Heather bounced her way down by them and refilled their beers. "How did you guys do?" she asked.

Jack answered for both of them, "Not so fuckin' good."

Then one of Heather's favorite songs started playing, "Kryptonite," the Superman song, and she danced and side-stepped herself away to the next customer.

Mick noticed Don opening the door under the counter. He removed the bucket of Crisscross money and went back to the office.

Jack started telling Mick some jokes, but he was only politely half-listening. Jack could go on and on sometimes. Don came back out and started taking out the garbage. First he emptied the wastebasket with the losing tickets, and then the garbage cans with all the empty beer bottles. He took them all out through the beer room to the dumpster out back. It was just a little after midnight and Mick was feeling good. He felt he did a good job of nursing his beers and would have no problem hanging around until closing time.

Jennifer never came in that night, so Mick figured he would just see her in the morning. Now Mick started to watch the clock. He thought if I get out of here by two and I gotta be back by eight, that's only six hours. Figure an hour to get to sleep and another to wake up, shit, shower, and shave—that leaves four hours to sleep. That's doable. Why's Jen want me to stay until closing anyway?

Mick was thinking to himself, Jen must be short in her books. Don is the night manager. When she bought the bar, she kept him on with Debbie, Jack, Betty, Craig, and Carla. Jackie and Heather were the only two new waitresses. Heather is Jen's girlfriend, and Jackie is Heather's. Mick thought he hadn't seen anything unusual that night, or had he?

Follow the money, he thought. That's what the FBI would do. But he didn't know how Jen kept her books.

Boink! It hit him like a bright light. If Jackie rips her tickets up and throws them in the garbage with the beer bottles, and the other girls drop them in the slot in the counter with the money for the tickets—but they pay off the winners out of the cash register! No wonder nothing adds up right. Don took the winning tickets and the money into the office, but he was never in the office long enough to add up anything. Did he throw them out with the garbage?

Jack was about to start another joke, when Mick excused himself, quickly finishing his beer and saying, "Gotta go." He knew he was supposed to stay, but he wanted to check the dumpster.

He got in his car, a Pacific green Thunderbird LX, and pulled it around back and stopped by the dumpster. It was overflowing. Mick saw what he was looking for right on top: the bag from the wastebasket with all the losing tickets—or was that all? He grabbed the bag and threw it in his trunk. He figured he would examine the contents at home. If tomorrow Jen asks why he left early, he'd just have to explain he had a hunch.

When Mick got home, he put the bag on the dining table. It was just off the kitchen. Almost feeling foolish—he would for sure if he didn't find what he was looking for—he undid the tie wrap and partially poured the contents onto the table. He sifted through some used bar napkins, and there they were: the winning tickets, right on top of the losing ones.

This was too easy, Mick thought. A procedural error, maybe. It's not proof. How stupid can Don be, or how clever? If he's the drop man, then who might be the pick-up man? Are they one and the same? Maybe the lucky guys in the morning are in on this. Maybe the dumpster diver will hit after closing. Maybe go back to the bar to see if the pick-up man will hit tonight? There's plenty of time, at least another hour until closing.

Mick was thinking of going to the donut shop for a bite and coffee. It might be a long night. He scooped the tickets back in the bag. Gotta give them back to Jen in the morning, he thought, or when I see her.

It was almost closing time when Mick pulled up in a neighboring steakhouse parking lot far enough away that nobody should notice him parked back there, staring at a dumpster.

There were a few cars still in the lot when Mick saw a dark police cruiser slowly drive through. Heather's pickup truck was there, and Debbie's Pontiac. Mick didn't know what kind of car Don had, but he knew he would find out as Don would be the last to leave.

Mick's eyes were getting heavy, and he was about to nod out. He wasn't used to this kind of thing, sitting and waiting. Suddenly his coffee was gone and he discovered the girls and Don had left. The parking lot was empty. Mick only had the radio to keep him company.

He started to look for a corner to piss in, or he thought maybe he should just go home. Maybe it wasn't a "drop." Maybe there would be no pick-up man. Errors in procedure—maybe that's all it was. Well, he thought, it wasn't a complete waste. He had found a fault in the system. It would be a neat little scam if Don was in on it: throw out winning numbers at night, then bag 'em and cash in the next day—*over and over.* Maybe there's more than one bagman? How do you catch them?

The squad car pulled in the lot again, creeping along. Mick slid further down in his seat. This time, the cop stopped by the dumpster. He got out and started looking through the garbage. Then, Mick thought, he's leaving. No, he's just going back to the squad for a flashlight. Now he's searching through the garbage with purpose.

Mick already had what he was looking for locked in his trunk. He couldn't believe his eyes. A garbage-diving copper!

Mick snickered. So, he thought, was this how Don paid off the cops? Was this a skim operation?

He was far enough away so he couldn't see the cop's face, but his body was on the thin side. It had been five minutes now, and the cop's still searching. Mick scooted down even lower in his seat, so low he could no longer see out or be seen. He stayed hunkered down for about ten more minutes before poking his head up again. He saw that the garbage-diving copper was gone.

With the coast clear, Mick started his car and pulled out in the opposite direction. When he got home, he thought enough to call Jen and leave a message on her answering machine: that he would be late getting in the next morning because he was out late, but he would explain when he saw her later. All he could think of now was sleeping in.

"What do you mean it wasn't there?" the mayor bemoaned.

"Just like I said. I looked and looked. It wasn't there."

Standing at attention, mostly cowered—even though the mayor was his uncle—the young officer Ben Smide feared him.

"Well, I'm going to find out what happened, and you better be right. Now get out of here," the mayor warned.

The police station was right next to city hall, and Officer Smide had just got off duty.

The mayor skimmed profits for years that way from his partner. He justified his thefts by supplying the protection. The only reason the mayor sold the place was because his partner was tired of working, and the mayor didn't want his own name on the liquor license. The business started dwindling when the mills went bankrupt. He thought it would be a good time to get out of the game.

Then Jennifer fixed the club up, and business was better than ever. The mayor thought for sure she would go under. As he held the note for the mortgage, he made money off the place anyway. Plus, Don helped him skim money off the top to pay for his protection—Don and his coke operation. Now the mayor wanted the bar back and was willing to do whatever it took to drive Jennifer out of business. The mayor really didn't have any headaches, except one: how to keep his new girlfriend happy. He was drunk when he promised her the place, and now she was hounding him for it.

The mayor had met her at the strip joint, otherwise called a gentlemen's club. He was in love after the first lap dance. She let him cop some cheap "feels" at first, but they got more expensive as he put more and more money in her G-string.

Copulation was what life's all about, the mayor had thought, and later that night the same stripper sent him to heaven. He thought, Damn the wife! She never made him feel *that* good, ever!

When Officer Smide left, the mayor got on the phone and called Donald.

"He's sleeping," his wife explained.

"I don't care what he's going. Get him on the phone now!" the mayor roared.

A few moments later: "Ah, who's this?" Don's voice answered.

"It's John, dipshit! What happened to the package?"

"Wha… what are you talking about? I left it out as usual."

"You sure?"

"Yeah, I'm sure."

"Well, Ben said it wasn't there."

"I don't know nothing about that. But I put it out!"

"OK, maybe he couldn't find it, the asshole." The mayor paused. "When is the next time you work?"

"Wednesday night."

"OK, no more slip-ups, right?"

"Ah, yeah. Right."

Click went the phone.

The mayor punched the phone again. "Marilyn, put me through to Jake."

"The mayor's on line one," she said.

"Yeah, John?"

"Jake, how many drunks you bust last night?"

"Jesus Christ, John! You just have me the mandate yesterday!"

"And I told you the town needs the grant money. Get on it, will you?" *Click!*

Asshole, John thought.

CHAPTER 4

Mick didn't roll out of bed until noon the next day. He gathered himself, yawned, and jumped in the shower.

Jackie was still at the bar when Mick got there. "Jennifer wants you to call her at work," she said. "Here's the phone and here's the number."

Mick punched in the numbers and a receptionist answered, "Watts Décor."

"Jennifer Tuttle, please," Mick said.

"Please hold." "Hello. Jen Tuttle."

"Hi, Jen. It's Mick."

"Well, what happened to you?" she said in a demanding tone. "I give you an advance. You leave early. You get there late. Well?!"

"Didn't you get my message?" Mick queried. "What message?"

"I called you last night and left a message on your answering machine! Basically, I was up all night watching your dumpster, and I told you I would be late this morning."

"No, I didn't get your message, and what in God's name are you watching my dumpster for?"

Mick looked about and there was nobody within earshot, except Jackie, and she was pouring his coffee right in front of him. Mick didn't want just anybody overhearing what he was about to say, so he whispered in a soft tone, "I caught Don putting winning Crisscross tickets in the dumpster for a bagman."

"What?! Put Jackie on the phone." Mick did.

Jackie's head started bobbing up and down in "yes" motions, as if she was taking orders. "Here," she finally said. "She wants to talk to you again."

"Sorry, Mick," said Jennifer. "Heather must have erased the message last night. She stayed over. I want to see you at my house at seven tonight, OK?"

"Yeah. Sure thing."

Jackie went over by the Crisscross container and removed it from under the counter and carried it back to the office. When she returned, the phone rang, she picked it up and said, "Golden Door." She started bobbing her head again, then stopped and said, "OK" and hung up the phone. "Don't say anything about this to anyone," she said to Mick.

"OK."

"We're temporarily out of pull-tabs."

Jackie scurried away as the guys playing pool were flagging her for beers. Mick thought, The hell with the coffee. He walked around the bar, poured the coffee down the drain, and helped himself to a cold one.

Mick grabbed the TV remote and put on the stock market report. "Shit," he said as he saw all the indicators were down.

That night he met with Jennifer and he brought his bag of Crisscross pull-tabs. Jen greeted him at the door. They went to the kitchen counter, Mick opened the bag, and explained what he saw—but was interrupted before he got to the part about the cop dumpster diver.

"You know," she said, "I knew something wasn't right. I was considering letting Don go anyway, but I didn't because he does a good job handling all the bands, and he has a lot of friends that he brings in. But everybody is replaceable."

Jennifer took a deep breath and sighed. A look of disappointment enveloped her face.

"Mick, how do you feel about adoption?"

His jaw almost dropped open.

Shock and bewilderment suddenly became reality. That was twice she'd asked him that. What is she getting at, Mick wondered.

Being caught off-guard, all he could spit out was, "I never gave it any thought."

Jennifer looked up at Mick. He could see tears welling up in her eyes.

"Did you know that I was an adopted child?" she asked.

"No," he responded.

"Well, it's true. And now I have this desperate urge to become a mom myself. What's the sense in becoming a success if you don't have anybody to leave it to? You know what I mean?"

"Yeah, I guess."

"This state won't let gay couples adopt, so the bottom line is: I need a man to marry me so I can adopt a baby."

Bang. Direct hit! The floor just dropped out from under Mick's feet. He was falling, tumbling through the air, his mind spinning dizzily. What was the meaning of this, he thought. When was he going to crash and burn? His throat suddenly went parched. Gotta buy some time, he thought. Open mouth and insert foot. I can't think right now!

"I think I need a drink," he said.

Mick got up to fetch himself a beer. He stuck his head in the fridge, searching. The cold air slapped his face. Come to your senses, man! he thought. He grabbed a beer and thought he should have a whisky, too. A good Scotch whisky. Make it a double on the rocks.

He opened the can and took a swig. "Ahhh." He looked over at Jen, who was studying him.

"Do you have any Scotch?"

"Yes, in the pantry there." Jen was pointing to the door on the left. Mick opened the door and found a full bottle of Chivas Regal. That'll do the trick, he thought. He knew where the glasses were in the cupboard, so he helped himself. Putting a glass under the ice dispenser, he filled it with cubes and then Scotch.

Jen and her big puppy dog eyes were still staring at Mick. It felt like X-ray vision, going right through and looking at his soul. He sat back down at the kitchen counter with her. He needed time to think. This whole thing was not clear to him at all. He took a gulp of whisky. It gagged him, burning his pipes on the way down. Goose bumps formed on his arms. His whole body shivered. Mick exhaled a big "ahhh," as he shook his head. His eyes were slightly glazed over, and there was a big question on his face.

"You will be well compensated, Mick," she said.

"How's that?" he coughed, still stinging from the whisky.

"If you would take over Don's job at the bar, I could pay you a thousand a week."

"Are you sure you know what you're doing?" Mick asked.

"Yes, I have it all planned out. We can fly to Las Vegas and get married. I will take care of all the adoption proceedings. I've already started the paperwork, but it will probably take a year for the adoption to be completed. If after that time you decide you don't like the situation anymore, I will give you an amicable divorce and a bonus. Any way you look at it, you can't lose, and you will always have your freedom. You can come and go as you please and have all the girlfriends you want. I know you like your freedom and I like mine. This will be a Platonic relationship—no strings attached."

"Yeah, I'm kind of getting the picture, but I don't understand it. I gotta think this over. I got brain-freeze right now. Let me sleep on it." He took another swig of Scotch. This time it went down a lot smoother.

"What does Don do there anyway?" he asked finally, biding his time to think. I've gotta have rocks in my head for even considering this, he thought. But I'd be making a grand a week. How hard could it be? Would she drive me crazy? What else have I got to do? It could work out. No strings attached. I'd have all my freedom, or would I? Better get it in writing—a prenuptial agreement. Put my mind at ease. Yes, that's the ticket. There may be hidden charges. She may change her mind; change her attitude. She's being sweet now, but you never know how fast that can change. Yeah, get an agreement in writing. That's the ticket. No hidden charges. She foots the bill for everything.

His thoughts were interrupted by her ramblings of what Don's duties were: back the bar, book the bands, count the cover charges, pay the bouncers, tally the receipts, and keep the customers happy. But she left out the real reason why she was firing Don. She knew he was dealing cocaine out of her office at night.

Let Mick think he's a hero, she thought. It's easier to control men that way. She imagined she had enough friends to inform her of what's going on when her back is turned, although they did miss the pull-tab scam. She already had Mick looked into from all the angles she knew. She also knew he was handy, an excellent craftsman, honest, polite to a fault, quiet, and reserved. A man that commanded respect and didn't do drugs.

She didn't care if Mick didn't know anything about the bar business. It might prove out to be better that way. She could train him to run the bar the way she wanted it run.

Jennifer didn't fool around when it came to getting things done. She fired Don the very next day, without explaining why. She gave him two weeks' severance pay, and no hard feelings.

Too generous, Mick thought.

She bought a new security system with remote cameras aimed at the bar, the registers, and one rotating camera for the parking lot. It took Mick the better part of a week to install all the equipment.

Mick felt at home in the bar. Find a job you love, he thought, and it doesn't seem like work at all. Debbie showed him how to book the bands—standard contracts and all that goes with them. Jackie showed him how to enter the debits and credits in the books. A regular auditor filed the monthly receipts.

By the end of the week, Jennifer's proficiency was showing. She had her attorney draw up the prenuptial agreement, and she gave it to Mick to read over. She had tentative plans to fly to Las Vegas and get married there.

The power and energy women get, Mick thought, when their minds are set on something, especially having a baby! Their excitement radiates like nothing else.

CHAPTER 5

"What do you mean you were fired?" The mayor, who was on the phone with Don, wanted to know. "Why did she fire you?"

"I don't know."

"Did she get wise to our scam?" "I don't think so." Don paused. "She didn't say anything, and she gave me two weeks' severance pay."

"What are you going to do now?"

"I don't know. I was hoping you would find me a position."

"There's nothing open right now that I can think of. Why don't you lay low for awhile till something comes up? Take a vacation."

"I can't afford a vacation."

"Well, you would be able to if you quit blowin' all your dough up your nose!" The mayor hung up.

The mayor took a cigar out of his humidor, leaned back in his chair, and fired it up. That fuckin' cunt, he thought. The mayor puffed on his cigar, pondering. How do I get that cunt to sell me the bar back? She's paying her bills, so foreclosure is looking dim. Hmmm. Attack her liquor license? Send in some minors and bust her? No. Maybe I could get away with it once, but she's got a lawyer—pay the fine and start up again. That would take too much time anyway. Send in some bikers to tear up the joint? No, don't get any insurance people involved. Ruin her business base? Start busting the regulars for D.U.I.—that's politically acceptable. Nah, they're my old customers, and I'll want them there when I take over. That's only a small part of the business anyway. Hmmm. Maybe just make her an offer? No, stupid. She didn't buy it and make all the improvements to resell it. Besides, she would want to charge me an arm and a leg that way. I want it back for a song and a dance. Make her feel like I'm doing her a favor is the way to do it.

Hmmm, he thought as he bit down on his cigar. Brown stain dribbled on his chin. His mind was churning as he mindlessly chomped on his cigar like he was chewing tobacco. His drool finally splattered his shirt. Set up a drug bust, but how? Attack her liquor license, but how? I could have Don run it for me. Get my Susie Q on the liquor license and I would be in like Flint again. But how? Don wants a job. I'll give him one.

The mayor called Don back. "Look, Don, this is what I want you to do. I know you're still dealing that shit, and I want you to go back in the

Golden Door and I wanna know who all's doing drugs. I wanna know who all the lezzies and queers are. I want you to report to me directly, understand?"

"Yeah."

"Good."

The mayor picked up the phone again and punched the number of his nephew, Ben Smide.

"Uncle John! What's up?"

"I was wondering, in your last meeting, did Jake ever go over the new seatbelt law and the new D.U.I. limits with you guys at the station?"

"Yeah, he did."

"Did he tell you to stake out Ridge Road and the Golden Door?"

"He told us to patrol Ridge Road. He didn't say anything about the Golden Door. Why?"

"Well, the town needs extra revenues or we're going to blow our budget. So how many you bust out there?"

"A couple dozen seatbelt violators and one drunk."

"OK. Look, when you get a chance, stop in my office."

The mayor was thinking. Jake just doesn't listen to me anymore, that ungrateful shit. I made him what he is! the mayor fumed. He relit his cigar. If you want to do something right, do it yourself, he thought.

The mayor picked up the phone again and called his stripper friend.

"Hello?"

"Hi, honey. It's John. I gotta see you tonight."

"I have to work tonight," she said.

"Can you take the night off? I'll make it worth your while."

"Nooo, 'cause I might lose my job."

"Dammit! Why don't you just quit?"

"I will once you get me my own place, like you promised me."

"OK, OK. I'm working on it. I just need more time. Rome wasn't built in a day, you know. I still gotta see you. Can you come by my office?"

"Yeah, but I thought you said never come by your office?"

"Yeah, yeah. Never mind that. I got a headache that only you can cure. So come over as soon as you can. I got to talk to you about the Golden Door anyway."

"I'll be right over then. Your office is right next to the police station, isn't it?"

"Yeah."

"Give me a half-hour then, and I'll be there."

"Good. I'll be looking for you."

She knew where the police station was—she was locked up in it before—but he didn't have to know that. Now, she thought, I'm doing the mayor. And she giggled to herself.

She dressed casual, as proper-looking as she could. She left her duffel bag full of dancing outfits and sex toys in her car. She wouldn't be needing them today.

The mayor must have seen her pull into the parking lot, because he waved and ushered her through the side door. Like the big fat rat he was, he snuck her in his office without going by the receptionist.

His office stank of cigar smoke, even with the air-conditioning on. He sat down in his big office chair behind his cluttered desk.

"Come here and sit on my lap," he said.

She knew what he wanted and she knew what she wanted. She paused to think of a story line. Then she went over and sat in his lap, putting her arm around his shoulders.

"Ooh, what am I going to do, Johnny? I called the vet today to see about getting my cat neutered, and they want eighty dollars. Can you believe that? I don't have that kind of money. Maybe I should throw the cat out? But I love him so."

"Don't worry about the cat. Worry about me!"

"What!" she exclaimed. She stood up and glared at him.

"Here, here. I'll take care of the vet." He reached in his pocket and pulled out a wad of hundreds. "Here's one for the cat, and here's one for you."

"Thanks, Johnny." She stashed the cash in her cleavage. Then she sat back down in his lap and started to gyrate her hips. "Nice big office you have here, Johnny. I like the way your nice big chair swivels and rocks with me. Don't you, Johnny?"

"Yeah, yeah."

She started swaying and rocking her hips a little faster now. He reached up and cupped her breasts in his hands, pinching her nipples painfully.

"Oh, Johnny. You're getting so big and hard. That's a nice big trophy over there, Johnny. Did you shoot that bear, Johnny?"

"Yeah."

"I can feel how big and hard you are, Johnny. Do you want to show me how big and hard you are?"

"Yeah."

Susie Q got off his lap and on her knees. She reached in and undid his belt and zipper, then pulled his pants down to his ankles. He put his hands on her head and pulled it down to him.

"Gobble, gobble," he demanded. "Gobble, gobble."

That weirdo is actually trying to sound like a turkey, she thought. I'll turn him into a turkey all right.

When she finished draining him, she got up and said, "Is your headache gone now?"

"Ye-ahh."

He was out of it. His eyes were closed. He was all sprawled out in his chair, arms dangling over the sides, pants still down around his ankles, and his belly rolls protruding. She looked at him and shook her head.

What a disgusting sight of a man, she thought, then turned around and left him, exiting the way she came in.

He was so distracted he forgot to tell her he needed her to do him a favor. He wanted her to spy on the Golden Door, too.

CHAPTER 6

It was Mick's second week on the job, and he almost had it down pat. His hours were changed to nights and weekends. More importantly, he was having fun. It got to be busy work, sometimes hectic, but fun just the same.

That Saturday Jennifer and Mick had a meeting. Her profit margin rose considerably since Mick took over. She thanked him for doing such a good job.

Mick had his attorney look at the prenuptial agreement, and he said there were enough escape clauses in it that he could get out of the relationship any time he wanted. So Mick signed it. Not that Jennifer would stick it to him anyway, as she was an honorable person, forthright and sincere as a woman possibly could be.

She had the itinerary all planned: five days', four nights' vacation package to Las Vegas. Her secretary made all the arrangements for three—Heather was going along as a witness.

Right, thought Mick. He doubted if that was the only reason.

Jennifer pulled out an advertising pamphlet from a local jeweler and said, "Pick one out, Mick."

He knew he didn't want a wedding band, but he did find an impressive ring. One big diamond in the center, surrounded with small diamonds in a square inlay pattern—a 24-carat ring. "How about this one?" he asked as he pointed it out.

"OK." She even had a gauge with her to measure Mick's ring finger size.

"Which one are you getting?" he asked.

She flipped through a couple pages and pointed. "This one." It was another ring that had no prospects of being mistaken for a wedding ring. "We'll leave Monday morning at 9:00 A.M. I'm having a limo pick us up at my house. I'll see you then. I have errands to run." She gathered up her papers, gave Mick a big smile, and left.

That night, "Tookabite" was the band playing. The band played at the Golden Door regularly, every other month. Mick had never met them personally, but he'd heard them play before. Debbie was still taking care of the bands, and would be until Mick returned from "vacation." It was a typical band: two guitars, one bass, and a drummer. The drummer looked like a little kid in back of the drum set. Debbie explained that the lead-singing drummer was really a girl.

Mick was surprised by that revelation. Her get-up, sound, and looks fooled him. And Mick was a hard person to fool. He'd had a lifetime of experience, and not much got by him. She played hard, sounded good, and the house was always packed. That was the only thing that really mattered.

Then Mick saw Don walk in with two girls, one on each arm. That part didn't surprise him. But Mick didn't think Don had the balls to walk into a place he was fired from. Not to mention that his wife sometimes came in the Golden Door, too.

At any rate, Mick didn't want any confrontations or "a scene" with him at all. So Mick helped himself to a beer and disappeared into the back office where he could relax and watch things on the new monitor. Jack was on the door with bouncing duty.

The TV screen was split into four frames. Mick could watch the parking lot, and remotely control the other cameras to see what was going on. He double-checked the tape recorder to make sure it was working and, while checking the monitor, there was Don. Mick didn't even have to move the cameras. He was standing on the opposite side of the bar, near the pool room. He had a wad of cash in his hand, and he was buying drinks for his girlfriends and a couple of regulars he used to serve.

Mick really didn't know Don that well, as they had never conversed much, but the girls he was with were both knockouts—with plenty of knockers. The one blonde was caressing his hair, and the brunette was draped on his arm. Mick smelled a rat. No particular reason—the scene was just out of place.

What if his wife walked in and started a row? Mick thought. What if his wife walked in and just shot him? These were things he just didn't have training for. What would happen if this? What would happen if that? Mick was busying himself with contemplations. Isn't this like it always is in life? You get a good thing going and somebody always comes along and fucks things up! Mick was wondering if his thoughts were all on the paranoid side, or was it the reality side?

He watched them for quite a while. They were just partying. Don was spending his money freely, buying four, five, six drinks at a crack. When his lady friends got up to dance and show off their equipment, Don would just stand on the sidelines and talk to whoever was near. Maybe he got a new job already, Mick thought, or maybe he wanted to show off his buxom friends. Whatever. As long as he didn't start any trouble, he was welcome.

Mick's beer was long gone, as he kept himself holed up in the office for over an hour. The chair he was sitting on started to feel hard. He needed to walk about for a bit. Get the ass bone moving, he thought. Get the blood circulating. Mick walked out to the bar.

"How's it going?" he said to Debbie as she whisked by.

"The coolers need to be stocked and the garbage needs emptying," she said in a cursing tone as she whizzed by again.

Mick went into the beer room and stacked four cases of beer on a two-wheel dolly, rolled them out, and started restocking the coolers. They were pretty empty, so Mick put a little extra hustle in it to catch up. All the garbage cans were full, so he emptied them next. He rolled out four more cases after that.

"We're out of vodka and Jack Daniels," Heather chimed in.

Mick was really moving there for awhile. Before he knew it, he had to empty the garbage yet again.

"Last call for alcohol!" Debbie shouted out.

Whew, Mick thought, 'bout time. It sure does fly when you're having fun.

When Mick finally slowed down, beads of sweat poured out of his forehead. He noticed his undershirt was drenched, too.

"Last call for alcohol!" Heather hollered out. The band had quit playing and was putting their instruments away.

The crowd thinned out real fast, and there were only a few stragglers left. The Donald and friends were gone. Mick was so busy he didn't notice when they'd left.

The girls did though. "Did you see him? His wife is going to find out, but I'm not going to tell her!" The girls were gossiping among themselves. Even though they didn't mention his name, Mick knew who they were talking about. "Those hussies were all over him! Did you see that one sitting in his lap? He was grinning ear to ear!"

The band's gear was all packed up and they were going to pick it up in the morning, so they left it on the stage. Mick let the last one out the door and locked up. The girls were counting their banks and tips. Mick thought it seemed they did all right that night. He went behind the bar and made himself a well-deserved drink—double Chivas on the rocks.

CHAPTER 7

The limo was already there when Mick pulled up and parked in the driveway. He handed his suitcase and leather duffel bag to the driver, who placed them in the empty trunk.

"Are the girls awake yet?" Mick asked the driver.

"Yes, sir. They should only be a few more minutes."

Mick went to the door and rang the bell before walking in. He figured he would have time for a cup of coffee. Women always take more than a few minutes, he thought. There was one suitcase at the door ready to go. He saw Heather scamper up the stairs in her bathrobe and disappear into the bedroom.

Mick went into the kitchen. Coffee was already made, so he helped himself. Jennifer came down the stairs with her suitcase.

"Ready to fly?" she asked.

"Yeah," Mick said.

She placed her suitcase next to the other one by the door.

"Heather, are you ready yet?" she hollered up the stairs.

With no reply, Jennifer went to the coffeepot and poured herself a cup. "I think I'll join you. She might be a while yet. She needs her vitamins to get her motor started in the morning. You could have stayed over last night if you wanted, you know. I have a room all made up for you downstairs. You can use it any time you want."

"OK, OK, but I'm comfortable where I'm at. I have everything I need at home."

She gave Mick a wink and a smile. "I just wanted you to know you're welcome to stay here any time you want."

They sipped some of their coffee.

"Heather! What's taking you so long?" she hollered upstairs again.

"I'm coming! I'm coming!" Heather hollered back.

Mick carried Jen's bags out to the limo. Heather followed with hers.

"All loaded," Mick said to the driver, who was holding the backseat door open for the ladies.

The girls sat next to each other, and Mick stretched out on a side seat. "Where's the champagne?" he asked.

"Mick, if you wanted champagne, you should have brought your own," Jen replied. "They charge extra for a wet bar. You'll have plenty of time in

Vegas to drink all the champagne you want. We'll be there before you know it, so relax."

"It's just my first ride in a limo," he said. "I thought it was complimentary."

Mick turned to look out the window. They were on the expressway now. Take Jen's advice, he thought, and just relax. He released his body and sank into the cushy leather seat, as he watched the scenery flash by.

Mick had driven that road many times over the years, but he got a different perspective on it while looking sideways through the windows of a limo. The girls were talking on the rear seat, mostly just Heather gossiping about the customers. She wanted to throw some parties at the club, too. The bikini contest she wanted to run grabbed Mick's ear, but he didn't respond. He kept staring out the windows.

Heather leaned over to give Jennifer a kiss, but Jen rebuffed her advance. "Not now," she whispered.

Jen and Heather had vacationed together many times before. Jamaica, the Bahamas, Virgin Islands—all the trendy resorts. As long as there was a beach and ocean nearby, they loved suntanning together.

This was their first trip to Las Vegas, however, and Heather was all excited about it. Mick had been there before. He liked the way it had evolved into a premiere vacation destination. The grand resort-casinos were really beautiful, and they kept on building them. No shortage of money in that town—for the owners anyway. Mick brought a couple thousand with him, but he promised himself he was going to take it easy.

Jennifer's eyes were weaving between Heather and Mick. She was only half-listening to Heather now. She did give her the go-ahead on the bikini contest, but she didn't care for all the rhetoric about the customers. She'd heard it all before, and it was sounding like the same tape being played over and over.

She was thinking about Mick and how her experiment was going to play out. After all, she thought, Mick was a lot older than she was—that must be why he was so reserved. He'd never even tried to hit on her, as many a man had tried and failed.

She pictured him naked that day at the pool, and that twinge of nerves he set off between her thighs. The electricity felt like nothing she had ever experienced before. She should have been mad at him and scolded him good, but with his demeanor he would have laughed it off. Then she did remember she'd had that sensual feeling before.

She hadn't even been owner of the bar yet. She was checking out the customer base before she bought the place. At Heather's insistence, she played Mick a game of pool. She remembered the electricity flowing that night. She was a bundle of nerves, twinges of shocks. She didn't know where they were coming from, so she dismissed them and blamed the booze—intoxication.

Now she looked at him and thought: it's the way he moves, effortlessly, smooth, with confidence. He's not moving now, just sitting in the seat looking out the windows. The aura of nonchalance exudes from him—was this his attraction? She wondered for a moment if she would ever again see him naked. There it is again—nerve shattering impulses from knees to crotch, lightning bolts moving that fast, and gone.

She thought, I bet if I asked him, he would clean the pool naked again. No, no. You don't want to gamble like that again, now do you? She caught herself grinning and shook her head to get rid of her thoughts.

"Did you bring money to gamble with, Mick?" she asked.

"You bet," he replied.

They arrived at the airport with plenty of time to spare. They went through the security checks and bypassed the lounge. Mick didn't feel like drinking—not at the extravagant prices they charge at airports. They finally boarded the plane after a lengthy wait. The girls sat together and Mick was across the aisle.

Just as well, he thought. He started daydreaming about winning the big jackpot and flying home first-class instead of coach. Take it easy now, big fella, he thought to himself. Remember, you promised yourself to watch what you do. Don't get crazy with bets. Yeah, yeah. But it's still nice to dream about winning once in a while.

The plane taxied down the runway, made a turn, and the engine thrust kicked in. Mick was staring out the window, as the plane quickly picked up speed and catapulted itself into the air. Smooth, thought Mick. A nice smooth take-off.

A couple hours later, he was thinking the same thing about the landing—smooth, nice and smooth.

The hotel had a courtesy bus waiting curbside, just beyond the exit doors of the airport. The three of them loaded their luggage onto the bus and took their seats. It was a bright and shiny afternoon, and not oppressively hot. They were going to be staying at the Flamingo. Jennifer picked it out of a brochure advertising fifteen acres of Caribbean-style water playground. She did love her islands.

They checked into their rooms on the fifth floor. The girls had their own, and Mick was down the hall.

Jennifer asked Mick, "Do you want to have lunch after we freshen up?"

"OK," Mick replied. "Call me when you're ready."

Mick packed light. He brought his best Italian-made suit, which he immediately hung in the closet with his dress shirts. His casual dress jeans he slid into the drawer. His duffel bag he put on the chair.

His mind started wondering and wandering. Was he doing the right thing? You thought this all out before, he reminded himself, but it's still not too late to back out of the deal. But what else do I have to do? Nervous anxiety was pumping through his head, but it didn't show. He turned on the TV and stretched out on the bed.

This could be the best deal of your life! he began thinking. What have you got to lose? What surprises are in store? How is this all going to pan out?

The phone rang, interrupting his thoughts.

"Yeah?"

"We're ready!"

"OK, I'll be right out."

There at the Paradise Garden Buffet all the food looked inviting. Mick sparingly filled his plate with little samplings of his favorites. The girls picked mostly seafood and salads. They sat where they could look out the windows at the waterfalls.

"Nice view," Mick said.

"Yes, it is," Jennifer replied.

"Dee-lish!" Heather added, referring to the food.

"After lunch, I would like to go get the marriage license, and get that out of the way so we can party tonight," Jen said. She was looking at Mick for a response.

"Sure," he said.

"I reserved the chapel for noon tomorrow," she added.

"I'm going to sun by the pool while you guys are gone," Heather said.

Mick hailed a cab in front of the casino. He held the door open for Jen to get it.

The cab driver asked, "Where to?"

Jen said, "To the Clark County Marriage License Bureau."

"Right away!" the cabby replied.

They got their license in no time at all.

"That was easy," Mick said.

"Yes, it was," Jen responded. Then she added, "You know, I hope you can put up with my little quirks. I really think this arrangement will work out for both of us, and, if you ever find a woman for yourself, I will respect your choice and let you go without a fuss. It's just that I have to adopt a child. I have this motherly need I have to satisfy. Do you understand? I really do appreciate what you're doing for me."

"I think I understand."

She stretched upward and gave Mick a kiss on his cheek in gratitude. They walked to the corner cab stand and rode back to the hotel.

Mick felt like gambling. Jen went looking for Heather at the pool. Mick strolled through the casino, getting his bearings. He found the sports book. It was baseball season and the room was practically empty. Maybe, he thought, he'd just come back for a night game. He had better check the schedules. Not much going on in the card room either, he thought.

He found the blackjack tables down past the roulette and crap tables. The few that were open were full. He thought of just going to the bar for a beer, when the Keno corner caught his eye. Why buy, he thought, when I can sit there and drink free?

He sat down in the Keno gaming area and was filling out cards to play when a waitress came over and asked him if he wanted something to drink.

"Yes," he said. "I would like a beer."

She smiled and left.

He played four cards, five dollars apiece. He sat back down as the waitress came back with his beer.

"Thanks," he said, giving her a dollar tip. Yeah, he thought, what do they mean "gamble and drink free"? It always costs you something! Maybe I should have ordered something more expensive, like a Chivas on the rocks. No, he thought, no need to get in a stupor the first night in town. After all, you're getting married tomorrow! No hangovers, please.

The game had started while he was sipping his beer. He looked up at the board and some of his numbers were already lit up. Let's see, he thought as he looked down at his cards and picked up the one with some of his birthday numbers on it. Three numbers were picked already, two more to go. A fourth lit up and, with ten more chances to go, it started looking good. Come on, he thought, one more please, please....

Before he could think, pretty please with sugar on it, there was the fifth number. All right! Wow! he thought. First time for everything! Now I can afford my own Chivas. He laughed to himself, finished his beer, and went up to the counter to cash in. Don't be stupid now, he cautioned himself. Quit while you're ahead.

The clerk had to call the manager to double-check the winning ticket, and then produced the dreaded tax form that had to be signed. Still, Mick had scored a sixteen-hundred dollar hit, almost doubling his bankroll. Good start, he thought. Is this a sign of better things to come, or what?

Jennifer found Heather and decided to go get her swimsuit on and join her suntanning. When she returned, Heather inquired, "How did it go?"

"Just fine!"

Heather applied some suntan oil to Jen's back. They both were a little spent. They could blame it on jet-lag or weeks of hard work. All they wanted to do was lay around the poolside, relaxing, and gathering rays.

Mick had a different idea: take the money and run. He left the casino before temptation grabbed him. He went to his room and called the spa for an appointment for a massage. A deep therapeutic is just what the doctor ordered, he thought. He hit the gym for a bit, then the steam room and sauna melted all his tension away. He was starting not to care about anything. He was enjoying the ride, the vacation, Vegas.

The masseuse did a job on Mick. He felt all rubbery—so loose it felt like walking in a dream. He did walk. The sun went down, and he took a deep breath of cool night air. He wished he had brought his camera to take some pictures of the beautiful fountains along the Strip.

He wondered what the girls were doing. Probably having dinner, he thought. Mick was tempted to eat—prime rib was on special everywhere—but he wasn't hungry. He was enjoying the way his body felt, refreshed and relaxed.

Tomorrow is the big day, he thought. How will my life change? Will she be able to pull this adoption thing off? What if I meet a woman I really like? Would she understand the situation? Time will tell; time will tell. He went to his room and called it a night.

The next morning the phone rang. It was Jennifer.

"Where were you last night?"

"What?" He was fully awake and had already showered, but the question caught him off guard.

"We were looking for you in the casino."

"Ah, I didn't know I was supposed to meet you there."

"Well, I assumed you were going to be there. You said you wanted to gamble."

"Oh yeah, right. I thought I would take it easy the first day, so I got a massage."

"Oh, well. As long as you didn't ditch me and leave town."

"Why would you think I would do a thing like that?"

"Oh, I don't know. Edgy nerves, I guess."

Sheesh, Mick thought.

"Well," she asked, "do you want to have breakfast? There's plenty of time."

"Yeah, champagne breakfast," Mick said.

"OK, I'll arrange everything. G'bye."

Ten minutes later the phone rang again.

"Hello?" Mick answered.

"We have reservations at the Flamingo Room. Are you ready?"

"Yeah, I'll be out in a minute."

Mick was dressed in casual jeans and dress shirt. He had laid out his suit on the extra bed. He planned on wearing it for the ceremony. He wanted to look his best, figuring she would want photos.

The best part of this wedding was that he didn't have to pay for anything. He guessed that kind of made him a gigolo—without the sex part. Mick smiled at the thought.

He left his room and knocked at theirs. Heather opened it and said, "Hi!" They were ready to go. Jen grabbed her purse and they headed for the elevators.

The Flamingo Room was all done up in pink—tablecloths, chairs—a real eye-opener. The girls loved it. Mick ordered a bottle of pink champagne to go with the room and eggs benedict. The girls were all smiles and chatty as usual. Jen would turn to Mick and give him a wink every once in a while. They all shared the champagne, and Mick thought the girls' faces were getting a rosy color, or was it the rooms' colors being reflected? Mick was thinking of ordering another bottle but, when he inquired, the girls said no.

Jen turned to Mick and said, "I hope you don't mind, but I wrote my own vows. They're very simple, really. I just can't do anything negative, like, 'I will honor and obey.' That just won't work for me."

Mick shrugged his shoulders. "I don't care. It's your dance party!"

"Good. The wedding chapel is down the hall on the other side of the building. Do you think you'll be able to find it all right?"

"Sure. How early you want me there?"

"A quarter to twelve."

"OK, I'll be there." Mick stood up to leave and added, "You got the check? I got the tip." He took a ten-spot out of his pocket and laid it on the table.

Before he left, Jen asked, "You do have a suit, don't you?"

"Oh yeah. I came prepared."

"Good." She gave him a wink and a smile. "We'll see you before noon then."

Beautiful woman, Mick thought. Too bad this wasn't going to be a real wedding.

Mick was looking good in his suit. On his way to the chapel, several women looked him over. He stopped at the lounge on the way, as he had plenty of time to get there. When the bartender came over, Mick ordered a double Chivas on the rocks.

Mick got his drink and noticed that a woman a couple stools over was giving him the eye. She was alone, so Mick smiled back and went over to her. "Mind if I join you?" he asked.

"No. Sit down."

"My name is Mick."

"I'm Marie. Are you in town for a convention?"

"No, just partying."

"That's nice," she said.

Marie is a nice-looking woman, Mick thought. Vegas is full of them. He noticed all the rings on her fingers, with not a wedding ring in sight. Single, he thought. Yes, probably divorced.

Her neck was draped with jewelry too. Mick thought she must be well-off, judging from her attire. He looked at his watch: eleven-thirty. Only fifteen minutes to go. Damn it anyway, he thought. He wanted to stay and talk to her longer.

"Look, Marie," he said. "I have some business I have to take care of now. Can you join me for dinner tonight?"

"Yes, that would be nice."

"Where would you like to dine?"

"How about the Alta Vista?"

"OK. Is six o'clock a good time for you?"

"Yes."

"Shall we meet right here then?"

"That'll be fine."

Mick looked at his watch once more and finished his drink. "I'll see you then. I gotta run. Bye," he said as he scurried off.

He made it on time. The girls were already there, sitting on a bench outside the actual chapel. Jennifer was tapping her toes anxiously. They stood up as Mick approached.

"You look very nice, Jen," Mick said.

"Thank you. So do you. I mean, you look handsome."

She was wearing a white satin dress and a tiara made of flowers. Even Heather had a dress on. Mick thought it was funny he'd never seen either one of them with a dress on before. This wedding thing must really be special to them.

The minister was inside the chapel waiting for them. Before they went in, Jennifer gave Mick the ring he was supposed to put on her finger.

The music theme of "Here Comes The Bride" started playing. Jen grabbed Mick's arm and they started walking down the aisle, stopping in front of the minister.

"We are gathered here today," he began, "to bring together Mickey Swift and Jennifer Tuttle into the union of matrimony. In the spirit of new life, happiness and harmony, and the joy new life can bring. Repeat after me, 'With this ring, I thee wed.'" And then he slowly read the vows for each of them that Jen had written.

"With this ring," they each said in turn, "I thee wed."

As they exchanged rings, the minister said, "I now pronounce you man and wife. You may kiss the bride."

Mick kissed her lips. "How's that?" he whispered.

Jen blushed royally.

The minister signed the certificate and handed it to Jennifer with her credit card. "If you'll turn for the photographer, I'll have a complimentary photo sent to your room. Congratulations!"

"OK," Mick asked Jen after they'd left the chapel, "that's over and done with. Now what?"

Looking at Jen, he noticed tears beginning to well up in her eyes.

"Oh, Mick," she said and then suddenly kissed him on the lips as if it meant something, "thank you. You don't know how much this means to me!"

Mick was taken aback by the extra kiss, and so was Heather, who was looking on courteously.

Mick wiped the tears from her eyes and said, "Come on, let's go. It's time to celebrate. Let's get some champagne." They left the chapel area and headed for the lounge.

Mick ordered a bottle of brute champagne. "This time it's on me," he said.

Jennifer's smile returned, but her eyes were still somewhat puffy. They emptied the first bottle in no time flat, so Mick ordered another one. The girls were trying to agree on what to do next. Changing their cloths was first on the list. Then go gambling or back to the pool.

"How was your massage, Mick?" they asked.

"Great."

Heather definitely wanted one of those. Then the shows. Which one did they want to see first—the "Jubilee" at Bally's, "Le Cabaret" at Paris, or did they want to cruise the Strip in a trolley? Mick was noncommittal on anything. He had a date with Marie. But, he wondered, would she show up? That's another whole question. If he mentioned it to the girls, and she didn't show, that would be a little embarrassing. But if he didn't mention it, and she doesn't show, no harm done, he thought.

The girls decided on getting a massage first and then go gambling later. Mick decided to gamble now, and hopefully get lucky later.

He went first to his room to get out of his suit. Then he went to the casino, bypassing the slots, craps, Caribbean stud, and "Let It Ride" tables. He settled on a blackjack game. Mick started out conservatively, with just two hundred. He figured if he lost he would quit, and still be ahead of the game.

A couple hours later and the action was mostly back and forth. He was relatively close to being even. Mick looked at his watch: still enough time for one more shoe. He told himself that, after the shoe, he would take a dinner break, with or without Marie. Mick finally hit a blackjack, first hand out of the shoe. He was playing ten or twenty dollars a hand all day. The next hand he hit a double-down, and he was back even. Some more back-and-forth hands, and then Mick hit three twenties in a row. Now he was up sixty bucks.

No, he thought, don't count your money now—the shoe is almost over—that's bad luck. Like the gambler song says, "Don't count your money till the dealing's done."

Then the dealer busted three in a row.

Only a couple hands left, Mick figured, by looking at the discards.

They exchanged a few more hands, and the shoe was done. Mick grabbed his chips, threw the dealer a chip tip, and excused himself to cash in at the cashier. A little over a hundred won is better than losing one, he thought. He went to the lounge a little early to wait and see if Marie showed up.

Mick ordered himself a beer and started to watch a baseball game on one of the TVs strategically located throughout the bar area. He was thinking about how the bar was doing back home, when he was tapped on the shoulder.

It was Marie.

"Hi," she said.

"Hello," he replied. He gave her a quick look-over as she sat down next to him. "You look lovely," he said.

"Thanks."

Mick didn't have to flag the bartender, as he was over as soon as Marie sat down.

"What'll you have?" he asked.

"A vodka and cranberry."

"Comin' right up."

"Glad you could make it," Mick said.

"I told you I would be here. You're a very handsome man, you know."

Caught off guard again, Mick didn't know how to reply, so he changed the subject. "I'm from the Chicago area. Where are you from?"

"L.A."

"That's a hop, skip, and a jump from here. You must come here often. What do you do?"

"I'm a journalist, so be careful what you say." They both laughed heartily. "And what do you do?"

"I'm a manager for the Golden Door Lounge."

"You must know a lot of interesting people?"

"Why yes. Yes, I do." Mick was almost tempted to start telling her about the real reason he came to Vegas: to marry a gay woman so she could adopt a child easier. He thought, if that's not an interesting—or different—story, then I don't know what is.

Better change the subject again, he thought, because she didn't need to know that. She might get the wrong impression, or it might sound too kooky and scare her off. Hopefully, she's just horny and wants to get lucky—like me, Mick thought. Be careful what you say to her. That is a warning worth heeding.

"Are you ready for dinner now?" he said finally. Besides, he noticed her cocktail was empty and he wanted to check before flagging the barkeep.

"Yes, I am."

"Where is the Alta Vista?"

"Just follow me."

"Lead away, my fair lady," Mick said, smiling broadly.

The Alta Vista gave Mick the feeling of an old Italian villa—garlic aroma in the air, flagstones on the floor, hanging trellised arbors surrounding the walls. They both ordered filet mignon wrapped in prosciutto, as Marie recommended. Mick ordered a bottle of rosé with their meal.

"This is delicious! Good recommendation," Mick said.

"I knew you would like it. It's one of my favorites."

"Do you work for a newspaper?" Mick asked.

"Yes and no. I freelance."

"That must keep you busy?"

"Very. But I can afford to pick and choose, more or less." She reached for her pocketbook and gave Mick a business card.

"Thanks," he said.

Mick's keen senses were dulled, as he was mesmerized by the obvious beauty of Marie and her intelligence. He never noticed Jennifer and Heather coming into the restaurant, stopping on the descending flagstone stairs after spying Mick and his date, staring, turning on their heels, and leaving.

Looking at Marie's card, he said, "Well, if I ever come up with an interesting story, I'll let you know." He tucked her card into his shirt pocket.

Trying to keep the conversation going, he asked, "Do you gamble?"

"Of course! I play slots, roulette, and blackjack."

They were both staring into each other's eyes, measuring things up. Mick broke the stare first.

"I made a little bit playing blackjack this afternoon," he said.

"Oh, would you like to play a little more?"

"Sure, why not." Mick picked up the check.

"I'll get the tip," Marie said. They got up and left for the casino.

The casino opened some new tables for the night crowd. Mick and Marie sat down at the first blackjack table devoid of players.

"I like to play third base," Mick said.

"So do I," Marie replied.

"Well then, you take it," Mick said courteously.

She played the position perfectly. When she hit, she won. When she passed, the dealer busted. When Mick had eighteen, the dealer had seventeen. When the dealer had nineteen, they had twenty. They started hot and stayed that way.

They were having a good time. She was betting a little more than Mick, but they were both up substantially. Mick's luck was running hot. Now, if he could only bed this beauty, he thought, his day would be complete. They were having fun, laughing and congratulating each other: "Nice hit!" "Nice hit!" It's real easy to have a good time when you're winning, but the ever-skeptical Mick privately started to wonder. All good things must come to an end, he thought. Be careful. The cards are due to change.

Behind Mick stood Jennifer and Heather.

"Mind if we get in?" Jen asked.

"Of course not," Mick said, surprised.

"Looks like you're winning," Heather added.

"Sit down. The shoe is almost over." Mick was needlessly worried, as he scaled back his bets.

"Where have you been?" Jennifer innocently asked.

"Let me introduce you. This is Marie. Marie, this is Jennifer and her friend Heather. Marie and I had dinner earlier and we just started playing."

"Hi, Marie," Jen said.

"You know each other?" Marie asked Mick.

"Oh, yeah. We flew out together. She's the owner of the Golden Door where I work."

"I see."

The dealer couldn't help but eavesdrop as he was trying to concentrate on shuffling the cards.

"Am I getting between something here?" Marie directed the question to Jennifer.

"Oh no. We were just married today, that's all."

Marie picked up her chips and threw one to the dealer.

"Cad," she said to Mick.

"No, wait! You don't understand!" Mick got up to chase her. He gave up instantly, realizing it probably would be a waste of time.

The dealer was grinning ear to ear, trying to keep his composure.

Still standing, Mick had his fists on his hips giving Jen a disgusted look.

"Now what did you go and do that for? We were getting along famously. You promised you wouldn't interfere with my love life!"

The still-grinning dealer missed his last shuffle, sending cards flying—some even off the table. "Card down!" he called out to the pit boss.

Mick picked up his chips as well.

"I'm sorry, Mick. I didn't mean it. I'm sorry," Jen was saying to Mick as she followed him closely.

Heather called out "Stop, Mick!" as she quickly bounced her way in front of him.

Jen grabbed hold of Mick's arm. "Let's go to the lounge," she said. "I'll buy us a drink. Come on," she begged, tugging Mick's arm.

Heather excused herself. "I think I'll go play some craps."

"Come on, Mick," Jen repeated. "People are staring!"

Mick threw his arms up in the air. "Oh, all right." He was fuming inside, though. This better be good, he thought, whatever her excuse is.

Mick was ready for a double. Her smile was no longer able to cut through his anger. She picked out a table away from the bar.

"We can talk here," she said.

The waitress came and went with their drink orders.

"What do you think you're doing?" Mick squarely asked. "I had a good thing going with Marie."

"Well, I know, but…." The waitress came back with the drinks and quieted Jen.

Mick took a hit as soon as the waitress set down his drink. It was a good hit too. His body shivered. His spine went taut. Goose bumps formed on his arms. "Well". She said. Well what?" he bit back with a strong fervor.

"Well, I don't know. I feel funny, I guess."

"Guess what? I feel funny too. I could've gotten some loving tonight that I need, and you ruined it," Mick said angrily.

"I said I was sorry."

"Being sorry doesn't get me any loving, now, does it?" Mick continued, "It's only the first day. What's tomorrow going to bring? Maybe this was a bad idea. Maybe we should just get an annulment and be done with all this business."

"No, no please. I can make it up to you," Jen said.

"And how do you plan on doing that?"

"Well…"

"Well what?" Mick was so flustered, he wouldn't even let Jennifer finish what she was trying to say.

"You're not helping me."

"Not helping what?"

"Can you just listen a minute?"

"OK, I'm listening."

"I don't know how to say this right. This isn't easy for me. But... I thought you might like to consummate the marriage with me."

"What?"

"You heard me. I thought if you promise to be gentle with me, we could consummate the marriage."

Mick was in shock. Dumbfounded. His face was a blank, as if he just had a stroke. His brain couldn't process this information.

His natural reflexes took over. He took another swig of Chivas. He was still speechless, until tears started flowing from Jen's eyes.

"Now, Jen." He handed her the bar napkin.

He needed another drink, so he emptied the one he had. Jen hadn't touched hers yet. No matter, he thought, as he flagged the waitress.

"One more, please."

Mick just looked at Jen awhile. "Do you know what you're doing?" he finally asked. The question just popped into his head.

"I think so," Jen answered.

"I thought you said this was going to be a Platonic relationship?"

"Yes, but you're making me have desires again. I don't understand it myself." She started to cry again, then excused herself. "Wait right here. I'll be right back."

While Mick was by himself, he contemplated the new situation. I gotta have rocks in my head, he thought, for even considering this. Is this girl nuts, or what? How can you ever satisfy her? Remember those escape clauses in the prenuptial agreement. If you have sex with her and she changes her mind again, what kind of repercussions can you expect? You're opening a whole new can of worms here. What a dilemma! Or, are you just being paranoid? She's a bundle of exotic emotions—can you handle it? OK, start over. What if she just wants some loving? Did this wedding thing set something off in her?

She was coming back. Mick studied her graceful sway.

"Feeling better?" he asked.

"Yes, thank you," she responded as she sat back down. She had a drink and inhaled deeply. "Yes, I feel much better now. You know I was married once before, and he wasn't very nice to me. Do you think you can be nice?"

"I'm nice to everybody."

"I don't know if I can satisfy you, but I'm willing to give it a try." She looked sad, pathetic, like a virgin who was going to have sex for the first time. "Well, I would like to spend more time with you. We were married today, you know, and I am sorry I ruined your date. I was just jealous, I guess. Why can't we have our honeymoon and have some fun?"

Mick was still contemplating, filing all this new information away in his filing cabinet upstairs. He really didn't know what to make of it. His temper had subsided with the curiosity of it all. A bird in hand is better than two in the bush, he thought. This certainly will be a memorable day.

"OK, let's party," he said.

Jen's smile returned to her face. "Where do you want to start?"

"Right here." Mick flagged the waitress over. "Give us another round."

"Do you want to gamble some more?" Jen asked.

"No, not tonight," Mick responded.

He felt he was taking a big enough gamble on the relationship. Jen's a hard woman to say "no" to. Don't press your luck, he cautioned himself, there may be more surprises around the corner. He then suggested room service, a wedding cake, champagne, and hors d'oeuvres.

"OK," Jen said meekly.

On the way to Mick's room, she asked, "Can I stop in at my room for a minute? I would like to get a nightggown."

"Sure, but you won't be needing one," Mick grinned.

She stopped at her room anyway. She wanted to look sexy and feel comfortable.

Mick called room service. He ordered two bottles of champagne, four fresh strawberry shortcakes, and two shrimp cocktails.

"Why did you order four strawberry shortcakes?" Jen asked.

"You'll see," Mick replied.

Jen went to the bathroom to change into her lingerie. While she was changing, Mick went to his duffel bag and retrieved a prescription container of sildenafil citrate, or Viagra. He'd never used it before. He was waiting for the right place and time. He'd had some concerns about performance failure when he was drinking. He certainly never expected any "head" from Jen to get him started. So, he popped a pill. The instructions were to wait half an hour before stimulation.

Room service knocked at the door. Jen was still in the bathroom. Mick's order was on the cart. The waiter rolled it into the room, and Mick signed the receipt.

Jennifer came out in a sheer satin pink gown. She stood there blushing sheepishly. Mick made a twirling motion with his finger, so Jen did a pirouette.

"Absolutely lovely," Mick said. "Champagne, anyone?"

"Yes, please," she said.

Mick popped the cork and poured the champagne into the glasses. "Let's toast to us and the spirit of new life!"

They clicked their glasses together.

"Very tasty stuff," she said.

"Plenty more where that came from," Mick added.

As she was standing there, Mick maneuvered himself around back of her, put his arm around her waist, and started kissing the side of her neck and nibbling at her ear. His hand moved to the flat of her belly, as he moved the slick satin material in circular motions. She tilted her head back and moaned quietly with approval.

He then moved his hands up to cup her breasts. He gently moved his fingers over her nipples, massaging the satin into them. He then stood back to remove his shirt. She turned to him and kissed him, driving her tongue into his. Her hand dropped to his belt buckle, where she wrestled with the fastener to pry it undone. He was wearing red silk boxers.

"Oh my," she said, upon making the discovery.

His trousers fell effortlessly to the floor. He stepped out of them while they were still embracing. Her hand dropped down to his genitals. A strange and different feeling for her, especially through silk boxers. She cupped his testicles gently, bouncing them in her fingers. She felt him rising. Amazing thing, she thought. She hadn't felt a man for a long, long time. Maybe too long.

She couldn't help thinking about the disgusting things her first husband had made her do. She swore to herself then—never again, never! But this felt so much different now. Maybe all men weren't like he was.

She was feeling Mick's penis grow. It was getting heavier now, stiffer, and longer than her hand. They were still lip-locked, as their tongues were dancing with each other.

She pushed him away for a moment to catch her breath, and to take a drink of champagne. While she was emptying her glass, Mick did the same and quickly refilled them.

She sneaked a peek at his shorts to admire her handiwork. Mick's bulge pointed straight out, like Pinocchio's nose under a tent. She smiled at him. How do men walk around with those things, she wondered, almost giggling at the thought.

"These stem glasses don't hold very much," she said while extending hers for Mick to fill up again. From the look of things, she thought, he has plenty to fill her up with, too. She felt ready now. Her desires were in full bloom.

Jen set her glass down on the nightstand next to the bed and pulled down the covers. She removed the satin nightie from her shoulders. Her sheer bra and panties were the only obstacles left, Mick thought. His eyes soaked up the sight.

"You're absolutely beautiful," he said.

Her cheeks were blushing as she slipped into the sheets. Mick went to the service cart and took two of the strawberry shortcakes and put them on the nightstand. His boner was standing at full attention.

"Let me see you," Jen said, tugging at his shorts.

Mick dropped his drawers, and then she twirled her finger. So, Mick did a pirouette for her.

"Absolutely beautiful!" she exclaimed, giggling.

Mick pulled the covers all the way off the bed. "We won't be needing these," he said.

Scooting up to her, he placed his mouth directly on the sheer bra covering her nipple. He gummed at it until it was perky, and then he moved to the other one. Reaching behind her, he undid the clasp like the skilled craftsman that he was. He brushed away the shoulder straps and discarded the garment. At last his prize was before him to suckle, but he wanted to tease her a little first.

Quickly he got up and went to the ice bucket, and grabbed the biggest cube he could find. He came back with it completely in his mouth and lay down again, placing his mouth on her bare nipple. His tongue played with the nipple as his lips suckled. The cold and heat made her nipples even more rigid and protruding. She moaned consistently with pleasure. Mick was successfully completing his mission.

His hand then moved to her panties, and he ever so lightly ran his fingers between the elastic and the flat of her belly, until he saw her muscles twitch. Then he knew he had the right spot.

Her eyes rolled back in her head and she arched her back. "Oh, Mick!" she cried. "Oh, Mick! Do me, honey. I can't stand it any more. Do me!"

Her body started to buck wildly, but Mick wasn't finished yet. Now he slid his hand down between her thighs, and then ever so lightly ran his fingers upward from her knee, slowly up and up.

Those lightning bolts were shooting through Jen's nerves now, like nothing she had ever felt before. The tingling sensations were driving her mad.

"Oh, Mick! Stop! I can't take it any more. Oh, Mick!" Of course, she didn't really mean stop, as he had just started on her other thigh.

Her love juices were flowing now as Mick caught her aroma. He slowly slid her panties down, as she was twitching and bucking to help get them off. She wanted him. She needed him. She wanted him now.

She never thought she would feel this way. As Mick mounted her, she spread her legs. She reached out for him to guide him in between her folds. As he slowly entered her, she moaned, "Oh my. Oh, Mick!"

He then wiggled himself from side to side, while slowly plunging deeper and deeper. The swelling heat lingered there, deeper than any cold plastic dildo had ever gone.

His pelvis was toying with her clitoris, as he rocked back and forth across it. He then slowly pulled back until his swollen head hit the spot.

"Oh, oh!" she cried. "You're so cruel to tease me like this!"

Using short strokes, he had her clawing at his shoulders. Then he went deep again, and she clamped her muscles around his shaft as if she never wanted him to leave. His side-to-side gyrations were becoming too much for her to handle. She started to buck at him.

"Faster, faster please!" she cried. "Come on, baby, come on! I can't take it any more."

He started to speed up. His long strokes were purposeful. All the way deep, she could feel herself stretch to accommodate his size. Pulling back, he could feel the rim of his head touching her on the spot. She started gasping for air. Faster and faster he moved now. She could feel his balls slapping at her thighs. The deeper he drove, the better she liked it.

He paused deep inside her now as he arched his back. She felt him swelling even more. As he quivered, she felt a sudden gush of liquid heat. He moaned huskily. Still wiggling, he moaned again.

Then they both lay still.

Oh my, Jen thought. What have I done? This experiment has surpassed my expectations. How did he do this to me? How can I ever say no to him now? Why am I worrying about enjoying myself?

She realized she'd never felt this good before.

Mick rolled off her. She reached for her glass and drank. Her mouth felt parched. She then got out of bed to fill up her glass again. She looked at Mick. His eyes were closed. Was he done? she wondered. That's the problem with men, she thought. When they're done, they just roll over.

She looked at the full length of his body lying there face-up. Gorgeous, she thought. On the tip of his "head," she noticed a drop of his life-milk, sitting there like a shiny pearl. His stiffness had dwindled some, but he was still swollen. She thought, I'd sure like to ride him now. Can he do it again? He's just laying there. What if I...? No. My "ex" gagged me like that. He forced me. I swore I'd never do that ever again.

She continued her reverie. Don't blame Mick for that, she thought. He's a real sweetheart.

Mick's muscle pulsed suddenly, sending up another pearl drop.

Should I give him some pleasure? she wondered. Would he think less of me? He's pleased me, and I'd like him to again. As I understand it, his little head is at its most sensual level right now. Maybe if I teased him like he teased me, it will come back to life. Then I could take him for a ride.

She sat back down on the bed, looking, and then reaching. She put her fingers around his base, standing him straight up. She looked at his face. His eyes were still closed. The pearl drop was still there. Well, she thought, "in the spirit of new life...." She then closed her mouth around it, sucking it upwards. Hmmm. She squeezed his base and gave it a small jerk. Suddenly another pearl popped up. Hmmm. She put her lips around the rim of his "head" again, and started sucking very slowly. Mick opened his eyes.

He could feel his erection coming back. His blood was filling himself up again. He thought, those pills work great!

I did it, Jen thought, smiling to herself with pride. Then she mounted him.

"Ready for a ride, Mick?"

"You bet!"

Her breasts were dangling in front of his face. As she moved on him, they swayed to and fro. He caught them in his hands and took turns sucking each one, bringing both nipples to rigid points. Then he would turn them loose again to sway with her motion. Great view, he thought.

She rode him like there was no tomorrow. She got herself "off" a couple of times before Mick came again. She was exhausted now. She collapsed on the bed.

They slept good that night.

When they awoke the next morning, Jennifer showered and dressed first. The whipped cream had melted all over the now-soggy shortcakes, the ice had melted around the shrimp cocktails, but there was still a full bottle of champagne. Mick took the bottle off the cart and called room service to pick up the rest.

Jen asked, "Why did you order four strawberry shortcakes?" "I'll show you tonight if you come back over."

"Well, I don't know," she responded. "Heather might be upset if I do this again. That reminds me. Not a word of this to anyone about last night, OK? Promise?"

"OK, I promise."

"Heather and I are going shopping today, so we'll meet up for dinner, OK?"

"OK."

She gave Mick a wink and a smile before leaving.

Mick had a free day. What to do? he asked himself. He didn't feel like gambling any more. He could get another massage—why not? He called for an appointment. The quickest he could get in was that afternoon. He felt hungry now. He did get a good workout last night. He grinned to himself at the memory of it all. He sure did her good. She'll be back for more.

He was thinking of steak and eggs now, or maybe prime rib. On his way out, he went by the bar where he met Marie. If he ran into her, he thought, he would apologize and try to explain, as if that would do any good. She wasn't there anyway. He thought, too early to start drinking anyhow.

Mick thought about eating somewhere else that day. He went outside and waited for the trolley. He took it to the Riviera. He had stayed there the last time he was in town.

He was more familiar with the surroundings. He changed his mind about steak, and ordered scramble eggs with minced ham instead. He'd bought a newspaper and settled in a booth to relax. He sipped his coffee and lost his thoughts reading about other people's problems.

When he returned to the Flamingo, he walked by the bar again. No, no Marie in sight, he observed. Then he thought, they were having a good time until Jen broke it up. What's with that woman anyway? Expect more surprises, he thought, even though it worked out all right last night. What did she mean by "if you can put up with some of my quirks"? Will she be more demanding of me now? Maybe I did her too good, Mick wondered.

He was going to the workout room, then have a sauna and get a massage. He brought his swim trunks with him because he felt like taking a swim and getting some sun out by the pool.

Relax and enjoy yourself, he thought. Maybe you'll bump into Marie poolside. If Jen catches you together again after last night, be careful. Or, be prepared for fireworks. She might be a very possessive woman. Then he thought, oh, don't worry about it. Mick did his workout, got another massage, went to the pool, swam a few laps, and parked himself in a lounge chair. The scenery was great, with the fountains and all, and there was the other scenery, too—the walking kind. Mick soaked it all in with the sun.

While they were shopping, Heather quizzed Jen.

"How was he?"

"Fine."

"Was he gentle?"

"Yes."

"Did you enjoy it?"

"Yes."

"Did you tell him you were taking fertility drugs?"

"No."

"Are you going to do it again?"

"I don't know."

"Do those pills make you feel horny?"

"Heather, stop." Jen gave her a disgusting look after that question.

When Mick finally headed back to his room, he knocked at the girls' door to see if they had returned from shopping. Jennifer answered it.

"Hi! Come on in," she smiled generously at Mick.

"I was wondering if you'd made any plans for dinner tonight. I'm in the mood for some prime rib."

"We haven't thought about it yet," said Jen, "but I'm sure we can agree on a place that serves prime rib."

"Look what Jen bought me," Heather said, sticking her hand out and moving her fingers so Mick could see her turquoise ring and bracelet. "She got me this, too!" she added, putting her thumbs in the armholes of a leather vest with floral embroidering.

"Very nice! Very nice, Heather," Mick said. "Well, look, I have to change clothes. When you two decide where you want to go for dinner, give me a call."

"OK, Mick," said Jen. "I have to make some other calls first. I'll let you know when we're ready."

Mick turned and left for his room.

The leftover bottle of champagne he put in the bucket with fresh ice, just in case he needed it later. He then took a shower, turned on the TV, fluffed up the pillows, and laid back.

When the girls finally called, they'd decided to go to Conrad's Steak House. Mick ordered his prime rib, and the girls split an order of herb-marinated rack of lamb, with beluga caviar. With dinner they all split a bottle of burgundy wine.

"I've got good news and bad news, Mick," Jen said. "Heather and I have to fly back tomorrow. Debbie was arrested last night for D.U.I. I called my attorney and wired bond money for her, but she's pretty shaken up and depressed about the whole thing. So Heather has to relieve her for a few days. You can stay on if you like. No sense in ruining your vacation, too."

"Sorry to hear that," Mick said, "but if you're going, I'm going too. I don't want to party here by myself."

"Whatever you want, Mick," said Jen. "We're going to do some gambling tonight. Care to join us?"

"Sure, why not?"

The girls first stopped at the slots. Mick watched for awhile, until he got bored.

"I'll be right back," he said over the incessant pings and dings of the machines. He went back to the bar where he met Marie. Last chance to apologize, he thought. No need—she wasn't there. Oh, well. Then he remembered he still had her business card in his shirt pocket. Maybe, he thought, I'll write her.

He ordered himself a Chivas on the rocks. When he went back to the girls, they had moved on. Heather was at a craps table. Mick heard them before he saw them.

"Yahoo! Rub my butt for luck, yahoo!"

The rest of the table was cheering for her too. A noisy crowd, she had them all rubbing their butts.

"Yahoo! Rub your butt for luck!" She had a good roll going.

There was no room to squeeze in, so he meandered around until he parked at a Caribbean stud table. The way his luck was going, he thought maybe he might even hit that ever-elusive royal straight flush.

No such luck. He quickly dropped a deuce and moved on.

The dice must have run cold, too. The girls had moved on and the crowd had quieted down. Mick spied them at a blackjack table. Now, he thought, they're playing my kind of game. As he walked up, Jennifer was taking more money out of her purse. They must have lost at craps too, Mick thought, because they had no chips left. Jen slid a couple hundred to Heather.

"Mind if I join you?" Mick asked.

"No, sit down," Jen said.

Mick chipped in a couple hundred for himself. The girls hit a pair of blackjacks first hand out of the shoe.

"Yahoo! Rub my butt!"

Oh boy, Mick thought, here we go. They both threw the dealer a tip.

An hour later, Mick was up a little over two hundred. He managed to win back the money he lost at the stud table. The girls, being ever so generous with their tips, were about even. Every other hand, they were either betting for the dealer or throwing him a chip. Mick thought to explain to them that the object of the game is to win. Tip if you leave a winner. The dealer isn't going to tip you if you lose.

Well, at least they were having fun, Mick thought, and that's what it's all about. It's Jen's money. Who am I to criticize?

Tired of seeing them give all their money away, Mick planned on excusing himself after the shoe was over. It seemed to him that Jen and Heather were quite content playing cards.

"What time are we leaving tomorrow?" he asked.

"Noon," Jen responded.

"I'll see you in the morning then." Mick wasn't really that tired, but, gauging from Jen's response, he figured she wasn't planning on sleeping with him tonight. It was Heather's turn for her affections.

Mick stopped at the bar again on his way to his room for a nightcap, and to check if Marie was there. She wasn't. Why are you still looking for that woman? Mick questioned himself. She was charming, and beautiful after all, but that only means she's harder to catch. Why knock yourself out over something that didn't happen? He wanted it to happen, though. He thought, how's that saying go? Don't cry over spilt milk? She would have dumped you anyway, he told himself. You can't even afford that woman's upkeep.

He was still contemplating things when the bartender snapped him to. "Would you like another drink?"

"Yes. Yes, I would. Same way. Double Chivas on the rocks."

Mick was up early the next morning. After he showered, he packed his things, including the full bottle of champagne he never opened. He went downstairs to Lindy's for breakfast rolls and coffee. He leafed through the Las Vegas newspaper, skimming the stories while sipping his coffee. He wondered if Marie ever wrote a story for the Las Vegas paper. Get over it, man, he thought to himself. You're going home today.

"Are you still married?"

Mick heard the question from a familiar voice behind him. He turned to see Marie standing there with her arms folded across her chest like a teacher ready to scold her students.

"Ah, no—yes. I mean… Won't you sit down? I want to apologize for what happened. Let me explain."

She grudgingly sat down. "This better be good. And don't bother explaining if it's not the truth. I don't want to hear any lies."

"Do you want breakfast or coffee?" Mick asked.

"That's what I came in here for," she replied.

Mick flagged the waitress. "Can we have some more coffee here, and whatever else she wants?"

"Fresh strawberry crepes, please."

Hell, she even likes strawberries, Mick smiled to himself at the thought.

"Look," Mick said. "It's like… a marriage of convenience. She wanted a husband so she can adopt a child easier."

"That's an odd way of doing things," Marie said.

"I know, but she's gay," Mick continued, "and the adoption agency won't let gay couples adopt."

"I see. Very interesting. And I believe you're telling the truth, unless you're the best liar in the world. Nobody could invent such a hoax. Why didn't you tell me this before, up front?"

"Well, I hardly know you, and I really didn't think anybody would understand. After all, it does sound a little kooky."

"It sure does! But maybe it would make an interesting article? I'll have to do a little research on the subject."

Her breakfast came. "Looks good," Mick said.

"Yes, indeed."

After she finished eating, Mick went on to explain about the verbal dating agreement and the prenuptials—his out card, if things got unbearable. Marie seemed to understand, but Mick realized he missed an opportunity with her, as she was leaving that afternoon, too. So even if Mick stayed over on his "vacation," the timing was all wrong. At least he felt better about telling her the truth. You never know when there might be a next time, he thought.

She did leave him an opening.

"Let me know how it turns out," she said.

She reminded him of love lost in the past. Mick was self-conscious in his youth. He was afraid he couldn't afford to have girlfriends. Yes, he loved them. Yes, they were beautiful. Yes, he let them slip through his fingers. He thought it's about time he closed his hands to hold on tight, but he didn't know how to do it. He was lost. He couldn't do what he felt like doing. He felt like holding onto Marie and going to California with her. But it was true, Mick hadn't found his way yet.

Marie picked up the checks—she insisted. He got the tip. When she reached out her hands to say good-bye, Mick took them in his. He felt the magnetism there as they gazed into each other's eyes. He felt the warmth of her hands. He saw the warmth in her heart through her eyes. He started to feel he made a mistake with Jennifer. Don't let her go, he thought. Bad timing again, he realized.

He felt lost, even though he knew where he was going. Not dejected, not rejected, just lost. Don't let her get under your skin, he thought about Jen. Don't do anything stupid. You got a job to do. Remember, he thought, the grass is always greener on the other side of the fence.

Once he got to his room, he called the girls to see if they were up and about yet. Jen picked up the phone.

"We're going to breakfast. Care to join us?"

"No," he declined. "Just give me a call when you're ready to leave for the airport."

CHAPTER 8

The flight home was uneventful. Mick passed on trading up for a first class seat. He knew the girls had lost, so he didn't want to seem pretentious. After all, he never did tell them about his luck at keno. When they got home, he thought, he would give the champagne to Jennifer. Maybe they might need it some night. She had been acting normally since their dalliance, or more like it was no big deal. She still gave him a wink and a smile, when Heather wasn't looking, which, he thought, was probably a sign meaning whenever Heather's around, he's not going to be getting anything.

In the back of the limo, the girls were sharing stories of what happened when they were pulled over by the cops. They could be wasted to the max, and the cops would always let them go. Their good looks must have carried a lot of weight, Mick thought.

Now Debbie was in trouble and Jen seemed a little perturbed. She was asking, hadn't she bought enough fund-raising tickets from the chief? With the understanding he'd be laying off the customers, let alone the hired help?

Mick wasn't saying much about this kind of business, as he usually never did, but now he offered, "Maybe she was in a different town, or got in an accident?"

"No, that's not what happened," Heather countered.

"Well, I'll find out," Jen said.

Mick kept his opinions to himself the rest of the trip. When they retrieved their luggage from the limo's trunk at Jen's house, Mick opened his suitcase to remove the champagne bottle and gave it to Jen. "For the house," he said.

"Are you going to the bar?" she asked.

"Yeah. I could use a few brewskies."

"Well, we'll be along later. I want to unpack, check my messages and things."

"OK," Mick said. "I'll see you later then."

Mick drove his car to the Golden Door, walked into the bar, and sat down. Jack the bouncer was bartending.

"Hi, Mick," he said, reaching into the cooler for a bottle of Mick's regular beer. "How was the trip?"

"Fine," Mick said. "So, what's happening here?"

"Not much."

"What happened to Debbie?" Mick countered, being more specific.

"Oh, that. I don't know. The cops got her down the street somewhere. That's all I know."

He moved on to another customer. Mick turned his attention to a ball game on TV. The first beer went down fast.

Jack came back, "You're running on empty."

"Yeah. Guess so."

He got Mick another beer. "Hey," he asked, "do you know what they call a lesbian dinosaur?"

Mick's face went blank. "No," he said.

"A lickalotapuss."

Mick smiled, feeling a little relieved.

"Do you know what they call a gay dinosaur?"

Mick just shook his head.

"A brontosoreass."

Mick grinned. Enough stupid jokes, he thought. Jack must get them from his kids. Jack then took off to serve another customer.

Jackie appeared out of the back room and went right over to Mick.

"Hi," she said. "I just got off the phone with Jennifer, and she told me to tell you don't wait for her. She has some business to take care of and, oh, you don't have to work tonight. I already made arrangements. Jack is pulling a double and Heather is relieving me."

"Sounds good to me," Mick said.

"How was Vegas?" she asked.

"It was nice."

"Did you win?"

"A little bit."

"I'm going to go one of these days. Well, see you later. I have more books to balance."

Mick turned his attention back to the ball game, and then Jeff Bonds sat down next to him. He was an out-of-shape ex-boxer, too young to be an "alkie" but he was one nevertheless.

"How's it going, Mick, ol' buddy?" he asked, slapping him on the back. "Hear ya went to Vegas. Ya lose your ass? You're back mighty quick. If I had some money, I'd go out there and never come back. I got a system figured out."

Jack came over and poured him a double Hennessey.

Good thing Jeff walks everywhere, Mick thought. His apartment's just down the street, and so's his job. Good customer though. Spends lots of money. He'll spend his last dime on booze.

Jeff lost his driver's license years ago, and never bothered trying to get a new one. He was forever bumming rides, if he had to go somewhere, which automatically made him a pain in the ass.

"I hear ya got Donny's old job," Jeff said.

Jack interrupted. "Hey, Jeff, did you hear the one about the traveling salesman?"

Thanks for breaking in, Mick thought. He didn't feel like answering or explaining anything to a blabbermouth like Jeff.

Jack was ready for him anyway. As soon as Jeff finished his first drink, Jack poured him another.

"You see," Jack begins, "this salesman hails a cab at the airport. And he's never been to this town before, so he asks the cabby, 'Where can I get fucked in this town?' The cabby says, 'It'll cost you a hundred though.' So the salesman says, 'Yeah, OK. I just want to get fucked.' So the cabby pulls up to this hotel and says to the salesman, 'Go up to room 13 and knock on the door. There's this fine-looking woman with a great body and big boobs. She'll ask if you're a cop. Ya gotta say no, then slip her a hundred under the door, and she'll fuck you all you want.'"

"'Yeah, yeah,' says the salesman. 'That's what I want.' So he pays the cabby and goes up to room 13 and knocks on the door. This sweet sexy voice asks, 'What do you want?' The salesman says, 'I want to get fucked.' So she asks him, 'Are you a cop?' 'No,' he says. So she says, 'Then slip a hundred under the door.' So he pulls out his wallet and takes a hundred dollar bill out and slips it under the door. So, he's standing there waiting for her to open the door. Two minutes go by and the salesman is getting antsy. He's pulling at his crotch and everything. So he knocks on the door again. 'Hurry up!' he says. Then the sweet sexy voice asks, 'What do you want?' He says, 'I want to get fucked.' The sweet sexy voice says, 'If you want to get fucked again, slip another hundred under the door.'"

Jeff broke up with laughter. He had to hold his gut, and he almost fell off the stool laughing.

"Good one, Jack," said Mick. He also took that opportunity to leave. "See ya, Jeff, Jack."

Mick went home to unpack and take a nap. "Jet lag," he said to himself. He was kind of tired. Maybe, he thought, he'd come back out later that night. He didn't. Once asleep, he slept the rest of the day and night away.

The next morning he was awakened by a phone call. It was Jackie.

"You'll have to open this morning, Mick."

"Huh? What?" He was caught off guard.

"I had to bail Jack out of jail."

"What?"

"I said I had to bail Jack out of jail. I was up all night."

"Yeah, that's what I thought you said. What the fuck is going on? Twice this week our bartenders get busted? What the fuck!"

"I know, I know," said Jackie. "Jen called me last night. She was too pissed off and too tipsy to do it, so I had to. Now I have to get some sleep. So will you open this morning?"

"Yeah, yeah. Sure thing."

"OK. Then I'll see you later. Bye."

Mick checked the clock. Just enough time, he thought. He jumped in the shower, shaved, and away he went.

Betty the cook pulled up as Mick arrived.

"Good morning," she said. "Where's Jackie?"

"She won't be in this morning," Mick said. "She had to bail Jack out of jail last night."

"Oh, OK."

Mick unlocked the doors and made the rounds, turning on the lights. Betty did her rounds in the kitchen, turning on the grills and fryer.

Customers were already gathering at the front door, peering in the windows with their hands shielding their eyes from the reflected glare. Mick checked the clock. Five minutes to go, but he left them in anyway.

As they settled in their seats, Mick turned on the TVs and made a pot of coffee for himself. He went behind the bar for a couple draft beers two customers wanted.

"Got any Crisscross tickets?" they asked.

"No. We have a new game, Lucky Poker," Mick said.

"No thanks," they said.

Then Mick recognized them. They were the same two guys cashing in the winning tickets that first day he worked with Jackie.

That got Mick thinking: Were these guys tied to the dumpster-diving cop? Was the cop pissed off now? Is that why our bartenders are being picked on? Or are these just wiseguys? Who is that cop anyway? Never did get around to telling Jen about that part. Now's the time. Next time I see her.

Mick went about his business, wiping down the bar and tables, and setting out ashtrays. The coffee was done, so he poured himself a cup. The two guys finished their drafts and left. Mick cussed at himself. He should have tried to find out who they were and what they wanted. Too late now, he thought. But he resolved to be ready for them next time.

At that moment, The Donald was on the phone with Ben Smide.

"You got the wrong guy last night," he told him. "The guy I want busted is Mickey Swift. He drives a green '97 T-bird. That faggot's got little stuffed animals in his back window! You can't miss him."

"I thought you said he closed the bar?"

"I did, but I don't know what happened. He must have switched shifts or something. I know he's there now. If you want, go by and check out his car."

"I'm not going over there now," said Officer Smide. "I'll just have to get him later. Keep me posted and use my cell phone next time."

Ben didn't like talking to him while on duty. He always said, "You never know who might be listening in." Not that he was real worried about it. After all, he was clout heavy, with his uncle being mayor and all. Actually he was doing the mayor's bidding, and he was promised he'd be the next chief of police if everything worked out as planned.

Mick was back in his groove. He busted his ass getting through the breakfast crowd. He didn't have time to answer all the "Where's Jackie?" questions all morning long.

With the lunch crowd due in, he was glad to see Carla. She normally came in from eleven to five, and sometimes pulled relief at night. Carla was a sweet young thing, half Mick's age, with straight blonde hair cut square at her shoulders. She was also a newlywed who still wore her ring to work. The girls all told her she'd make bigger tips without it. "So?" she'd always say while flashing it with pride. There's a lucky man somewhere, Mick thought.

Then he looked down at his own ring. Oh yeah, he was married now. He almost forgot already. He smiled to himself at the thought. It was going to take him awhile to get used to the idea. He'd been a bachelor for so long. He thought he'd better check again with Jen that night about having his own girlfriends. Nip the hassles in the bud if you can, he thought. It makes for smoother sailing. Besides, he had to tell her about the dumpster-diving cop, too, and see what she might make of it.

The mayor called Don at home. "You got any information for me yet?"

"No, not really."

"Come on now. Somebody's got to be dealing drugs out of that bar besides you?"

"No, sometimes the groupies that follow the bands around bring some in, but that's about it."

"I heard you're bitchin' out Ben for busting the wrong guy," the mayor said, changing the subject.

"Well, yeah. I told him the right guy, but something got fucked up—that's all."

"Who's the guy you want busted?"

"The asshole that took my job, that's who! He doesn't know his ass from a hole in the ground, and that fucking dyke hires him!"

"You mean, he doesn't know he has to pay for protection."

"Yeah, that's right," Don quipped.

"Well then, he'll have to learn the hard way, or my name isn't John Quibly!" The mayor hung up the phone.

Mick and Carla worked through the lunch crowd without breaking a sweat. Jennifer had called to inform him that Heather and Debbie would be working the night shift, and to make sure the coolers were stocked for them.

"Mick," she said, "you'll have to double back and close tonight, and stock the coolers again for Jackie in the morning."

"Yes, dear" was what Mick felt like saying, but he didn't dare. He realized she was just shuffling people about until the work rotations stabilized. While she was barking orders, he couldn't get a word in edgewise. So he resolved to wait for a more opportune time to talk to her.

Debbie and Heather came in for the evening shift. Mick was relieved. He wanted to ask Debbie what happened to her, but never got the chance. Asking private questions in a busy bar can be a tricky thing to do, especially if you like privacy. He assured himself he'd find out soon enough.

Off duty, Mick sat on the other side of the bar and had a beer while watching the local news. It felt good to sit down. His feet were starting to ache.

Then, like a brain flash, he suddenly realized that if Heather was there, then Jen would be home alone. He decided to go there instead of to his own place. He did want to talk to her anyway, and feel her out—would she be in the mood for making love again? After all, she did invite him to stay there whenever he wanted. He thought he could use a nap before coming back to close. He could also use a romp in the sack. He thought, Only one way to find out!

Mick parked in the driveway and rang the doorbell before letting himself in. She should really lock the front door more, he thought. Anybody could walk in on her.

"Hello!" he said huskily.

He heard music playing outside. He walked through the kitchen out to the patio deck. He found her talking on the phone, catching some last-minute rays before the sun set. Jen turned her head as she heard him approach and gave him a silent wave.

Mick turned on his heels, went back to the kitchen, and raided the fridge for a beer. It looked to him like she was taking care of some kind of business, as she had all kinds of papers and folder strewn about.

Mick took a stroll around the pool. He didn't want to put himself in the position of eavesdropping on her conversation. It looked to him like the pool could use another cleaning. Jen was still yakking away on the phone, so he put down his beer and picked up the skimming net. He started scooping the leaves out.

Jen finally hung up the phone, and he hung up the skimming pole.

"What's up, Mick?" she called out.

Mick grabbed his beer and went over to where she was sitting on the picnic table bench.

"Have you talked to Jack yet?" he asked.

"No, not yet."

"I never mentioned this to you, but that night I saw Don throw away the winning Crisscross tickets, I waited out behind the steak house; and I saw a cop rummaging through the garbage, as if he was the pick-up man. He might be pissed off because his share of the take is gone."

"Mick, I already talked to Chief Weasley on the phone. He says it's out of his hands. He said something about a mandate from the Secretary of State."

"I was just kind of wondering if it's the same guy. That's all."

"Don't worry. My attorney will take care of everything." She started gathering her papers and things. "Well, I'm going to take a shower now."

"You want some company?" Mick saw his opening for what he really wanted.

"No, I'm going to the bar tonight. I want to get good and buzzed. I've had a hard day." No comment from Mick. That statement answered his question. "Are you going to stay here? You have to close tonight, you know."

"Yeah, I think I will. I'll probably take a nap, so make sure someone calls me to make sure I get up—just in case."

"All right."

Mick settled in on the couch in the den. He turned on the TV and started watching a movie. He nodded off before Jen was finished with her shower.

Don and Jeff were seen conversing that night at the end of the bar. Heather and Jennifer were oblivious to them, but Debbie noticed. Where are his girlfriends tonight, she wondered. She never liked Don anyway. He was always cheating on his wife, or trying to. He hit on her a few times, too. Now the both of them were drinking doubles like there was no tomorrow. She wouldn't have been surprised if they both fell flat on their faces.

What are they cooking up, she wondered. They were never this buddy-buddy when Don was working there. She also noticed that Don had a big bankroll. She'd never seen him buy so many drinks before. How did he do it, she wondered, especially now that he wasn't working?

Mick was awakened by gunfire on the TV. He did some stretches on the couch before getting up to check on the time. He thought of taking a shower in the guest bedroom, but then he realized he didn't have his gear with him. The hell with it, he thought.

He ran a brush through his hair. He didn't have any toothpaste or mouthwash with him either. He figured he'd have to bring his own personal hygiene kit next time, if he was ever going to have that "at home" comfortable feeling.

It just turned midnight. Mick decided to go back to the bar early, two hours before closing time. It was karaoke night. Sometimes the singers are good for a hoot.

Someone was butchering a song when Mick walked in. If he had been a paying customer, he would have been tempted to make a U-turn and walk right back out. Then he spotted Jennifer at the bar talking to Ed and Linda. Ed had a cue stick in hand and was probably between games. Ed and Linda were an older couple, partners in a supply business. The bar bought all of its paper goods and cleaning products from them. They were good regular customers. They'd always spend some of the money they made right back.

Jen and Linda were doing some engaging chitchat, as Mick stood there, ordered his beer, asked Ed if he wanted to play pool, and didn't get any recognition until he tapped Jen on the shoulder.

"Oh, hi!" she said, before turning back and resuming her conversation.

Ed was waiting for his pool partner to return, so Mick turned his attention to the next karaoke performer. She was dressed in a calico-print mini skirt with black leggings and a country style leather jacket. She chose a song by Fleetwood Mac and did an excellent job of imitating Stevie Nicks. Hope she does another one, Mick thought, as he applauded along with the rest of the crowd.

Mick's eyes followed her off the stage. She went over by Heather. They exchanged a few words and Heather pointed her finger in Jen's and Mick's direction. Mick picked up on the clue. She wanted to talk to the owner or manager about something. He decided to save her steps. He grabbed his beer and went over to them instead.

"Hi! My name is Mick."

"I'm Dawn."

"You did a wonderful job on that song. You're not an amateur, are you. Are you going to sing another one?"

"Yes, I could do that. Are you the owner?"

"No, I'm the manager. The owner is right over there."

"Can you buy me a shot?"

"Sure. What'll you have?"

"Southern Comfort."

"Heather," Mick said. "A shot of Southern Comfort for the lady."

"Coming right up," she said.

Dawn explained. "I used to be in a band, but we had a falling-out and I'm looking for another gig. I have one now but it's only one day a week. I have a son at home, so I need to make more money. I have to find another place to work."

"Do you play guitar?" Mick asked.

"Oh, yes. I fly solo. You can catch my act next Wednesday night. Here's my flyer." She handed him a piece of paper. "I play at Jolly Roger's, eight to midnight."

"Thanks. I think I will."

Mick was smitten with Dawn already. She had a twinkle in her eye. She was cute and sexy, with long brown wavy hair that flowed down to the small of her back.

Mick was a sucker for a smile. If he had been younger, he certainly would have hit on her. Of course, he thought, you never know until you try. So he dismissed the age difference.

Dawn went back on the stage to sing again. She chose another Stevie Nicks tune, "Stand Back." Her mannerisms were nothing like Stevie's—no spinning or twirling—but Dawn sounded just like her. When she got to the part "Take me home, I need a little sympathy," she was looking directly at Mick, sending shivers up and down his spine.

"Take me home, give me a little sympathy," she sang.

Was that an invitation? Mick wondered. If it was, he thought, he would certainly jump on it. The crowd applauded vigorously when she finished. On returning, she asked Mick, "How did I do?"

"You were great. Fabulous! I plan on being at your show next Wednesday. If you play as well as you sing, I'm sure we'll find a spot for you."

"Could I have another shot?"

"Sure thing." He flagged Heather over. "Give Dawn another shot of Southern Comfort."

When Heather returned with her shot, she said to Dawn, "You really sound good. Will you sing another one?"

"Not tonight. It's late and I have to get home. I have to get my son off to school in the morning. Good night. Thanks for the shots, Mick."

Quit dreaming, old man, he thought. She's too good-looking and talented. She's gotta have a ton of suitors. He wondered, Why was she alone anyway?

Dawn practically got mugged on the way out. Just about every Tom, Dick, and Harry in the joint made a pass at her. Mick thought, Lots of competition, but good for business.

Wednesday nights were the Golden Door's jam nights run by the Crawdaddies. The mike was open, so Mick thought she might fit in real well with those guys. But she was already working that night. The only other thing that was open was Sunday nights with the dart tournament. He decided to catch her show first and then figure out what to do.

The following Wednesday Mick was there. The Jolly Roger's was on a rural farm road—out in the sticks, as it was said. There wasn't much traffic on the outside or inside. The bar was decent enough: a long bar that ended at the dance floor. Beyond that was a smallish raised platform where Dawn was setting up her amp and speakers. She strummed her guitar and did some mike checks, "Testing, one, two, three."

It appeared to Mick she was ready to play, but she wasn't. She went to the bar and ordered a shot. She hammered it down, while the bartender was getting her a beer chaser. She looked down the bar, eyeing the few customers. She finally recognized Mick, who was sitting in the middle, and waved him over.

"Sit here with me," she said.

"Becky, this is Mick from the Golden Door."

"Hi, sweetie," the bartender said. She was a long lanky country girl complete with Southern drawl. "Pleased to meet ya!" She held out her hand for a shake. Mick took it and gave her a one-pump.

"Same here," he said.

"Glad you could make it," said Dawn.

"My pleasure."

Dawn pushed her shot glass at Becky for a refill. She complied. Mick thought, This girl really likes her shots. Liquid courage, or something else?

Dawn made her way to the stage, propping open her guitar case with a sign pinned to the lid: "Tip freely and often." She started flipping through some loose-leaf papers. They weren't in a binder and were in complete disarray. She found what she was looking for and placed the paper stack on one of her speakers and used her beer bottle for a paperweight.

She started with some mellow songs, "Sarah" and "Gypsy" by Fleetwood Mac. Mick noticed her guitar playing was decent.

She took a swig from her paperweight, shuffled the papers around, lit a cigarette, took a couple drags, and stuck it in between the strings at the end of the guitar neck. How amateurish, Mick thought.

Then she started again with Janis Joplin tunes: "Piece of My Heart," "Me and Bobby McGee," and "Get It While You Can." She not only sang them well, she sang them with feeling. She had that strong raspy texture in her voice, Mick thought. Of course, her cigarette burned itself out and the butt was still stuck in the strings.

Dawn took a break and sat down next to Mick at the bar. Some guys came forward and threw some bucks in her guitar case.

"All right, Dawn!" one of them said.

"Can I buy you a shot?" said another, as they crowded around her.

"Give us a shot!" the tallest one bellowed out to Becky, as he elbowed his way in between Mick and Dawn.

She took the shots gratefully, and whammed them down without a shiver. Mick had to slide his stool over to regain some elbow room.

Mick had wanted to talk to her. He wanted to tell her the bit with the cigarette looked tacky and not very becoming of an artist with her talent. She must have needed a break, as she got up and went to the restroom. Her fans in close pursuit almost went in with her.

When she came out, she took her beer bottle from the bar and went back onstage. She did some John Hyatt and other country favorites in her next set. Almost after every song, the tall guy was bringing her a shot on a tray and throwing money in her guitar case.

How can she handle it all? Mick wondered. Why doesn't she turn some of those shots down? She'll never last all night, he thought. The booze was starting to show on her guitar playing, as she missed some chords from time to time, and when she forgot her lines she would just laugh it off.

Mick was starting to get pissed. That tall obnoxious bozo kept buying her shots and she kept drinking them. Mick had seen enough. She obviously can't control herself, he thought, and the music is suffering. He finished his beer, dropped a fiver in her case, and headed toward the door.

"Don't go!" she blurted out. "Wait! Wait!" She hurriedly put down her guitar and stepped off the stage. "Let's go outside. I want to talk to you."

They walked outside.

"Why are you leaving so soon?" she asked. "Didn't you like the show?"

"You have a lot of talent," he said, "but I can't put you onstage at the Golden Door drunk."

"Well, I'm sorry," she said, "but this is how I make my money here. I have to drink to make tips. Would you give me another chance?"

"Well, I don't know, I'll have to think about it."

With that, she gave Mick a hug. "Thanks," she said.

That hug felt good to him, and his heart started to melt in her arms.

"You want me to come by for karaoke?" she asked.

"Yeah, do that."

"See you then, then." She broke off smiling.

At that moment the tall dude staggered out to the parking lot.

"Oh, there you are!" he said. "Come back in and have a shot." He grabbed Dawn's arm.

"Look, mack," Mick said. "Let go of her. We're talking business here."

"Buzz off, you old fart!"

With that, Mick's arm extended with a snap. His fingers were curled in a half-fist, and the palm of his hand struck the drunk right between the eyes on the bridge of his nose. It happened so fast, with so much force, that he didn't see anything but stars. The blow sent him reeling. When he landed, he just lay there spread-eagled on his back in the gravel—out cold.

Mick stood over him a minute, ready to give him another whack if he dared to get up again.

"Mick, don't," Dawn said. "He's my best tipper. I can handle him."

Mick looked down at him again. He was still out cold. "When he wakes up, tell him I said it's impolite to grab a lady."

He got in his car and watched Dawn run back inside the bar. The bozo was trying to get to his feet. He flopped one more time, face first into the gravel. Ouch, Mick thought. That must have smarted.

The tall man then propped himself up on his hands and knees. Mick decided it was time to go. He spun his tires in a hillbilly style of bravado, sending plumes of dust and stones flying. Mick thought, Have a little insult with your injury, bozo.

As Mick drove back to the Golden Door, he did some more thinking. Dawn could be a star with a little coaching, maybe even a recording artist. She'd need her own songs, though. He wondered if she had any written. She could definitely be good for business, Mick thought, if he could get her to clean up her act. He also realized that might be easier said than done. He'd have to get Jennifer's approval first—cover all the bases in case it backfires.

Back at the Golden Door, the Crawdaddies were having their jam. Mick thought about Dawn. She probably needed to get set up with a new band. He wondered, Where would she make a good fit? He decided to ask the lead singer if he knew of a band that was looking for a female singer. Meanwhile, he thought he'd see if he could develop her on Sunday nights. Entertain the dart players. Maybe they'd stick around longer.

Mick called Jen the next day and tried to explain what he planned to do. He asked if she wanted to hear her sing. No, she was too busy.

"Do whatever you want," she told him. There was a silent chill in her tone. Mick thought it might just have meant: Don't bother me with trivia.

It was an unusually busy night for karaoke. The crowd was having fun laughing, singing, and joking with one another. The Donald was in again, and Jeff was his lapdog for as long as the booze kept coming. Dawn wasn't there yet, but it was still early.

Mick went about his business. He made sure the coolers were stocked and the trash containers empty. He was caught up, so he got himself a frosted glass, filled it with ice, and went over to the bar's soda gun and shot himself a Coke. He started watching the karaoke singers. Most of them were gathered at the tables in front of the stage. They would take their turns and cheer each other on. Mick thought there must be some kind of "ism" for behavior like that, but he couldn't think of what it might be.

Then Dawn sauntered in, hips a-swaying, and sat down in front of Mick standing behind the bar.

"Hi!" she said.

"Sorry about the other night."

"That's OK. Glad you could make it."

"Can I have a lite beer?"

Mick went and got her one. She didn't put any money on the bar yet, so he politely said, "I got this one." But he was thinking, If you think I'm buying you shots all night, you're crazy.

"Thanks, Mick," she said. "I had to bum a ride from my babysitter to get here. If I can't find a ride home, I'll have to take a cab."

"What happened to your car?"

"The moon roof flew open on the highway. I thought I was going to die or crash or something."

"How does a moon roof fly off?" he asked her.

"Not 'off,' open. Like, straight up! It's twisted and bent. I can't get it closed. The wind rushes in like crazy. I can't drive more than 20 miles-per-hour."

"Oh," said Mick, "maybe you want me to fix it for you?"

"Can you? I don't think you can."

"Why not? Is the glass broken?"

"No."

"Then I can fix it."

"OK, that would be nice." She smiled. "Do you want me to sing you a song now?"

"Whenever you're ready. But you may have to wait your turn. There are other people."

"Yeah, I know."

Mick was surprised when she did finally get to sing. She chose a song by the Box Tops called "The Letter." The song was way older than she was. Mick remembered it from when he was a kid. It was a simple song but not her forte, he thought, even though she sang it well. Maybe it was because of the change of pace? Maybe it was a song she just learned? Mick thought, Or maybe she just wants to have some fun.

"How was that?" she asked upon returning to her barstool.

"Fine, just fine," Mick said. "That's a fun song."

"Yeah, I know. I just felt like doing something different. A little variety never hurts."

"Look," Mick said. "I can hire you to sing on Sunday night, on a trial basis. But we do things different at the Golden Door. You won't need your 'tip' sign. I'll pay you one hundred dollars a night, or twenty-five an hour, for four hours, eight to midnight. We have dart tournaments on Sunday, and I would like to see if you can build up a following. Of course, we have some other rules we all have to follow, like bartenders aren't allowed to drink until they finish their shift."

"OK," she said.

"This isn't Jolly Roger's," Mick continued. "So, I don't want to see you getting into drinking contests with the customers while you're singing. I'm not saying you can't have a beer to wet your whistle, or a shot once in awhile to soothe your throat—that's different. You know what I mean. And meanwhile, if everything works out, I'll look for a band that could use a female singer. I should be able to hook you up with someone."

"Don't worry, Mick. Everything will work out. Thanks, by the way." She smiled again. "I think I'll sing another song now. I'll be right back."

Dawn walked up to the karaoke D.J., spoke with him for a minute, and then walked out the door to the parking lot. When she came back, she was all happy-faced and jovial. She bounced right up onstage and belted out a Grace Slick imitation of "White Rabbit."

Through all the applause and cat-calls, Mick thought, This girl can sing!

When she came back to the bar, where he was now sitting, she asked, "Mick, could you drive me home?"

"I don't see why not."

"Great! Can I have a shot now?"

Mick's eyes temporarily glared at her, but they were softened by her smile. He flagged Debbie over. "Give her a set-up."

Dawn took turns singing with the others until the night was over. Mick watched her work the crowd. She easily made friends with everybody. She's a real entertainer, he thought. She made friends with Debbie and Heather, too. They were all giggling and laughing. She even helped Debbie bus the tables.

Mick locked the doors. The girls said their good-byes. Mick beeped his car alarm, and Dawn got in.

"Nice car," she said. "Moon roof and everything. Perfect! How do you work the CD player?"

Mick pushed the play button. "Where we going?" he asked.

"Turn right and take Ridge Road to Route 20."

A Led Zeppelin song came on, "Dazed and Confused."

"Perfect!" she said.

They were down the road a ways when she reached over and put her hand on Mick's thigh. It gave him quite a start—a nice start. He felt his nerves tingle with delight as she caressed slowly. He felt his blood heat up and the swelling, too.

He smiled as he drove. Then she took her hand away.

"I want to thank you for everything you're doing for me," she said.

"My pleasure," he replied.

She reached for her shoulder bag and took out a plastic bag full of "weed" with rolling papers. Oh shit, Mick thought to himself. He checked the rearview mirrors. He saw no cars or cops.

He felt like saying something to her, but chose to ignore what she was doing. When she finished rolling a joint, she brushed off the top of her skirt.

"Open the moon roof, Mick," she said.

She fired up the joint, as he pushed the button and the tinted glass roof slid open. She took a few hits and tried to pass the joint to Mick.

"No thanks," he said.

"Oh, don't be like that. You can't tell me you've never smoked a joint before. Don't you want to love me tonight?"

Mick didn't know how to respond to that. He had a slight case of brain-freeze. Then it came to him.

"What red-blooded American wouldn't?" he said.

"Well, here then." She held out the joint for Mick to take, as if this was some kind of sexual ritual of hers. Smoke it and you will get laid, he thought. He wavered briefly. No contest.

"Oh, what the hell," he said. Then he took a hit. It was a little stronger than he thought, and he immediately gagged and coughed.

"Whoa," he finally said. The aroma stuck in his nostrils before the open moon roof sucked out the smoke. He took another hit and held the smoke in his lungs longer this time, before coughing it back up again.

"Here," he said in a damaged voice. He passed the joint back to Dawn, and her hand returned to his thigh. Just like magic, he thought. His smile and arousal returned, too.

"Now, that didn't hurt, did it?" she teased. "Turn left at the stop sign."

Mick realized one thing: he didn't recognize his surroundings anymore. The street he was on was forest-lined and dark. The car glided along. He saw some lights up ahead. When he reached them, she said, "Take a right into the trailer park. Then left on Hickory Drive. My trailer is the one on the right, the one with the lights on."

She had decorative lighting along her walkway that led to a porch with hanging Chinese-style ornaments and baskets of flowers. Dawn opened her door and turned on the inside lights. For a trailer, Mick thought, this was pretty snazzy. She had framed jigsaw puzzles mounted on the walls, and fancy figurines in a curio cabinet.

"You want a beer, Mick?" she asked.

"Sure."

She went to the fridge and got two. "Come on, big boy," she said.

He followed her into the master bedroom. She set the beers down on the night table and neatly folded down the sheets.

"Well, what are you waiting for?" she asked.

Mick undressed himself as she went into the bathroom. She returned in a see-through negligee, pausing in the doorway. The lights in the background illuminated her goddess outline perfectly.

Mick had slept dreamily that night. He was awakened by some chattering in the kitchen. Looking about, he found his clothes neatly folded on a chair. He hurriedly dressed and followed the voices. He found Dawn having breakfast with a little boy.

"Good morning, Mick. This is Danny. Danny, this is Mick. He's here to fix mommy's car."

Oh yeah, Mick thought to himself. He had forgotten all about it.

"Hi, Danny," Mick said.

"Hi," the boy quietly replied.

"Now hurry and finish," Dawn said to him. "You don't want to miss your school bus."

"OK, mommy."

"I think I'll have a look at your car now." Mick excused himself and went outside.

Now that he saw it, he believed it. The moon roof was bent almost straight up. Mick surveyed the damage. He wiggled the window about. He straightened some bent pieces. He deduced: This will never work again.

He went to his trunk and got out some screwdrivers and a rubber mallet. He started prying and pounding until the window lay flat in its place again. Then he went back to his trunk and got some duct tape and sealed the window all around. That should hold it, he thought.

As he finished, he looked up to see Dawn and Danny walk to the corner so he could catch the school bus. When she returned, Mick explained that the replacement parts and dealer labor charges would be more than buying a whole new moon roof, but that his repair should hold through wind, sleet, rain, and snow, until she wanted to get it replaced. She thanked him and promised to be at the Golden Door on Sunday.

Mick got in his own car and drove off. Strange the way things work out sometimes, he thought. As he drove home, thoughts of Dawn and how the night had transpired made him feel strange.

CHAPTER 9

As Mick got closer to home, he realized he needed gas. He pulled into a station with a car wash. His T-bird was due for its weekly bath anyway, so he gassed up and pulled around by the vacuum. He spotted seeds and debris on the floor and seat, all from the night before.

He was vacuuming over the upholstery and carpeting when a plastic bag full of pot suddenly stopped up the end of the hose. What the hell did she leave this shit under her seat for? he wondered. He murmured to himself, "Idiot!"

Then he looked further and found the rolling papers, too. He stuffed everything in his shirt pocket, finished vacuuming, and drove through the car wash.

When he got home, there was a message on the answering machine: "Call Jennifer A.S.A.P." Then he realized he didn't even have Dawn's phone number. Now who's the idiot? he thought to himself. How unprofessional were you last night? Then he wondered what Jen wanted. He bet that Heather probably told her about him taking Dawn home. So why should he care anyway? She said "do whatever you want," and he did just that.

He called her at work. "Jennifer Tuttle, please," he told the receptionist.

"Who shall I say is calling?"

"Mickey Swift."

"Just one moment please."

"Hello, Mick." Jen got on the line.

"Hello."

"Mick, darling, I've arranged a meeting with the adoption support center in Indianapolis next week. We have to sign up and be interviewed. The whole process will take about twelve months. So the sooner we start, the better. And don't you think it's about time you moved some of your things over to the house? I mean, I really want your company more often. Eventually the agency will send agents over to interview us there. I want to make sure you're comfortable by then. Don't you think that will work out better?"

"Yeah, I guess so."

"Good then. I'll see you later this evening. Bye now!"

Oh my God, what have I gotten myself into, Mick thought. He was starting to feel the inevitable noose tighten around his neck. Shake it off, man, he thought to himself. Don't let your paranoia get the best of you. It could be fun, after all. It was in Vegas, remember? Yeah, he thought. I remember Marie. Now there's Dawn. Just take it one day at a time. Remember, you've got nothing to lose. What did she mean "our house"? He thought, Hey, that wasn't part of the pre-nup!

A phone call came in to the mayor's office.

"John Quibly speaking."

"Susie said to call you when the deed is done. The bag is under the seat. When do I get my money?"

"Hold on, dearie," the mayor said. "You say Susie sent you?"

"Yes, that's right."

"Well, I'll need a few days to check out your story. But if what you say is true, you certainly will be rewarded. Tell Susie to give me a call." *Click!* The mayor then dialed out. "I want you to pick up that guy Mickey that we talked about. I hear he's got pot under his car seat. Treat him like a drug dealer. Get him as soon as you can, got it?"

"Yeah, I got it." *Click!*

The mayor dialed out one more time. No answer, but the machine went on: "Sorry I can't come to the phone right now. The dancing queen has danced out of sight. Leave a message after the beep." *Beep!*

"Goddamn it! You're never home any more." *Click!*

The mayor decided to pay her a visit at the Industrial Gentleman's Club that night. He sat there at his desk tapping his fingers on the glass top. He wanted to get laid, his fingers started tapping faster, and his brain was percolating with frustration. Bitch has been avoiding me lately, he thought. I want a blow job now and fuck her later. His fat fingers tapped faster. Goddamn old lady, he thought. If it wasn't for her I could be getting laid all the time.

He got up off his chair and went to his mahogany bookcase. That part of the office was floor-to-ceiling law books. He hadn't read any of them in years, but it looked impressive to visitors. He opened the bottom cabinet and pulled out his hideaway bar. He took out a bottle of Jack Daniels and a rocks glass. He had a compact refrigerator right next to the desk, but he preferred his whiskey straight. Ice was for sissies, he thought.

He poured himself a stiff one and sucked it up. He poured another one and sat back down behind his desk. He took a cigar out of his humidor, grabbed his cigar guillotine, and chopped off an end before lighting it with his special gold-plated lighter.

He mulled things over, and then picked up the phone. "Lizzy honey, I won't be home till late tonight. I have some business to take care of."

"What kind of business?"

"Same ol' mundane political stuff."

Click! His wife hung up on him.

Fuckin' bitch, he thought. I'll kill her one of these days.

He went back to his bar and poured himself another whiskey. Fuck this, he thought, I'm going to the titty bar. Gotta see my Susie. He walked by the receptionist and said, "I'm gone for the day. I've got business to take care of."

It was only 4:30 in the afternoon, but he couldn't wait until 5:00. He had that itch. Whenever the mayor got antsy, he had to satisfy himself as soon as possible. He got into his white Cadillac and drove to the next town, where there was a strip club in the industrial district.

He would never allow such a place in his own town. All his holier-than-thou preaching helped get him elected in the first place. "I'm going to clean up this town" was his slogan. He laughed to himself. If only they knew, ha! He thought back and started remembering—and laughing some more. That seemed to him so long ago. If only they knew, he thought to himself while laughing out loud. He started laughing so uncontrollably, tears were welling up in his eyes.

His stomach tightened up. "Whew!" He had to exhale to stop himself. He wiped the tears from his eyes and sucked up a big breath and exhaled again. "Whew!"

The mayor pulled into the Gentleman's Club. Carefully he parked as far in the back as he could. He didn't want to be so obvious as to advertise his presence. Not that it mattered, as he had almost as much clout as the governor. Nobody could touch him, he thought. Nobody.

He walked in and asked the doorman, "Is Susie Q in yet?"

"No, not till 7:00."

He went to a booth in the rear. It was darker back there, and the girls had more freedom for personal shows. There was also a back room just off to the right. That's where the mayor planned to get serviced that night.

The waitress came over to take his drink order. She was wearing a bustier and thong with high heels.

"Give me a Jack Daniels in a rocks glass, no ice, and a beer." Reaching in his pocket, he pulled out a wad of bills, threw her a twenty, and said, "Keep 'em coming." Reaching in his other suit coat pocket, he took out his cell phone and called Don.

"Hello?"

"Hey, Don, it's John. I'm down at the industrial club. Come on down. I want to talk to you."

"OK. I'll be there in fifteen minutes. Bye."

The next girl got up on stage and started strutting her stuff to the tune of Bloodletting's "Concrete Blonde." Her boobs were bouncing and twirling tassels in opposite directions. How do they do that? the mayor wondered. That's a healthy set she's got there, he thought. I'll have to send for her. Then he got into the song she was dancing to: "I've got the ways and means…" *ta-dum, ta-dum, ta-dum.* "I've got a lot to think about…" *ta-dum, ta-dum, ta-dum.* "Oh yeah, oh yeah." She was spinning on the pole now, making all kinds of suggestive moves. Then she took her top off. The mayor started to clap and whistle. She then slowly wiggled out of her mini skirt, exposing her G-string. It was her chest that mesmerized the mayor.

He called the waitress over. "I need a lap dance from her," he said pointing.

"That's Miranda. I'll send her over."

"Get me another whiskey, too."

When Miranda finished her routine, she went to the dressing room to change outfits. She came out when she got the message.

"Hi. My name's Miranda. What's yours?"

"John."

"You want a lap dance, John?"

"Yeah."

"I'll need a twenty dollar tip for that, John."

"Yeah, yeah." He swung his massive legs out so she could mount them.

As soon as she sat on his lap, his hands wrapped around her and roamed until they were planted on her breasts.

"No touching!" she told him, as her hips began to gyrate.

He paid her no mind, beginning instead to squeeze her nipples through her halter top.

"Are you trying to get me in trouble?"

"Don't worry, sweetie. I know the owner and the cops, too.

"I don't care who you know. I said no touching! Those are the rules."

"Damn the rules, girl."

She pulled his hands away.

"I'll give you a hundred if you go in the back room with me," he whispered.

"I don't do that either," she said.

"Why not? Susie Q does."

"Then you'll just have to wait for her then." Miranda was still gyrating her hips, but she couldn't feel his arousal. "Come on, John, what's wrong with you? Your time is almost up."

He pushed her off his lap. "*You're* what's wrong. Here's your twenty. Thanks for nothing."

Don was standing right there as Miranda grabbed the money and left.

"What's wrong, John?"

"Oh, nothing. The bitch was just another one of those fucking dykes." He purposely said it loud enough so Miranda would hear him. She turned around and gave him the finger. "See? That bitch has balls!" He broke out in laughter.

"You want to go someplace else?" Don asked.

"No, no. I'm waiting for Susie. She's the only one that does me right."

You and everybody else, Don thought, but didn't dare say.

"What did you call me for, John?" he asked while sitting down in the booth across from the mayor.

"Did you find out if anyone is dealing drugs out of the bar yet?"

"No."

"What the fuck?" He stopped as the waitress came over. "What are ya drinking, Don?"

"Just a beer, thanks."

"Fill me up too, honey." He pulled out another twenty. "Keep the change." He said to Don, "Everything costs twenty bucks around here," and started laughing again.

Don laughed too.

"Let's see now, where was I?" said the mayor. "Oh yeah. I got a call from a girl today. She said 'the deed' was done and I owe her money."

"Yeah, me and Sue found this singer to help set up Mickey like you wanted."

"Good. I've got Ben working on him now. Can you trust this broad?"

"Yeah, sure. She needs the money bad. Cokeheads always do."

"That reminds me. Where do you get your drugs from?"

"Some guy in the Heights."

"And if I wanted to buy a package as a gift for Susie, you can get it for me?"

"Sure. Sure thing."

The mayor passed Don his cell phone. "Ask him how much for a key or a pound—whatever you call it."

"Sure, sure." Don was surprised by the request, but he punched the number anyway. "Hello? Hey, Bean, I got a customer who wants to buy a key of coke. How much? Eighteen hundred? No? OK, I'll get back to you on that." He clicked off and gave back the cell. "Twenty-four hundred, John."

"OK. I'll let you know when I want it. Let's watch the show."

"Hey, can you give me an advance, say, five hundred? The old lady kicked me out of the house. You're lucky you caught me today. She let me in to pick up some things. She also froze the bank accounts, changed the locks, and everything. I had to move into the trailer park. Now she wants a divorce, says she's tired of me whoring around. Oh well, I'm tired of the bitch anyway. Best get it over with. Well, what do you say?"

"Yeah, yeah. All right. I wish I could get rid of my old lady too." He reached in his pocket and peeled off five one-hundred-dollar bills. "Here."

"Thanks, John."

"Pay off that broad singer with that, too. I don't want her calling my office any more."

"John, I didn't give her your number. She must have got it from Sue."

"OK, I'll talk to her about that."

The mayor's attention went back to the stage when Susie's song started playing: "You Can Leave Your Hat On" by Joe Cocker. His eyes got big as Susie started dancing. His smile grew too.

"I'll show you what love is," the mayor sang along.

Susie turned her back on the audience, keeping her legs apart but straight, bending at the waist until her head was between her knees. The move always made her ass stand out, and she was proud to show it off.

Susie was a little bolder than some of the other dancers. As she worked the crowd, everybody sooner or later got a personal close-up view of all her assets. She would wiggle her tits so close to a guy's nose, it looked like she was slapping his face with them. By the time she finished, her G-string was always full of bills.

I gotta get her to quit this job, the mayor thought. I want her for myself.

When she finished, she came over to him. "Hi, big boy," she said. "You want a lap dance?"

"Yeah!" he said.

She mounted his legs but gave Don a private wink.

Don said, "I'm going to go now. Have a nice time, John."

The mayor didn't answer him, as he groped Susie's chest. "Ride me, honey. Ride me," he panted. Soon it was going to be time for the back room.

He stayed for a few more hours. He couldn't get enough of her or her show. His mind was willing, but his body was getting weak. He felt like taking her to a motel room and savor the woman, instead of just the quick hits she provided in the back room.

"See you tomorrow," she promised.

Better leave it at that, he thought. Besides, his senses were numbing from the liquor. He waved good-bye as he staggered out the door.

He drove about a half-mile before a police car flashed its lights.

"Oh, shit," he mumbled to himself.

He didn't even bother getting his license out of his wallet. The officer knew who he was.

"Sorry, mayor. You were weaving all over the street. Are you all right?"

"Yeah, I'm fine. Just a little tired, that's all."

"How about I give you a ride home?"

"No, no. I'll be fine. Thanks." He pulled away and slapped himself in the face. Wake up, he thought to himself. Only a mile to go.

CHAPTER 10

Mick moved some of his clothes and personal effects into Jennifer's house. It was his last trip. He had his arms full of clothes when he got to the three steps leading down to the den and his room. He stepped on the cat's tail, which sent Mick tumbling.

The cat screamed and so did Jen.

"Oh! Are you all right?" she asked when she got there.

"Yeah." Mick was more embarrassed than bruised. He started to pick up the clothes that went flying. "Ah!" he moaned as he stepped. "Must have twisted my cat stomper."

"Mick," Jen said in a scolding tone, not appreciating his comment. She picked up her cat. "Are you hurt, my sweet pumpkin?"

Like the cat could answer, Mick thought. Wish I could get some T.L.C. like that. Meanwhile he was wincing in pain with every step.

He flopped down on the bed with all his clothes. He lay there for a moment wiggling his foot. Nothing broken, he thought. Better take some aspirin.

He hobbled over by his gym bag to get some pain killers. Should get some ice, too, he thought. He hollered to Jen, "Can you get some ice out of the freezer and wrap it in a towel?"

"In a minute," she called back.

Mick turned on the TV and lay back down on the bed.

"Here," said Jen when she came in with the ice in the towel. "Does it hurt?"

"I can feel it throbbing," Mick said. "I better not close tonight."

"Oh, OK. I'll get somebody."

He peeled off his socks and put the towel wrap on his ankle. The ice felt good. After while it felt too cold, so he had to constantly shift the ice pack around. When the ice started melting, he called out to Jen for another towel to soak up the drips.

"Don't get used to the maid service," she quipped, with a smile, throwing the towel at him.

Mick stayed in that night. He tried to keep his foot elevated—a tip he learned from a doctor show on TV. His ankle was numb from the ice, but it was becoming a pain always having to adjust the homemade ice pack. As the ice melted, the weight changed and the pack would slip off this or that way. He'd already made three trips to the freezer drawer for more ice. On his last trip he thought about setting up a chair and putting his whole foot in the freezer, but then he couldn't watch TV. So, he dismissed the passing fancy.

He had used up most of the ice in the freezer by that time anyway. The hell with the ice pack, he thought. It's time for a nightcap. He put the rest of the ice in a rocks glass and filled it with Chivas. Then he gingerly limped his way back to bed.

Mick slept good that night, but for all his preventive measures his ankle had swollen badly by morning. The first few steps he took in getting out of bed were painful. He went right to his duffel bag and swallowed twice the number of aspirins he would normally take. So much so that his mouth went dry and he couldn't swallow them all. The leftovers started to dissolve on his tongue. He wasted no time . The need to wash them down led him straight to the bathroom sink. He turned on the faucet, lowered his head, and took a big drink from the running water. Ick, he thought, and bent down and took another drink. Now he needed mouthwash, so he limped back to the bedroom, got his duffel bag full of toiletries, and placed them on the bathroom counter. Might as well shower while I'm at too, he decided.

After his shower, he dressed and hobbled up to the kitchen and helped himself to some orange juice. That nasty aspirin flavor still lingered somehow, even after the mouthwash and brushing of his teeth.

The girls weren't around or up yet, so Mick really didn't know if Heather was with Jen or not. He certainly didn't hear anyone come in the night before. He rationalized that, well, he didn't get a piece but he did get quiet.

He put his empty juice glass in the sink and went back to bed. He did nod off again, and when he awoke he could still feel his foot throbbing. I'll have to get to the drug store for something stronger than aspirin, he thought.

Mick was developing some hunger pain, too, but he didn't feel like raiding the fridge, although he was sure Jen wouldn't have minded. He really didn't feel like making a mess or doing the dishes.

His ankle was swollen but he wasn't crippled. He figured he would go to the Golden Door for breakfast. He had to get out to the drug store anyway. Then he got a brainstorm. He would get a cooler and fill it with ice from the bar, and then he could stick his foot in it like he'd seen the pro athletes do.

Once Mick had a plan, he was a man of action. He grabbed a cooler out of the garage and with a limp he was off. When he got to the bar, he parked his car by the back doors. They were closer to the ice machine. He wouldn't have to carry the cooler so far that way. He limped in with the cooler in hand. It was a slow morning. Betty the cook and Connie were talking at the end where the kitchen meets the bar.

Connie only worked one day a week on Saturday mornings. That was all she wanted to work because of babysitting her kids and things. Betty noticed Mick's grimace and limp with every step.

"What's the matter with you?" she asked. "Have a rough night?"

"No, just a swollen ankle," Mick replied.

"I hear if you eat too much Viagra, the swelling will go to the wrong places," Betty quipped.

"Very funny. You got me good on that one," he said.

"What happened?" Connie inquired.

"If you really must know," he answered, "I tripped over Jen's cat."

They both laughed.

"You want some coffee, Mick?" Connie politely asked.

"Yes, please."

"Are you ordering breakfast this morning?" Betty asked.

"Yes. I'll have two scrambled, double bacon."

"OK."

Jim the painter came in and sat down next to Mick. They exchanged good-morning pleasantries. Connie came back over and took Jim's order, which never varied much—a half order of biscuits and gravy, nuked coffee, and his usual "painter's omelet."

Mick asked him again, "Did you get the light for the church yet?"

"No," was Jim's reply. "I still don't know what kind they want."

Mick had offered to install it several weeks ago. It's a good thing they still haven't got it, he thought, because it'd be hell trying to climb a ladder now.

His ankle was still throbbing. He couldn't fasten his sandal strap earlier that morning, so he slipped it off and placed his bare foot on the brass foot rest. The coolness of the rail gave him some temporary relief.

His breakfast came and Connie refilled is coffee. Jim and Mick ate in silence, periodically looking up at the CNN newscast. "Looks like they're still killing each other in the Middle East," Jim said.

"Yeah, it's a never-ending story," Mick said. "They keep blaming each other's religion, but it's always over the land. They just use religion as an excuse to murder one another. It's just like the Hatfields and McCoys.

Even after the Palestinians get their own state, they'll be killing each other for another hundred years or so, till the next generation finds something else to fight about."

"Amen to that," said Jim.

"I'll never see the end of it in my lifetime."

"You're right, Mick. It'll take them a hundred years at least before there's peace."

"What pisses me off is they just tore down the Berlin wall, and now the government is using our tax dollars to build a wall separating the Israelites and the Palestinians. They claim good fences make good neighbors. But any excuse to take my tax money is what it's really all about. I can't talk about it any more. I'm just aggravating myself."

"Well, see you later," Jim said. He put a fiver on the bar. "I gotta run. Lots of work to do."

"See ya," Mick said. He was finished as well.

"More coffee?" Connie asked.

"No thanks, but I need my cooler filled with ice though."

"OK, no problem."

Mick put a fiver on the bar himself, to cover his own tab and tip. Connie had the cooler half full in six scoops. "Be a sweetheart and carry it out to the car for me, OK?" Mick asked.

She obliged, following him to his car. Mick forgot to bring a bath towel to protect his car seat, and he knew he didn't have one in the trunk. It was full of tools. "Just put it on the passenger seat," he told her. He'll just have to clean the seat later, he thought. "Thanks, Connie," he said.

"No problem, Mick."

He drove off to the drug store. He shopped through all the pain medications, comparing prices, reading labels, figuring out what does what. He wanted pain relief and an anti-inflammatory. He couldn't decide between generic ibuprofen—which was cheaper—or Advil, which was on sale. The hell with it, he thought. He bought them both.

Mick went home dragging himself and ice chest back to the den. He turned on the TV and added some salt and water to the cooler. He got some more bath towels and put his foot in the ice.

"Whoa!" he said out loud.

The shock of the cold hit him so severely that he had to take his foot right back out. Too cold, he thought. Almost unbearable pain. How can the pro athletes stand it, he wondered. He put his foot back in, and was able to keep it there a little longer this time. He kept putting it in and out until the foot became more acclimated to the cold. He was finally able to leave his foot in the ice as it became numb.

He was looking through the TV guide. He saw that two ball games were on that afternoon. He knew he'd be going back to the bar to watch them. He was bored already. Sitting with his foot in an ice chest wasn't high on his list of exciting things to do.

The National Anthem was just ending when Mick arrived at the Golden Door. "The land of the free, and the home of the brave" was blaring out of the TVs, signaling the start of the ball game. He limped over and sat on the corner barstool, where he could have a good view of all the TV sets. The regulars were already there. Kenny was decked out with his Cubs shirt and baseball cap full of memorabilia buttons. Big Ricky with his Sox shirt was sitting with Denny. He had his Sox shirt on, too. They were already yammering back and forth, trading barbs on who the best team was.

Jack and Michelle were bartending now. Connie's shift was over. Michelle was a die-hard Cub fan and always took sides with Kenny. If there wasn't a good sports argument going on, she would start one. Not too long ago she was a hefty girl, but then she took up running and lost a hundred pounds. Now she ran in every marathon she could.

Mick was a paying customer that day—officially off duty. He thoroughly enjoyed sitting on the customer side of the bar to watch a ball game. Like a slice of American pie, he thought, some consider this better than going to the game in person. On TV there's all the replays to watch and you never get rained on. Mick liked joking with the guys, going over play-by-plays, ridiculing the professionals when they made an error—all the time wishing they were in their shoes.

It was a camaraderie among men, almost like religion. Have a few beers, he thought, share a few laughs. Mick could have stayed home and watched the same game, but that's not even close to being the same thing.

"Whoo-whoo!" Michelle cheered. "Sammy just got a home run. Did you see that, Denny? Whoo-whoo! Go, Sammy, go!"

"Oh yeah, they're winning now, but the game ain't over," Denny countered. "Betcha they get beat."

"You're on for a dollar," Michelle said.

"OK, now we're talkin'. Get me another beer while you're here. 'Hee-hee.'"

When she came back with Denny's beer, he said, "Sure ya don't wanna up the bet to include some lovin'?"

"You're already losing three-to-nothing, and besides, you don't have enough money to get in my pants. I'm an expensive woman to keep. Nothing but first class for me!"

"If you're so first class, then why would you bet on losers like the Cubs? 'Hee-hee,'"

Denny mocked. By then, half the bar was laughing too. Denny was getting his digs in. All the kidding was in good fun, and, when the Cubs lost the game in the ninth, Denny said he was going to frame the dollar Michelle gave him. Then he tipped her three times as much. "It's been fun," he said as he left.

Jeff Bonds was sitting at the other end of the bar. He was not being his usual boisterous self. He was following instructions: If he saw Mick drinking in the bar, he was to give his buddy Don a call. Jeff had sneaked outside during the fifth inning and made his call from a public phone. Then Don made his phone call to the mayor, who called Officer Smide.

Unbeknownst to Mick, there had been a dark maroon unmarked cruiser making his rounds through the parking lot, noting the cars there. The ball game was over, Mick finished his beer, said his good-byes, and left.

He didn't get far before: "Bwoop-bwoop!" It was the sound of the cruiser behind him, lights flashing, wanting to pull Mick over. He looked in his rearview mirror and saw a dark squad with semi-hidden blue and red lights flashing on the dashboard. A skinny officer emerged from the squad. When he came up to Mick's door, Mick thought he hardly looked old enough to be a cop.

Mick already had his driver's license and insurance card out of his wallet. "What'd you pull me over for?" Mick inquired.

"You weren't wearing a seatbelt," the officer replied.

"I just now undid it to get my wallet out." He handed him his IDs.

"Do you have your vehicle registration?"

Mick's anger was already building up because of the pimpiness of the stop and the smirk on the cop's face. "Don't shoot me," he said. "I have to reach in my glove box."

Mick wasn't kidding either. There had been a rash of cops killing motorists in the news lately. It seemed to him that if you reached for anything or had a cell phone or a wallet in your hands, a cop had a built-in excuse for murder. "I thought he had a gun" was their automatic excuse. "I was protecting myself." It always worked at bench trials to get cops acquitted.

Mick looked about but couldn't find what he was looking for. It had been a long time since Mick was pulled over for anything. He didn't know where his registration card was. He gave up the search.

"I can't find it," he said.

"Step out of the car," the officer said. Mick got out of the car. He was wearing a regular short sleeve shirt, matching shorts, and sandals. "Come over and stand here," indicating to Mick to stand in front of his squad car. "Where have you been?"

"I was watching a ball game," Mick answered.

"I need you to stand on one leg and count to ten thousand. Like this: one one-thousand, two one-thousand, up to ten. Do you understand?"

"Do you understand how swollen my ankle is?" Mick bent over at his waist and pointed. "Can you see I can't even buckle my sandal strap?" He demonstrated the obvious, as one strap was buckled and the other was undone.

"Stand on your good foot then."

Mick gave him a look of disbelief but did it anyway. "One one-thousand...." He counted off to ten thousand. "There you go," he said.

"Now I want you to come over here and walk heel-to-toe on this line."

So Mick did as he was told. He walked heel-to-toe along the line, swollen ankle and all. "There you go," he said.

"Now I want you to blow into this breathalyzer." He unwrapped it and put it in Mick's mouth, so he blew.

"You're under arrest," the officer said. "You registered point-0-8-2.." Mick was getting madder by the second. "Turn around and put your hands behind your back."

Mick did and, *click-click*, he was now wearing cop jewelry.

"Do you have any sharp objects in your pockets?"

Mick didn't answer.

"Spread your legs."

Mick didn't move. Then he felt a kick in his swollen ankle that almost toppled him.

"I said spread 'em!"

His backup squad pulled next to them as Mick said to the arresting officer, "You don't believe in the Constitution, do you?"

Mick got no answer but his temper was still building. "I want an ambulance. I don't believe your test was accurate. Actually, I believe you're a lying thief. How much money does the tow company kick back to you?

You can't answer my question, can you? Who do you work for, some Jewish Nazis? I get it now. We have some blue shirt Nazis working for the Jewish Nazis. You certainly don't believe in the Constitution, and that's a fact!"

Mick was venting a build-up of high blood pressure. The cop led him to the rear of the squad and sat him down, but left the door open as he called for an ambulance. Then the two cops went over and started searching Mick's car. He watched them from the squad. Good thing he took that bag out that Dawn left there, he thought.

When they returned, the backup cop had Mick's wallet in his hand. He started leafing through the wallet, and Mick could hold back no more. It felt like he was getting raped.

"And what are you stealing?" Mick demanded, only to be grabbed by the throat and choked. As he was being choked and pushed back farther in the squad, the cop started to grill him.

"Where did you get all this money? Where are the drugs? What are you high on?"

Lucky for Mick, the ambulance pulled up and the cop had to release his grip.

"You got a good one this time, Ben," the cop said as he slapped the arresting officer on the back with praise.

The ambulance paramedics came over with a gurney, and Mick was strapped in for the ride. He was loaded into the ambulance, and Ben Smide got in too.

"Where are you taking me, to the gas chambers?" Mick was still venting his satirical quick wit.

One of the paramedics didn't see the irony or sarcasm in Mick's comments.

"We're taking you to the hospital," he said. "We want to help you. Now what's your name?"

"See the blue shirt Nazi over there. He's got all the information you need."

"Where do you live?"

"I already told you, see him." Mick couldn't point. His hands were cuffed behind his back and strapped to the gurney. He was very uncomfortable and his blood pressure had risen to its boiling point.

"I'm here to help you." The paramedic was persistent.

"If you're here to help me, then leave me alone!" Mick blurted out.

Finally the questions stopped. Mick's mind was still racing though. He saw the cops searching his vehicle like they were looking for something. All this for a seat belt, he thought; how pimpy can you get? Was this a set-up? Strange, strange things have been happening lately.

Mick couldn't put a finger on it though. He never did get a chance to talk to Debbie or Jack about their busts. Nothing to brag about, he guessed. In all the years he'd been going to the Golden Door, he'd never heard of anyone getting busted. Now, all of a sudden, everyone was. Strange, strange indeed, he thought.

The ride in the ambulance was uneventful after the grilling, but it started right up again at the hospital.

"What's your name?" a nurse asked.

"See him," Mick replied.

"What is your address?"

"What the fuck is the matter with you people? I already told you this cop has all the info you need!" Mick was in no mood to cooperate with anyone.

"Watch your mouth." Ben Smide finally spoke up.

"How about loosening these cuffs? You've cut off the circulation in my hands." Mick got no response, but a doctor came over.

"Which foot is swollen?" He asked.

"If you can't see which one is swollen, I don't want you touching me." Mick had no mercy on anyone. He was unrelenting. He was in pain, he was uncomfortable, and he was being babysat by a crooked cop who constantly wore a crooked shit-eating grin.

The doctor told the nurse to take Mick's blood and put his foot in a cast. The nurse came over with a syringe to take his blood, when Mick hollered out, "What are you doing? Injecting me with AIDS? You blood-sucking Jew Nazis!" Mick's brain was thundering over his helpless condition. He was in a very surly mood.

The nurse was in no mood either. She called for two orderlies who rolled Mick over and held him down until the nurse took his blood. When she was done, another nurse came over and fitted him with a temporary cast.

Lying on his back again, Mick still couldn't get comfortable. The cuffs were digging into his wrists. There was a constant pressure. His muscular chest and shoulders made it impossible for him to get comfortable.

"I have to go to the bathroom," he told the officer. He really didn't have to, but he wanted the cuffs loosened. One of his hands was going completely numb.

"You're going to have to hold it until we get back to the police station,"

Ben said. "I'm not going to take the cuffs off, and I'm not going to hold it for you either."

Mick settled in the best he could. It seemed like an eternity to him before the nurse came back with the blood-work results.

"What did you arrest him for?" she asked the officer.

"He wasn't wearing his seatbelt and he didn't pass a field sobriety test."

"Don't try to justify yourself, motherfucker." Mick was testier than ever.

"How do you fill out this release form?" the nurse asked.

"I'll fill it out for you," Ben replied.

The orderlies came back and wheeled Mick back out to the squad car. They gave him a pair of crutches and a prescription for pain to take with him. On the drive back to the police station, Mick noticed he wasn't buckled into the back seat. He envisioned his head slamming into the squad's cage if the driver slammed on the brakes and, to add insult to injury, Mick noticed the cop wasn't wearing a seatbelt either.

Mick knew it was going to cost him anyway, se he might as well get his money's worth and have some fun giving everyone a hard time and a day they'd never forget. After all, he felt he needed witnesses to verify he had a swollen ankle at the time of his arrest, feeling the officer violated his rights as well as the proper procedure for detaining a handicapped person.

He also realized it was useless to complain. The crutches were given to him as a matter of hospital procedure, even though he didn't need them. They were just padding the bill, he thought.

Upon arrival at the police station, Ben was free to get his digs in. He took Mick's crutches away and tried to make him hop into the jail.

"Come on, hop, asshole," he said.

Mick turned cold and didn't respond to any of his tauntings. He knew he was staring straight into a video camera. He stored the information in his memory bank. He figured he may use it someday at the trial.

When it came time to make his phone call, he called the bar and left a message for Jen to come and get him. The bail was eight hundred dollars, and he was well short of that. While Mick stewed in the clink, his thoughts returned to Debbie and Jack's busts. Was this cop the same cop? he wondered. Was this the dumpster-diving cop? He didn't know for sure, but he did know something was wrong—big time.

Jen didn't get around to bailing him out until the next day, and Mick's fury hadn't been diluted any. While she was bailing him out, the cop on duty was all smiles. They're always polite and happy whey they have your money in their hands, Mick thought. It was a task for him to keep his temper and mouth in check. If it wasn't for the presence of a lady, he would have ripped into the desk sergeant, too. He got his walking papers and was adding it up already: eight hundred for bond and one hundred-twenty-five to get his car back. Mick was not a happy camper.

When they got to Jen's car, he put his crutches in the back seat.

"Well? What happened?" she asked. But before he could answer, she went on. "Good thing I have a lawyer on retainer. Half my staff needs him." Jen was a little miffed too. "Damn it anyway! I buy all their charity and special events' tickets that I never use. What more can I do?"

"You know then, I think they're laying for us," Mick finally got a word in.

"Yes, someone's got a bug up their ass. Well, what happened?"

"He must have been casing the lot and saw me limp out of the bar," Mick responded. "He said he pulled me over for a seatbelt violation. I want to find out if he's the same guy who got Debbie and Jack."

"It won't make any difference. You'll have to plead to reckless driving and go to traffic school."

"No, I won't," Mick said. "The seatbelt law has to be in violation of the Constitution."

Jen didn't say anything.

"How can the government force anyone to buy safety equipment," Mick continued, "and then force you to use it? The Constitution guarantees me that I have the right to protect my own self, but that I also have the right to protect myself against government. These people are professional thieves! I wasn't far off when I called that cop a blue shirt Nazi. They're just dictators."

"That's not the way it works, Mick." Jen interjected. "It's not worth fighting over. Even if you're right, it's cheaper just to cop a plea."

"Exactly! The problem with this system is nobody has the money or the guts to fight for their rights."

"Simmer down, Mick. It's not the end of the world. You can talk to my lawyer and see what he has to say." Jen pulled into the tow truck lot so Mick could get his car. "Do you want your crutches?"

"No," Mick replied. "I'll meet you at the house."

They both said "see you later," and Jen drove off.

CHAPTER 11

Earlier Ben Smide was on the phone with the mayor. "He didn't have any dope in his car," he was explaining.

"Did you look under the seats?"

"Yeah."

"And you're sure?"

"Yeah, I'm sure. That guy gave me nothing but shit. I sure wish I could have found something on him. He nailed me for getting kickbacks from Tony's Tow. He called me a lying thief and a blue shirt Nazi—'working for the Jewish Nazis' is how he put it. Who the fuck is that guy?"

"He called you a blue shirt Nazi, did he? Well, I'll show that motherfucker what a Nazi really is!"

"What are you planning on doing?"

"I don't know yet. I need some time to think." Click! I think I need a drink, the mayor thought to himself. He went to his hideaway bar and poured a stiff one.

He started humming to himself, "ta-dum, ta-dum, ta-dum," and thinking: I made myself a drink. "Ta-dum, ta-dum." I'll walk around. "Ta-dum, ta-dum." I've got a lot to think about. "Ta-dum, ta-dum." He then did some sort of aborted-effort dance with himself, wiggling his huge backside like a stripper. He thought it was a good thing he was by himself, because even he knew his ludicrous imitation was laughable.

He sat back down at his desk and took out his cell phone. He hit the memory button and looked up the number Don called to inquire about the coke. This is too simple, the mayor thought as if to applaud himself. He wrote down the number. He decided to trace it later for the name and address.

That fuck Don, he thought, is playing me for a chump. That singin' bitch never put no drugs under that guy's seat. If you want to do things right, you'd better do them yourself, he thought.

The mayor called Ben Smide back. "Ben, I want to see you in my office as soon as you can. I've got a job for you."

When Ben came over, the mayor offered him a drink.

"No thanks," Ben said.

"Suit yourself."

The mayor started telling Ben a tale about him and the chief, and how they used to rob drug dealers "back in the good ol' days," as he put it. But the chief, he said, was too old and looking forward to retiring. "He'll have to be replaced someday, Ben."

He was laying on the fatherly advice thick, like an old pro.

"The thing is, I'd like to see you get his job, but first we have another job to do. I have first-hand information about a drug dealer out in the Heights. Even though it's out of our jurisdiction, I've got clout with the sheriff. I want to go out there and scope the place out. We'll get the van out of my parts warehouse. I've got a telescopic camera that can read plate numbers a block away. We'll find out who these fucks are. They're easy marks. That's how I cleaned up this town. Nobody does nothing that I don't know about. It's a win-win situation. Either we bust 'em or rob 'em. You can keep the accolades or the money. Are you with me, boy?"

"Yeah, you bet, John. Count me in."

"Good. Let's go."

The Heights was a rural area, mostly farm land. The houses were sparse and set off the street with large stands of trees separating spacious lots.

As it happened, they cruised slowly past the house they were looking for. It was an average brick ranch, with attached garage and neatly trimmed lawn. They were in luck. The garage door was open and they could see a 'Vette inside. There was also a new Ford 4x4 pickup out on the driveway being washed by a Mexican.

"Perfect," said John. "Pull over down at the corner." He got out his telescopic camera and started taking pictures. "That's got to be him. It looks like an easy mark. Make one more pass by the house. I want some close-ups."

As Ben cruised by, John was clicking away.

"Perfect!" John bragged. "See that 'Vette in there? I bet that boy never worked a day in his life." He started rubbing his hands together in a greedy fashion. "This will be a piece of cake."

"Yeah," Ben agreed. "Did you see that Mexican's house? It's nicer than mine! He sticks out like a sore thumb. What's he doing out in this part of the country anyway?"

"You know, what we should do is come back in a couple hours and check for cars again," John said. "First, we develop the film, run the plates, and get his name. See if we can dig up a warrant or rap sheet on him."

That they did. They ran the license plate numbers through the D.M.V. and came up with "Juan Beamer." He owned both vehicles. Then they checked for a police record—nothing. They checked the county tax records and found he didn't own the house. Typical drug dealer, they deduced, and probably an illegal alien.

"Perfect," John said again. "All's we have to do is wait down the block on him. When he makes a move, pull him over in the unmarked car. Cuff him. Put him in the back of the squad, get his keys with his IDs, drive him around for an hour or so, and I'll search his house for the drug money or drugs or weapons. You never know what you might find. Cut him loose when I'm done, and the beauty of it all is: drug dealers can't complain to nobody—especially an illegal alien, or they'll send him back to Mexico. Nobody would believe him anyway."

"Beautiful plan, John," Ben said. "I wonder how much money he has stashed."

"Could be a hundred thousand. You never know."

"Damn! Let's go back and check on that house again."

"OK, let's go. But first, I need a drink." As the mayor poured his drink, his mind drifted. Ta-dum, ta-dum, ta-dum. I'll walk around, ta-dum, ta-dum. I've got a lot to think about, ta-dum, ta-dum. Oh, yeah. He started laughing to himself. Should have fucked that bitch and I will, or my name isn't John Quibly.

Mick unwrapped the cast as soon as he got home. He took some more pain pills, and he found there was still ice floating on top of the water in the cooler. He stuck his foot back in it.

"Ah, ooh," he mouthed.

Jen was scurrying about in the kitchen, cooking or cleaning or something. "You want a sandwich, Mick?" she hollered down to the family room.

"Yeah, sounds good!"

She brought it downstairs with a beer. "How's my little crippled jailbird feeling?" she asked with a wry smile.

"Ha. Ha," Mick mimicked laughing. He was hungry though. She had made a ham sandwich with lettuce, cheese, and mustard, neatly cut in half with some potato chips on the side. He wolfed it down faster than he could savor the flavors. "That hit the spot," he said. "Thanks."

She took the empty plate up to the kitchen and came back downstairs and sat with Mick on the couch. She put her hand on his knee and said, "You know, I've never made love to a jailbird before. Are you in the mood?"

Surprises never cease was the thought that flashed through Mick's mind. "Is that a trick question?" he asked. "Sure, I'm in the mood."

"Then I'll start up the whirlpool and you can come upstairs with me." She grabbed his hand and said, "Come on, honey."

Mick yanked his foot out of the cooler in an instant and barely tapped it dry with a towel and followed Jen's lead upstairs. He had never been in her bedroom before, even though he'd heard about the whirlpool. It was extra large—plenty of room for two or three. She opened the faucets and poured in an assortment of bath oils, which filled the air with a sensual fragrance. Then she added some bubblebath. As Mick looked around, he saw a big double bed on the other side of the room. Her whole bedroom was decorated impeccably.

He put his hand to his face and realized he had day-old stubble and needed a shave. His gear, however, was downstairs. He looked around on the bathroom counter but didn't see anything he could use. So he decided to say, "I need a shave and my gear is downstairs."

"Don't worry, Mick. I'll take care of everything. Now here, give me your shirt." She reached for the buttons and undid them. He was still in his shorts and she undid the button and zipper. They dropped to the floor and he stepped out of them.

"Go ahead, climb in!" Jen urged.

Mick removed his briefs and gingerly stepped inside the whirlpool. Jen turned on the water jets and bubbles started rising. The water felt different to him, silky, slick, and fragrant. He was used to plain old shower water. He stretched out and let the water jets massage his legs and back. Jennifer set a tray of utensils and accessories on the edge of the bath and lit candles at the other end.

As she was busying herself, Mick slid down, submersing himself and soaking his hair. When he wiped the suds from his face and eyes, he found the lights had been dimmed. The gentle flicker of light from the candles completed a very sexy atmosphere.

While he was relaxing, Jen disrobed and slipped in behind him. "Do you like?" she asked.

"Another silly question," he replied.

"Scoot over here so I can wash your hair."

"OK." He slid right over on cue.

She took some lavender Herbal Essence shampoo and applied it to his hair. She worked up a lather and her fingers probed his head like a pro. The scalp massage and swirling waters relaxed Mick's tension away. He felt all his muscles just melt.

With all anxieties removed, he floated in heavenly bliss until he was awakened by a splash from a retractable spray nozzle. The shampoo was being rinsed.

"Now give me your hand."

Mick sat up a little and she took his hand. She took a cuticle remover tool from her tray and started poking his fingernails. Mick's instant reaction was to pull his hand away.

"Hold still," she said. "Look at these nails. They're all rough."

As she poked his fingers, he noticed how her breasts swayed in the suds with the rhythm of her strokes. Partially hidden by the bubbles, her nipples still stood out.

"I've never gotten a manicure in a whirlpool before," he said.

"Oh, I do it all the time," she replied. With his free hand he scooped up some suds and started to massage one of her breasts. She looked up at him and smiled. "Wait until I'm finished. There's plenty of time to play." He withdrew his hand but not his eyes.

Then she got out the emery board and went over every finger again. "There now. I'll polish them later. We must do something about your whiskers. Come on now over to the sink, before you turn into a prune."

She had foam and Lady Bics in the mirrored medicine cabinet. "This should do the trick." She squirted the foam in her hand and applied it to his face. Then she gently started to shave him. "Don't move," she warned.

Mick was beginning to wonder what all the primping was about, but he didn't mind. He was starting to enjoy the special attention. She carefully went over every inch of his face with the razor, and then felt with her hand to see if she missed any stubble. Then she would go over it again.

"There," she said. "Smooth as a baby's bottom."

She led him over to her bed and pulled down the covers.

"Get in," she said. "Mind me now. This is your play room. There is no sleeping in here."

"OK," he said.

"I have a surprise for you. I'll be right back."

When she left the room, he wondered: What surprise does she have in store for me now?

Jen came back with a bottle of champagne, the one from Vegas, and a plate of fresh strawberry shortcake. "I went shopping yesterday, and I couldn't resist."

Mick's eyes lit up at the sight. She opened the bottle and poured the champagne into two stemmed glasses.

"Here." She gave Mick a glass. She had always wondered why Mick ordered such room service in Vegas, so she asked, "Does strawberry shortcake give you extra energy?"

"Kind of," he responded. "When you finish your drink, I want you to lay down and close your eyes."

She was puzzled by the request, but the curiosity of the sexual adventure was giving her goose bumps.

It was Mick's turn to pamper when she lay down. His eyes devoured her beautiful body. He bent over and gave her a kiss.

"No peeking now," he said.

He had no use for the cake, but he considered the whipped cream and strawberries to be a delicacy. He used a spoon to scoop up the whipped cream and put some of it on one nipple, some more on her other nipple, and then topping each off with a strawberry. Jen's apprehension was starting to run wild. Then he repeated the steps on her belly button and upon her well-trimmed bush.

"Now," he said, "you look good enough to eat."

Right then he dove in with his mouth and tongue, tasting, teasing, prodding, lapping, sipping, inhaling—nothing was wasted. Before long Jen was crying for mercy. "Stop," she would say, only to contradict herself with, "No, don't!" She was moaning profusely. She then blurted out, "Oh! I love it! I love you! Don't stop! Oh, what have I done?"

Jen was in a state of euphoria. Her mind was flying between reality and ecstasy. This can't be happening to me! she thought. Oh!

Her nerves were lit like a multicolored string of strobes.

Mick stopped tasting and climbed up her body to penetrate her tenderness.

Jen was confused mentally and physically. She couldn't tell what she wanted anymore. She bucked her hips at him. "Come on, honey. Come on!" She tightened her pelvic muscles around his swollen strength. "Come on, honey!"

She found his rhythm and bucked with him. With a flood she felt his love heat explode within her.

"Oh, honey!!" she bucked at him some more to encourage him to stay on and up, but he was exhausted and spent. He rolled off.

"I think we need to shower," he whispered.

"Not now! Hold me," she moaned.

Jen didn't realize her hormones were changing. She was confused, yes, but new life was forming deep within.

CHAPTER 12

Ben and the mayor went back out to the Heights that night. John left his trademark white suit in the office closet, while changing into a dark blue windbreaker with a shoulder holster and snub-nose .38 special underneath. They were taking Ben's unmarked cruiser this time.

The mayor opened up his wind bag on the ride over. "We've got to get an M.O. on this guy," he said. "Most small-time drug dealers go out partying at night to sell their wares. Big-time dealers sell out of their homes during the day. We have to find the best time to crack him. We have to get him when he's alone—no witnesses—that's the important thing. Pull him over on one of those dark country roads. I know this guy's got a kilo for sale. He's big time, probably armed and dangerous. We have to be careful. I smell a hundred grand on this guy. He ain't no small time."

"Yeah," Ben finally got a word in. "It really pisses me off. Those drug dealers are making millions, while I work my ass off for peanuts."

They drove by the house. The front room light was on. The 4x4 pickup was in the same spot, but the garage door was closed. No other cars in the drive meant no visitors.

They sat in the cruiser for an hour down at the corner, watching the house.

"Nothing moving," Ben said.

"Yeah, I'm getting bored too. Maybe we should call it a night. I need a drink anyway."

"Why don't we just go up to the door and bust him?" Ben's impatience was getting to him.

"No, he might panic and pull a pistol. Too messy. We have to get him in his car. That way, he won't know what's up until it's too late."

"Yeah, I guess you're right," Ben said apologetically. He'd been daydreaming about all the things he could do with a hundred thousand dollars. Go on a cruise to the Bahamas. Find himself a whore and party for days on end. Buy himself a new house and car. Get a new fishing boat. Or, better yet, buy a hunting and fishing lodge on a good lake. Yeah, that would be heaven, he thought.

His daydream was interrupted when the mayor said, "There he is!"

Ben snapped to. "Oh, yeah!"

The mayor started to rub his hands together greedily. "Let's get him."

The pickup backed up and stopped, pulled forward with a half turn, backed up again and pulled forward, completing a driveway U-turn. Then the driver pulled out onto the road, going in the opposite direction of the cruiser, giving him no chance of seeing the squad.

Ben started to laugh with anticipation. "Did you see he's not wearing a seatbelt?"

"Well, you got better eyes than mine, but let him get a mile down the road before you pull him over."

"You got it, John."

"This is perfect," said the mayor. Again he started rubbing his hands together with nervous energy.

Following a mile down the road, Ben said, "I do believe this guy's speeding." He turned on his squad lights and pulled the unsuspecting Juan Beamer over.

John Quibly had it all figured out. When Ben put the cuffs on the guy, he would get out of the squad and step to the rear, so the victim wouldn't get a good look at his face when he was being put into the back seat. Ben would drive him around, leaning on the prisoner to show him where all the drug dealers lived and who he got his supplies from—if he wanted to go free. While he really didn't expect any cooperation from the drug dealer, he just needed an excuse for the delay.

Meanwhile, John figured he would drive the truck back to the house and ransack it, and if Ben thought he was going to let him keep all the money like he promised, then Ben was a bigger idiot than he thought. If the mayor found a hundred grand, Ben would be lucky if he got ten.

John was trying to figure out where he would stash the cash without Ben finding out. He was daydreaming about the money too, and how to hide it from Ben and the old lady. He could buy back the bar outright, if he had the cash and a place to launder more cash.

While John was dreaming, he was watching Ben in the spotlight from the squad. Then he saw an extra flash and then the sound of gunfire reverberating.

"Oh, shit!" he said to himself, as he climbed out of the squad and rushed over to Ben. He was standing there like a frozen sculpture with a drawn pistol.

"What happened, Ben?" the mayor asked emotionally.

Ben just stood there staring at the dead body. He had shot Juan in the head. His body was slumped over the shift console.

"Oh, shit!" the mayor said when he saw the carnage. "Put your gun away," he ordered the zombie-like Ben.

"I… I thought he had a gun," the whimpering rookie said. He was staring at a cell phone that landed on the lap of the deceased.

"Snap to, Ben!" barked the mayor. "It'll be all right, don't worry." He started to look down the road. No car lights in either direction. "Come on, Ben. Get back in your car and put the gun away!"

John grabbed his arm and tugged. "Get in your car and give me some rubber gloves. Come on, move it!"

Ben snapped out of his trance and followed John back to the squad.

"Turn off those lights!" John demanded further.

Ben reached in the glove compartment and retrieved a box of latex gloves. "What are you going to do, John?"

"Stop your sniveling and listen up. We're dumping the body back at his house, and we're looking for the money as planned."

John put on a pair of gloves and stuck an extra pair in his pocket. "I want you to drive back to where we were parked before, and wait for me."

"OK," Ben said meekly.

John went back to the truck and shoved the dead body head-first over the console until it lay crumpled up on the passenger side floor. Then he made a U-turn and a bee-line back to the house.

He found the garage door opener on the sun visor and let himself in, parking next to the Corvette. He took the keys out of the ignition and let himself in through the utility door.

The mayor's adrenaline had built to a crescendo. His heart pumped extra hard with every light he had to turn on. Wearing his clean pair of gloves, he only turned on the ones he thought necessary and moved with the stealth of a fat cat. He was careful not to disturb anything that wasn't necessary. He found the master bedroom and looked around—nothing. He found the walk-in closet and turned on the light. "Bingo!" he whispered to himself.

There was a triple beam scale on top of a dresser cabinet inside. He opened the top drawer. :Bingo!" he whispered again.

Inside the drawer he found a gram scale and various sizes of pre-wrapped bags of white powder. Coke or crack—the mayor didn't care. He stuffed the little bags into a bigger bag.

Then he opened the next drawer and found bags of cannabis. He went back to the kitchen where he found trash bags. He returned to the bedroom where he loaded his finds into one of the black plastic bags. The rest of the dresser drawers were filled with socks and underwear.

Now, where is the money? he wondered. Look for a suitcase or duffel bag. He checked the top shelf of the closet first—nothing. Then he looked under the bed—nope. Back to the kitchen he went, searching the cabinets—nothing. He set his garbage bag full of goodies down by the front door. He looked around the furniture. Everything was neat and in proper order. He thought, Now where would a dealer hide his cash?

Sweat beads were forming on his forehead. He knew he didn't have all night. He had to find it now, or kiss it good-bye. He wiped his brow with his sleeve. If he got caught now, he realized, he would have a hard time explaining his way out of this one.

One more pass, he thought to himself.

He went back down the hall to the master bedroom, stopped inside, and looked around again. It was there somewhere—he could smell it. But it wasn't in that room. This guy wouldn't keep his cash in the same room with his stash, he thought. So he went into a second bedroom across the hall and turned on a light. It looked like an office, with a computer, printer, and fax machine sitting on a desk. He checked the desk drawers, the closet, the furniture—nothing. He tugged on the drawers of a file cabinet. It was locked. "Damn!" he cursed in a whisper.

He was going back to get the keys which he left dangling in the utility door to see if there was a cabinet key among them, when his cell phone rang. He looked at the ID number. It was Ben. "Yeah?" he answered.

Ben was blubbering. "What's taking you so long? Everybody's looking at me!"

In reality, only two cars had driven past while John was searching, and neither one had noticed the parked cruiser at all.

"Fuck!" the mayor said. He'd forgotten that the rookie was probably a basket case by now. "I can't find the fucking money! That's what's taking me so long. Give me five more minutes and, when you see me walking down the drive, come pick me up. No, no. Never mind that. Just wait right where you are. I'll be there in five more minutes." Never send a kid, he thought, to do a man's job.

He went back to the kitchen, when the house phone rang. The mayor grabbed at his heart. The unexpected ring instantly fried his nerves. "Fuck it," he whispered. "I'm otta here."

His heart was pounding madly now. He rushed to pick up the goods and exited the front door. He hurriedly waddled down the walkway and drive as fast as his fat stubby legs could move.

Ben saw him when he crossed the road and started the cruiser. He met him half-way. When John jumped in, he set the garbage bag down at his feet. He was huffing and puffing like he just ran a marathon.

It took John awhile to catch his breath. He took off his latex gloves and shoved them in his pocket. His hands were all sweaty and his forehead dripped.

"Fuck," he said. "I'm getting too old for this." He grabbed his heart again which was still pounding. He sucked up all the air he could, and exhaled slowly. "Fuck. I couldn't find the money, but I found his dope."

Ben was feeling a rush too. He was doing 70 m.p.h. in a 40 zone.

"Slow down!" John ordered. "And calm down. The last thing we need is to get in a wreck."

Ben eased off the gas and turned on the main highway, heading for home. He was in a state of silent shock. Both hands were firmly clamped on the steering wheel, his knuckles were turning white, but he couldn't feel the pain.

"Take me back to the office, Ben. You hear me?"

"Huh? Oh, yeah. I hear you."

"Snap out of it, man! Everything will be just fine. You hear me?"

"Yeah, I hear you."

"Dealing drugs is a dangerous game. That guy got just what he deserved. Don't let it get under your skin."

"Yeah, OK."

They pulled into city hall's parking lot. The mayor grabbed the bag of drugs. "Come on in and have a drink," he said. "It'll be good for your nerves."

"Yeah, OK."

Ben was still in a comatose condition. He usually didn't drink, but he was in such a state of fog that it was easier just to follow orders.

The mayor put the bag on top of his desk and dumped out the contents. "That guy must have been a small-time dealer. My guess is there's only five grand worth of shit here."

Ben just stared at it, while John went to his bar and pulled out a bottle of Jack and two shot glasses. He filled them both and gave one to Ben. They clicked them together.

"Better luck next time," the mayor said.

They downed the shots in unison. The mayor took his in stride. Ben gagged slightly. "Ooh," he mouthed, and his body shivered.

The mayor filled the glasses again.

"What are we going to do with this stuff?" Ben asked.

"I'll figure out something," John said.

"Can you sell it? I sure could use the money."

"No, we can't sell it. Well, maybe." The mayor's mind was whirling again. He wanted the dope to use a drops against the Golden Door. Arrest them enough times, he thought, then he would have an excuse for the liquor board to revoke their license.

He needed Ben to do that, and he knew it. Now, he thought, how to pacify Ben and keep him in line—that was the question.

"Have another shot, Ben," he said with a friendly smile as he poured him one. "We gotta lay low on this for awhile. See what happens when they find the body. It should hit the news in a few days. I'm sure they'll blame it on a gangland slaying. Why did you shoot him anyway?" Before Ben had time to answer, the mayor continued, "If you would have stuck to the plan, you could have asked him where the money was. I know I smelled it in there, but I couldn't find it."

Ben was staring again at the dope on the desk. "I wonder what it's like," he blurted out.

"What what's like?" the mayor demanded.

"To snort cocaine."

"Go ahead and try it. It's overrated, that's for sure." The mayor slipped up with his "overrated" comment. That meant he'd done it before himself.

Ben was in a state of depression. He realized he'd just murdered someone, and that it was no accident. But he didn't realize exactly what a state of depression was, nor that he was in one. "Don't shoot me" were the last words out of Juan's mouth. Ben decided he wasn't going to take any shit from anyone ever again.

He opened a package of coke and spilled some on the desk. He licked his finger and stuck it in the little pile. He put the glistening white powder in his mouth for a taste. It reminded him of novocaine at the dentist's office. He rolled his tongue around and it felt a little numb. He repeated the steps, but this time he put the cocaine on his gums.

He smacked his lips together and paused, thinking what's the big deal with this stuff? He thought it was just like an anesthetic.

"You're supposed to snort it, not eat it," John said, as if he were reading the questions in Ben's head.

"Here." The mayor took out a credit card and chopped up the powder and arranged some of it in a thin short line. He then took out a hundred dollar bill and rolled it up into a fat straw. He handed it to Ben. "Go ahead, snort it." So he did.

Then Ben stood back and sniffed the remnants in his nose up into his head. His nose started to run, and he sucked up the drainage too. Now he felt better.

He then took the card and made another line for the other nostril, and snorted that up as well.

"That should do the trick," he said. He started to smile, and then his somber mood was gone. "What's all the hype about? Ain't nothin' special about this. It's just like novocaine."

"But it is special," John countered. "You just snorted up a hundred dollars' worth."

"What?" Ben asked in disbelief. "I would never pay a hundred dollars for that!"

"I know, but some people will," John said. "That's why I like my whiskey." He poured them both another shot. "Cheers," he said.

John was cheery now. He knew he had Ben right where he wanted him—under his thumb. "Take some home with you if you want, but don't get caught. It's illegal to have this stuff, and you know how the cops can be."

That comment struck Ben as funny, and he started to laugh hysterically. John joined in the laughter. Ben had to hold his stomach, as it was cramping up. When he finally calmed down, he took two packets of coke and put them in his pocket. John cleared the desk of dope, putting it back in the bag and storing it on the shelf in his closet. He took off his shoulder holster and swapped jackets again.

"One more for the road," he said, as he poured two more shots.

It wasn't until Monday afternoon that Juan's body was found. Two men from the company came to the house when Juan didn't report in or answer his phone. The insurance investigators called their boss to inform him: "He'd dead, as in murdered."

"Empty the file cabinets. Remove the computer and all the disks before we call the police," their boss told them. "That's company property and we don't need the sheriff snooping around into our files or operations."

Ralph Swanson was the investigating manager of the insurance company's division that the public never hears about. He met with the C.E.O. and other top executives to digest the information and discuss how to proceed. It was decided that the case was probably due to a robbery: murder for drugs. This was a clandestine operation, as the drugs were used as an investigative tool. The operatives and management would naturally have to deny any knowledge of this arrangement, but since Juan was one of their own and in their safe house, a complete investigation was ordered.

They deduced that the killer was in their files, and that this wasn't a crime of happenstance. They also wanted to plant disinformation with the newspapers and media, partially to deflect any of their own culpability but more so to instigate a belief among the killer or killers that they missed "the big score." The idea was to plant twenty thousand dollars, which they would have used as reward money anyway, just to get the chatter started and see who slips up.

"Get on it right away," said the C.E.O. "Double time for all agents. Hit all the hot spots and get on those files," he ordered. The meeting was adjourned.

Ralph, as chief investigator, picked up $20,000 in cash from the accounting department, signed out as reward money, and went directly to the safe house. His other operatives were almost finished removing company property.

"When you're done," he said with authority, "take all the equipment directly to my office." He then started taking pictures of the scene and the body.

"Anything else?" one of his men asked.

"No. I'll handle it from here."

The money was banded and placed in a plain paper grocery bag. Ralph stuffed it inside the pickup in the garage, under the driver's seat. He was careful not to disturb the body or anything else. Satisfied he could do no more, he called the sheriff's department.

"I want to report a murder. His name was Juan Beamer. My name is Ralph Swanson. Juan was one of my employees from Swanson's Landscaping. I'll wait right here till you arrive."

CHAPTER 13

Rule Number One had now been compromised: playground only. But Jen didn't seem to mind when Mick woke up next to her. Just the same, he felt out of place. He gathered his clothes and went back downstairs.

He started the coffee pot brewing and then took his shower. Jen had a cup in hand when Mick returned.

"Good morning," she said with a smile.

"Good morning," he returned.

She was dressed in one of her business suits. Her black leather briefcase was at her feet. She was ready for work.

Fresh out of the shower, Mick had a bath towel wrapped around his waist. He was pouring a cup for himself, when Jen sneaked up behind him and tugged at his towel, which unwrapped and fell to the floor. Mick spilled some of his coffee as he set the pot and cup down too suddenly on the counter. He instinctively grabbed the towel off the floor and covered himself back up.

Jen laughed heartily. "My, my," she said, as Mick's face flushed. "You embarrass easily for a naked pool man."

She laughed again and Mick joined in.

"You got me there," he said.

"And what are your plans for today, my beautiful naked pool man?"

"I don't know. I guess, since I'm already naked, I might as well clean the pool."

"Sounds like a plan. Too bad I won't be here to enjoy the show. I'll call you later." She gave Mick a kiss, put her empty cup in the sink, and left with a smile on her face.

Jen is acting differently lately, Mick thought. He didn't understand that gay or lesbian thing anyway. Was it a phase some women go through? Must be a phase, he thought. She sure doesn't act gay around me.

Mick couldn't find a word that seemed to fit right. He didn't know how to describe his feelings for her either. She was growing on him, and he was starting to feel better about their relationship. Before, he had been a "Doubting Thomas," never believing such a relationship would ever work out. He still had his doubts, but not as many. Seeing is believing, he thought. That is the saying in the "Show Me" state. Mick had only previously driven through Missouri, but he knew the state was proud of its motto. In most cases, he reasoned, that saying runs true in everyday life experiences.

He finished his coffee. He thought about having another cup, as there was some left in the pot. No, he decided, save it for later. He turned the switch off on the appliance.

He looked out the sliding patio doors at the pool. Yeah, he thought, it is a good day for a swim. The sun was shining and the morning seemed quite warm.

He slid back the door and stepped out on the patio. His ankle felt a lot better. It was still a little swollen, but he no longer limped. He walked up to the pool's edge and quickly looked around for any gawkers, as if it mattered. He knew the area was kept private by the solid board fence.

He dropped his towel and dove in for a morning skinny-dip.

Mick was enjoying the freedom of no trunks, as he swam lap after lap. Maybe, he thought, those nudist people have a good thing going. No, maybe not. He knew he could never get naked in front of children.

After tiring from swimming, he got out of the pool and set up the automatic skimmer and hoses. He figured he'd let that do the dirty work. There wasn't much debris floating on the surface anyway, just a few leaves and bugs. He retrieved the net and fished those out quickly, replacing it when he was finished.

He heard the patio door open and looked around. Heather was standing there, gawking at Mick in all his glory. After he picked up his jaw from the concrete, he dove right back in the pool.

The cool water knocked the red from his face. His towel was on the other side, but Heather was kind enough to make a U-turn.

Mick wasted no time jumping out and retrieving his towel. Oh well, he thought, busted again. He half-laughed to himself.

Heather was on the phone and didn't even look at him when he walked by to get to his room. He felt a cold stare through his bedroom door as he dressed, and his ears were burning too. She was probably on the phone to Jennifer, he reasoned. He wanted to avoid any confrontation, so he simply waved good-bye and left by the front door. Let those two work it out, he thought. It's safer that way. He still had to work with Heather that night at the Golden Door, so he hoped this incident wouldn't evolve into any bitterness.

Ah, he thought when he arrived back at his place, home again. Or, was this home-away-from-home? Anyway, he had things to do. He started with his laundry.

Mick was right about one thing. Heather had been on the phone with Jennifer, but they didn't have a big row or anything of the sort. Heather was every bit a free spirit, even more so than Jennifer. It was true, they both loved each other but, like any other lovers, they had their differences too.

When Mick showed up that night for his shift, Heather and Debbie were already there. It was pool tournament night, and Jack was running that. The bar was a little slow, but the action was expected to pick up later.

Heather didn't seem terribly upset, but Mick sidestepped her anyway. What he really had on his mind was that cop. He pulled Jack aside the first chance he got for a little privacy and inquired about his bust. Who was the cop and what did he pull Jack over for were Mick's top questions.

Jack got pulled over for crossing the center line, "which was total bullshit!" he said emphatically. He said he got a warning ticket for that, but a real ticket for not wearing a seatbelt and another one for D.U.I.

"My kids are going to go hungry for awhile because of that one," Jack complained. "That cop fucked me over real good, but I don't know his name."

"Let me know the minute you find out, OK?" Mick asked.

"I sure will."

Jack went about his business lining up pool players. Mick went about his, going to the beer room and wheeling out a dolly full of cases to restock the bar.

When he finished, Mick tried to pull Debbie off to the side. "I need you to tell me about the night you got busted," he asked earnestly but quietly.

Her voice went up an octave. "Can't you see I'm busy?" she snapped.

"Debbie, it's important." Mick was trying to calm her down.

"The lawyer said I have to plead guilty to reckless driving, and go to traffic school. I have to pay $500 for the ticket and $600 for the school!"

"I know, I know." Mick was using his best soothing voice. "What I need to know is, who was the cop?"

"What difference does that make?" She was still chomping at the bit.

"I need to know if it's the same guy that got Jack and me."

She calmed slightly. "I don't know his name."

"Will you look at the ticket for me?"

"Yeah, sure. It ain't gonna make any difference though."

"You never know," Mick said. "If there's a pattern here, it might prove profiling. Why did he stop you in the first place?"

"For a seatbelt violation!" Her voice started rising again. "I don't know how he could tell if I was wearing a seatbelt in the middle of the night!" She was storming now, and she jetted off to get a customer another beer. *Sheesh*, Mick thought. Trying to get some simple information around here is like pulling teeth. He noticed that the garbage cans were full, so he busied himself emptying them. He started thinking about that pimpy cop and the seatbelt bullshit.

That law has to be a violation of one's Constitutional rights, he reasoned. The very thought of it started Mick's blood pressure to rise. I'm in charge of my own safety, he thought. Second Amendment: the right to bear arms. So therefore a man can protect himself, his property, and his own liberty!

Then his mind drifted off on another tangent. The founding fathers of the country, he thought, agreed to fight the tyrants and so will I. Mick decided to look up the Constitution and the Bill of Rights on his computer tomorrow. He promised himself: I am going to fight this thing. No plea bargain for me, and I don't care what it costs!

His thoughts were interrupted by a phone call. It was Jennifer.

"I heard you got caught with your pants down," she snickered.

"Yeah, sure did." His face started to blush as he glanced in Heather's direction. She was busy serving customers and didn't see his embarrassed expression.

"Well, everything is cool," said Jen. "I explained to her that it was my idea."

"That's good."

"How's business?" She changed the subject.

"Steady, but not crazy crowded."

"Are you coming home tonight?"

"Ah, if you want me to."

"I want! Are you caught up on your work?"

"Yeah."

"Then tell Debbie you'll be back in an hour. I want to see you. I'm home and I'll be waiting."

"OK."

Mick wasted no time in getting over there. He'd heard a sexy tone in her request. As he drove, he got excited with anticipation. He pulled into her drive, jumped out, opened the front door, and called her name. But all he heard was music out on the patio.

The pool lights were glowing in the darkness. He slid the patio door open and was standing right where Heather had stood earlier in the day, and he was witnessing something very special.

There was Jennifer, in all her glorious beauty, swimming in the buff.

Her dark hair fanned out on the water's surface and her buttocks glistened in the moonlight. She stopped long enough to invite Mick.

"Well, don't just stand there," she smiled. "Come in!"

She was a beautiful sight and Mick was undressed in a flash. He dove in, swimming to her and greeting her with a tongue-twisting kiss. She was more than willing to return the passion. There they swam together freely and gracefully as dolphins, as playfully as sea otters.

She had it planned all right. When their pool foreplay hit a crescendo, she pointed out a comforter blanket that she had previously laid out on the lawn. The glory of the night was spent there under the shining full moon. One hour quickly turned into two.

"I have to get back to work," Mick said.

"Oh, don't go," she instinctively said.

Jen didn't want to let him go. It was just that she was so comfortable laying outside, wrapped in Mick's arms. His body heat warmed her soul. It was an unusual feeling to her, a warmth and comfort she hadn't ever experienced before. As she snuggled with her man, her eyes were closed but she saw the moon. It was brighter than she had ever seen it before, but her eyes were closed. She felt Mick's warmth, but she had goose bumps. Her heart was purring right along in a comfort zone that she'd never felt before. She didn't understand it. All she knew was that she didn't want to let Mick go. It was a heavenly blissful evening until he ruined it by reminding her he had to get back to work.

"The girls will be mad at me, not you," he explained.

She relented with an "Oh, all right" in a disappointing tone. She realized he was right, and had a job to do. "You are coming back tonight, aren't you?"

"Yeah, sure thing."

They kissed again, and he left her smiling.

Mick hurriedly raced back to the bar. Dirty looks were coming from everyone but Jack. He had restocked all the coolers once already in Mick's absence and emptied the garbage. He was also running the pool tournament. He was all smiles though.

"So, where ya been, Mick?" he asked teasingly with a big old ear-to-ear grin.

Mick answered sheepishly. "I had some business to take care of. But thanks for backing me up."

"No trouble, bro," said Jack.

Mick was glad to see closing time roll around. He gave Jack a twenty from his own pocket in gratitude. Heather and Debbie left with nary a word. Mick helped himself to a beer and sat at the bar watching sports highlights on TV until they started to repeat themselves.

He was also pondering things. He didn't have Dawn's phone number, and karaoke night was tomorrow. Is she going to show up? he wondered. What was he going to do if she did show up? Turn her down, he figured. The girl was trouble, and that he didn't need. Why did she leave that pot in Mick's car? This was a real good question. He was thinking that something was going on, and it bothered him. Besides, he thought, things are going great with Jen. So why mess it up with trouble?

He answered most of his own questions himself. He finished his beer and locked up. He was cautious enough to scan the parking lot as far into the distance as he could, looking for another kind of trouble.

Mick did sleep downstairs that night. He was too tired, too pooped to pop, all passioned out. He needed a good night's sleep to recharge his batteries. He imagined Jen needed the same, as she was already sleeping anyway. He figured morning would arrive soon enough.

As it was, he slept in. He didn't wake up until quarter-to-noon. When he got to the coffee pot, he found a note: "Here is my lawyer's card. Give me a call at work."

He did call the lawyer to set up an appointment. Then he remembered the promise he made to himself. He went home and looked up the U.S. Constitution on the Internet.

He logged in on AOL and punched up www . usconstitution . com. He waited a minute and the website popped up on the screen. There was a lot of things to choose from. He started with the Bill of Rights. He scanned the monitor and knew this was what he wanted. He hit the print button. Then he repeated the steps and printed out the entire Constitution. He thought back to a time in high school which was the last time he had read the document. That was then when he had to read it. This was now, he thought, when he wants to read it. Again, and on his own time.

Mick imagined that most people take it for granted and have never read it. But fighting for freedom and liberty is a never-ending battle, he thought. Freedom needs constant vigilance. He was thinking of a quote from James Madison. He wasn't sure of the exact quote, but he knew the meaning of it. Mick felt like he was fighting for a cause now. There was something inherently wrong with laws like passenger restraints. It sounded to him like the end of freedom, like laws made up by dictators who make profit by violating Americans' Constitutional rights. Such people don't even have the courage to call it a "safety" belt, Mick reasoned, because they don't want to be liable when people get killed in one.

When he finished with the Constitution, he printed out the Declaration of Independence. That was short and quick—only one page but every bit as important. The more pages his printer spat out, the more patriotic Mick was becoming. He then printed out all the Amendments.

He didn't have to read far. The First Amendment covers freedom of religion, speech, the press, the right to peaceably assemble, and to petition the government for a redress of grievances. The Second Amendment assures the right of the people to keep and bear arms. Mick reasoned this meant that a person has the right to protect himself, his family, and his property.

There is a dangerous precedent being set here, he thought, when the government can force people to buy safety equipment and make them use it. What's next, he wondered, bulletproof vests? You might get shot by a drive-by gangbanger. Or how about gas masks? You might open a letter containing anthrax. Or how about making everyone dress like Arab women? You might get skin cancer from the sun. Mick started to laugh at his own silly exaggerated thoughts.

Getting back to reality, Mick figured the right to protect yourself— that's the key. There has to be plenty of case law to back that up. The government has the right to protect the public, but an individual has the right to protect—or not protect—himself. That's the ticket, Mick thought. He was gathering his thoughts together so he would know what to ask the lawyer when they met.

His thoughts further delved into the disability act. Even though he didn't know much about it, he felt that there's something inherently wrong with a cop who makes a guy walk heel-to-toe with a swollen ankle. Then he thought: the "fix" must have been in place. That cop had no intention of passing me on any of those tests, Mick thought, but he must have violated some procedural rule with that walking demand. So this was another question for the lawyer.

"Bad boys, bad boys. What you gonna do when they come for you?" That cop show theme song just popped into Mick's head. The video cam! That TV show suddenly reminded Mick that most squad cars use video cameras to record every stop an officer makes. Did his cop have one and was it running? Mick wondered. He knew that the camera in the jail was running. They always run for security. He reasoned that if his cop had one running, it would show the cop baiting him, trying to make him hop to jail. How ridiculous is that? Mick thought. Especially when he was in a cast and walking on crutches. He knew that that's the videotape he needed to prove how he was treated on the street.

While Mick was contemplating his case and the Bill of Rights, there were other future discoveries looming in the newspapers. One headline read: "Drug dealer found in mob style slaying." It didn't make the front page. It was semi-buried on page two of the local news section of the Times. Parts of the story went on to read: "gunshot to the head," "close range," "drug paraphernalia found," "$20,000 confiscated by the sheriff's department," "neighbors stunned," "saw or heard nothing," "police investigating," and "no known relatives."

Ben was in the mayor's office.

"See? I told you," the mayor said pointing to the article. "You have nothing to worry about. They don't have a clue. I'm just sorry we missed out on the cash. I knew it was there. Better luck next time." He threw the paper in his wastebasket.

Ben just sat in his chair, head bowed, staring at the floor.

The mayor continued his lecture. "It'll all blow over in a few days." He started pacing back and forth as he preached. He yammered on and on, giving his prophecies on Ben's bright future. He wanted a drink, but it was still too early even by his standards. "Go home. Relax. Get some sleep. You look tired."

Ben got up. "Yeah, maybe you're right. I'll see you later." Still looking dejected, he shuffled his feet out the door.

Damn! How did I miss that money? the mayor thought. He was still pacing, sometimes talking to himself. "Fuck it," he said. He pulled out his hideaway bar and poured some whiskey. He was wound up tighter than a baseball. He was worried.

"That Ben," he said aloud. "Sometimes he looks like he's going to crack up. The kid has no self-confidence. Gotta keep building him up." He downed his whiskey. I gotta change the scenery, he thought. There's nothing to do here today. I think maybe I'll head down to the strip club. Yeah, he thought, that's what I should do. I'm gonna go see my Susie Q.

CHAPTER 14

I t was karaoke night. Mick, Debbie, and Heather were there as usual. Heather was bouncing around, and Debbie was just as energetic.

New day, Mick thought. All's forgiven. Life at the Golden Door forges ahead. Everything's back to normal.

He was wondering if Dawn was going to come in. Yes, he had pipedreams about turning her into a recording star, but dreams like that can be very fleeting. He reminded himself that, really, he's got it made. He's got a good job and, much to his surprise, Jen is actually fulfilling his sexual needs too. He wasn't sure how long this would last, or if it would get better or worse. But he did see the logic of sticking with a good thing.

As it was, Dawn never showed up that night and Mick was kind of relieved. He wasn't quite sure how he would break it off with Dawn. If she smiled seductively at him, he might melt. He believed it would be real easy for him if she never showed up again. Besides the age difference, there would be constant competition for her affections. Mick didn't like dealing with it. He figured that girl could get two men fighting over her every single day of the week without even trying.

Mick was more into a comfort zone. He wanted his women to be there because they wanted to, not because they had to.

He couldn't help noticing The Donald though. He was drinking shots— that was normal—but it was how he was drinking them. There were no women draped on his arm. There was no Jeff to laugh at his jokes. He had an obvious case of "the shakes." But he wasn't shaking from the D.T.'s. They were inside-the-gut nerve shakes.

Mick didn't know it, of course, but The Donald had read an article in the Times. He did figure that Don had experienced something and was drinking to kill the pain. He noticed it was dead serious drinking. Very somber. Just the pound-the-shots-down-and-don't-bother-me-I'm-serious blues. The keep-the-shots-coming-and-don't-ask-me-a-question-or-I'll-bite-your-head-off blues. That's hard drinking. The only time his eyes left the shot glass was to tilt his head back and chug a beer chaser.

Mick was glad when he finally left. Don had radiated down-in-the-dumps. When everyone else was having a good time, Don was definitely a clash to the party atmosphere.

Mick heard through the grapevine that Heather had moved in with one of her girlfriends near the dunes on Lake Michigan. He guessed it was because of him, but he really didn't care. Some things are just out of a person's control, he thought. And he found that out again when he drove to Jen's house that night and found a strange car in the driveway.

When he let himself in, he discovered Jen had female company, so he went to his room, turned on the TV, and wondered what was going on upstairs until he fell asleep.

Mick slept in again, and when he awoke the house was empty. Maybe it was just as well he didn't find out what was going on all the time, he thought. The strangeness of it all might cause extra stress that he didn't need. But just the same, he was always curious. He couldn't understand what gay women see in each other—or gay men in men, for that matter—and he doubted he ever would.

He sat at the kitchen counter, having his morning joe and staring aimlessly out the windows to the patio. He noticed a slight drizzle outside, and he got up and opened the patio door. Yes, it was raining, he realized, and yet it was sunny. The sight of a rainbow fired him up faster than the coffee. He hadn't seen a rainbow in—he couldn't remember how long.

He ran out to his car to get his camera. He found it behind the driver's seat. He couldn't see the rainbow from the front of the house, so he ran back by the pool and…. Voilá! He snapped off six shots and felt very satisfied. He looked up and let the light rain splash his face. He even stuck his tongue out like a little kid trying to catch snowflakes. He suddenly wished he could live his youth all over again. He remembered it was so much fun.

You never realize how good you have it, he thought. You're always wanting to grow up fast, and then, when you get there, you find out that it's not necessarily a very nice place. But it's what you make of it, he thought. That's the most important part. Hopefully, tragedy never comes knocking at your door.

Mick went back into the kitchen and put his camera down. He wiped the rain from his face and watched the rainbow until it disappeared. Was this an omen of good things to come? he wondered. Then he started to think about the adoption Jennifer was planning. She hadn't spoken of it lately. Did she want a boy or a girl? Mick deduced, Girl. How would she grow up? Would Jen hide her own sexuality from the child and let her grow up normally?

He slapped himself on the head, as if that would knock out any negative thoughts. Don't even worry about it, he thought to himself. Any child she raises will have a better chance at life than one running loose on the street. Have faith, he thought. Jennifer is a kind, warm, and caring woman, quirks and all.

The summer shower passed. The wood deck and concrete patio were almost dry already. Suddenly he felt like swimming. The pool's right there, he thought. Might as well use it. This time though, he went and put his trunks on. He didn't feel like getting surprised again.

Mick dove in the pool and did lap after lap at workout speed, until he was exhausted. Then he stretched out on a chaise lounge to dry off. He thought it strange how the swimsuit felt funny to him now. He grabbed the leg parts and squeezed out the excess water. After awhile, he flipped over onto his stomach. Boredom was setting in fast. He had no clue how Jen and her friends could lay out in the sun like this for hours on end.

When he got up, his trunks were still damp. He went into the house, hung them behind the bathroom door, showered, and dressed. It was too early to go to work, so he turned on the TV. Ah, he thought, a Cubs game. He settled down on the sofa and watched.

CHAPTER 15

Ralph Swanson was analyzing Juan's computer files. Juan's main assignment had been auto theft, chop shops, jewel thieves, and other high-price crime. He had helped set up a sting operation for a jewel theft ring led by a retired lieutenant from the detectives' bureau of the Chicago Police. He had received his information through a coke customer trying to sell diamonds or watches for drugs. Juan had made transactions like that every chance he got.

Ralph wanted to make sure his murder wasn't a retaliation hit, even though all the men in the jewelry ring were already in jail. He searched through the miles of files by starting with the most recent and working backwards. He figured the killer's name was in there somewhere.

Juan was one of Ralph's best agents, and he had never lost an operative before. So this case stuck in his craw. The forensic investigators reported that he was shot in the driver's seat of his own vehicle and then moved to the passenger side, according to the blood splatter evidence. The common theory was that he must have been murdered elsewhere and his truck driven back home to his garage. That meant that the killer knew where he lived. All that was missing from the house were the drugs. Every other pawnable item was left behind. This told Ralph he was looking for a desperate drug user, or maybe a down-on-his-luck drug selling gangbanger. Unless of course it really was retaliation.

Ralph had his assistants going over all the phone records, trying to match up persons and places. Juan kept his drug sales in code, and Ralph was deciphering that now. He wanted to find the killer, or killers, and tighten the noose around their creepy little necks himself.

The mayor was having a grand old time at the strip club. He'd been parked there all day long. While he waited for Susie Q, he had all three of the dayshift strippers give him lap dances, and he was becoming bolder and bolder in taking indecent liberties.

These dalliances of his were becoming a daily affair. His mayoral duties were put on the back burner. As long as he got his kickbacks from the business community for steering lucrative city contracts their way, he was happy and so were they. He wasn't up for election for two more years, and he figured his reelection was in the bag anyway—the bribe bag. On days like these he laughed to himself. He could care less about the politics of meeting groups or kissing babies. He thought that was all just a pain in the ass.

His sexual desires were the most important things to him now. But as his physical abilities waned, his mental desires increased tenfold.

The Donald suddenly showed up at the mayor's table. "I thought I would find you here," he said. "Oh hi, Don," the mayor mumbled. "What the hell do you want?"

"I'll get right to the point. I need a job or another five hundred advance." "What for?"

"For doing your dirty work!"

"What you talkin' about?" The mayor was loaded. He didn't realize how plastered he was. He was just partying with the dancers., each and every one. He'd had a drink with all of them, and always Jack Daniels with no ice—that was for sissies. He was longing for his Susie Q. Here she'd just stepped onstage, and Don was in his face.

"I'm talking about my dealer getting whacked the other day," Don complained. "And with no supplier, I can't make any money!"

"Not my problem." The mayor's eyes opened wide, but with a scornful look. "I wanna watch the show now. Get the fuck otta here."

"No, John. I don't think you understand. You need me. Your scheme to get the Golden Door back isn't going to work without me. Now I need money to find a new supplier, and you're going to give it to me."

"You already fucked me with that singing bitch. She never dropped no drugs."

"Yes she did. Your man Ben screwed up somehow. At any rate, I had to pay her off."

"Now look what you did. You asshole. You made me miss Susie's first act!"

The tempers of the two con men were beginning to boil.

"Give me five hundred and I'll get out of your hair," Don demanded.

"I don't have it with me. Come back tomorrow."

"Give me a hundred then."

The mayor didn't want to argue with him anymore. Don was creating a scene. So he reached in his pocket and carelessly pulled out a wad of bills. He was going to give him a hundred, but he was holding a thousand at least. Don saw his chance and snatched the wad in an instant.

The mayor started to rise out of the booth in protest, but was shoved back down.

"You're drunk," Don said, as he stuffed the cash in his own pants' pocket.

"What do you think you're doing?" the mayor protested in vain.

"Sit down and shut up. I'll tell you how it's going to be. I'm sick and tired of your bullshit." Don was standing over the cowering mayor. "Susie's not going to touch you unless I give the OK, understand? I own the bitch. You catch my drift? And you are going to buy back the Golden Door and stop fucking around with all your games. You got that?"

"What's the matter, boys?" Susie interrupted.

"We were just talking about buying the Golden Door, weren't we, John?"

"Yeah, that's right," John said.

"Give him a free ride tonight, Sue. He's paid his dues."

"OK, Don."

"Never mind tonight," the mayor was bowing out. "I'm not in the mood."

"Oh, come on, Johnny," she purred. "Won't you do it for me?"

The mayor was tempted.

"No, no. I have to get going." He climbed out of the booth. "I've had too much to drink today anyway."

He was making excuses now. He knew he could never perform in his condition of silent rage. Don had ruined all his fun.

"Save that thought for tomorrow, sweetie."

"OK, Johnny, if you say so." She gave him a pat on his ass and went to her dressing room to change for her next act.

"I'll see you later," Don said to the mayor in a demanding tone.

The mayor said nothing as he watched The Donald walk out the door. Who the fuck does he think he's talking to? the mayor thought to himself. He must really be desperate to get up the nerve to talk to me like that. Doesn't he understand that I am the boss, and I'll prove it to him too.

He braced himself in the doorway, as he watched Don drive off, and then he staggered out to his Cadillac.

I'll show that motherfucker who's boss, he thought. He doesn't own Susie, I do.

He probably thinks he can shake me down forever, just because I'm married and the mayor. Well, he thought, have I got news for him! He drove to city hall and let himself in the side door. He went straight to his closet and retrieved his shoulder holster. He wanted to feel the power. His adrenaline started to percolate. It wasn't "liquid courage," it was pure power that he felt. It was power that he needed. A gun strapped to his body made him invincible. He swapped his suit coat for the windbreaker. To prove he was thinking rationally, he put on the latex gloves that were still in the pockets. Then he opened his stash bag and put some packets of coke in the pockets where the gloves used to be. Now he was ready, he felt, ready for anything.

First things first, he figured. He was going to have to confront Don and get his money back. He was insulted the way he'd snatched his money right out of his hands. Nobody had ever done that to him before, and he was dead certain that it would never, ever happen to him again.

The second thing is, he thought, I'll prove that he doesn't own Susie. I'll make him eat those words. I've got the power.

He thought briefly of taking a drink before he left, but his adrenaline rush pushed him out the door. No time to waste, he told himself.

The mayor drove straight to his parts warehouse and climbed into his service van. When he got to Don's trailer park, he cruised up and down the street looking for Don's car. He knew he was in the right park, but he didn't know the right trailer. After two passes, he concluded that Don wasn't home yet.

It dawned on him that Don had all his money. "He's probably drinking on my money, that fuck!" he said aloud. On a hunch, he took off for the Golden Door. And when he pulled in the parking lot, there it was: Don's silver striped Chrysler. The mayor kept driving around and finally left the parking lot.

He's probably getting good and soused, the mayor thought. He could feel himself sobering up, as his blood rush was rising. He drove down the street to the 24-hour donut shop and bought a large black coffee at the drive-thru window, but all he had to pay for it was the van's tollway change. He was preparing himself to wait Don out.

Inside the Golden Door, Don was partying down. Jeff was at his side and they were laughing and joking. Don was in a state of euphoria. He thought he'd just pulled off one of his greatest cons ever. He felt like bragging about it, but didn't. He knew he could ruin the mayor's career if he didn't play ball. And right now, he still needed the mayor. Don looked around at everything inside the Golden Door like as if he owned it already.

He turned to Jeff and said, "See that smug ass Mick over there doing my job? That prick. He'll be the first one I fire once I get the place back. You can bet on that."

Jeff dismissed the bravado, but he let Don order more shots and beers for the two of them.

Mick was going about his business, restocking the coolers and whatnot, when he noticed Don and Jeff tying one on. That didn't bother him much anymore—as long as they didn't cause trouble—but he couldn't help marveling how much Don's demeanor had changed from the other night when he saw him last.

Oh well, Mick thought, live and let live. But he still felt uncomfortable enough with this changed scene that he took every opportunity the rest of the night to hide in the office and watch the monitor, which was part of his job anyway.

The video monitor's four-way split screen was not made for entertainment, and one could fall asleep real easy in front of it. Mick decided he would much rather be out helping the customers to party heartier. A white service van did catch his eye, however, as he watched it on the screen pull slowly through the parking lot. Still, he thought nothing of it until he looked a second time and noticed an older man with balding gray hair driving it. The van kept cruising through the parking lot but didn't park. He turned his attention back to the interior cams, but there was still nothing unusual going on.

His mind drifted a little, as he hoped Jennifer would call him for a quickie. That won't happen very often though, he thought, so he felt all the more lucky it happened that first time. He sat back in his chair, smiling at the memory. The girls were in a snit that night and probably complained to Jen. Some women just won't let a guy have any fun, he thought. On the other hand, he realized that from their point of view, this was a business and somebody had to be here to run it.

Tired of sitting in the chair and bored with watching the monitor, Mick got up and joined the crowd. Kenny was there ripping off pull-tabs. He'd hit a hundred-dollar winner earlier, but he spent it right back. He seemed determined to empty the card container that night. When he succeeded, Mick went back in the office and got a new brick of pull-tabs. There were some four thousand cards in a case. Easy money for the bar, he thought to himself. Guaranteed profit.

Some people just plain enjoy trying to beat the odds and get lucky. Mick wasn't sure if Kenny was addicted to the game or just played it for something to do. It seemed to Mick that if Kenny wasn't pulling tabs, he was playing pool. The bottom line was: he spent a lot of time and money doing what he liked, and that added up to a valued customer.

Don and Jeff were laughing boisterously in the corner. Jeff could be a stand-up comic, Mick thought. He told the funniest stories sometimes. Mick also noticed that the girls were flying behind the bar as usual. Everybody seemed to be in good spirits, except him. He had to take out the trash.

Not that he was in a bad mood exactly. He was just still pissed off about the way that cop treated him, making him walk heel-to-toe with a sprained ankle. It was as if that cop enjoyed giving people pain. He's like a masochist, Mick thought while he emptied the garbage cans.

He went back to the office to look again at the parking lot video cam. He was starting to wonder how many times, and when, the cops might come cruising through. Was the cop who busted him that same dumpster-diving cop? Mick wondered. He was starting to think those two were one and the same guy. What's he want? Mick wondered. He surely wasn't about to pay off any cops.

As he watched the monitor again, his mind drifted back to the time he was sixteen and his first driver's test. He remembered it like it was yesterday. The driving inspector deliberately told him to pull over, making him cross over two double yellow lines, and then hitting him up for five bucks or he couldn't pass the test.

"You see, kid, my boss is in the tower," the inspector had told him.

"What tower?" Mick asked.

Welcome to the real world of shake-downs, Mick reflected with a smile. He had recognized it even then, and he was watching it happen all over again now. And he was pissed off then and he was pissed off now. He remembered what had made that incident even more memorable. A few months after he got his license, the secretary of state died in office, leaving behind two hundred thousand dollars in cash stuffed in a shoe box.

Now, thirty years later, Mick was following in the news how the latest secretary of state-turned-governor was being busted by the F.B.I. for issuing licenses to unqualified drivers who paid bribes. Apparently, Mick thought, there's a lot of money to be made in violating the Constitution after all. The F.B.I. shuts off one way for politicians to steal money, so then they create another: ticketing for seatbelt violations.

It's all about making money, Mick thought. And politicians don't care how they get it or who they steal it from.

He was staring into the monitor, wondering if the seatbelt law had been tested yet in the Supreme Court. No, he didn't think so. But the government deliberately violates the Constitution to prevent certain freedoms, and there's a lot of money to be made in violating the Constitution. Mick reminded himself of all the fines the government had never returned to people after police roadblocks were found to be unconstitutional. Only the government can make a profit by making up rules that violate the law of the land. No, he thought, that's not exclusively true. Lawyers make profit too, and so do special interest groups, lobbyists, and of course the lawmakers themselves and politicians who use them to their own advantage. Mick was answering his own questions all the while he was staring blankly at the monitor. And the monitor may as well have been blank, because his mind wasn't registering what his eyes were seeing. All he knew is what he felt: the government gets away with this because nobody has the time or money to challenge it.

Mick's eyes were trained on the screen, but in his mind's eye he saw five children being burned alive. All trapped in a burning van by their seatbelts. Some of them could have escaped the ravaging fire and climbed into the rescuing arms of their parents, but they couldn't escape the seatbelts or the law.

He may have been dreaming, or this was a nightmare, but in Mick's gaze he saw Al Capone-like insurance companies bribing congressmen so they'll pass these unconstitutional laws. What do they care? They all ride in limos, he thought. All they want is the money, and they don't care how many people they burn alive to get it. They must justify this stuff with odds, Mick was thinking, like gamblers do. The odds are with you if you wear a seatbelt, so the hell with the Constitution and your rights. No, we don't want you free to think for yourself; the odds are better if we think for you. Believe us, Mick imagined the politicians saying, "When we empty your wallets, it's for your own damn good. The odds are in our favor. We always win. We are the law. Praise the odds!"

His eyes were still staring at the monitor. It may as well have been a blank blue screen, as he saw only what his mind wanted him to. He was thinking of the Wilson family's five children, whom the news recently reported were strapped inside a burning van while their parents were unable to free them from their seatbelts. This incident was vividly implanted on Mick's mind because he had known the family. They'd lived just down the road from him. The thing that bothered him most now was the fact that the truck that hit those kids was driven by an unqualified driver whose company had paid a bride to have him licensed.

In Mick's mind he saw the parents' arms being burned by the flames as they tried to reach their children, who were struggling and wanted to be free. He saw devils dancing and laughing on the roof of the van as the children screamed. The devils were wearing blue shirts, and on their shirts were badges—brightly shining badges with the Star of David covered by a swastika. As the devils danced, the children's cries were silenced one by one. The devils had horns and faces. Mick knew he had seen them before, but the flames were too bright to let him see them again. In his mind, he blinked and squinted to try and get a better look...

"Mick!"

He jumped from his chair.

It was Debbie. She'd burst into the office and startled him out of his nightmare.

"Jeff puked all over the floor. Get the mop!"

"Damn! OK." He was suddenly brought back to the real world.

Mick filled the mop bucket with soapy water and wheeled it out to the bar. The two jokers had left, leaving their trail behind them. He tried to suck up his breath and hold it, so he wouldn't have to smell the foul air. That didn't work, so he mopped as fast as he could before the pungent smell chased more customers away. For those brave enough to stay, he bought a round of drinks.

Debbie and Heather were mad, too. It seemed amazing to Mick how a little thing like that could clear out a bar. The rest of the night dragged on to the point where Heather was allowed to leave early.

Mick had the chance to ask Debbie if she'd looked up the name of the cop that busted her.

"No, not yet," she said.

"It's important," Mick reminded her.

"Yeah, yeah. I still say it's not going to matter."

"Humor me then. Just do it for me."

"OK, OK. I'll look it up tomorrow."

"Thank you," Mick said. "I'm going to fight my case and I want to know if it's the same cop. I'm trying to see if he's stalking the bar."

"OK, OK." She turned to walk away and stopped. Then she looked back at Mick and said, "If you're going to fight 'em, sucker-punch him once for me."

"You got it, babe."

Mick went home—to his home—after he closed that night. No particular reason, other than he felt the need for a little space. He wondered if he should move all of his things over to Jennifer's or keep the other home going for a retreat or safety haven. He knew or had the feeling that he might need it again someday, but he also realized it would be more economical if he just lived at Jen's.

But what if I run into another woman I like? he wondered. What if Jen stops loving me after she completes this adoption thing? Too many "what if's," Mick thought, shaking his head. I'll bet she won't even miss me if I stay away a couple of days—or, like they say, will her heart grow fonder? He wondered, still shaking his head, how everything was going to pan out. He'd discussed this subject with himself before, and he was always able to answer with: You got a good thing going so far, so don't do anything to screw it up. Give her the benefit of the doubt.

He wondered about everything for the rest of the night, until he wondered himself to sleep.

CHAPTER 16

The Donald's body was found two days later. A deputy sheriff found him. The ink wasn't dry on the divorce papers he was trying to serve.

The deputy saw that a car was there, but he couldn't hear the door bell ring when he pushed the button so he knocked on the door. It popped open under his fist. A horrid odor punched him in the face.

At first he just hollered in, but then pushed the door open wider. After grabbing his nose to close his nostrils, he peered inside and saw the bloated body on the couch. He then walked in to examine it closer.

On closer examination, the deputy saw blood caked in his hair and the pool of blood that had dripped down his face. There was a gun in his hand and small bags of white powder on the coffee table. He miked up the transmitter on his shoulder and called the station.

"Deputy McGuilicudy reporting. Dead body found. Apparent suicide."

Soon the tiny trailer was buzzing with police and investigators. The state and local police were there. The chief, big Jake, represented the Griffith Police Department, and he had Officer Ben Smide rope off the area with yellow crime-scene barrier tape. There was a crowd of onlookers building up outside the trailer, mostly mothers with babies in arm and toddlers tugging at their skirts. Ben tried to shoo them all away.

"There's nothing you want to see here," he shouted.

Hank Williams was the county sheriff. He had his forensic team dusting for prints and going over the body taking pictures and swabbing for DNA samples. They bagged the gun and ballistics tests were ordered. They took the suspected drugs off the coffee table and put it all in an evidence bag for future testing.

Ben entered the trailer and announced to Jake, "There's a reporter outside from the Times. What do I tell him?"

The chief gave him a you're-supposed-to-stay-outside glare. "Tell him to wait until we're finished."

While Ben was in there, he gathered all the visual information he could and then informed the reporter of Jake's command.

"You know what's odd?" Sheriff Williams said to Jake.

"What's that?"

"The way his pockets are turned inside-out."

"The way what?" Jake wasn't sure what he was driving at.

"His pockets are turned inside-out. That ain't right."

"Why's that?"

"If you were going to commit suicide, why would you pull your pockets inside-out?"

"I don't know. Maybe that's where he had his dope."

Ben came back inside the trailer. "The coroner's wagon is here to transport the body to the morgue."

"Tell them to wait till we're finished," Jake barked. Then he turned back to the sheriff. "Look, this guy's been a doper ever since I've known him. He's down and out. He lost his job and his old lady's divorcing him. So, he blows his brains out. Case closed."

"Maybe you're right," the sheriff answered.

"I know I'm right!"

The technicians came over to them. "We're finished now."

"OK, Jake," said Williams. "Tell your man to let the coroner's guys in here."

Everybody stepped outside for some fresh air. It was hot and stuffy in the trailer, and filled with the smell of death.

Mick, Debbie, and Heather were doing their regular things when the gossip filtered in and started a wildfire: The Donald committed suicide over some stripper. The Donald killed himself because of his impending divorce, because he was drunk, because he was high. His poor wife. Serves him right.

"I would have shot him, if she'd only asked," was one comment Mick heard. "The chickenshit shot himself," was another.

Everybody has an opinion, Mick thought to himself, except the right one.

Nobody except Ben Smide suspected the mayor. He had seen those coke packets before, and his were already empty. He knew right away the drugs were a plant. That's the mayor's M.O., Ben thought.

He also thought the gun, too, was a plant. He figured he could prove it to himself the next chance he got to see the empty holster in the mayor's closet.

"Hah!" Ben muttered to himself. It's all even now, he thought. He has the noose around my neck, and I have the noose around his. It's all even now!

Ralph Swanson placed a call to the sheriff's department, inquiring about the new case. He saw the article in the Times. He was wondering if it was more than just a coincidence that two men were shot in the head that week.

Ralph's assistants had tied in all the phone records, and he himself had deciphered the computer codes. The computer connected the two dead men. There were weekly phone calls, and weekly drug buys by one Donald Strapp, now deceased, the apparent suicide.

Insurance investigator Swanson wanted to make sure that he and the sheriff were on the same page. One case was clearly murder; the other seemingly a suicide. He and Sheriff Williams discussed the various possibilities. Was this now a case of murder and delayed suicide? Did Donald Strapp kill Juan Beamer? And then himself? Was it the same gun? Do ballistics results show a match between the two guns used? Whose dope was found and did any of the finger prints match? Have autopsies been completed? Did any toxicology reports come back from either one?

The sheriff didn't have complete reports yet from all investigating units, but he promised to keep Mr. Swanson apprised of any new information as it came in.

The girls were somewhat depressed for the rest of the week, after the sheriff's investigators got through grilling them. "What was he doing here?" they wanted to know. "Who was he with?" "What time did he leave?" "Did he say or do anything unusual?" They had never been through anything quite like that before, and felt quite helpless in believing their answers were of little help.

After their grilling, Debbie and Heather looked like as if vampires had sucked out all their blood. They had no energy. The famous "party animals" were etherized. Mick knew it would take them a week at least before they snapped out of it. He thought of throwing a party to celebrate life and living and all, but that wasn't his call. He figured he'd try running it by Jennifer to see what she had to say.

She beat him to the punch. She had recognized the state of despair, too, and before Mick had the chance to ask her, she announced to the entire bar that she was throwing a "just because" pool party the following Sunday. Everyone was invited.

"Why?" customers would ask.

"Oh, just because," she'd reply. It was just what the doctor ordered. Jen had impeccable taste. She had the food catered with a Hawaiian theme. She ordered things that weren't available from the Golden Door's grill—like a whole roast pig. There was a magnificent veggie dish as well, on a fancy tray with radishes meticulously cut to look like roses. It was so pretty that nobody wanted to disturb the tray by snacking from it.

The beer and spirits came from the bar, and there was no shortage of bartenders. The blender ran non-stop making pitchers of Margaritas and Mai-Tais. Only the part-time employees had to work the real bar. The girls all felt sorry for them.

Mick jumped in and joined a volleyball game that was going on in the pool. Everyone was having a good time.

Heather got out a squirt gun as big as a bazooka. If people weren't wet from the pool, she made sure they got wet anyway. She squirted everything that moved. The mischievous little girl inside her came back to life. There was even a "Bud party" going on in the garage. "What's a party without a little Bud?" the girls joked.

Jennifer had all her girlfriends over, so Mick was never able to get next to her as she entertained her friends. No one besides Heather ever suspected they were man and wife. That was the strangest part of their relationship, but Mick was getting used to it. He was able to handle her apparent indifference. He knew that when her girlfriends were around, she was different. He also knew that when they were alone, she was different again.

The chef who came with the rotisserie announced that the pig was done. He set out a tray of freshly sliced pork on the table. There were instant takers piling pork high on their plates—just like Congressmen, Mick thought. The first tray didn't last long, but the chef was proficient enough. He set out another tray right away. Mick thought, This guy's fed wolves before.

It was a glorious day: perfect weather, delicious food, Jen going around all smiles. She was in her glory, and all her guests complimented her profusely. The party was a huge success—just what the doctor ordered. They celebrated life and living. Mission accomplished.

CHAPTER 17

Mick read a terrible story in the newspaper the next day. A child had been burned alive. "Freak accident," the headline said.

"The driver had pulled off onto the shoulder of I-65 to change a tire. A truck hit the car at the end of a construction zone. The impact knocked the car off the jack and severed the man's foot. The truck dragged the car which burst into flames. The man hobbled on the stub of his leg after the car because his son was strapped in a seatbelt inside. Another trucker stopped to assist with a fire extinguisher, but to no avail," the story read. "The child was dead."

Mick cut out the article and put it in a folder. He figured it might prove useful to show a jury just how dangerous a seatbelt can be—if his case ever came to that.

More to prove a point, Mick thought, it shows how this whole thing is just a numbers game, a gamble. Lawmakers betting on the odds against such tragedies happening. Mick wondered if that shouldn't be the main focus of his case. It's impossible to save everyone's life in accidents, he thought, seatbelts or not. Air bags are also killing people in small fender-benders. All these "safety requirements" are taking away from the plain old best advice of just "drive carefully."

People are always speeding along with reckless abandon, Mick thought, but it is still possible to save the Constitution from traitors who want to destroy it. Freedom is as precious as life itself, he reasoned. The Constitution guarantees every citizen's right to protect one's life, liberty, and property. Mick wondered, Why do all these lying, thieving, murdering dictators who hide under the "safety" cloak want to destroy it?

Mick was becoming obsessed with the Constitution and with his own case. These issues started to consume all his idle mental moments. He had to force himself to keep busy—working, playing, doing anything—or else his mind went right back to that lying, thieving, blue-shirted Nazi cop and the way he treated him, the way he stomped all over Mick's Constitutional rights.

"No, no, Mick. Don't try to argue about the safety of seatbelts." He was talking to himself again, but then he continued thinking: That's immaterial. Better to argue the Constitutional side. The government in this has shown a complete disregard for a basic personal freedom—one's right to decide for himself what's safe and what's not. Where has all the liberty gone? he wondered.

Mick's blood pressure was rising. He felt a need to argue his points. He wished he'd become a lawyer. He could see himself in court, passionately arguing for the Constitution point by point. In order to get rid of all the Timothy McVeys of the country, you have to get rid of all the socialist Reno-like dictators too!

The mayor skipped going to city hall for a couple of days and was getting antsy. He headed back out to the strip club. He felt his Susie Q was calling. His head was ringing with: Johnny, come on, Johnny. Give it to me! His fanatical infatuation with her was pulling him in like a magnetic force that he couldn't resist.

He parked his Cadillac in the back. He was over any regret about Strapp already. Greedy bastard, he thought, should have never grabbed my money. He got what he deserved. I'm justified. Nobody is going to get in between me and my Susie Q.

She cringed slightly when she saw the mayor walk in. She'd read the paper too, after her girlfriend prompted, "Did you see this? Don committed suicide!" Somehow it didn't seem real to Susie. The story caught her completely off guard. All the things the two of them planned had come to an end. She was going to run a high class prostitution service, and he was going to be a bookie for high rollers. They would have been millionaires in no time. She'd dreamed of vacations in the Bahamas, sailing in their own cabin cruiser. She thought, How could he run out on all those dreams and plans?

Now she had to deal with the mayor all by herself. She detested him and most of the other men who stuffed money in her G-string. From now on, she decided, she'd push him harder: no bar for her, no nothing for him. I'll take him for all he's got, she thought. If he doesn't deliver, I'll make him take a hike.

As soon as she finished her routine, the mayor flagged her over.

"Hi, Johnny," she said. "Did you get me that bar yet?"

"No, but I'm working on it."

"I'm tired of hearing promises, Johnny. I'm beginning to think you have no intention of buying me anything."

"No, that's not true. These things take time. I'll get it for you, I promise."

"Well, I don't know," she sighed. "There's another guy that comes in here, and he's promising to buy me a bar too. That's all I hear. Promises, promises, promises. And I'm getting tired of being lied to."

"No, I mean what I say. I'll buy you that bar. They don't call me Honest John Quibly for nothing."

"How long will it take you to get it?"

"A couple of months. Even if the deal closed tomorrow, it would still take a couple of months. There's contracts and lawyers, loans and insurance, licenses and fees—it all takes time."

"Well, fine," she said. "Get busy with it then, and don't come back till the deal is done." She walked off in a deliberate huff.

"Come back!" he called after her.

Susie ignored his call and made a beeline for her dressing room.

"Damn bitches!" the mayor mumbled to himself. He was mad and embarrassed. He slugged down his drink and steamed out the door. He hustled out to his Caddy, gassed it in reverse, and squealed the tires. He slammed on the brakes and gassed it in Drive, bouncing down the parking lot apron and onto the street.

"Fuckin' bitch," he muttered. "Doesn't she realize I'd do anything for her—including murder?" Suddenly he slowed his speed. Get a grip on yourself, he thought. Bottom line? I got to get that bar back. He thought, I'll make that dyke-ass bitch an offer she won't have a chance to refuse.

Sheriff Williams received fingerprint reports from the state lab that left him baffled. The prints on the cocaine packets were identified as Juan Beamer's. The prints on the gun were from Donald Strapp, but there were no prints on the bullets. Ballistics were inconclusive, as in the .38 caliber bullets were fired from two different guns. The evidence was not adding up to murder-suicide. Not exactly "case closed."

The sheriff looked up Ralph Swanson's phone number on his Rolodex and told him the murder-suicide case would remain open. He would fax him the pertinent lab reports, out of professional courtesy. Privately he wondered why the insurance investigator even wanted the reports. A landscape employee, a dead dope dealer, and a dead out-of-work bar manager. The sheriff wondered, Dope dealer or user or both—where are the partners in crime? Dealers need suppliers, and dealers need customers. There's got to be more people involved. But who? He mulled the information over before assigning the murder-suicide case to the homicide division.

⟵———◉———⟶

Mick kept his appointment with Jennifer's attorney, Andrew Traylor. He was a smallish man, intelligent looking and wearing bifocal glasses. Behind his desk were piles of manila folders, and others were heaped on top of his already stuffed file cabinets.

He held out his hand to shake. "Mr. Swift, you're here for a D.U.I.?"

"Yes, that's right."

"Sit down, please. Did you take the breathalyzer test?"

"Yes."

"And what did you blow?"

"Point oh-eight-something."

"Just enough to get you arrested, eh?"

"Yeah, I guess so."

"Any prior convictions?"

"No."

"Good. I can get you off with reckless driving."

"I wasn't driving recklessly," Mick said. "So, I don't want to plead to reckless driving."

"I know, but this is the way the system works," said Mr. Traylor.

"I don't care how 'the system' works," Mick retorted. "I care about my Constitutional rights. I believe the cops are profiling the bartenders at the Golden Door. They're busted three of us already this month."

"Maybe you're right, but fighting them isn't practical. I can get you off with a five-hundred-dollar fine. I only charge $125 an hour as a favor to Jennifer. If you want to fight the case, I would need a ten-thousand-dollar retainer, and there would be no guarantee that you would win. Do you have that kind of money to throw around fighting for your Constitutional rights?"

"No."

"I didn't think so."

"How about if I do some of the leg work?" Mick responded. "Like, say I want a jury trial. What's the next step?"

"Motion for discovery."

"OK, and if I wanted to make a motion to dismiss because the cop was profiling the bar, or because the seatbelt law is unconstitutional and violates the Bill of Rights?" Mick's voice rose excitedly and Andrew raised his eyebrows, now peering over the tops of his glasses.

"Whoa, soldier!" he said. "You're talking a whole new ball game there. I suggest you take the cheapest way out. Haven't you heard the saying, you can't fight city hall? Don't be foolish. You don't have the money to fight them, and I don't have the time. Go home and cool off. Call me back when you come to your senses."

Mick thanked him for his time and left disappointed. Can't afford justice, he thought, so that's how the con game works. He was almost talking to himself as he walked to his car. Make up laws that violate the law of the land, he thought, and then make it impractical to fight 'em. Nice system they got going for themselves, the fuckin' dictators.

"Did you see his face turn sour when you mentioned the seatbelt law violates the Bill of Rights?" Mick asked himself as he got in his car. You may be right, he thought, remembering what the lawyer told him. But it's not worth fighting for? Bullshit! The Bill of Rights is worth fighting for, Mick thought, and I'll fight those fuckers if I have to do it myself! He made another promise to himself as he drove off.

He pulled into the parking lot of the first bar he saw. His nerves were on edge. He wanted a beer to calm himself down. Mellow out, Mick, he thought to himself.

The first beer went down smooth and fast. For the second, he took his time as he transferred his attention to the TV news.

Ben Smide finally caught up with the mayor. It seemed to Ben that whenever he called or stopped by, the mayor was gone. He had used up all the coke he had and decided he liked it and now he wanted the rest of it. Ben thought, John could keep the marijuana for his "drops" and plants or whatever other traps he wanted to set up.

"Hey John," Ben said as he walked into the mayor's office. He had a chip-on-his-shoulder attitude that day. He walked right up to the mayor's desk, putting his knuckles down on its hard polished mahogany top and assuming an authoritarian posture.

"What can I do for you, Ben?" the mayor asked.

"We need to split up the drugs from the Beamer hit. You can keep the mary jane and I'll take the coke."

"OK," the mayor said, and got out of his chair and went to his closet with Ben right behind him. As John reached up for the stash, Ben peered in and saw the empty holster.

Just like I figured, Ben thought to himself. John plugged Don and left the evidence. Smart move, Ben thought, if the gun can't be traced back to him, which is probably the case.

The mayor set the black bag on his desk and dumped out the contents. He quickly separated the pot from the cocaine, and then put the pot back in the bag and returned the bag to the closet. By the time he turned back around, Ben had already stuffed all the coke packets in his pockets.

"All square?" the mayor asked.

"Yeah, all square," Ben replied. Then suddenly he asked, "Why did you whack Don?"

Unfazed, the mayor answered, "Same reason you killed Juan."

"Oh" was Ben's only response.

"By the way," the mayor continued, "are you still available for hitting drug dealers?"

"Yeah, sure. Make sure they have money next time."

"He *had* money," John responded. "I just couldn't find it, that's all."

"Yeah, I know. But you know what I mean. Let's make it a big score next time."

"You got it, kid!" The mayor patted his police officer on the shoulder in praise. Then he opened his office door and herded him out, since that day's business was all concluded.

John decided he needed to go back to the industrial strip club. He had to talk to his Susie Q and make her see the light. After all, he thought, she was a reasonably greedy woman. He figured he could make her understand.

With Don gone he would need a new spy, someone who understood the frailties of men. Corruptible people are easy marks, he thought, and I can teach her the tricks of the *other* trades.

He did get her attention, too, when he flashed the biggest wad of hundred dollar bills she ever saw.

Yes, he got his lap dance and more. They were all kissy-face once again, and then he asked her a question.

"Do you know who I can buy a key of coke from?"

"Gosh, Johnny. I didn't know you were into that kind of thing."

"There's a lot of things you don't know about me."

"Yeah, I know who you can get some coke from."

"Now, I don't want a little dime bag, baby. I want a whole kilo or pound. Can your guy get me that much—at a reasonable price?"

"Absolutely."

"Good. Here's my cell phone. Call him right now and find out how much it is."

She took his phone and punched out another drug dealer's death warrant.

CHAPTER 18

Mick was beginning to feel the need for some loving.

Jennifer worked days; he worked nights. He hardly saw her during the week; and, if she was entertaining on the weekends, it was impossible to get next to her. He decided he'd like to seduce her the very next weekend, *but how?*

Do something different, he thought. Maybe a day-trip getaway, or, better yet, a whole getaway weekend. Better check with her now, he thought. She might already have other plans. Or, he wondered, maybe she doesn't want to go away with *me.*

No harm in trying, he thought. "Ask and find out," he told himself out loud. He picked up the phone and punched the numbers for her office.

The receptionist answered, "Watts Décor."

"Jennifer Tuttle, please." "One moment please… sorry, she's not at her desk right now. I'll transfer you to her voice mail."

Damn, Mick thought. Talking into those machines was not one of his favorite things to do. It seemed so impersonal to him. Modern technology, he thought to himself, get used to it, buddy.

"This is Jennifer Tuttle," her voice announced. "Your call is important to us. Please leave a message after the beep. I will get back to you." Beep!

"Hi, Jen, it's Mick. I, I was just wondering if you would like to get away for the weekend. I have a couple of nice places in mind. Think about it. We can talk more when I see you. See ya. Bye."

For some reason Mick talked with a nervous quiver in his voice whenever he left messages in answering machines. He realized this and always tried to overcome it by thinking positively. He concluded that he didn't do it often enough to get accustomed to such cold machines, no-face machines, no-personality machines. He doubted he ever would.

Jennifer was right about getting Mick to do whatever she wanted. She gave him a taste of her love and he was looking for more. What was supposed to have been a Platonic relationship blossomed into something else. She knew she was an attractive woman, and she was also a skilled manager. With a cool coyness she skillfully played men like instruments— pluck their strings and they all make music for her affections. She had the power indeed to influence whatever results she wanted. She was the same way with women, too. Gay or straight, it didn't much matter.

She was struggling now though. Her motherly instincts were affecting her behavior. Now when she saw another attractive woman—the type she used to hit on—she was indifferent. What was once an insatiable desire to seduce other women had waned into nothingness. She wondered whether it was the hormone pills her doctor prescribed for her, or was it Mick?

She did let those "I love you" words fly in moments of heated passion. She questioned herself, Do I really mean it? Mick is uniquely different from everyone else. Jen wondered if he was why she argued with Heather, in some kind of self-destruct manner.

The adoption she'd been planning was of the utmost importance to her—being adopted herself just magnified her feelings. Being a successful woman, she also knew she could afford it. The need to take care of the innocent, just as she herself was taken care of (especially by her adoptive mother), was paramount in her life.

She knew she was starting to think about Mick more than she should—even at work, where her diligence used to never let up. Between meetings, she would sometimes wonder if he was cleaning her pool. She laughed about it sometimes. She thought about what a bold, unabashed man he was. She liked how he overcame his natural shyness, thinking, for example, of how he cleaned her pool. Mick always commanded respect without effort.

Jen wondered how he would be as a father. She knew he had put his other kids through college, but those were his kids. How would he be with an adopted child? she wondered. She figured his manners would remain the same. He's set in his ways, she thought. Her mind drifted to the way he made love to her. It brought a smile to her face. She knew she was rather pleasantly surprised by his methods, but she also knew she thoroughly enjoyed their sexual romps together.

What had started as merely going through the motions of consummating a marriage had now suddenly become something else. This was very satisfying to her, but it was an odd feeling. She would have never believed it was possible. She had trouble understanding sexuality in her youth, and now she was having a hard time understanding it again—but maybe for different reasons.

She broke off her reverie and listened to her voice mail. So, she thought, he's planning something. Hmmm, a little getaway. Hmmm…

She knew what she wanted: champagne and strawberry shortcake.

Hmmm, she thought, sounds good to me! But I also like surprises, so I'll let him choose. "Surprise me," I'll tell him.

Jennifer's smile grew into a full-fledged grin. She started to feel giddy as a schoolgirl over the prospects of a date. In anticipation, she fantasized about whatever goodies he might have up his sleeve.

Mick, on the other hand, passed the day cleaning the pool with his trunks on and taking a swim. He also found some interesting articles in the newspaper, and those he cut out and put in his folder.

Jen was in dreamland all day. She lacked concentration and even made a few typos on her computer. Her assistant was on the ball though. When she made Jennifer aware of them, Jen said, "Oh, sorry. I think I need a vacation." That was her rationale.

Right after work, and for the first time in a long time, she was anxious to hit the expressway traffic. She was going to the bar that night to see Mick.

The traffic was particularly brutal, so Jen was relieved when she finally walked into the Golden Door. She was in good spirits, so when Debbie served her usual lite beer, Jen ordered drinks on her own tab for all the regulars.

Debbie knew exactly what to do. As she passed out the drink chips, she added it all up in her head as fast as any calculator. The tab came to just over thirty dollars. Jen gave her two twenties, and a wave of her hand told her to keep the change.

Expensive bottle of beer, Jen thought.

She realized she was too generous at times, but she enjoyed doing it. After all, she was the owner. She knew that regulars were the lifeblood of her business. But more than that, she really did like them as people. She took her beer in hand and went stool-to-stool, stopping to chat with every individual. She always left them laughing, or at least with a smile. She knew how to mix business with pleasure. She loved to socialize, but that wasn't what she came for.

So, after finishing cheering up all the customers, she wiggled her "follow me" finger at Mick, and the two of them headed back for the office.

Jen closed the door behind them. "So, you want to get away for the weekend?"

"Yeah," he said. "I was thinking it would be nice."

"Are you going to surprise me?"

"Huh?" The question caught him off guard. He actually hadn't planned on surprising her, but he knew it could be arranged. "Well, yeah. I can surprise you."

With that, her smile grew and she wrapped her arms around him, locking him to her in a passionate kissing embrace.

Mick was the surprise one, as her kiss almost sucked the breath from his lungs. For the moment, he almost toppled backwards as he was forced to take a half-step back to balance himself. Her hands slid up to the nape of his neck to hold his head as she darted her tongue about with his. Mick was slowly running out of oxygen, as Jen's passion was unrelenting.

He had to gently push her away. "Wow!" he exclaimed. "I'll have to surprise you more often!"

"Yes, I think you should." She kissed him again. This time she dropped her hands and grabbed his butt cheeks, pulling his pelvis to hers. After another passionate couple of minutes, Mick had to come up for air again.

When they separated, she said, "I think you need the night off."

"That's always a good idea," Mick said smiling. He had a good idea what she wanted, and so did she.

"I'll call Jack and see if he can come in," Jen said. "Meanwhile, why don't you go see if the girls are set up for the night."

"You got it!" He was off to stock the coolers.

A few minutes later Jen came out of the office and went over to Debbie. "Jack is coming in to relieve Mick," she said. They both looked over at Mick, who was bending over and loading the cooler with beer.

"Look at that ass go," Debbie said.

"Yeah, and I'm taking it home."

"Have fun!"

They both giggled.

Jennifer strode over to Mick, interrupting him briefly as she whispered her private message, "Jack is coming to relieve you in five minutes. I'll be waiting at home."

Mick smiled broadly at her. "I'll see you in a little bit then."

She gave him a wink and a smile before walking away.

Five minutes seemed like an hour to Mick. "Come on, Jack, hurry up," he muttered to himself. Anticipation was sometimes the best part of reality, he thought. He was pacing from behind the bar to the window. He would peer out into the parking lot, looking for Jack's van to pull up, and then he would go all the way back to the office just to look at the spot where Jen and he had been making out earlier. Then back to the window he'd go. His heart was pounding with nervous energy, and his legs were pumping like pistons in an engine.

"Come on, Jack!" he kept saying, only half to himself.

Debbie noticed Mick's fleet feet but didn't say anything. He suddenly made a detour during his next trip, going around the pool tables to the beer room—just to look.

Everything is OK here, he thought.

He went back out to the window, and then he saw the van pulling up. "All right, Jack!"

Mick went back behind the bar. "Jack's here," he told Debbie. "See ya later."

"OK."

Mick whisked right past Jack as he was entering with a "Hi, bye," and he was gone as quick as lightning.

Jack moseyed over to Debbie. "What's with Mick?"

"I don't know. For a grown man, he's been acting like he's never been laid before. Maybe he's in love?"

"Oh" is all Jack would comment on that.

Debbie hit that observation on the head. Mick was flying high as a kite, but he was driving as carefully as possible. He was happy about the way everything was turning out. Looks like I made some right decisions, he thought to himself. He really did want to make the whole affair work.

He pulled into the driveway and scurried up the walkway. He let himself in, and the scent of lilacs greeted his senses. There was a candle burning on the table, lighting the way upstairs.

"Jennifer, I'm home! he announced, as he made his way up to her bedroom.

There he found a vision of beauty. She was wearing a long flowing purplish silk negligee, with nothing left to the imagination underneath.

He went to her and they kissed. His hands took hold of the silk as he caressed her body with the fine fabric.

His hands glided all over with ease. Her hair was let down to her shoulders, which he brushed aside to spread his kisses along her neck. Then she tilted her head back, exposing more. His hands were now exploring the small of her back, as his kisses trailed down to her breasts.

"Oh, Mick!" she cried. "Do you love me?"

He stopped for a moment to look into her sparkling hazel eyes.

"Yes—yes, I love you."

"Take me then. Take me now!" She took his hands and led him to her bed—their bed.

CHAPTER 19

While Jennifer and Mick were wallowing in the ecstasy of love, the Golden Door was visited by two gorgeous women, Susie Q and Miranda.

John had explained to Susie that he missed Don terribly, because he was his eyes and ears, and the plan was for Don to be the manager after John bought back the bar. All he really wanted the bar for was to launder his ill-gotten gains down to his account in the Cayman Islands, where he planned to retire.

Susie was taken in by this line because that was what she wanted to hear. That was what she wanted to believe. John admitted that Jennifer didn't want to sell him the bar, but he conveniently left out the part where he'd never bothered to ask. But now it was Susie's turn to find out the comings and goings at the Golden Door.

So she and the mayor had come to terms. He wanted to know everything about the new manager. What time was he there, what time did he leave, who was dealing drugs in the place, when did the dyke owner come and go, and who were her girlfriends? Susie didn't like that dyke term he used, as she had had a few trysts that way herself but gave it up because there was no money in it.

The mayor's list of things he wanted to know went on and on. His jaw had flapped like a well-oiled machine. He would have still kept going, but she finally rolled her eyes up and said, "All right already! I get the picture."

Then he further explained that all she had to do was catch the dyke violating the law so he could have her liquor license revoked, and then the bar would be all Susie's.

She took the bait—hook, line, and sinker—but she wasn't that slow. She talked her Johnny into slipping her a couple of those hundred dollar bills he was flashing.

"I've got expenses, you know," she said. And then she got him for a couple hundred more, for a little of this and a little of that, but mostly she hit him up for *that.*

Susie Q really didn't like what her Johnny was asking her to do, but she did like the sound of the results: money. Money, she thought to herself, justifies everything. He had it and she wanted it. Susie had a powder problem herself, an expensive powder problem. Deep down, she knew she was leading a dumb life. For all the money she made, she had none.

Easy come, easy go, all for blow, she thought. Blow this, blow that. Yes, she knew her life was dumb, but that was why she needed the blow—to make herself numb.

Susie missed The Donald too, but not that much. She knew her career as a dancer would be short-lived. She was aging faster than she knew, faster than she wanted, too. Her legs would ache. Lines were forming on her face, or so it seemed to her. She felt she was getting tired. She needed stability, a regular income. She was tired of all the hustling, tired of giving lap dances, tired of this and tired of that, and especially tired of that.

One more hustle, to get a place of her own, she thought—that would set her free. One more hustle, she thought, just one more. She felt tired. Deep down sewer-hole tired.

Susie Q and Miranda sat down at the bar in the section where Jack was working. When he came over to take their orders, she said, "Hi. Two Absolut Vodkas and orange juice, please."

"You got it," Jack replied.

Miranda was a Spanish girl with long straight black hair. A foxy looking girl, she was relatively new to the stripping business compared to Susie, but she was well-informed and knew how to play the game. Susie's plan was to get Miranda a job there waitressing. Her instructions were: "Do what you have to do and you will be rewarded." From there Susie would have all the inside information her Johnny would ever need.

She and Miranda had worked out their own deal. "Report only to me," Susie told her. She was simply quoting the same instructions the mayor had given her.

Jack came back with the drinks. "That'll be five dollars."

Susie gave him a twenty. "My name is Sue. This is Miranda. What's yours?"

"Jack."

"Hi, Jack. Is the manager in? My friend is looking for a job."

"Hi, Jack," Miranda said with a flashy smile.

"The manager isn't here tonight," Jack explained. "Come back tomorrow and he should be here. But I don't think he's looking for any help right now."

"Oh, OK," Susie said. "We'll come back tomorrow. Nice place you have here," she added.

"I like it," Jack responded.

Susie spun around on her barstool and looked at the stage. It was "D.J. Night" at the Golden Door. Even though she had been there before with The Donald over by the pool tables, she was now looking at the stage from a completely different angle. There was a lone D.J. spinning CDs on a big stage under dim colored lights. She saw the stage in a different light. She saw herself up there dancing under a spotlight.

She would need to install a twirling pole right there in the middle and build a little catwalk, so she could strut her stuff out to the tables and gawkers in the audience. Yes, she figured, that's all she would have to do after her Johnny got her the bar. She would have strippers every night of the week. The hell with the bands and the lovers dancing, she thought. She would have wall-to-wall men, panting and wanting and paying. They'd be stuffing cash into her girls' G-strings, and she'd be stuffing their cash into her register.

Laws didn't mean anything to men like Johnny, with all his protection and clout. Susie figured she could turn this pop stand into a real money maker. Yes, yes, there she was. She saw herself crystal clear right there in the middle of the dance stage, under the spotlight, slithering on her pole.

After she got the clientele she wanted, Susie then figured she could become a madam. She would be a first class madam, and treat her girls right. First class everything; no pimps allowed, especially the kind of pimps she was used to working for. Yes, she definitely saw herself in the spotlight.

Jack interrupted her visions of grandeur when he asked if they wanted refills.

"Yes, by all means!" When he returned with their drinks, Susie said, "My, you're big enough to be a bouncer."

"I am," Jack said, "on Friday and Saturday nights."

"Hmmm," Susie smiled, "I've never bounced on a bouncer before." She sat up and craned her neck to get a look at his crotch. "I bet that would be fun."

Miranda started to laugh as Jack's forehead broke out in a sweat.

"My wife thinks it is," he said with a thanks-but-no-thanks smile. All the same, he did walk away wiping his forehead and grinning a grin that lasted the rest of the night.

The two women left after that, leaving Jack the biggest tip he had ever received. They waved to him, too, as they sauntered out the door.

The next morning Jennifer woke up wrapped in Mick's arms. She felt good about the night before. It was a glorious night, but her stomach felt queasy, nauseous. It was like nothing she'd ever felt before.

She slipped out of his arms and went to the bathroom. It was like dry heaves. She wanted to throw up but her stomach was empty. She drank a glass of water and was going to brush her teeth, but then suddenly she had to drop to her knees and hug the porcelain.

In a matter of minutes, she recovered her composure. She started to ready herself for work. As she was going through her routine with facial cleansers and such, she spied her sanitary napkins and instinctively tried to remember the last time she needed them. Her mind started racing backwards in a marathon of thought. It wasn't since way before the Vegas trip, she realized.

"Oh my God!" she gasped.

She grabbed her belly and leaned forward to look at her eyes in the mirror. They were bloodshot, like as if she'd been on an all-night binge.

"Oh my God. Could it be true?"

She felt her stomach again to make sure it was still there. She gently massaged it while looking down, rethinking whether it could be true. She didn't think it was possible. She thought something was wrong with her. She was still holding her stomach as a flush filled her face.

She looked back into the mirror and saw a glowing face. A face with no makeup was glowing—her face, right there in front of her. It seemed to be getting brighter and brighter, like an early morning sunrise, the dawn, the beginning of eternal bliss.

If she knew the words to "Zippity Do-Dah," she would have sung it. She was having a wonderful day, and it had just started.

As she finished readying herself for work, she thought of calling in to take the day off. She pondered over her schedule. What's so important that her assistant couldn't handle? she wondered.

She was dressed and ready to go, and then she glanced over at Mick peacefully sleeping. She gave him a wink and a smile that he never saw, but somehow she knew he felt it.

Although she wasn't hungry, she started the coffee brewing and raided the fridge for bacon and eggs. Soon the kitchen was full of aromas, like a country café. As she cooked the bacon, its particular aroma wafted upstairs and silently stirred the sleeping Mick. While the bacon sizzled, Jen picked up the phone and left a voice mail for her assistant: "I won't be coming in today."

CHAPTER 20

John called Ben into his office.

"I've got a number to trace," he said. "It's gonna be a nigger's though. See that Gary prefix? And when we get the address and check it out, we gotta use the van. I don't want none of our squads out there. They would probably use 'em for target practice. You never know what you'll run into in that town. I don't have any clout there—don't want any either. They got a lot of dope though, and more money than you or I can count."

"Right," said Ben.

"If he's a big-time dealer," the mayor continued, "he might have some pals to contend with. Also, I'm thinking of appropriating some high-tech surveillance equipment for the police department. We can test the equipment out for ourselves."

"Sounds good to me," Ben said.

"All right then. Here's the number. You know what to do with it."

"Sure do." Ben took the scrap of paper with the phone number on it from the mayor and left.

Mick was enjoying his breakfast while Jen drank coffee. "This is dee-lish!" he said.

"You're welcome."

"How come you stayed home today?" he asked.

"I don't know. I felt like it, I guess. I think I'm excited about going away this weekend. I thought we might get a head-start. Where are we going anyway?" She paused. "No, don't tell me. Surprise me."

"OK."

"Will I need my swim suit?"

"Maybe. Pack one just in case. Is Jack going to fill in for me?"

"I'm sure he will. Which reminds me I have some calls to make. Excuse me."

Jennifer grabbed her valise full of business papers and spread them all out on the coffee table in the den and started dialing. Mick, making himself useful, did the dishes. Well worth the price of admission, he thought.

They were a hundred miles into Michigan when the radio station's transmitter signal began to fade. Mick hit the CD player button. Jefferson Airplane's "Surrealistic Pillow" came on. Dreamy music for a dreamy woman, he thought.

Jen sat there peacefully, saying nary a word. She'd let her seat recline when she first got in. Actually, it was the first time she'd ridden in his car. For most of the ride she had her eyes closed, totally relaxed, day-trip dreaming. When "Somebody to Love" started playing, she perked up briefly to look at Mick, who was studiously navigating the highway.

It was hours later when they reached Arbutus Beach in Otsego County. Mick pulled over for gas and to stretch his legs.

"Hungry yet?" he asked.

"Not really," Jen replied, "but I suppose I could use a bite. Are we there yet?"

"No, we have a couple hours to go."

"Then I think it would be a good idea to eat then. That looks like a nice place." She pointed to the Beach Café across the street.

Jen had the perch dinner and Mick had the walleye. Both meals were very satisfying and reasonably priced. But Mick wasn't going to be his regular penny-pinching self that weekend.

Even though he'd never been to Mackinac Island, he'd heard nice things about it and decided to check it out. A grand adventure, he thought, on a grand island. He had heard, and saw pictures, of the Grand Hotel, sitting high on a cliff. As an adventurer, he failed to make reservations though, which was just the way he did things. There must be room in a place that big, he thought. Typically a fly-by-the-seat-of-your-pants and hold-on-for-adventure type of guy, Mick had done things this way his entire life. He thought, Why stop now? Yes, he was set in his ways, but he was a proud man right then. He had a beautiful woman to share adventures with.

Dusk had settled in, and a weary Mick knew he was close to his destination. He spotted an inviting lodge, called the Old Mill Creek Motel, and pulled in. He noticed a dignified Jennifer sitting placidly next to him. If she wasn't laying back utterly relaxed, she was looking out the windows gathering in the splendid views. Once in awhile she had commented on the beautiful scenery.

She never did ask where they were going. Was that a sign of trust, Mick thought, or devil-may-care laissez-faire? The industrious socialite go-getter didn't have to call the shots for once, or make the plans or call for reservations. She seemed to be in a mood of sedated relief.

Mick had never seen her so peaceful, with him or herself. Actually, he realized that this was the first time they had been completely alone together for any extended period of time.

Little did he know why she was at peace with herself, but her mind was busy as a beehive. But it was a fun busy. Was it going to be a boy or a girl? she wondered. What will she name him or her? What would the first kick feel like? Would the delivery be difficult? Would it hurt? Oh, who cares, she thought, as long as it's healthy. When will the baby take its first steps? When will it cut its first tooth?

Jen's mind was as busy as that of any expectant mother. She knew she would have to buy all the books she might need, of course. When should she inform Mick? She wondered. It's too early now, she thought. She figured she'd have to buy a test kit first, and see a doctor second. Better be 100% sure before you tell Mick, she thought. Then she wondered to herself, Are you still going to adopt a child?

Yes, Jennifer was at peace with herself and everything else. She was a proud woman that day. She was now on the adventure of a lifetime, and she was proud to be on that adventure with a kind and understanding man—her man. My man Mick, she thought.

"Do you want to wait here while I check in?" he asked.

"Yes," she shyly replied.

He was in and out in a matter of minutes.

"That was fast," she commented.

"Yeah, she must have seen me coming," Mick said. "She was ready for me. Our room is over there." He pulled around the bend and parked.

They both grabbed their overnight duffel bags and entered the motel room. Jen gave the place a quick inspection. "Very quaint," she said with satisfaction.

"Do you want me to bring in the rest of your things?" he asked.

"How long are we staying here?"

"Just for the night."

"Then I have everything I need, thanks."

"There's a lounge around the corner. I could use a beer about now," Mick said.

"Yes, good idea. It was a long drive, so let's walk, OK?"

"You got it."

As soon as they left the room, Jen grabbed Mick's hand. When he looked at her, she gave him a wink and a smile. He smiled right back. Hand in hand they strolled, arms gently swaying as if in a breeze. As they walked, they talked. She confessed that it felt good to get away, and commented on how fresh and clean the air smelled.

The lounge was done up in log cabin style. The walls were abound with taxidermies, mostly of mounted fish of nearly every local species—perch, pike, walleye—and of animals like badger, beaver, and bear. The lounge was also decorated with old traps, bows, and arrows. The scene was set to remind people of the old days. There was one round unlit fireplace right in the middle of the room. It very well could have been an old hunting lodge, redone with a stone façade added to the front.

It wasn't very crowded, so when they sat down in a booth off the bar, a waitress appeared immediately to take their drink orders. Mick could smell steak sizzling on the grill. The aroma almost made him order one for himself, but after eating earlier he just wasn't hungry enough. He did ask Jen if she wanted to order hors d'oeuvres. She nodded yes and picked up a placard standing next to the napkin dispenser.

"I think I'll have a shrimp cocktail," she said.

"Sounds good. I'll make it two."

The waitress came back with their drinks and caught them holding hands over the table. They quickly pulled their arms back as she approached.

"You kids on your honeymoon?" she inquired politely.

"Er, no. Not exactly," Mick blurted out.

The lights were low enough that nobody noticed Jennifer's cheeks blush rose red.

"We're, uh, just visiting—er, vacationing," Mick tried to explain. He then quickly changed the subject with, "And we'll have two shrimp cocktails too, please."

The waitress wrote it down, smiling broadly, and walked away wondering.

On the walk back, Jennifer saw a flash of light between the stars.

"Did you see *that?*" she exclaimed.

"See what?" Mick asked.

"*That!* There goes another one. Shooting stars! Did you see them?"

"Oh, yeah. Is it me or do the stars look brighter out here?"

"Oh, they're just beautiful!" She put her arm around his waist and leaned her head on his shoulder. "Oh, everything is beautiful. What a nice night!"

They strolled along, arm in arm, connected physically and mentally. Without saying a word they were bonding, telepathically fusing their commitment to each other. Mick opened the door of the room and she kissed him right there on the threshold. He instinctively scooped her up in his arms and carried her inside, kicking the door closed with his foot as they entered.

The next morning they were off, and in short order they were upon a massive bridge. It reminded Mick of the Golden Gate Bridge.

"Are we going to Canada?" Jennifer asked.

"Oh, no," he replied. "We're just crossing the Mackinac Bridge."

"Oh, it's beautiful!"

Even as he drove, Mick reached for his camera and started clicking away.

"Leather and Lace," another Fleetwood Mac song, started playing on the CD player. Jennifer sang along, and Mick soon joined in. He was a great fan. He figured Stevie Nicks had the power to turn any man on.

"Give me your leather, and take my lace," they both sang. Mick glanced lovingly at Jen when the tires started singing their own song as they rode over the bridge's iron grates.

"Some people are paranoid about crossing this bridge and have to be driven across by a toll attendant," Mick explained.

"No, you're kidding," Jen replied.

"No, really. I saw a feature on a TV program—I forgot which one, but it was something like '20/20.'"

"Where are we going?"

"You see that big while building on that island?"

"Where? I don't see it."

"We'll be there soon enough."

"Did you make reservations?"

"Ah, er, no."

Jennifer's business sense was taking over. "Well, don't you think you should call and make them?"

"Oh. Well, sure."

Once they'd passed over the bridge, he followed the main highway and the signs until he found the ferry boats. He pulled into the Star Line parking lot and, to appease his lady fair, went to the pay phone to make a reservation.

"Grand Hotel," the receptionist answered.

"My name is Mickey Swift, and I would like to make reservations for two this evening."

"Double bed or king size?"

"King size."

"It also includes a five-course dinner."

Mick wasn't expecting a dinner to be included, so he instinctively asked, "How much is it for one night?"

"Four hundred" was all he needed to hear to start a lump growing in his throat. The receptionist went on explaining the dollars and cents and what the other amenities were. Mick could only half listen. His mind was in sticker-price shock. He'd been used to motel bills, not hotel. That lump in his throat was getting bigger.

The thought occurred to him: cancel. Tell Jen they're all booked up and stay somewhere else. Then "you cad, you cad" echoed in the back of his mind. He remembered what Marie had called him in Las Vegas. Then he remembered his winnings there. He knew he could afford it. Blow some dough, you cheapskate, he thought to himself. It's for a good cause. He glanced over at Jennifer. Now there's a good cause, he thought.

It was hard for him to do, but he gulped down that lump, which to him sounded like a bowling ball rolling down an alley. Then the pins scattered—strike! Now, with his mind made up, he was free to think clearly.

The receptionist had just finished explaining the amenities, and Mick said, "That'll be fine. What time can we check in?"

"Twelve noon."

"Thank you." Mick walked back over to Jen and with a big cocky smile said, "We're all set."

He loaded the luggage on the boat and away they went. He had his camera out for the ride. He snapped off a couple more shots of the bridge and a few of Jen. The boat that was ferrying them to Mackinac Island was more like a speed boat, and the fantail it threw up in its wake was bigger than the boat. The water spray and the sunlight combined made a rainbow prism, if looked at from the right angle. He took a picture of that, too.

Jen's hair was fluttering in the breeze, so she searched her handbag for bands to fasten her hair in a ponytail. She put her sunglasses on too. Then she spotted the hotel.

"Is that it, Mick?"

"Yeah."

"Well, take a picture. It's beautiful!"

It appeared to be an extremely long white building, almost like a replica of the White House with extended wings. It had a dome in the middle and a lone American flag flying proudly on top.

Mick took several pictures of the building, as well as the marvelous looking Victorian mansions that flanked it atop the same bluff.

They were soon docked and off the boat. They had a valet take their bags up to the hotel. Jen wanted to stay in town awhile and wander through the quaint little shops. More than once she commented on how beautiful the town was. All she knew about Mackinac was that they raced boats there from Chicago. She never realized they didn't allow cars there, nor that there were so many quaint buildings and stores. She was in heaven.

There were flower baskets hanging or flags flying at nearly every shop. People were walking or leisurely biking, and many kids were in strollers. She stopped whenever she saw a baby in a buggy, making sure to say hello as she cooed for the infant. She marveled at all the stained glass ornaments and water color paintings. She couldn't figure out which painting she was going to get or where to hang it in the house.

They made their way to the livery station, climbed into a horse-drawn carriage, and were off for the Grand Hotel.

As they drew closer, the enormity of the building made their eyes dilate. Jennifer was ecstatic with joy. She couldn't believe the size of just the front porch.

"It must be as long as a city block!" she exclaimed. "Just look at all those flowers!"

They checked in but rather than going right to their room, they strolled about getting their bearings. As soon as Jen spotted the serpentine-shaped swimming pool, she knew what she wanted to do. Likewise when Mick saw the sauna and whirlpools, he knew what he wanted to do.

After a swim and sauna, they were both refreshed; but Mick didn't want to dawdle the day away doing things they could do back home, so he suggested touring the island on horseback—which Jen ixnayed, but settled on a carriage tour.

Mister Virtual Tourist was at it again, taking pictures of everyone and everything. Mick wanted to savor the experience and justify the expense. He particularly liked the old fort, complete with the antique cannons and musket rifles. Jennifer sat passively floating along on the springboard-cushioned carriage seat while Mick snapped away. He'd already used two rolls of film and was working on a third.

After they completed the tour, they went back to their beautifully appointed room. The king-size bed had a golden canopy with matching drapes. The room was made up in a way that made one feel truly special. They cleaned up and dressed for dinner. Mick had never eaten a five-course dinner in a five-star restaurant before and was looking forward to it. He specifically saved his appetite all day long and was famished.

Jennifer loved the dining room. From the crystal chandelier to the white tablecloths and the lace doilies decorating the tables, it looked as if Martha Stewart herself had arranged it all. Mick was indifferent to the décor; he was just plain old hungry. He could still smell the steak he'd passed up the other night, and he really didn't care if they served it on a paper plate—as long as the steak was thick and juicy.

The food was plentiful: soup, salad, fresh baked bread, appetizers, dessert, and the main course. It was all a bit much even for a man like Mick to consume. Jen picked through her meal daintily, but all the same her plate was also clean in the end.

They could hear an orchestra playing. When they went to investigate, they saw people dancing. It dawned on Mick that they had never danced together before. He knew that omission would be corrected right away. A place with this kind of elegance and style, he thought, simply implores couples to dance.

Just off the parlor in the Terrace Room they went, and didn't miss a beat of the big band sound. They instinctively took to the dance floor and started to sway with the swing music. During the second dance, Jennifer whispered in Mick's ear, "Thanks for bringing me here." Mick just smiled back at her.

They danced every tune for what seemed to him like an hour, before sitting down for a rest and a cocktail. After another dance session, they took a leisurely stroll out to the front porch for a breath of fresh cool evening air. When they reached the corner of the hotel's porch, they saw a group of people with telescopes peering into the twilight.

"What are you looking at?" Mick queried one fellow.

"The Perseid meteors in the constellation Perseus," he replied.

"We saw shooting stars last night," Jen added.

"My name is Mark" the fellow said. "Would you like to look through my scope?"

"Hi, Mark," she responded. "I'm Jennifer and this is Mick."

She bent over to look through the telescope. It was set up on a tripod and already focused, so Jen got an eyeful of shooting stars. Mark went on further to explain that, in this case, the meteor shower she was looking at was from the Swift-Tuttle Comet.

Jennifer straightened right up and looked at a shoulder-shrugging Mick and then back at Mark. "You mean these shooting stars come from a comet named 'Swift-Tuttle?'"

"Yes, that's right," he said.

"Well, I'll be! Thanks for letting me look through your telescope, Mark."

"Any time."

As they walked away, Jen tugged on Mick's arm. "How about that? We have a comet named after us! Our union is blessed by heavenly bodies."

"I didn't know you were into astrology."

"I'm not really, but I read my horoscopes. Besides, it's all in fun, don't you think? Anyway, it ties us together more. It's like you were heaven-sent. Don't you see? We're 'a match made in heaven'? Well, that's the way you make me feel."

"That's nice."

Mick wasn't nearly as excited about the revelation as Jen was. He knew the comet was named after the astronomers who discovered it, but he didn't dare burst her bubble over useless trivia. If it made her feel good, he was all for it. Besides, he thought, it is kind of cool to have your names attached to a comet.

He pointed to the sky. "There's another one." Mick's mind took off like a rocket-man. "What do you think it would be like flying through space at a million miles an hour?"

"You can't go that fast in space."

"Why not?"

"I don't know." She playfully elbowed him for kidding her.

"It's a million light-years to Mars," he said.

"No, it's not."

"I heard it in a song."

"So?"

"So how long do you think it would take to get there?"

"I don't know," Jen replied, "but it wouldn't take a million years."

"Do you think there's life on other planets?"

"Not in this solar system, but I'm sure there's life out there somewhere. Look at all those stars! Into infinity! I'm sure there's a celestial phenomenon like Earth out there somewhere. We're really just a bunch of atoms and

DNA stuck together, and the same atoms we have here are out there."

"OK, already," Mick said, being secretly quite impressed with Jen's grasp of such things. "Maybe you're right. Who really cares anyway? It's not like we're going to jump into a spaceship anytime soon."

"Just look at the enormity of it all! Doesn't it make you feel small and insignificant?" Jen was on a roll. "It's supposed to be a fun thing to think about. Imagine what the Greeks, Romans, and Egyptians did at night. They had no TV to watch, so they watched the stars—until they probably got so bored and fell asleep."

"I'll bet that's not the only thing they did at night." Mick gave her a big hug. "Come on, let's go." He gave her his best "let's do it" smile, and she smiled back.

"Yeah, let's go," she agreed. "Do you want to order some champagne and strawberry shortcake?"

"You bet I do!"

The next morning Mick awoke drained—physically, mentally, sexually. Jennifer had turned into a tigress. All doubts had been vanquished that night, as he secretly had to pop a "pole pill" to satisfy her. He let her believe it was all her doing, and she couldn't have been more delighted.

But now he was slightly lethargic. He wanted to roll over and blow some more Z's, but he could hear the shower running and smell the sweet smell of whipped cream still on him. The aroma and the thought of sharing a shower with Jen stirred his "good morning muscle" back to life. Either use it or lose it, he thought. So he rolled out of bed and headed for the shower.

"Want some company?" he inquired.

Jen slid open the glass door. "Sure, come on in!" Her eyes opened wider when she noticed his growth. "Don't forget to bring your friend!" She gave him a wink and a smile.

He wasted no time entering the shower. After a little soapsuds foreplay, she made him enter her. As they sang the song of love, Jennifer was seeing shooting stars all over again. She imagined heavenly bodies intertwining, shining, shining like she had never seen before. There they were, united in a Roman chariot behind two white stallions flying after the Swift-Tuttle Comet. Water from the meteor shower sparkled as the tiny droplets burst into newborn suns, scattering across the sky. Faster and faster they raced. Mick was cracking his whip as they flew. They were now racing at the speed of light. Mick cracked that whip again and again. When the tip of that whip snapped, it sparkled like fireworks on the Fourth of July. Streams of colors flew out—crimson reds, bright oranges, crystal blues and greens, sparking her nerve endings like lighting the fuse.

The stallions caught up to the comet and took a nip at its tail. The meteor shower's moisture splashed at their faces. It tickled, and twinkled like the morning dew. They both felt the thrilling quake and eruption of Mount Ecstasy—the heat—that warm and comforting heat—the flowing lava, that oozing, flowing lava, filling the valleys and crevices. Mick pulled back on the reins and guided the chariot down, landing in the sea of tranquility!

As the water poured down on their bodies and Mick withdrew, panting like a race horse that just won the derby, Jen's smile grew and she said,

"Well, good morning to you too!"

They packed and readied themselves for departure, but not before the breakfast feast. After all, Mick reasoned, it was all-inclusive. He also realized how petty worrying about the price was. He'd had a grand adventure on Mackinac Island at a Grand Hotel.

Jennifer wanted to make one more stop before they departed. She wanted a souvenir from the Artists' Gallery down by the boat docks. She chose a watercolor painting by one of the local artists. She told Mick it reminded her of the love of nature, and it reflected her interest in impressionism and realism. The painting also showed astonishing beauty and conveyed a miraculous life energy.

"When I see this painting hanging on our wall," she said, "I will always remember our weekend together."

They hopped the ferry back to Saint Ignace, loaded Mick's car, and pulled out onto I-75. When they got to the middle of the bridge, Jennifer waved bye-bye to Mackinac Island.

CHAPTER 21

hile Jen and Mick were headed for home, Ben Smide was invited to the mayor's house for a meeting of the minds.

The mayor had a palatial home in the affluent part of town. Most notable was the way the driveway split in two, like a snake's tongue, making two ramps that enabled him to have a two-car garage under his three-car garage. It was a four-level home, but the mayor himself was long ago banished to the bottom two. After the wife caught him cheating on her for the third time, this was all they could do to live amicably.

Mrs. Quibly loved the snobbery of being the mayor's wife and didn't want the D-word to spread among her upper-class social clubs. She had John over the barrel in many ways. So into the basement he went, sharing with her only the next level's kitchen and living rooms for entertaining. Also banished with him was his taxidermy collection of dust-collecting animal trophies.

These animal heads and other trophies lived in the recreation room, complete with pool table, bar, and giant screen projection TV. Ben's eyes almost popped out of their sockets when he saw this. It was just how he'd wanted his own hunting and fishing lodge to look. But it was the mayor's antique mahogany gun closet that lured Ben's eyes for a closer examination.

The mayor unlocked the glass doors and allowed Ben to scope out his collectibles, along with his other killing machines. Ben didn't bother with the shotguns. He grabbed the AK-47 and aimed it across the room.

"I'll bet you could do a lot of damage with this baby," he said.

"Yeah, you're right about that," the mayor went along. "Too big to be practical for what we want to do though. Here, have a look at these." He slid open a drawer which held an assortment of pistols, Colt six-shooters, Smith & Wesson nine millimeter automatics, a Baretta with a silencer, a Luger with an infrared scope, and a Derringer.

"Where did you get all these?" Ben asked.

"Mostly from drug dealers. The chief and I bagged them. But you ain't seen nothing yet." He slid open another drawer and there it was: a fully automatic Uzi.

"Wow!" Ben picked it up.

"There's a lot of firepower there," the mayor said. "We got the drop on him, and he never got a shot off. It's the drug dealer's dream machine—and that might just be what we're going up against. Take whatever you think you'll need for the job. These weapons are untraceable." He paused. "So, you have the joint all scoped out?"

"Yeah. It's a gas station that went out of business. Now it's a front for RAP Cartage Company. It's half boarded up with a fenced-in storage yard. Could've been a chop shop at one time. There's a 'tune-up and oil change' sign outside. The cars that pull in there only stay for five minutes—in and out and gone."

"It's a front all right."

"So, what's your plan?" Ben asked.

"We'll set a fire in one of those old abandoned buildings on the other side of town to divert the police," the mayor said. "There's only six of them on duty at any one time—when they're awake."

They both laughed.

"I'll be listening on the police scanner," the mayor continued, "while you go in there and see what they're hiding."

"You know if anyone lives near there?"

"Nah. Nobody. There used to be strip malls on both sides of the street, but they're all boarded up."

The mayor opened up a closet door that held all his camouflage hunting clothes. On the far side he had an FBI jacket and on the shelf an FBI hat.

"Wear your bulletproof vest and cover it up with this." He pulled the jacket off the hanger and handed it to Ben. "I have a fake search warrant you can use. If you flash it in front of them, I figure they'll give you no problems."

"OK, let's roll."

They turned off the expressway onto Broadway. They drove two blocks to 25th Avenue and made a pass at the garage front. "There's his Continental," the mayor said. "They're open for business."

The mayor was driving and he sped off. Ben had already made a molotov cocktail. They made two right-hand turns and headed for the east side of town. There was now row upon row of old abandoned buildings in what was once part of a hustling, bustling middle-class steel town community. With the mills all but closed down, the only things that kept the town afloat were the recently legalized gambling boats.

They pulled up to a nondescript building that had previously been vandalized, as the plywood window was now removed. After checking briefly for witnesses, Ben threw in the firebomb, and they were off.

They turned on their police scanner to listen for response to the impending fire. They made it all the way back to Broadway before the first dispatch was aired.

"We're all set now," the mayor said.

It was the middle of a Sunday afternoon. Traffic was light and speeding was easy. Ben was cocked and ready for action. The mayor had a new piece in his holster. He was locked and loaded and ready for back-up duty.

Their adrenaline was pumping, a cold and calculating adrenaline. They each had their reasons for taking chances. They had justified themselves beforehand with talk like: "drug dealers don't deserve to live," "drug dealers are the scourge of humanity," "look at all the lives they ruin," and "all's fair in love and war."

The mayor pulled the van right up to the front door and Ben burst in screaming, "FBI! Don't move! I have a search warrant and you're all under arrest!"

Bob Jackson was looking down the barrel of an Uzi. He put his hands up immediately. From around a corner came a guy and his girlfriend.

"What's going on?" the guy asked.

"Put your hands up!" Ben commanded. "You're under arrest."

Ben ushered the three of them to the rear of the garage. "You can make things easy on yourselves," he demanded, "if you tell me where the drugs are."

The girl was shaking and about to cry. "In the back room," she blurted, pointing to a storage room door.

Then a spray of bullets from the Uzi splattered blood on the wall behind them, and down to the floor they fell.

Ben went to the door and opened it. He was greeted by gunfire.

He took two shots in the vest before splattering the room with automatic gunfire.

When the smoke cleared, he saw what he came for: several bricks of cocaine sitting on a desk. On further inspection, he saw a satchel. He kicked the bloody body out of his way. Looking into the satchel, he saw the cash.

Ben slung the Uzi over his back and grabbed the satchel and two bricks of cocaine. He ran back outside to the van and deposited the loot inside.

"Come on, let's go!" the mayor said.

"No, wait! There's more!"

The mayor was getting nervous. He heard the gunfire and wondered if anyone else did, or who else might stumble upon the scene. Ben ran back in and took four more bricks of coke.

"That's plenty. Let's get out of here!"

"But there's more!" Ben hollered.

"Let's go while the getting's good."

"No, wait! One more trip."

"Hurry up then!" The mayor nervously looked around to check and see if anyone was coming. He looked in the rearview mirrors, out the back window of the van, and bobbed his head out the driver's window to double, then triple-check.

Ben ran back into the storage room and the man on the floor grabbed his pants leg and cried out, "Help me!"

Ben looked down and drew his service revolver. Pow! He shot him right in the head.

"Try to kill me, motherfucker?" He cursed over the dead man's body. He kicked him one more time to move him out of his way and took four more bricks of coke.

"All right, let's roll!" Ben ordered the mayor as he jumped back in the van.

Just in the nick of time, too. As they pulled out, another customer was pulling in.

"What dem white dudes doin' out here?" the driver asked. "Dey muss be lost, dat's fo sho!"

"Why's Bob's door open?" the other one asked back.

They parked and went in to witness the carnage.

"Damn!" they both said in unison.

They looked in the storage room when they saw smoke slowly climbing out of the top jam of the door. Inside they saw Slim Jim, or so they thought, as his brains were all exposed. The sight almost turned their stomachs to the point of vomiting.

"Let's git!" the driver said.

"Nah, I sees two keys yonder."

"Grab 'em den, an' den let's git!"

As he passed the body, the one going for the coke said out of reverence, "Sawry, Slim, but dees ain't gwine do you no good no mo." He grabbed the bricks and they split. As they sped away, the passenger had to roll down his window and vomit.

The police were eventually called by an anonymous caller from a public phone. The state police and lab technicians were called out because of the horrendous brutality of the crime. There were four dead bodies and no suspects. That was always an automatic call to get every available person immediately onto the case.

Sheriff Hank Williams was there, shaking his head in disbelief of the scene. A Times reporter and photographer were there, but they weren't allowed in. Crime scene tape was wrapped around everywhere.

With the emergency vehicles flashing their lights, congregations of people gathered to gawk. The police checked for witnesses, but nobody saw or heard anything. The lab guys were inside taking pictures, impressions of fingerprints, footprints, and anything else as evidence of what the killers may have left behind.

Back at the mayor's house, Ben Smide was counting a satchel full of money. It was more cash than he had ever seen at any one time. The mayor stashed the bricks of coke in his lockable deep freeze, for which only he had the key. Ben was busy counting the money, some of which was already banded and some was thrown in helter-skelter. All the fives and tens kept him busy, but he was enjoying himself. Actually, he was overjoyed, and oblivious to what he had done to get it.

The mayor went to his bar to make himself a stiff one.

"You want a drink, Ben?" he called out.

"Not now," was his reply. He was happier just playing with the dough.

The mayor gulped down the first drink and poured himself another. He turned on the small TV on the corner of the bar for company, and to drown out the noise of the gunfire that was still ringing inside his head. What did he shoot them for, he thought to himself. He was just supposed to rob them.

The mayor wasn't really surprised at what happened. He'd always figured Ben was a loose cannon. He remembered what happened to Juan Beamer. That was no accident, he thought. What did I get myself into, he wondered, and how do I get myself out of it?

Nerve-wracking beads of perspiration popped out on the mayor's forehead. He mopped them away with a bar towel. He poured himself another whiskey and got a beer out of the refrigerator. It had just turned 5 o'clock—time for the evening news.

There it was, headline news: "Four dead in Gary," "gangland slaying," "more news as it develops." Damn, the mayor thought, we hit the big time now. The sweat on his forehead returned.

Ben sneaked up behind him while his attention was focused on the TV and slammed the satchel down on the bar, startling John. "I think I'll have that beer now."

"Sure, partner." The mayor got off his stool and fetched one out of the fridge. "You'll have to learn to help yourself, Ben. You're part of the family now."

"Almost twenty thousand in there. Not bad for a day's work."

The mayor changed the subject.

"What happened in there?" "What happened!?" Ben raised his voice in indignation. "Those fucking niggers shot me!" He went back to the coffee table where he had counted the money and retrieved the FBI jacket and bulletproof vest. "Look here!" he shoved his fingers through the holes in the jacket and pointed to the pockmarks in the vest. "Those motherfuckers shot me with my FBI jacket on! I told them they were all under arrest. Who cares about dope-dealing niggers anyway?"

"Yeah, I told you it could be dangerous. You earned your money today."

"Yeah, I sure did." Ben gulped down his beer and went back to the fridge to get himself another. On the way back, he spied a shot glass next to a whiskey bottle. He stopped to pour himself one and slammed it down. After his body shivered from the whiskey, he poured himself another. "Ah, that tasted good. How much do you think that coke is worth?"

"I don't know," John replied. "Fifty thousand maybe."

"Is that all? I figured two hundred and fifty thousand."

"Well, it depends on how you sell it, package it, cut it—things like that. It'll take a couple of years to get rid of all that stuff. We gotta lay low until I get the bar back."

"What bar?"

"The Golden Door. Yeah, that's the one and only."

"So that's why you and Jake have me leaning on those people! I thought it was because they stopped paying the juice."

"That's part of it," the mayor said. "Everybody's got to pay their dues in this town. You let one off the hook and they'll all want off. That's how we keep the peace, around here and everywhere else. The palms have to be greased to keep the wheels turning. Otherwise, nothing would get accomplished."

"So you're planning on selling the coke in the bar when you get it back?"

"Not me. Don was going to do it—until I caught him doublecrossing me." The mayor paused. "You wouldn't doublecross me, would you?"

The mayor gave Ben a stern look waiting for his reply.

"No, no. Never."

"Good. So what are you planning to do with your money?"

"I was planning on buying a hunting and fishing lodge on a lake up north."

"Twenty grand ain't going to get you there. I thought you wanted to be the next police chief?"

"Yeah. I changed my mind about that. I can't get laid like I want with a badge on my chest. I found out the difference last week, when I went to this place called Miners Only. It's way out of town and nobody knows me there. Anyway, it's a rip-off of a cave theme. It's got lanterns and miners' helmets and all that. It was lingerie night, and this broad wanted money for a lap dance and I didn't want to give her any money, so I told her I had some coke. Her eyes lit up and she said, 'Show me, big boy.' So I made two lines right there on the table and she took a straw and sucked them both up. So I said, 'Hey, one was for me.' She says, 'Don't worry, honey, I'll make it up to you.' So she sits on my lap and does her thing and I had a boner in a minute. So I says, 'How about finishing me off?' And she says, 'I'll do anything for the rest of your coke.' So I follow her into the ladies' john and I give her the rest of the packet and she puts some on my pecker. Then she went wild on me. I mean she ate me alive! So, that's why I gotta go back to being a civilian. And I need some more coke. Mine's all gone."

Ben chugged down the rest of his beer, and the mayor said, "I understand perfectly, but don't you remember our deal from the first job? You get to keep the money and I keep the drugs. Just because I didn't find any money on the first job, we split the dope. Remember?"

"Yeah, but you got a quarter million in coke and I did all the work."

"Who got the phone number?"

"You did."

"And without the phone number, you'd have nothing."

"Yeah, I see your point, but it doesn't seem fair. I mean, if we're partners it should be a 50-50 split."

"You're right. Wait a minute. Let me think." The mayor got off his barstool to get another beer. He grabbed the bottle of whiskey and set it between them with two new shot glasses. He got Ben a fresh beer too. "Let's drink to 50-50 partners."

He filled the shots, they clinked glasses, and then they saluted each other.

"Maybe you might be interested in managing the Golden Door for me?" the mayor asked. "You can get a blow job every day of the week on a job like that."

Ben's eyes snapped to attention. "Really?"

"Yeah, really. You think about it while I come up with a new plan. I should have it all figured out by the end of the week."

"OK."

The mayor refilled their shot glasses. A wry smile appeared on his face. They clinked glasses one more time.

"Yeah, I'll have a new plan ready by the end of the week."

CHAPTER 22

Road weary Mick was a bundle of tension from the long drive, so Jennifer suggested stopping at the Golden Door to check on things and he was all for it. He knew a beer would go down real smooth right about then.

Jack was loading the coolers when they walked in. Heather and Debbie were running around behind the bar as usual. Jen had a few quick words with Debbie, who then started to pass around free drink chips to everyone in the house. Heather followed Jen back to the office, and Mick just plopped his butt down on the nearest barstool.

There was a night baseball game on TV that he started watching. He was still uncomfortable, so he arched his back until it cracked Then he did some torso twists and rolled his shoulders and cocked his head a few times. The cricks in his neck creaked and snapped. Nothing like barstool exercises, he thought. Better than watching Jane Fonda's workout video at home.

Mick would have preferred a chiropractor or masseuse, but he knew that this would have to do. Then he got off his stool and stood for awhile. He thought he might be developing a case of "flat ass" from sitting so long.

Debbie handed him a beer. "It's on Jennifer," she said.

When Heather returned to her station, there was evidence of a tear. Mick had no idea as to its cause. It could have been from extreme happiness or sadness, he thought. He knew she would never divulge information like that, but she quickly became lively and perky as ever and carried on gracefully.

Jack came over to Mick when he got the chance. "There were a couple of broads looking for you. They came in three nights in a row. They said they were looking for work."

"I don't need any more help right now," Mick said.

"Yeah, that's what I told them."

"OK. Thanks, Jack."

"No problem, man."

That first beer didn't last long at all, so Mick ordered another.

Jennifer was back in the swing of things. When she came out of the office, she paid Mick no never-mind and went straight to socializing with her customers. Just as well, he figured. He was into an exciting ball game—a

7 to 7 tie, two men on, two out, top of the ninth. The game went on tied until the Sox pulled it out in the eleventh inning.

Jen was still jabber-jawing with some ladies by the pool tables when the news came on: "Two men to be arraigned tomorrow in the Gary massacre."

"Good," said Jack. "They got those guys." He was standing within earshot of Mick but said it for everyone to hear.

"What happened?" Mick asked.

"They murdered four people," Jack replied. "Shot them up pretty good. Some drug deal gone bad."

"Oh."

The broadcast continued: "Police are still looking for a third suspect. The two men claim they're innocent, but police said they have matching fingerprint evidence and shoe prints from the bloody scene. They also have recovered two pounds of cocaine from the suspects." The explanation went along with film footage of the police walking the two handcuffed black men into the jail building. Their heads were lowered in an attempt to hide their faces from the TV camera. The voiceover concluded: "Both suspects have a long criminal record, police said." Then the telecast went on to other news.

Mick drank down his beer and was ready to go. He went over to Jen and tried to interrupt her conversation. She could go on all night, he thought, if he'd let her.

She turned and said, "In just a minute!"

But he had the distinct feeling she wouldn't stop anytime soon, so he went back to the bar and ordered another beer.

The newscast didn't provide the public with all the information the police had, of course. There was a third set of bloody foot prints. Yes, both suspects had passed polygraph tests, but their alibi about seeing two white men leave the scene of the crime didn't make sense. So the polygraph examiner marked the test results as inconclusive. There was a probability that those black suspects were used to lying, or they could have been so hopped up on drugs that they hallucinated. They could also have fooled the machine, which would do them no good in a court of law anyway, as the results of such tests were inadmissible. They were likely going to hang anyway. Possessing two pounds of cocaine with the intent to deliver could send them up the river for a long time.

What they had tried to do was unload the coke to an undercover insurance investigator who was employed by Ralph Swanson. Ralph was forced to blow his cover because "The Gary Massacre" case was so hot.

The forensic team did a magnificent job. They lifted twenty sets of fingerprints, all of which were traced to their owners in the fingerprint database. The irrefutable fact that the two suspects were still wearing the same bloody shoes at the time of their arrest positively placed them at the scene of the crime.

This quick police work was a godsend to the local politicians who were feeling the heat of their electors to solve the case. They spared no expense when people were terrified.

"Hang 'em! Hang 'em good and high," the Gary police chief told his men. "Find the guns. Search their homes, their cars, their bars, and their assholes. Get 'em to confess, and I don't care how you do it!"

He pounded his fist on the meeting room desk. "Who's their accomplices? I want answers and I want them now. There's a third suspect out there. Find him too!"

Ben and John were already drunk as skunks. They had been laughing and partying in the mayor's basement ever since they got the news of the arraignment.

"Fry them fuckers!" the mayor roared.

Ben chimed in, "Stupid niggers! They ain't got a chance beating that rap. Hah! The chumps! Ha-ha-ha-ha-ha!"

The two of them were really whooping it up.

"Hey, let's play some pool, Ben!" the mayor boisterously suggested.

"I'm pretty good!"

"So am I. I'll rack 'em. Eight Ball all right with you?"

"Yeah, sure."

John had to remove the plastic cover before he could rack the balls. His pool table was more for rec room decoration than anything else. It was so seldom used that it looked brand-new, even though it was twenty years old. There were cue sticks in the rack on the wall, but the mayor had a special case for his favorite. When he took the cue out, with its ivory and pearl-inlaid handle, one would think he was trying to do a Minnesota Fats impersonation. He did have fat little fingers and a rotund build, but even with a fancy stick and all, he still couldn't play worth a lick.

Both of them missed three shots in a row before the mayor knocked in a ball that was hanging on the corner pocket. If they knew how to play the game, one could say there were a little off. Yet they thought they knew how to shoot, but they couldn't.

Ben was thinking, Now we don't have to lay so low, since they busted the niggers.

"How about busting open one of those bricks?" he asked. "So I can have a little high time with that broad I told you about."

"Whatta ya need," bellowed the mayor, "A blow job? I can set that up for you. Ya gotta understand, there's a trick to makin' money off cocaine. An' that is, don't use it yourself. Once ya have the money, you can buy all the broads ya want."

"Yeah, I know," Ben said. "But doing coke is fun. It gives me energy like nothin' else I ever tried, and the cunts love it."

"All right. Jus' hang on a little longer. I'll get ya a broad meanwhile. Jus' wait an' see. You young peckers always got broads on the brain. Let me tell ya, when you're my age… you'll still be lookin' for cunt!"

Ben laughed.

"Let's play another game," said the mayor. "It's your rack."

Ben bent down to get the balls out of the return, and he fumbled around trying to get them all into the triangle. "How are you gonna get me a broad anyway?"

"Don't worry. I've got connections, remember? You come with me tomorrow and I'll set ya right up."

"Yeah. All right." Ben finally got all the balls inside the rack and the mayor broke.

Even though he was drunk, he was still feeling Ben out. He knew he was a trained killer, but would he go along with the plan he was concocting? John wondered. He knew the urge to kill would creep up on Ben again, but when? Just like it happened to him, he thought. First you're a boy with a .22 rifle killing squirrels in the woods, then possums, then the Army gets you and you're trained to kill men. Then somebody gets in your way, and they're dead meat. Then the game gets bigger—deer, moose, bear—and the thrill of the hunting game takes hold. The thrill of the kill. And it all gets bigger after that. Winning is the only important thing, the mayor thought. Just eliminate anything that gets in your way.

John's killing had been in remission for a long, long time—ever since that one summer. That summer that changed his life. Those draft dodgers had it coming, he'd told himself. They got in his way. He was just doing his duty, but that picture haunted him. It was still haunting him. Then, he thought, that Don got in the way. He fucked up my plans!

Now he realized the urge had gotten hold of him again. That urge kept creeping back into his mind, that cold-blooded urge that solved all his problems. He wondered, Will Ben do it for me?

The mayor thought he would. He knew Ben's weaknesses now. He pried them out of him with no effort at all. Now, he thought, wait for him to get hungry again and that urge will come back. He's living in denial now, but that urge is going to come clawing its way back.

John thought he had it all figured out. He was going to use Ben just like he used everybody else.

Ben started laughing, as he missed another easy shot. Then he started to stumble, catching himself with his hand on the side of the pool table. "Whoa, Nelly!" he said. John noticed him staggering as he made his way back to his stool.

The mayor wasn't in much better shape, but he did manage to sink two balls for the win. "You should learn how to play this game," he boasted after winning for the second time. They tried to play a third game, but Ben was staggering to and fro, so John made him sleep it off on the couch. It was the most intelligent thing these two men had done in months.

Pool wasn't the only game in town they didn't know how to play. There was a computer playing a game somewhere else. The computer was owned by the insurance company that employed Ralph Swanson. One of his assistants had found something, something very interesting. It may have been overlooked by others as being insignificant, but to that particularly curious assistant, it seemed important.

CHAPTER 23

Other than the two girls that promised they would do anything to get a job at the Golden Door, everything else was back to normal. That is, as *normal* as normal could be. Mick, for one, was a little different. He was heavy with contemplation. His first court date was creeping up on him fast.

When there was discussion with Jennifer, she asked him, "Did you talk to my attorney yet?"

"Yes, I did," was his reply.

"Well?" she had to ask.

"We didn't exactly see eye to eye. He wants me to plead to reckless driving, and I don't want to."

"So, your plans are what?"

"I don't exactly know, but I do know I want to fight the constitutionality of the seatbelt law."

He didn't know all the answers, and that led to frustration. And the frustration lit a fire in his belly, the fire led to a heated debate, and that left them both frustrated.

"It's very basic," Mick tried to explain. "It's about the purpose of the Constitution. The Bill of Rights was designed to protect me from the government's excesses and abuse of power. They have the right to protect the public, but they cross over that constitutional line when they force people to protect themselves. Passenger *restraints*—I don't even like the word. '*Restraints*' are for prisoners. It's the antonym of freedom. It's like going to jail every time I get in a car."

"But…" Jennifer tried to get a word in edgewise.

"Not to mention," Mick barged right on, "who really benefits from these unconstitutional laws—lawyers and congressmen. They're just lining their pockets with cash! There's no money to be made promoting freedom, but there is a lot of money to be made being dictators. The thing is, they know they make unconstitutional laws, but every politician out there bows to public pressure and the almighty dollar. And they're on a safety kick right now. All's they have to do is claim 'safety' and they think that gives them the right to violate my rights. As long as they're making money, they really don't care about you or me or the Constitution. The purpose of our founding fathers was to make the Bill of Rights so I can protect myself against the lying, thieving politicians. Law enforcement? Do you really believe a cop is going to give another cop a ticket for not wearing a seatbelt? That'll never happen. And that is how the special classes—the Nazi classes, the dictator classes—are created. Give them an inch and they'll take a mile. The government wants to end freedom while they brag about it. They want to end individuality and your freedom to protect yourself. Oh, and it's going to get worse, too. I read the other day that they want to pass a law against 'driving while distracted' which is going to encompass everything, like, driving with a cell phone, driving while drinking coffee, eating, putting on makeup, and even driving with pets—that aren't *restrained!* The list goes on and on. How would you like to be fined five hundred dollars for eating French fries?"

Jennifer was sitting quietly on the couch listening, almost sorry she ever asked. She had never seen Mick so upset before. He wasn't raving like a maniac or anything, but he was pacing the floor back and forth lecturing, and flapping his arms up in the air occasionally out of frustration.

"All the while," Mick raged on, "the *safety* police and their cronies are getting rich over violating my Constitutional rights! The point-oh-eight liquor law has nothing to do with being drunk or with safety. It's all about dictators getting rich and richer. The press—they just love to write about, oh, 'this guy was driving drunk over two times the legal limit' and 'this guy was three times over the limit.' That's all good press, but it really just means the legal limit is way too low. They're making criminals out of millions of reasonable, social people who like to go out and enjoy their lives. Three beers is all it takes, and the state says you're too drunk to drive. That's bullshit! The lying, thieving politicians are only out for themselves. Even Jesus Christ was done in by politicians! Pontius Pilot—I think it was—let a crowd of angry Jews crucify him for kicking the moneylenders out of the temple. How convenient for ol' Pontius. He just washed his hands of it! The bankers and the lawyers run this country—oh, sorry, I left out the insurance criminals—and every other corrupt official, too many to mention in a sentence. I ask you, who can I vote for to raise the legal limit back up to a reasonable level? Nobody! Who can I vote for to repeal the *restraint* law? Nobody! Chickenshit politicians are afraid to stand up for the Constitution and my rights. They have to go for what's popular to get elected. But that's the whole purpose of our Constitution. The only protection I need is from lawmakers and cops! I made a copy of the document. Would you like to read it?"

Jen was tempted to say yes, so she wouldn't have to politely sit there and listen to Mick's oration, but she finally said simply, "Wouldn't it be easier just to wear the seatbelt than to put yourself through all this aggravation?"

"Jen, that's not the point!" He threw his arms up in the air again, but continued his pacing all the way to the refrigerator to get himself another beer. He took a few swigs to quench his lecturing thirst. "Ahhh," he said, as the cool refreshing liquid salved his cotton mouth.

It acted like a tranquilizer, too, as he parked his butt in the easy chair.

"The point, Jen, is those Nazi dictators."

"I wish you would stop using that term. I have to get along with those people, or they would put me out of business. I do have a business to run, you know! I'm sure that they're just doing their jobs."

"OK, OK. But the point is, I've been doing the same thing my entire life, and suddenly they change the laws to satisfy their own agenda and to make me a criminal for continuing to do what I've always done! I don't like it. The system stinks of corruption on a daily basis. Every day I have to read about crooked politicians and their bribery scams. Plus, it just makes me sick to watch them stomp all over the Constitution to make a few bucks. No. I take that back. They're stealing millions of dollars!"

"They do it to save lives. Don't you think wearing seatbelts is a good idea?"

"Yes I do! If you're doing 80 miles an hour on an expressway. But, no, if you're going 30 to the store or cruising in a forest preserve. Seatbelts are a good idea. Freedom of choice is a better idea. Just because something may be a good idea doesn't mean it should become a law. Because I have good ideas of my own, and it won't cost the taxpayers anything."

"For instance," Mick continued, "in the name of public safety, let's make all public employees take lie detector tests—especially Congressmen; after all, they have a long history of corruption—and make them pay for it. Fat chance! They'll never give up their rights. I can hear 'em screaming now: 'Oh no! We're not giving up our freedom!' Freedom is propaganda! Pure Jewish Nazi—oops!" He quickly covered his mouth to show his mistake, and he apologized. "Sorry."

"Well anyway," he picked right back up again and barged ahead, "there are people in Washington that would love to eliminate the First and Second Amendments. What they want is all citizens to follow their lead, like mindless sheep, and never, ever complain—while they lead us into the gas chambers of apathy! For sure, they don't want you to have the right to protect, or not to protect, your own self. Imagine if 'the safety police' were in charge of this country. I can think of a million things more dangerous than driving around without a seatbelt. Take skydiving, for instance." Mick popped out of his chair.

Oh no, Jen thought, not again!

"Yes." He started pacing once more. His blood pressure was still percolating. "People die every year from that sport. So, let's make it illegal to jump out of airplanes! What would the Army do without paratroopers? 'Too bad, safety first!' The safety dictators have spoken. Or, how about mountain climbing? People die every year from that, too. So? 'No more mountain climbing!' The safety dictators have spoken."

Mick was now using a perfectly timed sarcastic voice that made Jen laugh. He went back to the fridge for a refresher. He continued by hollering from the kitchen.

"The point is, *everything* is dangerous. What sport isn't?"

He paced his way back to Jen.

"People fall over dead from just practicing football—oh, 'we gotta make that illegal, too.' Maybe they'll let us play baseball. I haven't heard of anyone dying from playing baseball. Or golf—no, not golf. You can get struck by lightning. At least baseball players have enough sense to get in out of the rain. I know! 'Thou shalt only play golf on sunny days.' The safety police have spoken."

Mick had Jen laughing to the point of tears. He was using voice variations that were worthy of a stand-up comic's routine. His oration was getting funnier and funnier. Even he was chuckling.

"On the bright side, there would be no more wars—too dangerous, by order of 'The Safety Police!'"

But Mick was serious. He knew every time any kind of freedom was eliminated, it was another death blow to the U.S. Constitution and another victory for the dictators making profit. They continued to wield all the power they could and, of course, make their money—as fast as he could say *lickety-split*—by taking bribes.

"It just amazes me," he continued, "how the passenger *restraint* law got passed in the first place by people who swore to uphold the Constitution of the United States. The Second Amendment allows me the right to protect myself. In a time-honored tradition, if someone broke into this house, I have the right to use deadly force to protect my life, liberty, and property. What confuses me is, the government is taxing me to assist in committing murder. It's a fact. They take my money and give it to people who want abortions. But the government has also decided that a woman has the right to govern her own body, so what do these dictators think they're doing when they're charging me to kill fetuses, and then turning around and fining me if I don't protect myself? These are life and death decisions made every day—and everybody should be allowed to make them. That's what freedom is!"

One of his comments struck a nerve with Jennifer. Her tears of laughter quickly turned to tears of despair. She had to excuse herself with, "I'm not going to listen to this anymore, Mick. You're paranoidly ill. I'm going to bed."

When she reached the top of the stairs, she gave Mick a look that radiated "don't even think of following me" while proclaiming "you're crazy if you think you're going to beat your traffic tickets on Constitutional grounds. Reality has spoken!"

He looked at her in bewilderment. She was laughing a minute ago. Was it something he said? he wondered. Maybe you talk too much, he thought to himself. Maybe not enough? He understood he wasn't talking about Armageddon. But, he thought, throughout history the Romans and all the other empire builders just naturally got too big for their britches and self-destructed from the inside out. And it could very well happen again, he thought, right here in this country. And it will happen again, he reasoned, if the people keep turning their backs on freedom. Absolute power absolutely corrupts, he thought, every single time.

Get over it, Mick, he told himself, you're thinking too much again. You're "paranoidly ill," remember? Maybe he should have asked her opinion more, he wondered. Like, what would you call a police force that set up roadblocks for safety checks? A modern-day, living, breathing Gestapo. Or, he thought, blue shirt Nazis. They don't have any respect for anyone's Constitutional rights. What would she prefer that I call them, pigs? That's so passe, but it's still true. Maybe I shouldn't have mentioned the Jews, or Jesus Christ. Did I offend her? Maybe I should have stressed that the government is trying to put her out of business, and it's going to get worse. They've turned all our employees into criminals. All our customers too, if they can't pass the .08 breathalyzer limit. That limit is way too low. Maybe I should call them, instead of Nazis, the "safety police dictators." That's nice and safe. That won't insult anyone's religious sensitivities. But I want to insult them to the max! For being traitors to the Constitution! "Jewish

Nazis" is just an oxymoron which represents the morons that make laws that are impossible to follow. Congressmen are just pussy-whipped by the M.A.D.D. mothers. And where were they during the Vietnam war? They would have been beaten to a pulp and thrown in jail by the blue shirt Nazis—that's where those M.A.D.D. mothers would be.

Mick was still unconsciously pacing as he mulled these things over. He was still restless. Arguing with one's self takes an emotional toll. He made his way to the liquor cabinet and poured himself a Chivas over ice. He needed to cool his jets. He wanted to calm himself down.

He was starting to think about going to bed himself. He noticed that, without even thinking about it, Jen just upped and went to bed. She gave him that "you just struck out; don't even think about it" look. How do women do that so naturally? he wondered. He made himself another drink. He was still wound tighter than a golf ball. He wanted to calm himself down even more. Then he remembered he had some Valium stashed in his room. He set down his drink and went downstairs. This'll do the trick, he thought, and popped the pill.

Jennifer meanwhile was lying in bed, wondering if she had made a mistake with Mick. He seemed to her to be losing his sanity over trivia. There must be more to it than that? she questioned herself. It's like he has been hiding a deep dark secret, she thought, that has erupted in frustrations. Has it only begun to show? How will he react when I tell him I'm pregnant How crazy will he be then? After all, that part wasn't planned.

She kept thinking, If he's so upset over traffic tickets, he might be mentally out of kilter? Or, worse, is he worked up to the point of having a stroke or heart attack? Then what would I do? she wondered.

Jennifer wondered how she could make him realize that it's useless to make his arguments in court. She knew he was delirious if he thought the Constitution was going to save him, while she worried herself to sleep over subjects that were important to her.

Mick put on some calming music. He went to his CD carousel and pulled out some Moody Blues. He liked the idea of a CD player. It was so much easier than flipping albums on a turntable. He loaded in five of his favorite disks and hit the play button.

He remembered his drink and went up to the kitchen to retrieve it. He refreshed it a little, then went back down and lay on his bed. The soothing orchestral sounds permeated his entire room. As he slowly drifted off, he heard the Moody's familiar verse, "I'm looking for a miracle to change my life!"

As he dozed lightly, his mind was still flying at breakneck speed—maybe a million miles an hour, or so it seemed. He tossed and turned, as he first saw himself as a preacher, giving a fire-and-brimstone sermon. He was standing on a soap box inside a used circus tent.

"Repent, sinners! Repent! Hellfire and damnation awaits upon you!" He saw himself throwing up his arms. "Praise the Lord and save your souls! I give you the Ten Amendments!"

A bolt of lightning shot down from the sky grabbing hold of each of his outstretched arms. A normal man would have died on the spot, but he was a preacher and this was no ordinary lightning bolt. It lifted Mick the Preacher up higher and higher. The lightning crackled and sizzled. The radiant emissions gave him wings. The lost souls were in awe at the sight. The devils at the back of the tent yelled, "Fake! Fake! It's a cheap trick. There is no Bill of Rights!" The Preacher clapped his freedom wings together, which stirred the atmosphere of positive ions to flash at lightning speed and fry the negative devil ions into smoldering bits of charcoal. Then he turned around to face the stone wall above the alter and lightning flew from his fingers and carved some very important words into the slab of stone.

As the Preacher hovered above the crowd, he could be heard to exclaim, "Go! Now you have your Ten Amendments. Protect your life, liberty, property, and freedom!"

Mick was awakened briefly. He felt his hands were hot and slick with sweat. He wiped them on the pillowcase as he fluffed the pillow. He looked at his hand for a moment and remembered himself as a little boy shuffling his feet across the wool carpet to build up static electricity, and then sneaking up on his sisters and shocking them with the jolts that flew from his fingertips. Yes, he zapped their arms good. "Brat!" they would holler out as he ran back across the carpet to do it all over again. Mick smiled briefly at the strange thought, then fluffed his pillow one more time and put his head down to rest.

The music was still playing, as he remembered the good old days spinning records, and the last verse he heard was: "It riles them to believe that we perceive the web they weave." As if he had wings, he felt himself floating across the room to play the flip side of his dream.

He tossed and turned while floating about. His hands were hot and his fingertips charred, but now he felt a different kind of heat. His face broke out in a sweat. There were flashbulbs from cameras. There was an intense heat from floodlights. All the world's stars were shining on him. As he floated around, he couldn't escape them, nor did he want to. He just wasn't used to all the bright heat, but there he was. He floated right into a courthouse. "The trial of the century," the press called it. Reporters hounded him for answers. They pummeled him with questions.

Even though Mick was sleeping in his T-shirt, it felt like he was wearing a stiff white starched shirt and tie. He made hapless gestures with his fingers to separate the choking collar from his neck. He entered the courtroom. The spotlights were blinding, but he kept a stiff upper lip. He felt as if he was lying naked in a suntanning bed. The floodlights were hotter than the sun, but he didn't sweat—not one drop.

The people in the gallery started to applaud as he strutted with pride and purpose to the attorneys' table. The judge sat on the bench dressed in a black-hooded robe with his sickle by his side, perfectly resembling the Grim Reaper.

"Glad you could honor us with your presence, Mr. Dream Team," the judge said sarcastically. "Where's your helpers?"

"I hold in my hand all the help I need," Dream Team replied.

"And what might that be?" asked the judge.

"A copy of the Bill of Rights."

"Good luck," said the judge.

Dream Team's client was there, U. S. Freedom, strapped to a whipping post. One strap went over his shoulder, the other around his waist. At his feet was a circle of firewood. The bailiff was nearby with a torch, ready for action.

"Prosecutor, what are the charges?" the judge asked.

"U. S. Freedom is a three-time loser. He still refuses to wear his safety bucklette."

"Boo!" went the jury. Every member of the jury looked the same. They all had blue shirts and "SSS" badges on.

"Objection!" Dream Team shouted.

"Overruled!" said the judge.

Dream Team continued, "My client is supposed to be tried by a jury of his peers."

The gallery broke out in applause.

"Order in the court!" the judge exclaimed while banging his gavel. "Don't you know applause is dangerous to your eardrums? One more outburst like that, and I'll have you all wearing ear plugs!"

As it was, the gallery was already laden with safety gear. They had to wear safety belts and safety helmets, just in case they got bored with the court proceedings, dozed, and fell off their chairs. Just like so many times before, the court was concerned with concussions, caused by blunt trauma of head against floor, and required this equipment to prevent them. Plus, the people were required to wear scuba respirators and bulletproof vests, just in case some crazed terrorist sneaked by security and attacked the courtroom.

"Objection!" shouted Marsha Bark. "The SSS has already decided that a trial by jury of peers is too dangerous to our system."

"Sustained," said the judge.

"Who is the SSS anyway?" D.T. inquired.

Marsha spoke out of turn and said, *"Why, they're the Secret Safety Service."*

"Well, they're not a secret anymore," D.T. countered. "So you might as well call them the 'SS.'"

"Nice going, Marsha. Now the whole world knows," reprimanded the judge. "Call your first witness."

"The prosecution calls Janet Renose to the stand." Marsha then directed her questions to the woman in the witness chair. "Will you please tell the court what you saw the defendant doing on July 4th."

"Well," the woman responded, "I saw him celebrating Independence Day. He had a lit cigarette in one hand and a sparkler in the other.""

"You mean he was smoking?" Marsha asked.

"Yes. That's a crime in itself, and having a sparkler is a crime too. You could burn yourself with either one of those. That's dangerous. So, I called the police to have him arrested. The police got there in the nick of time, too, because then he drove his car on the street without wearing his safety bucklette."

"Oohs" and "ahs" could be heard coming from the jury.

"Your witness, Mr. Dream Team," Marsha said and sat back down.

"Miss Renose," D.T. began, "what do you do for a living?"

"I work for the SSSSS."

"Can you elaborate? You have more S's than men in the jury."

"Yes. I belong to the Super Secret Socialist Safety Service."

"Well, now I know. And you socialists are not super secret anymore, so you might as well call yourselves the SS."

The gallery erupted with applause.

"Order in the court! Order in the court!" the judge repeatedly banged his gavel. "Bailiff, put down your torch and outfit the gallery with earmuffs. I warned you people about raising unacceptable decibels of noise."

When the bailiff finished, the judge said, "You may continue, Mr. Dream Team."

"Miss Renose, did you ever burn women and children alive?"

"Oh, my yes," she answered. "Lots of times. I had to save them from Satan, and they had dangerous guns."

D.T. continued. "The Second Amendment says…"

"Objection, your honor!" cried Marsha Bark. "That amendment was deemed too dangerous by the SS."

"Sustained," ordered the judge. "Don't you know that the Second Amendment was stricken from the Constitution as being too dangerous?" he said to D.T.

"Side bar please," D.T. requested.

"Approach the bench," said the judge.

Dream Team and Marsha Bark approached the bench, and the judge craned his neck for the best vantage point. "I'm bored, Miss Bark," he said.

She placed her hands under her breasts and flicked her finger under one, then another, as her tits bounced and bounced in turn until they bounced right out of her bustier. She bounced them for the judge and twirled them for the jury. Her tassels were still glued on her nipples from her night job, so everything was perfectly legal.

You could hear the "oohs" and "ahs" coming from the jury again.

After she tucked her assets back in, the judge asked, "Where did you get your law degree from, Miss Bark?"

"From Screw U."

"Ah yes, my old alma mater," said the judge. "And, Mr. Dream Team, where did you get your law degree from?"

"Cracker Jack U."

"Tsk, tsk," said the judge. "No wonder you don't know the Constitution was found to be antiquated and unsafe. You may proceed."

D.T. had a feeling that his case might be in jeopardy, but he had a trick up his sleeve.

"You seem to enjoy burning people, Miss Renose," he said. "How do you get away with it?"

"Not only am I the Secretary of State of the Socialist Safety Service, I'm also a prosecutor; and, as a prosecutor, I'm exempt from prosecution. So you see, I've earned all of my SS's, and you're not going to take them away from me. Bailiff, burn U. S. Freedom! I'm hungry. I'll eat him for lunch!"

"Hold off, bailiff," the judge ordered. "Now now, Miss Renose, you look like you've been grazing off the fat of the land again. Don't forget, I give the orders for lunch in my court."

"Sorry, your honor."

"That's quite all right, Miss Renose. You may continue, Mr. Dream Team."

For the first time, D.T. started shaking like he had the DTs. He realized he was dealing with the original SS. These people needed their bribe money before you got your license, and then you had to bribe them to keep it.

"I have a report here from the National Fire Protection Association," D.T. continued. "It says here that there were 368,500 vehicle fires, 470 civilian deaths, and 1,850 civilian injuries reported last year from those fires. Now, don't you think it would be prudent to return the freedom of choice, so nobody can blame our government for trapping all those people in straps and burning them alive, like the SS did?"

"No, I don't care how many people get burned alive," Miss Renose responded.

"Do you want to change the National Anthem's verse 'the land of the free and the home of the brave' to 'the land of the *restrain*ed and the home of the blame game?'"

"No," she responded. "That's up to our Propaganda Ministry."

"Now, Miss Renose," D.T. continued, "what were you doing on July 4th?"

"I was busy framing babysitters."

"Objection!" barked Marsha. "Plead the Fifth," she instructed her witness.

"I plead the Fifth Amendment," said Miss Renose. "I don't have to answer on the grounds that anything I say might incriminate me."

Of course, now D.T. knew this was one of the amendments still remaining—the one that gangster congressmen and organized criminal CEOs use. The thieves needed this one, so they saved it.

D.T.'s confidence returned. He thought he had his case in the bag. "Miss Renose, is that a bulletproof vest you're wearing under your blue blazer?"

"Yes, it is."

"Are you afraid of getting shot?"

"No."

"Then what's it for?"

"It's to protect my pet black widow heart and the cobwebs in my cleavage."

Then D.T. went over to his client, U. S. Freedom, and whispered, "All you have to do is claim the Fifth Amendment, and you can go free."

So, U. S. Freedom spoke up. "Your honor, I plead the Fifth Amendment."

"Eeeeek!" Marsha screeched as she put her hands over her ears. Then she dug out a billy club from her briefcase and smacked Freedom in the mouth. "Don't speak unless you're spoken to!"

"Objection, your honor!" shouted D.T. "Prosecution is badgering the witness! The accused has a First Amendment right to speak."

The judge looked away and pointed to the three monkeys on his bench: See No Evil, Hear No Evil, and Speak No Evil. Then Marsha smacked Freedom in the mouth again.

Marsha's fangs were now showing. She took her prosecution job very seriously. She went back to her briefcase and brought out her whip. *Crack-crack! Crack!* The whip was singing its song.

U. S. Freedom's back and chest were now bloodied.

"Objection, your honor! This is cruel and unusual punishment, banned by the Eighth Amendment," said D.T.

"Overruled. We do this all the time," said the judge. "You may proceed, Miss Bark."

Crack! Crack! Marsha seemed to be enjoying herself immensely.

Then a juror screamed out, "Oh, stop! You splattered blood on me! Now I have to go to the hospital! It may be AIDS-tainted blood!" The tip of the whip that tore through Freedom's flesh was laden with his blood.

"Eww!" cried another juror. "I have blood on me too. I have to go to the hospital too. I have to get checked out. Blood is dangerous!"

So the jury pool stood up and filed out one at a time. They all climbed into waiting ambulances and went to the hospital.

"Motion to dismiss, your honor," said D.T. "My client's First Amendment freedom of speech rights are being violated."

"Side bar," the judge ordered. "Mr. Team," he admonished, "there is no freedom of speech. The First Amendment was deemed too dangerous by the SS. We can't have people complaining about the way we do things. It might cause a riot and people could get hurt."

"Motion to dismiss then because my client's Sixth Amendment rights are being violated. We have no jury."

"Denied. I don't need no stinking jury."

D.T. started to worry about his case again. The Bill of Rights had failed him. He was desperate. He walked over to U. S. Freedom to console him. He was worn, bloodied, and tattered like an old VFW flag, but his resiliency astonished D.T. as he stood there proudly. "It doesn't look good," D.T. said to him. "Don't worry, Dream Team. I've been through worse times than this. If I wanted to, I could slip right out of this safety strap trap."

"You can? Then do it, man!"

Freedom raised his arms and bent his knees and slid right out. Freedom was free.

"If the safety strap trap doesn't fit, you must acquit!" D.T. declared.

The judge said, "Oh, goody goody. It's rhyme time." He patted his little hands together quickly and gently, like old folks do at an opera. "Acquit to wit: you're free to flee!"

"Objection, your honor!" Marsha barked. "I can rhyme too. Guilty as orange! Charged as orange!" Her voice cracked. Her shoulders slumped, like she was dumped. The case she knew, she blew. Nothing rhymes with orange.

Tap, tap, tap went the gavel. "Overruled. You're not well schooled. It's rhyme time. Don't interrupt, you ungrateful pup. You're a bore and it's time to score. I'm horny and corny, so off to my chamber or you'll be in danger. Do your strip for my tip. Hee-hee. Your judge got up and went wee-wee. It's all a lark, Miss Bark."

The gallery broke out in applause regardless of the danger. U. S. Freedom climbed up on Dream Team's back and spread his wings and they flew off to New York. They flew with flags waving, proud as can be, for everyone to see.

"Freedom was free," the people chanted. "Freedom was free, and you can't charge for that."

Back in his chambers, the judge consoled Miss Bark. "Freedom will never be free. The American sheeple don't have the will to fight for that. They'll be back."

Once Dream Team and U. S. Freedom reached New York with the new slogan, they were honored by a tickertape parade in Times Square. Little bits of shredded paper floated down from skyscrapers everywhere. Everyone was chanting, "Freedom is free. You can't charge for that. Freedom is free. Dream Team saved Freedom. Freedom is free! Freedom is free!"

As Mick tossed and turned, he was awakened by what seemed like tiny gavels pounding in his head. "Oh," he moaned. He went to put his hand to his forehead and hit himself with an empty tissue box. That startled him enough to open his eyes. He looked about his room to find it totally littered with ripped-up tissue paper.

He looked suspiciously at the empty box and the paper bits on the floor and wondered just what the hell happened last night.

He tried to think. Oh yeah, he remembered, I had a few nightcaps. He got up and stepped over the paper bits. What a mess, he thought.

He hoped Jen wouldn't see it, as he knew he'd have a hard time explaining this. He went to the hall closet and grabbed the vacuum cleaner. In short order he was finished. He picked up the tissue box again and gave it a curious stare before tossing it in the garbage.

Mick went to the bathroom for his morning shower, and was about to get in when he glanced at the full-length mirror on the back of the door. He noticed something about his naked body he admired. It was his tan, his deep dark brown tan. Cleaning the pool on a regular basis did wonders for his tan. Even when he turned around to check out his backside, he could hardly tell any outline from his briefs. Still admiring his tan, he hit the shower.

As he sudsed himself down, he wished Jen were with him now. He thought of their shower together at Mackinac. A smile came to his face as he started singing, "Freedom is not free! You must fight for me!"

He stopped, startled. Where did he hear that before? he wondered. He had tried to think of the song he and Jen had sung together, when that verse just popped out. He didn't know the tune or when or if he'd ever heard it before. But he thought it was catchy, so he tried it again.

"Freedom is not free! You must fight for me!" Has a nice ring to it, he thought, as he rinsed off.

CHAPTER 24

Ben's big day came. He was hobnobbing with the mayor, who was escorting him to the Industrial Gentleman's Club. It was all prearranged. Miranda was waiting there to service Ben. Susie Q had been bought and paid for by the mayor, regardless of her failure to supply him with all the inside information he wanted.

She was passively satisfied with all the money the mayor was forking over. He'd managed to render Susie into submission, even if it was superficial. But that was just step one for the mayor. He was already scheming up something new.

Ben came out of the back room with Miranda. He was in love. The mayor smiled. He had everyone under his control, just the way he liked it. He still had a problem to solve, but now he had more time to solve it in. The heat from the Gary massacre was way off base. He and Ben had nothing to fear. No news was good news in that case.

He did discuss with Susie her efforts to get Miranda a job on the inside—that would be perfect. But "that fuckin' Mick" wouldn't hire her.

"Who is that guy anyway? We couldn't seduce him into anything!" a flabbergasted Susie complained.

"Maybe he's the main fag in the dyke bar," the mayor reasoned.

A flash went off in Susie's head. "Maybe Miranda is asking the wrong person for the job. Maybe she should seduce the owner—what's her name, Jennifer?"

"Good idea," the mayor encouraged. "A dyke is always a dyke. Try it again your way, if you like."

The mayor started to laugh at his little joke. Susie just rolled her eyes, as if to say, Like, come on! Shut up!

Ralph Swanson was perplexed at that his assistant discovered. Three phone calls to three people who were now all dead. What were the odds of that happening? Pure happenstance? he wondered. Circumstantial evidence? Anyone could have used that cell phone, he thought. It was listed and paid for by the City of Griffith, Indiana. Official business? Ralph questioned himself. What would the mayor, John Quibly, have in common with dope dealers?

He was dying to get answers to all his questions. He knew if he ever presented his piddly pathetic evidence to a judge or state's attorney, he'd be laughed at—laughed right out of the courthouse. He would have to do the detective work. He would have to gather the evidence. Simple questions needed to be answered. Who called these people and why? he wondered. It made no sense at all. John Quibly? The mayor? A highly respected member of society? But Ralph could see that all the murders appeared to be drug related, at random even. It just didn't make any sense.

Follow the dog, he thought. See where he wags his tail. There must be a reason.

That's what led Ralph to the strip club. At that moment, he was covertly taking pictures of the mayor getting a lap dance by a local stripper. Nothing unusual about that, Ralph thought, just reckless. Many a politician has been caught in similar compromising positions.

Ralph had a special digital camera that used available light regardless of the darkness. No flash was needed. He had long been an expert at sneaking pictures, and he didn't have to sit there long before he had all the pictures he needed. But he didn't want to be conspicuous and leave too early, so he ordered another beer and enjoyed the show.

After awhile he was watching them out of the corner of his eye. The mayor and his male sidekick were preoccupied with laughing, joking, drinking, and groping the girls. So Ralph quietly slipped out unnoticed.

The pictures Ralph took only proved one thing: the mayor was a dirty old man. But what else was he capable of doing? he wondered. Ralph Swanson had no clue, no evidence to speak of, and only a bunch of useless know-nothing suspicions. He knew his work was cut out for him. But how to proceed? Call a meeting of the minds for sure, he thought. Put his best people on the case, maybe. Find out who those girls are, for sure. Search the mayor's office—Watergate style, maybe. The girls might be regular tricks.

Ralph had a lot of possibilities to ponder. For sure, he was going to follow the dog, to see where he wagged his tail. There could be other people, places, and things he was not aware of yet. Or, it could all be a wild goose chase and a tremendous waste of valuable man-hours.

After Ben and the mayor left, Susie Q and Miranda wrapped up their dance routines. They were counting all the money they made that night in the dressing room. Susie was plotting her own plot, when out-of-the-blue she suddenly asked, "Miranda, have you ever made love to another woman?"

"No," she said, a little surprised at the question, but then she added, "other than practicing kissing with a girlfriend. But I was only thirteen at the time, and that doesn't count."

"Yeah, I know. Why don't you come over to my place, so we can practice techniques on seducing Jennifer?"

"Sounds different. Maybe it'll be fun?"

"Oh, I have lots of toys," Susie said. "I *guarantee* it will be fun."

They both laughed giddily.

Miranda followed Susie in her car to her apartment complex. It was about five miles away, down off Ridge Road. It was an upscale place, complete with swimming pool and other popular features. Susie's apartment was well-appointed with modern décor. All her curtains were drawn tightly closed. The only one she ever opened was across her balcony door, when she would occasionally lie outside to sun herself.

Miranda didn't even compliment Susie on her neatly appointed furnishings. Something else was on her mind.

"Did you see a guy taking pictures of us at the club?" she asked.

"No," Susie answered, "but you always have to be careful. You never know who the perverts are. That's why it's best if we travel in pairs. Like that old pervert I had to entertain tonight. He always wants me to say strange stuff like, 'give it to your big daddy.' He's pretty harmless, but rich. Easy money, honey—that's the name of the game."

"Yeah, and that guy I was with—he's a little weird, too. He acted like he owned me—real pushy, like, I wasn't sucking his dick right. He didn't even tip me."

"In this business, honey, you either get the fuck or the shaft. That's why you gotta get the cash. You always gotta get the cash. Up-front!"

"Yeah, all those men. Are they stupid, or what? Twenty dollars a lap dance, just to give 'em a hard-on. They can do that themselves."

"Yeah."

"I guess it must be a macho thing," Miranda continued. "And they always sneak in a quick feel. They're always pawing at me."

"I know, I know," said Susie. "Well, after all, you do have a nice pair of boobs."

"Thanks!"

Susie reached out both her hands to cup Miranda's breasts. After a few moments of fondling, she sighed, "Real nice."

She moved closer for their first kiss. At first, Miranda felt awkward, but then Susie slipped in her tongue and fired up the passion. With expertise she used one hand to unhook Miranda's bra clasp, and dropped the other down to massage her crotch. Soon there were moans of enthusiasm.

Being expert strippers, they quickly and easily left behind a trail of clothing as they snaked their way into Susie's bedroom. Totally naked by then, Miranda was the first to plop on the bed, while Susie opened a drawer in the nightstand. As promised, inside there was an assortment of sex toys, but the first thing she retrieved was massage oil. Then she pulled down the bedspread and opened up the sheets, as Miranda twisted and turned her body out of the way.

"I'm going to give you a special treat tonight," Susie whispered, "so you'll know how it feels."

First she poured some oil into her palms, and then squirted some more on Miranda's belly and breasts. As she lay there spread-eagled, her body glistened from all the oil Susie so lovingly applied. Then the masseuse squirted some on her own body and scooted down between Miranda's legs. Then she poured a little more. Then Susie's legs thrust out, her body fell flat, and she did a perfect muff dive.

Miranda's juices were flowing now. Her belly muscles twitched and her hot spot tingled. Susie's outstretched arms cupped her breasts and her fingers urged her nipples to goosebump hardness. Susie's tongue probed and played with her clit until spasms came to Miranda's legs and her thick sweet moisture engulfed Susie's mouth.

Miranda's moans were getting louder. Her breathing was heaving heavier. "Harder! Faster!!" she cried.

It was an ecstasy Miranda hadn't ever felt before—a real first-time orgasm. Her hips wiggled in rhythm to Susie's lapping tongue. She shivered and shook. Her entire body convulsed.

Then it all stopped, and she was left panting.

Susie easily slid up Miranda's well-oiled body until their breasts met. She gave her a sweet kiss. "You think you could do me like that? Or do you want me to bring out my toys?"

Miranda was still floating around in an ecstatic state. The question didn't immediately register.

"I know what you need," Susie whispered. She reached in the drawer and pulled out a large and long double-headed dong. In fear, Miranda's eyes popped wide open.

"Oh no! You've got to be kidding me. That thing is so big!"

It was fatter than a billy club and looked just as lethal. She touched it to push it away, but it bounced right back and twirled around like a plastic slinky toy.

"It'll never fit!" They both started to laugh, as Susie mimicked choking it in a stranglehold.

"I have lubricant for it," Susie soothed.

Still bug-eyed, Miranda said, "No. No, let me do you first."

She had only known Susie for a month by then, but everything she'd promised had come true—moneywise, at least. So now Miranda felt like getting to know her a little better, as they switched positions. As she rose up off the pillow, she looked into the drawer and spotted a variety of vibrators and other exotic-looking gadgets. She suddenly had a feeling of excitement. She had the distinct feeling that, sooner or later, she would try them all— even the double-headed dong.

First things first though, she thought. Miranda was ready for her first foray into bisexual delights. As she slid herself down into position and zeroed in on her tantalizing target, she closed her eyes and drove her tongue home.

The two of them made a pact that night.

"It might be safer for both of us," Susie suggested, "if you move in with me."

"More economical, too," Miranda agreed.

Then they both played the rest of the night away, until total exhaustion finally consumed them.

That next Friday night they were reveling at the Golden Door. Susie Q had hopes of meeting Jennifer by seducing her with flirtatious body language. Starting with kissing Miranda and holding her hand in public, she thought, ought to do the trick.

They had worked that afternoon at the industrial strip club, and Susie had successfully hit the mayor up for a couple hundred dollars more for the both of them, plus another hundred "for expenses." He'd grumbled some, but relented after she explained her plan in the back room. After all, they both would be losing money by not dancing that night. Susie definitely knew how to get her money, and she wasn't about to do anything for free.

Inside the Golden Door, they were out on the dance floor "getting it on" with Promiscuous Behavior, a local band that played mostly the sounds and tunes of Santana, which was perfect for the two strippers to dance to. Miranda really let her long black hair fly. Being experts dancers at the bump and grind, she and Susie had no problem attracting more attention than they wanted. Guys were constantly trying to cut in, and all were rebuffed. Jennifer noticed the pair too, but she was too busy chatting at the bar.

Mick was restocking the coolers, and his other duties kept him hopping. It was a full house that night, so he had no time to dawdle.

After awhile Jennifer, being who she was, made her way to the table where Susie Q and Miranda were sitting and introduced herself. Susie, being the boldest, got right to the point.

"Do you like to party, Jennifer?"

Taking a moment, Jen responded, "Yes, I do."

"Are you into threesomes?"

Taking a moment longer, she said, "It's been awhile since I've done that."

There was something about Miranda that attracted Jennifer. The long black hair reminded her of when she herself was younger, and the way she used to party then. Both of these unfamiliar women had seductive smiles, but Jen usually preferred one-on-one for emotional purposes and stability. She thought about turning the obvious down, but then she thought about it again. She knew she had more important things to do, she debated with herself, but this would only be a fling. The more she debated, the more tempting it became. The temptation proved too much.

"Where do you live?" she asked cautiously.

"Down the road about five miles," Susie answered.

Jen really was trying to think of a reason to decline their offer. Then she looked at her watch, and figured she had enough time to play a little and still get back before closing time.

"I *could* party for a little while," she said finally.

"Good," said Susie. "Do you want to follow us?"

"Yes." She looked around briefly, and tried to be carefully discrete. "I'll meet you out in the parking lot in a few minutes." Then she gave them a wink and a smile.

Jennifer had a few quick conversations with other patrons for a couple of minutes, and then excused herself. She left without saying a word to anyone as to where she was going. Some things, she felt, she had to keep private.

Neither Mick nor Debbie saw her leave. Heather noticed, and thought it was very uncharacteristic of Jen, but she kept it to herself. She was mad at Jen before, but now she was furious. Nobody could tell, though, as Heather bounced around as usual with an agitated nervous energy—a fully charged energy that flowed quite naturally from her and lasted throughout the night.

Jennifer never returned as planned that night. It was almost closing time before Mick realized she wasn't there. He assumed she'd gone home. He closed as usual and had a few beers with the crew. Heather was the only one to jettison immediately. He didn't bother to look for her either, after he drove home, since Jen usually pulled in the garage and his car sat outside. Mick noticed nothing out of place, so he went straight downstairs to his bed.

He was awakened the next morning by the doorbell. It was an almost constant ringing. He tried to roll over and ignore it, hoping Jen would answer, but to no avail. Whoever it was, Mick finally realized, was persistent. It took him a minute to gather himself, thinking, This better be good or someone's head is going to roll.

He grabbed his bathrobe and, when he got to the door and opened it, saw two plain-clothed detectives standing there holding their badges out.

"Are you Mr. Tuttle?" the taller one asked.

"No, my name is Mickey Swift."

"Are you related to Jennifer Tuttle?"

"No, I'm her husband."

"Then you are related to her."

"Oh, yeah. I guess so." Cobwebs were holding back his thought processes. All this while his mind was saying, What the hell are you guys doing at this door, asking me questions on a Saturday morning? At the same time, his mouth was trying to respond to their inquiries. "What do you want?" he finally blurted out.

"We're investigating a murder." "Whose murder?" "Jennifer Tuttle's." "What the fuck are you talking about? She's upstairs!" He looked at the bottom of the stairway, and then back at the detectives. "You best be joking, cause you ain't funny. Just wait right here."

He left the door open and quickly hit the stairs, hollering Jen's name as he climbed them and got to her room. He froze, as he peered through an open door at an empty bed.

Then some kind of reality kicked him in the gut. His heart sank. His blood pressure started to rise. He stood in the doorway, staring at the empty bed. His throat went dry and tears welled up in his eyes. A sick feeling enveloped him. He couldn't believe it. His breathing became faster and heavier. He clasped his hands around his head, as if he could control the explosions going on inside. It took him several minutes to gather his senses and go back down the stairs, almost stumbling at the first step.

The detectives had walked right in and were waiting for him at the bottom.

"What were you looking for?" the tall one asked.

Mick just looked at him, trying to decipher the question among all the other thoughts clamoring inside his throbbing head.

"Jen," he answered.

"You're her husband?" the other detective asked.

"Yes, that's right!" Mick retorted, angry now.

"How long have you been married?"

"A couple of months."

"Then where did you sleep last night?"

"Downstairs."

"Then you don't sleep with your wife?"

Mick didn't like the way he was asking nor the tone of his question and its implications. He responded with, "I don't see how that's any of your business."

The tall detective interrupted. "We're investigating a murder. We have to get a statement from you, Mr. Swift, ah, Tuttle."

The stubby detective took out his pen and notepad.

"Where were you last night?" the tall one asked.

"I was at work."

"And where is that?"

"At the Golden Door."

"And what time did you leave?"

"About four in the morning."

"And what was the last time you saw your wife?"

"I'm not sure. Eleven, twelve, something like that."

"And who was she with?"

"I'm not sure."

"Do you own a gun?"

"No."

"Can we look in her bedroom?"

"What for?"

"For any kind of a struggle."

Mick's mistrust of cops was kicking in big time. He didn't like the questions or their implications, but in this case he felt his options were few and damning. He imagined what Jen would have said: "They're only doing their job."

He bit his tongue and replied, "No, I don't mind." He led them up the stairs to her room. "See for yourselves."

They entered the room, which was immaculately clean and tidy. They looked around while Mick waited at the door, already feeling the pangs of pain. He never did, or would, enter her space uninvited.

The detectives were looking for any sign of violence. Their trained eyes saw that there was nothing to be found in the room, and they walked out satisfied. But they still weren't through with their questioning. They all proceeded back downstairs to the living room.

"We'll need you to come down to the morgue to make a positive identification of the body," the taller one said.

Mick was afraid he would say something like that. He really didn't want to do it. In his worst nightmare, he didn't want to do it. He didn't want to confirm his disbelief. He didn't want to see anybody in a morgue, let alone Jennifer. The sickness came back, the queasiness. It was the queasiness of having to do something he never in his wildest dreams ever thought he'd have to do. He inhaled deeply, and sucked up his remorse.

"I'll have to get dressed," he finally spit out.

The detectives, being what they are, followed Mick to his bedroom—until Mick realized it and turned to say, "Do you mind?" He closed the door behind him, leaving them standing in the rec room.

"They don't sleep together," one said to the other.

"I wonder why," was the reply.

When Mick opened his bedroom door, the detectives were in position to peer inside, and they did. It wasn't nearly as neat as Jen's room, but right *away* Mick closed the door behind him, giving them both an angry look.

"I have to make a phone call before I go anywhere," he said.

They followed Mick up to the kitchen where he called Debbie.

"Debbie, it's Mick. You'll have to cover for me today. Call Jack and see if he'll come in early. Don't argue! Something's happened to Jen. Some detectives are here, and I have to go with them to check it out. Yeah, detectives. I'm afraid it's bad news. OK, good. I'll see you later."

"Who was that, your girlfriend?" the stubby dick asked.

"No!" Mick shouted back.

"Easy now," said the tall cool one. "He's just wondering why you slept downstairs is all."

"Well, it's none of his fucking business *what* I do!"

"Calm down, guy. He's just doing his job. We have a murder to investigate."

"Then let's get this I.D. thing over with," Mick said.

"OK, let's go. You can ride with us."

"No, I'll follow you." "Do you know where the morgue is?"

"No."

"Then why not ride with us?"

"I ain't going anywhere with *him*," Mick said angrily. "Like I said, I'll follow you."

"OK, OK," said the tall one. "Come on then."

As soon as the detectives got in their car, the stubby note-taker asked, "How do we get him down to the station? We've got to give this guy a polygraph. Or, at least interrogate him on our turf."

"I know," said the taller detective, who was driving. "I smell a big rat. He's married to her for only a couple months, he's sleeping in the basement, and he doesn't know he's a relative? And why two last names? Better check out the insurance policies."

"This could be a hired hit?"

"Yeah, exactly."

"We better check out this 'Debbie' at the Golden Door."

"Yeah, and everybody else over there too. That Donald Strapp suicide case originated from there, didn't it?"

"I think so."

"Maybe there was more to that than meets the eye."

"Is he still behind us?" the stubby one asked.

"Yeah. I don't expect him to make a run for it. Not today anyway. What we can do is follow up on some of our other leads, and invite Mister Swifty down to the station to verify other people's statements. Then we'll see if he slips up."

"Right."

It was a thirty-minute trip to the Gary city morgue. Mick followed the detectives inside and down a flight of stairs to a security door, where they identified themselves before being buzzed in. Without saying a word, they walked down a long, cold corridor. The sound of their shoes echoed hauntingly as they went. Mick had a feeling, a most uncomfortable out-of-place shouldn't-be-there kind of feeling, but suddenly there he was in the coroner's office building about to enter the morgue.

The detectives seemed naturally at ease. They'd been there many times before and were on a first-name basis with everybody. Mick could care less what their names were. He wanted out. Claustrophobia was setting in.

A man in a white smock approached him. "You're here to identify the body?"

"That's right." He tried to reply calmly, through a jungle of war-torn nerves.

"Right this way," the man said.

They all walked into another room, the strangest room that Mick had ever seen—and the coldest. It was colder than a freezer, and not just because of the temperature, and not because of all the stainless steel—but because of the men who worked there. The one they were following stopped at a table and pulled back the white sheet so coldly, exposing Jennifer's cold nude corpse.

He asked, "Is this Jennifer Tuttle?"

Now it was Mick's turn to freeze into ice. It was as if he'd been paralyzed instantly by being inserted in a cryogenic tube. His tears were waiting to flow into icicles, as they were already frozen on the inside. How could this happen to her? he asked himself incredulously. Who did this? I'll kill the motherfucker myself if I ever find out who. He swore this vow to himself as horrible terrors screamed through his head.

The coroner's assistant asked again, "Is this Jennifer Tuttle?"

I'll kill the motherfucker—motherfucker! was still echoing in Mick's mind, as if he was shouting in a canyon of abandonment. One tear ran down his cheek. He used his thumb to knock it aside, then another tear ran down the other cheek. He wiped it away. His sinuses started to drip. He pinched his nose with his trembling hand. His voice quivered noticeably.

"Yes. That's Jennifer."

His breath became quick and short, gasping, trembling, panicking as if he were lying upon his own deathbed. His heart was thumping, palpitating, pounding inside his chest. He turned and left the room quickly.

There in the hallway, Mick's whole body vibrated with hatred. His muscles tensed and his fists were clenched. He was ready to lash out. After a time, he was able to inhale deeply. His body was slowly being replenished with oxygen. He leaned his back up against the hall's brick wall.

The man in the white frock and the detectives came out into the hallway.

"Don't leave yet," he said. "I need you to sign some forms."

Mick glared at him with an icy stare.

"It's just a formality," the man continued.

"Come on, Mr. Swift," the tall detective said as he tried to place a calming hand on Mick's shoulder, which he immediately shrugged off. "Please try to cooperate."

Mick followed the men back into a small office inside the freezing room to sign the paperwork.

"You'll need to make funeral arrangements" was the last thing Mick heard before exiting his raging body down the corridor and into the outdoor air.

The detectives stayed behind. The coroner's assistant performed an autopsy and recovered the bullet that killed Jennifer.

"Gunshot wound to the head" was given as the official cause of death. The bullet was part of the evidence that would be transported to the crime lab for ballistics testing.

"One more thing," the examiner said to the detectives. "This was a double homicide. The victim here was pregnant."

They looked at each other quizzically. Then the tall one said, "Thanks, doc."

Mick made it back to the Golden Door, but he sat in his car. He sat there for a long time. He wanted to go in and have a beer. His throat was parched, but he was afraid to go in. There would be all kinds of questions that he didn't want to answer, nor did he even have any answers. He wondered, how was he going to tell the employees? How was he going to tell the customers? What was he going to do? He didn't feel like working there anymore. All the fun had been stolen from him. How could he function *period*?

All these things kept him in the parking lot. Fears. Fears he knew he would have to overcome. Fears of never being able to enjoy life again. He wasn't ready to deal with it all, but he knew he had to survive somehow. The people inside needed a place to work. The customers needed a place to go after work. The void. The emptiness of no Jennifer had only started to sink in. Oh my God, he thought, what am I going to *do*?

His body traversed a complete cycle of emotions. From disbelief to shock to rage, and now to depression. He started to blame himself. If only we didn't have that argument, he thought. But it really wasn't an argument. It was more like a one-sided discussion. If only I was there to protect her, he thought in angst. That was my job! And I didn't do it! How did this happen? Where did it happen? Mick was questioning himself and his very manhood. What could I have done to prevent it?

Without realizing it, he was playing the blame game. It was a deadly, destructive game. It was no fun to play at all. The longer he played it, the deeper his emotions sank into the abyss. He felt chaos. He felt a need to escape. He was choking. He was running out of much-needed oxygen. There was a noose around his neck. His throat was so dry, he could not even spit.

He didn't want to face the music, so he thought of just going home. No, not home, but far from home. No, farther. Farther away still. A different state. And he was just about ready to do that, when Debbie suddenly came out of the bar and walked up to Mick's window.

"What are you doing out here?" she asked quietly.

He didn't have an answer for her.

"We're so sorry," she said.

"Sorry about what?" His voice was cracking. It was impossible to hide his emotion.

"It's already on the news," Debbie said. "You know you can't sit out here forever, Mick. So you might just as well come in."

"Yeah. I suppose you're right."

He followed Debbie inside. The bar looked strangely different to him now. There was a kind of a hush. The customers all looked at him, but nobody said a word. Not one words. The TVs were on, but the jukebox was silent. Mick sat down at the corner of the bar nearest the kitchen, and Debbie brought him a beer—a much needed beer.

The aura of doom and gloom went out from him. Everyone saw it, and nobody dared to ask him those questions he had needlessly feared. Jack knew what to do. Without saying a word, he went to the liquor room and took out a new bottle of Chivas. He grabbed a couple of rocks glasses and filled them with ice. He poured one for Mick and the other for himself. Mick just looked at him and slammed it home.

All his dead nerves shuddered as the drink went down. As soon as he caught his breath, he said, "Thanks, Jack."

Jack poured him another and replied, "We're all here for you, buddy."

That affirmation struck at Mick's heart. His eyes welled up. He choked back the tears. He wanted to thank Jack again, but couldn't. He got up and went to the office, closing the door behind him. All that could be heard echoing like rolling thunder from the office, through the canyons of the kitchen, throughout the bar, all the way to the pool tables was: *"That dirty motherfuckerrrrrrr!!!"*

Mick collapsed in the chair and put his head in his hands and had a long-overdue cry. He had to let his emotions flow. All those poisons in his body had to go.

It would take him quite a while to regain his composure this time. He was emotionally, mentally, physically drained, but somehow refreshed. The human body works wonders repairing itself.

It's only another mountain climb, he thought to himself. The never-ending mountain ranges of life. There's always another mountain to climb, he reasoned. Some are just bigger than others. Positive thoughts somehow started to fill the void, after his poisons had been drained away.

He couldn't climb yet, though. It would take awhile longer before he could function—really function—again. Part of him was still in that cryogenic tube, frozen solid, to protect that most vulnerable piece of his heart.

He knew he'd never be the same again. After all, he reasoned, he was paranoidly ill, just like Jen said. He almost laughed at the thought. A slight smile crept upon him, the more he thought of her. The way she would wink and smile at him—it was kind of like her having an ice pick, and starting to chip away a little at his frozen heart. When Jen gets through with that ice pick, he thought, perhaps someone else will pick it up and continue chipping away—until his heart melts again. Mick couldn't keep it frozen forever. All it would take would be the love of another woman. But, not now. He couldn't bear the thought of anyone else. He had more important things to do now. He had to climb a mountain.

There was a knock at the office door.

"Yeah?" His voice was still quivering.

"Are you coming out of there? Or do we have to come in and get you?" It was Debbie. She cautiously opened the door.

"Are you all right?" she asked tenderly.

"I'll be right out," he replied. Then he took a tissue and blew his nose, tossing the paper in the waste can. "Hey, Debbie. Where did this Kleenex come from? It wasn't here the other day."

"Oh, Jen brought it in."

Mick stared at it for a moment and took a deep breath. Then he was ready to go out and face the music.

CHAPTER 25

Vital news has a way of traveling fast. The mayor knew Jennifer was dead. That's why he had his feet propped up on his desk. He was kicking back, smoking a stogie, grinning from ear to ear.

Problem solved! he thought, and his smile confirmed his thinking. He figured: The dyke has no heirs, no children, foster mother and father both deceased, no co-signers, nothin'! If his smile could have been any bigger, that cigar would've fallen right down his throat.

No bank would give her a loan for a bar, he reasoned. That's what makes contract mortgages so risky. But that's also what makes foreclosures so profitable. Now all he had to do was call his lawyer and file for foreclosure. And the best part was, he knew he'd never have to get around to asking Ben to eliminate his mortgagee.

Maybe Ben had already read his mind, the mayor mused, or maybe that other dyke bitch Heather just got herself into a hissy fit of rage. Who cares? he thought. Who cares who or how or when or why? The end result was still the same: the undickéd ole' witch was dead.

Ralph Swanson cared. He cared plenty. He cared about his operative Juan especially, but also he cared about The Donald, The Gary Massacre, and now about this Tuttle, too. Most of all, he cared about justice.

He gave his assistants the mundane tasks of doing background checks on both the strippers and Mickey Swift as well. He already knew the mayor had served two full terms in office, and now had two years left on his third. But he also knew it would be his last. In his hand he held a photograph. He knew if a picture like that were ever to be published, it would end anyone's political career.

What was he thinking of? Ralph wondered. Why would anyone risk his political career and reputation? Even if looks are deceiving, how could he explain himself out of this one? Fake photo? Fraud? Conspiracy? Nah, he thought. What other motives did the mayor have for risking this?

Despite the irrefutable evidence he held in his hand, Ralph still had more questions than answers. Now he was committed to get the answers. He was going to the Golden Door to find them.

First, he ditched the suit and tie. His experience led him to believe he'd get more forthright answers if he didn't look like a detective. Posing as a curious customer would probably bear more fruit. Catching people off guard with inquiring questions, he thought, would likely result in more truthful answers. Ralph then enlisted some volunteers to follow him up. He reasoned that curious people like to party, too.

Mick was busier than usual. He had so much more to do, which was always compounded by his indecision as to the right thing to do. For example, worrying whether to arrange a Christian burial or cremation was number one on his list. He called Jennifer's attorney to find out if she'd left any instructions in a will.

"No," the lawyer said, "no will so far as I know. I told her a long time ago she needed to get one."

After hours upon hours of internal debate, Mick decided on cremation. He thought it seemed like the easiest and best thing to do. He could then have her ashes in an urn and place it on the mantle over the fireplace. Or maybe, he thought, if later on the mood fancied him, he could scatter her ashes on Mackinac Island.

Then he called Jen's accountant to inform him of the situation. Then he called the attorney back to say he would be needing his services for traffic court after all. Mick had almost forgotten his court date was just two days away. Then he thought he would close the bar, give all the employees a paid day off, and hold funeral services at the house that Sunday.

After the services, he thought he would somehow try to celebrate Jen's life with a party. That's what she would have wanted, he thought. A party maybe with a tropical island theme.

"Yes, that's the ticket," he said to no one in particular. Mick thought for sure Jen would want it that way—celebrating her life with a party.

Mick wasn't the only one who was busy. Ralph Swanson made an appointment with the detectives assigned to Jennifer's case. He wanted to compare notes, go over the evidence, and then get back with the sheriff to go over Juan's case.

As they all poured over the evidence they had, they concluded that the person who had the most to gain from Jennifer Tuttle's demise was Mickey Swift.

"Who gets the life insurance benefit?" they asked. "Who gets the bar? The house? Who was sleeping in the basement? Who was uncooperative with police? With the detectives? And who had already gained the most from Donald's demise?"

Mickey Swift came up as the answer to all of those questions. He was exactly the suspect to whom they pointed their fingers.

But Ralph's nagging question still remained: "How does Mr. Swift tie in with those phone calls made on the city hall cell phone?"

The strippers were the key, Ralph decided. They could have easily borrowed the mayor's phone, with or without his permission. The ballistics tests weren't complete in Jennifer's case, but they were in Juan's. "Where's the gun?" Ralph asked. "What was Jennifer doing at that apartment complex? Could this Mickey slip out of work for extended periods of time unnoticed, and then slip back in again?" Yes, Ralph had discovered, the new manager of the Golden Door did hide out in his office for hours at a time.

So the three investigators decided to pick up the strippers. Maybe they'd talk, the men figured. Maybe they could lean on them until they cracked. Yes, the strippers were the key, but, as the men then discovered, both Susie Q and Miranda were gone.

Mick had a bout with depression that lingered. He no longer enjoyed his work. He had Jack fill in for him the rest of the week, and was considering promoting him to full time. He decided Debbie could be the new manager, as she knew all the ropes. His most immediate concern was resolving his traffic case and straightening out the loose ends of Jennifer's affairs.

Then the shit hit the fan.

He was meeting Jen's lawyer at the courthouse, all set to plead guilty to reckless driving, just like everybody else—including the attorney—wanted him to do, when the lawyer casually mentioned, "Then they'll drop the O.W.I. refusal charges."

"What?" Mick demanded to know.

"They'll drop the refusal to blow charges."

"Let me see that police report." Mick read it over and then said, "I counted nine lies in the first half alone! And here, the most provable outrageous like is in the second half. This part right here says I refused the breathalyzer test at the police station, and then I was transported to the hospital because I complained of pain. This reads like a cartoon. It's a joke!"

"It's not true?" Jen's lawyer asked.

"Number one," Mick countered, "I took the breathalyzer test right where this cop pulled me over on Ridge Road. Number two, I made him call me an ambulance, since I didn't believe him when he said I failed the test, and also because I was injured. And number three, I wanted verification and witnesses that he made me do all those walking tests with a badly swollen ankle! And look at this part here that says I was swerving all over the center line—three times it says that! But that's pretty hard to do when you've only traveled one block. I won't plead guilty to any of this! As a matter of fact, I want you to subpoena all the tapes from the police radio transmissions—all the audio and video from the police surveillance tapes, both on their cruiser and inside the police station, and all the log records from the ambulance company."

"That's going to cost you," the lawyer said with a dismayed look.

"I don't care what it costs!" Mick declared emphatically. His dander was up, his blood pressure was cooking, and his face was flushed with anger. "And while you're at it, file a motion to dismiss—because the seatbelt law violates my Second Amendment rights. I have the absolute right to protect myself, and I will determine when and where I'll use any safety equipment. Plus the fact that seatbelts and airbags can kill you anyway. What the hell gave the dictators that run this country the right to force me to buy such stuff, and force me to use equipment that can kill me?"

Mick was on a rampage. "The Bill of Rights was formed by our founding fathers to protect me from the very money-grubbing, lying, thieving, bastard dictators that run this overgrowing government!"

"I'm sure the seatbelt law has already been tested in the courts," the lawyer advised.

"I don't care. Do it again. I'm not bowing to these con artists!"

"Mick, Mick. Simmer down. If what you're telling me is the truth, I'll have a court order drawn up to get all the tapes and the ambulance records. If we can prove the officer lied, then they'll have to throw the case out."

"I want more than that. The author of this police report has perpetrated a fraud on this court, and I want to press charges. Make me a copy. What's this asshole's name?" Mick looked down at the report again. "Benjamin Smide. I want to know if this is the same asshole that busted two of my other bartenders for the same bullshit."

"OK, OK. We'll get a continuance today, and I'll file the motions later in writing. We'll know where we stand in about thirty days. Now just go sit in the courtroom until your name is called."

A brewing good fight was all it took to lift Mick out of his depression. His heart was pumping again. As he sat calmly in the courtroom chair, no one could see that he was seething. Real-life distractions took his mind away from the loss of Jennifer, if only for the moment. His glaring gaze was fixed squarely on the judge's bench. He then realized he forgot to press Debbie and Jack for the cop's name who busted them, but he knew that now he'd have time to correct the situation. For some reason, he remembered a quote from one of the founding fathers: "The price of freedom is eternal vigilance." He repeated this over and over in his mind. He thought, if he remembered correctly, those were the words of James Madison, one of the authors of the U.S. Constitution.

Once the judge took the bench and went through the swearing-in rituals, the time just flew. Mick's was the second case on the docket. When his name was called, both he and the lawyer approached the bench. Mick's mouthpiece got a continuance. He himself did not have to say a word.

Good thing too, Mick thought, as he was just in that kind of mood to let his frustrated feelings fly. He wasn't standing in front of the judge long enough to envision himself being arrested and shackled and thrown into the clink for contempt of court, but by the time he walked to his car he did.

His cantankerous side snapped him out of the blues. He felt energized again. I won't take any more of that bullshit from anybody, he promised himself.

He put the shifter into Drive and automatically headed for the Golden Door. While it was still fresh on his mind, he wanted to press Debbie and Jack to look at their tickets for the name of the cop who busted them. Mick felt a fight coming on, all right, and what he smelled was: lawsuit.

Dark clouds started to roll in from the west, as he headed right for them. Soon rain was pelting his windshield and he flipped on the wipers. Good, he thought, the grass is gonna turn green again. Then he reminded himself not to grow derelict in his household duties. Maybe, he thought, he should hire a maid. What are you gonna do with that apartment you're never in anymore? he asked himself. He decided to put those issues on the back burner. This wasn't important to him right now, but getting through the rest of the week was. The funeral services were happening on Sunday, and he still had to hire a catering service.

It was way too early for Jack to be at the bar, but Debbie was. Before

Mick could ask her the question he needed to help his case, she blurted out, "I need more help. Heather quit. She got herself a new job."

"Well," said Mick, "hire whoever you want. Is she coming to the services this Sunday?"

"I don't know. I didn't ask. Oh, and there's been some guy pestering me with questions about you these past couple nights."

"Hmmm. OK, thanks."

Mick started walking towards the office when he remembered he forgot something. He spun on his heels and went back to Debbie.

"Did you look at your ticket for that cop's name yet?"

"No," she said, "but I have it tucked in my purse."

"Good. Let me see it, OK?"

She reached under the bar and pulled up her purse, reaching inside for the ticket. There it was, that fairly familiar scribble-scratch signature of a barely legible name. It read: "Benjamin Smide."

"Thanks," Mick said. "That's all I need to know. Oh, and when you get a chance, put a sign on the bulletin board. We'll be closed Sunday for Jennifer's services. Everyone's invited to attend."

"What do you mean that fuckin' dyke bitch is married? You're out of your mind! Get real!" The mayor fumed into the phone before slamming it down. "Fuckin' lawyers," he swore out loud. Then he thought, That changes things.

Ben appeared at his office door.

"What do you want?" the mayor barked.

"Your plan isn't going to work, is it?"

"It'll work. It'll work!" the mayor said, raising his voice. "Just some new wrinkles thrown in, that's all. I, ah, I don't know who this pretend husband fuck is."

"His name is Mickey Swift."

"Mickey Schmickey. Who the fuck is that? Well, whoever he is, he ain't no match for me!" The mayor bounded from his chair and went straight to his hideaway bar. In two quick motions, the bar was open and he was pouring whiskey.

"And that ain't all," Ben said.

"And *what* ain't all?"

"The girls are gone." The mayor was just pissed off before, but now he was getting madder by the second. "What girls? Not my Susie Q?"

"I'm afraid so."

"That's impossible. She was making a living off me!" He stopped to slug down his whiskey and let his thoughts catch up with him. "Well, fuck the ungrateful bitch then. I'll find another one. And I've been meaning to ask you. What the fuck happened to that dyke bitch Jennifer?"

"I don't know."

"That's great," said the mayor. "Nobody knows nothin' and I just find out that fuckin' dyke was married to some mouse."

"This *Mickey*."

"That's right, Ben. That's the new fuckin' wrinkle. But maybe that fuckin' faggot can be bought out cheap. What's this world coming to anyway, faggots marrying dykes?" He stopped his rantings to pour himself another whiskey. "You want one?"

"No, not today. I want to talk about my half of the coke I got coming."

"No, not yet," said the mayor. "I don't want any loose ends. First, I'm gonna make that faggot down there an offer he shouldn't refuse. Just you wait and see. Susie will be back anyway. Something must've come up, that's all."

"I got more news for you. I don't think this Mickey's a fag. He's gonna be one tough nut to crack. That's the guy who gave me all that shit when I pulled him over."

"That's the fuck that called you a blue shirt Nazi?"

"Yup. That's him."

"Tough nut to crack, huh? Maybe I should talk to the boys about him then. We'll see how tough he is."

"You know I have my own plan, if yours don't work. But I want my half. Deal?"

"It's a deal."

Ben turned and left. The mayor made himself another drink and settled back down in his chair. Tough nut to crack, huh? My specialty! he thought pompously.

The news of the funeral services on the bulletin board was like a godsend to Ralph Swanson. Even though he had never met Jennifer, he had enough information about her to pretend he did. Coupled with some additional information from the detectives and the D.M.V., Ralph learned Jennifer's home wasn't Mick's primary residence.

Very suspicious indeed, Ralph thought, which called for very special treatment. He planned on having his crew visit the obscure apartment with one objective: search for the .38 special that killed Juan and Jennifer. The ballistics test confirmed both bullets came from the same weapon, and the autopsies showed both victims were killed by a single gunshot to the left side of the head.

Every second-rate burglar knows that funeral time is perfect for home invasions. Ralph gave his crew instructions: "Try not to disturb anything, but leave no stone unturned."

He felt he had his man now, but he had to prove it. Meanwhile, he would attend the services and look for clues in the house. He had a few questions for Mr. Swift, too.

That Sunday at 12 noon sharp, the preacher started, "We are gathered here today to honor the memory of Jennifer Tuttle." It was a somber audience. Jennifer's picture was displayed next to the urn on the fireplace mantle. Flower arrangements were so deep, they completely blocked the view of the ornamental brick hearth. Mick never realized she had so many friends. Some came from her primary job, some from the old neighborhood, and of course the rest were cast and crew from the Golden Door.

As the preacher spoke, the ladies had their hankies at the ready, and all eyes were already misty. One Ralph Swanson deliberately positioned himself at the back of the crowd. While all heads were focused on the preacher, he made his move and slipped upstairs. He had an excuse ready in case anyone saw him: "Oh, I was just looking for the bathroom." He'd had that one ready for years, but so far he'd never had to use it. He moved about the upstairs bedrooms, searching with stealth and efficiency.

The preacher ended his blessings with, "From ashes to ashes and dust to dust. With God's grace, let her soul rest. Now, Mr. Swift would like to say a few words."

Mick cleared his throat. He felt uncomfortable but he knew what he had to say. "Even though I've only known Jennifer for a relatively short time, I feel all the love in this room from each and every one of you. Because of you, I feel like I've known her all my life. We were brought together for a reason. We made a commitment together to adopt a child. I intend to honor that commitment in her name. Her love of life was so enormous. She was so selfless and caring. All I can say is that it was my honor and privilege to have known her at all. We are all part of Jennifer's extended family. So, in her honor, I would like you to celebrate life today. Jennifer would have wanted it that way. The caterers have set up a feast out on the patio. Please stay and join me."

Mick cut the eulogy short, as everyone was crying. Heather was the first one to give Mick a hug. Her mascara was running with her tears. "I'm so sorry, Mick," she sobbed.

Mick hugged her back. "I know. I know." He choked up, and he had to wipe back his own tears. "Look, Heather. We need you back at the Door. Jennifer needs you to help carry on."

"I can't."

"Yes, you can." Mick put his finger under her chin to lift her bowed head. He brushed back her tears with his thumbs and kissed her forehead. "Come back whenever you're ready. I'll have a surprise waiting for you. I know you're not working. You can't pull the wool over my eyes that easy."

She looked at Mick eye to eye and said, "OK."

The room was full of weeping, blubbering people, when Ralph made his empty-handed way back downstairs. A few men took turns shaking the preacher's and Mick's hands, congratulating them on the fine services. The reality of the grief had hit home for all but one. Ralph maneuvered himself into the utility room which led to the garage, his next target.

Debbie interrupted Mick's conversation with the preacher with a few quick "come here" flips of her wrist. When Mick got there, she whispered, "That guy I was telling you about, the one that was asking a bunch of questions about you—Ralph, I think his name is—just went in your garage."

Mick paused a moment. "Thanks, Deb."

He slowly made his way into the garage. Ralph stood there in the middle of the space, stunned when he saw Mick.

"Ralph?" Mick asked.

"Yes?"

"What are you doing here? The party's out back."

"Oh, I was just looking for a place to smoke a joint. Care to join me?"

"No. If you want to smoke a joint, I strongly suggest you do it in your own car." Mick hit the button to open the garage door. Ralph got the hint and started walking down the driveway, only to hear behind him, "And don't come back."

"Shit," Ralph muttered under his breath. I hope the other guys had better luck, he thought. He did notice the steely-eye stare Mick had given him. Not a man to mess with, was Ralph's impression. He wondered, What is that kind capable of doing? "Damn," he muttered to himself again. He knew he'd missed his chance to buddy-up to him. He still had questions for Mick, but he blew his chance. Time for a new tactic, Ralph thought. This is going to be a tough nut to crack.

The crowd had all finally made its way outside, and weeping was giving way to laughter and stories. Nice stories. Jennifer's old school chums were in one group, and her workmates were in another. Almost every conversation started with, "Remember the time?" Mick didn't need to listen in. He knew from their demeanor that they were all sweet stories. He was just glad to see they were all having fun again.

He made his way to the bar that was set up for the occasion, and took the bottle of champagne he had previously placed in an ice bucket. He opened it and poured two glasses. Then he went to the dessert table where he had specifically ordered strawberry shortcake. He took one and went back to the champagne. As if on cue, he borrowed that line from Humphrey Bogart and privately toasted Jen. "Here's looking at you, kid," he said aloud, spooning in some of the strawberry shortcake and then drinking down both glasses. A lonely tear dripped down his cheek as he savored the flavors.

Debbie came over and said, "I've got good news. Heather's coming back to work."

"Good," Mick smiled.

"What happened with that guy in the garage?"

"I sent him packing."

"Who is he anyway?"

"I don't know and I don't care. Care to join me?" Mick started refilling his and another glass with champagne and offered one to Debbie.

"Don't mind if I do," she said.

"To Jennifer!" Mick said.

"To Jennifer!" Debbie agreed, and they clinked their glasses together.

It truly was a beautiful day, sunny and somewhat cool. Most of the men wore their suits or sport coats comfortably. Mick gazed out at the pool and realized it was probably time to shut it down. Autumn was nipping in the air. It had seemed like the summer just flew by. He stood by the patio rail, carefully retracing those steps he took with his eyes. Those steps he took when he was so brazen to walk around naked while skimming the pool—to the spot where he stood when he first noticed that Jennifer was getting an eyeful. Then he retraced his movements to the spot where he was when Heather stumbled upon him. A slight smile creased his face as he remember his own folly.

He turned to look for Heather in the crowd. Ah, there she is, he thought. She was standing with Jack and his wife. She was laughing at something. Good, Mick thought, she's back.

He went back to the bar where Debbie was entertaining the loyal regulars. The bar was set up to be self-service, but old habits die hard. Debbie had taken charge and was busily mixing all the drinks. "Time for a Chivas on the rocks, Deb," he said.

"Coming right up, Mick!"

Mick felt like getting loaded that day. The worst of it was over, but even though he knew he didn't have to drive anywhere and could get as drunk as he wanted, he really didn't want to get flopping-down drunk.

He remembered the last time that happened. He hadn't even turned 21 yet. But he was already married with children. The wife didn't want him to go fishing with his buddies. He went anyway, over her protests. But that's not why he got flopping-down drunk. He just figured it was the combination of beer, wine, and sun. He mostly blamed the "Mad Dog 20-20" wine. It had been a fun day. They caught fish in the morning and water-skied that afternoon. But when it was time to walk up that gravel pathway to the cabin they'd rented, it was a whole different matter. His elbows were so bloody that day from flopping in the stones, he never forgot it and never drank that kind of wine again. But he knew that was then and this was now. Now he just wanted to get drunk and still stay dignified, if that was at all possible.

He knew he would cut himself off before he even got close to becoming drunk, but he just wanted to feel drunk. Drown your sorrows, Mick, he thought to himself. No, you know that won't work, but it's worth a try. He debated with himself. Then suddenly Jack tapped him on the shoulder, snapping him out of it.

"How you doing? Hangin' in there, bud?"

"Yeah. Thanks, Jack."

"Nice turnout."

"Yes, it is."

"Hey, look. I don't know if there ever is going to be a good time to tell you this, but Heather and me were talking, and we think Jennifer left the bar with those two girls that were looking for a job the other week."

"Is that right."

"I don't know if she did or not, but we just thought you should know."

"Let the cops handle it," Mick responded. "That's what Jen would have said."

"Yeah, I guess you're right."

"Thanks, Jack. Hey, what're you drinking? I'm buyin'."

"Well, it's about time you bought one!"

They both laughed.

Mick put his arm around Jack's massive shoulders and they bellied-up to the bar. "Deb, give me and Jack a Chivas."

Mick could pretend to be indifferent all he wanted, but Jack's information set his still-sober mind in motion. And what are the cops doing about Jen's murder? he asked himself. Snooping around in my garage? Mick parked Jack's info on his back burner.

"Jack, that reminds me," he said, changing his tune. "Who was that cop that busted you?"

"I don't know. I copped a plea. I got the papers at home."

"All I need is the cop's name."

"OK. I'll get it for you."

A couple from Jennifer's regular work walked up to Mick to shake his hand. "It was a very nice service," the man said. "Sorry we have to leave so soon, but we have a long drive ahead of us."

"Well, thanks for coming," Mick responded.

"Good luck," said the woman before they departed.

Slowly but surely the other couples followed suit. People Mick had never met before, and would never meet again, inevitably all said the same thing: "Good luck." He was still standing proud as the last guests left. There wasn't any food left over, which was a good thing. Debbie and Heather helped him tremendously with the clean-up.

Eventually it was time for them to leave, too. As before, Mick thanked them for coming and being so helpful. Then came the time he was standing on the pool deck all alone, staring at a neat-as-can-be pile of black plastic garbage bags.

Suddenly he felt he was naked again. Lonely and naked, standing in front of the whole wide world. Vulnerable and empty. What was the meaning of this? he wondered. Where does all the garbage go? He knew he'd put it out on the curb the next day, but the thought remained: Where does all the garbage go? His mind was playing tricks on him for becoming philosophical.

"To the big dumpster in the sky!" he proclaimed out loud. He looked skyward. "Where is that Swift-Tuttle Comet now?" he shouted, as if the setting sun was going to answer him. He studied the crescent moon that was starting to rise, and then cried out, "Jennifer, where are you?"

He was already naked with loneliness. "I want you back!" he bellowed, which followed with flowing tears. He raised his arms like Atlas carrying the weight of the world. He was trying to embrace her spirit. "Do you want me to join you? We belong together!!"

Mick's body broke down and he fell to his knees. His hands grabbed the railing on the way down. His head was bowed as if he were now in a church pew, praying.

He was gasping for air as his teardrops stained the deck. A cool breeze caressed his face. Gently it lifted his head back up. "No, no, nooooo," whispered the wind. "You have too many things to doooo. You must carry on for *meeee*."

He wiped his face with his sleeve before staggering back on his feet, holding onto the railing for stability. There was a throbbing in his knees as well as his head. He made his way slowly into the house, down the stairs, and crashed—a broken man on his bed.

CHAPTER 26

Ralph Swanson checked with his crew. "What did you find?"

"A lot of dust," was the response. "Otherwise, the apartment was clean. Junk mail was overflowing the mailbox, and the place didn't look like it was lived in for a pretty long while."

"Damn. OK, guys, nice work. I may have another job coming up for you. But I'll have to get clearance first."

"OK."

"I'll be in touch." Ralph hung up the phone. The strippers are the key, he thought. He then called the detectives to see if they had been interrogated yet.

"No," one of the detectives responded. "We haven't been able to locate them. We knocked at their last known residences at various times, but no luck. We can't even locate their cars. We checked with the owners at their strip club, and they haven't shown up for work for quite a few days. It looks to us like they just took off."

"Damn," said Ralph. "OK, thanks a lot. Wait a minute. What do you know about that Spanish one—that, uh, Miranda?"

"We got nothing on her but a green card. She may be illegal. You want us to see if we can get the I.N.S. on her?"

"It's worth a try. Hey, by the way. Are those their real names or just stage names?"

"Susan Q. Smith is on the one's driver's license. She was busted for prostitution two years ago in Cincinnati."

"What's the 'Q' stand for?"

"Beats me. That's all we got on her."

"OK, thanks again."

Desperate times mean desperate action, Ralph thought. He was tired of coming up empty. He would handle the next job himself, and to hell with getting permission. He wanted to be a hero and avenge Juan's death.

First he knew he had to go home and get his lock picking kit. Then get some rest, and then use the cover of late night darkness to do what he felt was necessary.

The mayor was getting antsy again, too. No Susie Q meant he had to find a new squeeze. On the plus side, he could put his Golden Door plans on hold. Let's see if this Mickey clown can cut the mustard, he thought. Who can I send in now to find out what's going on? he mused. Ben will want his half of the dope if it takes too long. Maybe there's another way to get rid of it, but how? He felt a headache coming on. A constant pounding was starting to develop. I gotta figure this out, he thought.

He could always call on the *boys*, but they would want half of the pie. How about the Swede? he wondered. He's an old dope dealer from way back when. No, he's also a dufus, the mayor remembered, but he could whack that Mickey fuck for me. No, no, that'll draw too much heat. Just make him an offer. Maybe he'll take the money and run. If he refuses, then what? Offer him more. Play it on the up-and-up for a change.

He figured he could slowly get rid of the coke and max out the profits. That alone would more than pay off the price of the bar. But then Ben said he had a plan. The mayor wondered what that was.

Ow! His head pounded. He put up his hands to massage his temples. Then he opened a desk drawer and took out a bottle of aspirin. He threw four tablets in his mouth. He wondered how he would be able to control Ben, if he went along with his plan. Ick. The tablets left an awful aftertaste in his mouth. He got up and went to his hideaway bar for a drink.

For the first time, the mayor was clueless as to what he should do. He wasn't used to not having a plan. He took a hard swig of whiskey.

Then it came to him. First things first, he thought. He went back to his desk and flipped through his Rolodex, stopping at the card of a realtor friend of his. He picked up the phone and punched in the numbers.

"Hey, Bob. This is John. I heard a rumor that the Golden Door might be for sale. It has a new owner that inherited the business. His name is Mickey something. Why don't you go down there and ask him what he wants for the place. Don't forget to lowball him, and mums the word on my inquiry. Just let him know you can sell it if the price is right."

"Sure thing, John. I'll get right on it. Thanks for the tip." Click.

If that won't work, the mayor thought, I'll have to consider Ben's plan. Damn! His head hammered him again.

Every time he thought of Ben lately, his head hurt. He was afraid he had a loose cannon on his hands. Gotta control that one, John thought. But then, the mayor always wanted to control everyone.

I'll bet his plan has something to do with that broad he met out of town, the mayor mused. That's an idea—buy a bar out of town. No, he thought, then he couldn't provide protection. Ouch! His head pounded him again.

He knew what he needed to ease his pain. He needed his Susie Q. Damn the bitch anyway, he thought, for leaving me. Now I gotta find another one. Nah, she'll be back. But when? Thump went his head again. He reached again for his aspirin bottle to pop a couple more. Why can't things run smoothly like I planned? *Pow!* His head was full of rolling thunder. He leaned back in his chair and closed his eyes for a moment. He couldn't remember the last time he had such a headache. He was hoping it would be his last.

Ralph Swanson finally got his hands on Mickey Swift's rap sheet: "Felony—destroying private property," it read. "Felony—resisting arrest, striking an officer of the law." Violent tendencies, Ralph thought, but is he capable of murder? Could he have hired a hit man?

Ralph considered himself to be a professional profiler. He wondered if maybe, when Mickey found out Jennifer was pregnant, he went over the edge? Why was he sleeping downstairs? He was only married a couple of months. Ralph wondered, Is he mobbed up? How does he tie in with the strippers?

That was one of the reasons why Ralph broke into Susan's apartment. He found that all the furniture was still intact. A couple of empty drawers meant she'd packed for a trip. To where? Ralph wondered. When he found her personal telephone-address book, he was looking for the name "Swift" or "Mick." There was one name written and underscored on an "S" page, but it said "Naomi Smith." Ralph thought, Mother? Sister? The address was in Cincinnati. Is that where she went? he wondered. He decided he'd let his fingers do the walking on that one.

As it was, the strippers were only wanted for questioning. Or, he wondered, were they material witnesses? Did they do or see the murder? And what do they have in common with Juan? Besides a ballistics match, Ralph knew he really had nothing on anybody. But he was tired of coming up empty. The strippers are the key, he thought to himself, over and over again. What was Jennifer doing at their apartment complex? He wanted answers, and he figured the only way he was going to get them was to find the girls. Everybody was guilty, he thought, until he proved them innocent.

◆———◆O◆———◆

Mick had already talked to Jennifer's attorney about incorporating the Golden Door and making the employees into equal partners. He knew he didn't want to work there anymore. Not because of the people or the job, but because he knew he could no longer enjoy himself. If it's no fun, he thought, then it makes work seem like work.

So when the realtor came calling, Mick sent him packing. Mick had other plans but wasn't sure how to work out all the details. And he had other problems to work out. He wondered whether he should he keep the house or not. He figured it was way too big for just himself. He needed a woman to fill it. But not just any woman would do. He needed one that would be willing to adopt a child—not an easy role to fill. But if he could do all that, he reasoned, then the house would be well-suited for its intended purpose.

He cancelled his apartment lease and moved his furnishings into one-half of the garage. From there he could filter in some of his belongings, and rummage-sale the other things that were no longer needed. He figured he would buy himself a working man's van and start up his own maintenance business. That was the type of work he'd always enjoyed doing, so that was what he decided he was going to do. He had a name for the company already picked out: Swift's Maintenance Service. He figured he would paint the name on the van himself. But of course, for all his best intentions and plans, some were just not meant to be.

Ralph Swanson had located Susie Q with the help of an affiliate in Cincinnati. The Gary detectives were on the case, but in a very unusual way. They were inspecting the furniture as the movers were moving it. The driver showed them his driver's log and the work order. The detectives realized they'd missed their chance to interrogate the girls within their jurisdiction. The furniture was being delivered to 833 Primrose Drive, Cincinnati, Ohio.

Was it flight to avoid prosecution? They thought so, but there was no evidence to support the claim. Ralph was equally livid when he found out. But he also knew all was not lost. It was just time to pull out the dirty trick bag.

He'd have the I.N.S. pick up Miranda, and threaten her with deportation if she refused to talk. He knew it was of the utmost importance to interrogate the strippers separately—if they hadn't already rehearsed an alibi. Their testimonies or sworn statements could then be analyzed for any discrepancies.

If Susie Q refuses to answer questions, Ralph thought, he and his man could make life perfectly miserable by leaning on her or anyone who employed her. He knew just the right guy to get the job done. He called his friend in the F.B.I. The first thing they found out is where the strippers went—back home to Susie's mother's.

The mayor was pissed when the realtor told him Mick wasn't interested in selling. "You can't lowball a guy who's not interested" was the way he put it.

"OK, Bob. Thanks. Maybe we'll try again later." Click. "Damn, damn, damn, damn!" bellowed the mayor.

He realized that now there weren't going to be any shortcuts to getting the bar back. "Damn!" he said out loud again. He also knew there wasn't any other bar in town for sale either. Ben's going to lose his patience pretty soon anyway, he thought. So, he might as well call him in to find out what his plan was.

The mayor decided to have him come to the house. Let him have one of those bricks of coke, he thought, and then see what he could do with it. Remind Ben to be careful and, even though we're partners, he thought, be sure to leave my name out of it—whatever he's got planned.

The mayor remembered Ben had gotten a blow job somewhere out of town, and he figured he could use one of those himself right about now. If nobody knows Ben out there, he thought, then it stands to reason nobody will know me either.

These thoughts stirred the mayor's groin to the point where he decided to go to the industrial strip club right then, to see if he could find a little action on his own.

It didn't take long for Susie Q and Miranda to find work in Susie's old haunts. Neither did it take long for the F.B.I.-guided cops to pick them up for prostitution. When Ralph found out, he was on the very next available flight to Cincinnati, Ohio. He wanted to be part of the interrogation team, and to be sure to get there before they bonded out.

The I.N.S. had Miranda buffaloed good about deportation. They had her convinced that the only thing that could save her now was her full police cooperation. The federal agents had her isolated in a small windowless interrogation room, complete with a one-way mirrored window for outside observation. When Ralph got there, the investigators had their tape recorder running and their pens and notepads at the ready. "

Now what happened that Friday night that Jennifer was murdered?" a male investigator asked.

"I did not have nothing to do with that," Miranda said. Then she just started bawling.

"Well, we don't know that," said a female officer, "unless you tell us. We have sworn statements that put you and Susan inside the Golden Door Lounge the night she was murdered at Susan's apartment complex. Why don't you start from the beginning and tell us what happened that night?"

"We were just looking for waitress work. And the manager Mick, he turned us down."

"Go on," said the female investigator.

"So then we heard that the owner of the lounge was gay. So we seduced her, because we thought that she would hire us."

"You expect us to believe a cockamamie story like that?" asked the male.

"It is true! I swear!"

"So, you two had sex with Jennifer the night she was murdered?" the female investigator asked.

Miranda paused, and looked embarrassingly at the male agent. The female understood immediately and gave her partner a nod that he recognized as meaning "time to leave." As soon as he left the room, she asked again, "Did you two have sexual relations with Jennifer Tuttle?"

"Yes," Miranda responded meekly.

"Well, now we're getting somewhere," said the female partner. "And how long did this activity go on?"

"For maybe a couple of hours, I think."

"Can you be more specific? Like, what time did she leave the apartment?"

"At about one o'clock, I think. She said she had to go back to the lounge."

"And then what did you do?"

"Nothing."

"What do you mean nothing?"

"Nothing. I stayed in the bed."

"And where was Susan all this time?"

"She was with me."

"You mean, the three of you had been together."

"Yes."

Ralph Swanson left his post behind the window-mirror and entered the room. "Hello, Miranda," he said. "My name is Ralph. I have just a few questions for you. I want to know about some phone calls. Did you or Susan ever borrow a cell phone from John Quibly?"

"No. I don't even know any John Quibly."

"You don't, huh?" Ralph pulled out some blown-up photographs from his file folder. He placed on the table in front of her one of Susie giving John a lap dance. "You don't know this man?"

"Oh, *him*. He is Susie's john. But I don't know nothing about no cell phone or phone calls."

"Are you sure?"

"Yes. I am sure."

"We're going to check out your story, you know."

"Yes, I know. But I have told you every thing I know already. I am not lying."

Ralph took his photo off the table and left the room along with the female agent to discuss the next line of questioning. Once outside, he said, "Her story is plausible, but make her go over it again. See if she slips up or changes anything, and ask her about Benjamin Smide. I saw the two of them go into a back room together. Probably just another customer, but he's a cop just the same. Here's some pictures. I have plenty of copies, so you don't have to worry about returning them. I'm going to go interview Susan now. Are they going to be able to bond out?"

"Susan can," she replied, "but Miranda is being held over for a deportation hearing."

"Good," said Ralph. "I'll get back with you after I'm finished."

"See you later then."

"Right."

Ralph only had to drive a couple blocks to get from the federal lockup to the city's. He introduced himself to the detectives who had questioned Susan.

"What'd she say?" he asked.

"Besides 'fuck you' and 'I want to see a lawyer,' she didn't say a damn thing."

"Do you mind if I give it a shot?"

"No, go ahead. She's been sitting on ice for a couple hours now. She's right down the hall."

The detectives led Ralph to the interrogation room she was in. Then they took their positions behind the one-way window.

Susie Q was sitting in a chair with her arms folded, looking every bit like a very unhappy customer, when the insurance investigator entered the room.

"Hello, Susan. My name is Ralph. You're in a lot of trouble, young lady."

"Fuck you! I want to see my lawyer."

"Oh, I see," he said calmly. "You're a tough babe. Well, tough babe, I got news for you. We're going to charge you with being an accomplice to the murder of Jennifer Tuttle."

"I didn't have nothing to do with no murder!" she practically screamed. "And you don't have no proof that I did! So, get your skinny ass out of my face. I want my attorney."

"An attorney isn't going to do you any good. Miranda already told us about you and Jennifer. But we only have you down for being an accomplice. We really want to hang the shooter."

He paused just long enough to let the information sink in, but she just sat there, arms folded and stone faced.

Ralph then took out a photo of her and John Quibly. "You know this guy?"

She looked at the picture but didn't bat an eyelash and never said a word.

"We have his sworn statement that you used his cell phone to call Juan Beamer, Donald Strapp, and another fellow better known as Slim Jim. And they're all dead. And now we have you fleeing the state to avoid prosecution. And you are also the last person to have seen Jennifer Tuttle alive."

Ralph was on a roll now. As he stood up and put his hands on the table to support his weight, he put his face as close to hers as he dared. He raised his voice and the level of his sincerity, as he continued, "So you see, little girl, you're an accomplice to murder and all I want to know is who the shooter is. Maybe you'd best start talking to me if you don't want to spend the rest of your life behind bars."

Susie was confused. She stared at the photos Ralph spread on the table. She didn't know anything about any *murders*. She had thought The Donald committed suicide. She didn't know any *Juans*. But she did remember calling Slim for a score—at the mayor's request. And now, she thought, he's testifying against me! Or, is all of this just bullshit?

She continued to think hard. While it was true that they'd left town because of Jennifer's murder, Miranda was hysterical with fear that *that pervert* was following her. As for that old fart in the picture, he could never get next to Slim Jim, let alone kill him. Besides, they had already arrested two guys for the hit on Slim. This Ralph punk is full of shit, she reasoned. He ain't got nothing on me, she thought. Regardless of anything, she knew she didn't have anything to do with any *murders*.

"I want to see an attorney," she finally said.

Damn, Ralph thought. His ploy didn't work. He thought he almost had her. He saw it in her eyes. But now he was just pissed again. One more time he came up empty. But he wasn't finished. Not just yet.

"I got more news for you," he said. "We already know the shooter's name is Mickey Swift."

"Go arrest *him* then. And get me my lawyer while you're at it."

Smart ass, Ralph thought, as he gathered up his photographs and left the room.

He asked the detectives outside, "How long can you hold her?"

"Twenty-four hours. All day. She has enough money on her to make bond."

"I almost had her!" Ralph exclaimed. "She knows something. I saw it in her eyes. I'll just have to take another crack at her later, that's all. Thanks, fellas."

"Any time."

One disappointed Ralph Swanson came up empty again. But he knew he was getting warmer. Now all he had to do was turn up the heat.

He talked to his friend from the F.B.I. to see if they had gotten any additional information from Miranda.

"Not really," he said. "She turned into a hysterical blubbering bag of tears. Claims some pervert was out to kill her. She didn't know anything more, as far as I could tell."

"Thanks," said Ralph.

He didn't want to call his office and report that he was returning empty-handed, so he figured he would talk to Susan's mother. Perhaps she could reason with her daughter, and try to get her to explain those phone calls. Ralph still felt Susie was holding back information, and he wanted to know what it was.

When he pulled up to the address on Primrose Drive, the first thing he noticed was a statue of the Virgin Mary surrounded by an arch of climbing roses. It was a smallish house, neatly trimmed in pink and white paint. Ralph's first impression was that she must be a religious woman. How does she deserve a daughter like Susie, he wondered. He rang the doorbell. A strikingly good-looking woman in her fifties answered the door.

"Can I help you?" she asked.

"My name is Ralph Swanson. I would like to talk to you about your daughter."

"Is she in trouble again?"

"I'm afraid so, ma'am."

"Come in then." She led him into the front room.

Ralph noticed a vast array of religious items, including statues, pictures, and crosses.

"Can I get you some tea?" she politely asked.

Ralph felt out of place somehow and declined the offer. They sat down on the sofa and he started.

"I'm having a problem reasoning with your daughter," he said. "I thought perhaps you may be able to help."

"I would like to, but, you see, she doesn't listen to me either. But you know it's all my fault."

"How so?"

"You see, I was an unwed mother. Her father left town before she was even born. You see, I didn't know he was already married when I got pregnant. He wanted me to get an abortion—quite naturally I refused. Susan was ridiculed by the neighborhood kids because of me. It was hard for her to grow up without a father."

"You shouldn't blame yourself, Miss Smith."

"It was my sin and this is my penance. Did she get caught prostituting herself again?"

"Yes, but that's not why I'm here. I'm trying to trace phone calls. I have reason to believe Susan was using the phone of one John Quibly."

The woman's mouth fell open and her eyes grew large. "That—that was her father's name," she confessed.

"Surely it's not the same man."

She gasped. Ralph just looked at her surprised.

"Of course," she continued, "after he abandoned me and she was born, I never told her her father's name. But on the birth certificate I gave her the middle initial 'Q' to remind me of my sin, and to spite him. An incomplete man doesn't deserve to have a child given a complete name from him. But surely it must be a coincidence. He has never send us a card or any support whatsoever. We don't even have a picture of him."

As if on cue, Ralph opened his folder and took out a copy of the picture he had taken and handed it to her. "Is this him?"

It only took her a second to study. "Oh my God! What's she doing sitting on her father's lap in her underwear? This is disgusting!" She threw the photo back at Ralph. "I think you should leave now."

"I'm sorry," he said. "I didn't mean to upset you."

She flipped her hands in a rapid shooing motion. "I don't want any of that filth in my house. Out! Out you go!"

Ralph was back-peddling his way to the door, apologizing on the way. Once outside, the door slammed in his face. "Damn!" he muttered under his breath.

As he walked to his car, another thought struck him. Holy shit! he thought. I've hit the smut jackpot! But how to use this ammunition to solve his murder cases was another question entirely.

He decided to go back to the jail and have another crack at Susie Q—Susan Quibly Smith.

He huddled with the detectives first. He figured he had to double check his information on John Quibly. He explained his concern for the possibility of mistaken identity. But that wasn't going to stop him from questioning little Miss Smartass again.

The matron retrieved Susan from her holding cell and escorted her back to the interrogation room, where Ralph was waiting for her.

"Oh, it's you again," she said. "I told you before, you ain't got nothing on me, and I want a lawyer."

"That's not what your mother said."

"You leave my mother out of this, you lying bastard!"

He took out the photo again and slid it across the table. "You know this guy, don't you?" She sat there with her arms folded. "Do you want to tell me about those phone calls now?" She was stone-faced. She said nothing. "I'm the guy who can help you get out of this mess, but you have to help me."

"I'm posting bond as soon as my 24 hours are up. So I don't need your help."

"That's where you're wrong, little lady. You see that man in the picture? Your mother says that's your long-lost father."

"You dirty bastard!" She stood up and whisked her way around the table, arms flaying in his face. He backed away in self-defense, but her nails dug into his cheeks anyway.

The detectives and matron, who were watching through the window-mirror, rushed to Ralph's aid. They restrained Susan's arms while forcing her back into the chair.

"You dirty bastard!" she screeched again.

Ralph put his hands to his face as he felt blood drip. "Like I said, you need my help." Then he said to the detectives, "I want to press assault and battery charges."

"You dirty bastard!" she lurched and screamed again at him as he walked out.

With Susie Q. Smith safely back in the lockup and new charges brought, Ralph hoped for a higher bond so she wouldn't be able to make bail. Keep her on ice for awhile, he thought, while he sorted through his options for his next move. It was obvious she wouldn't cooperate with him. So, he thought, he'd need to use someone else. A kindly female officer might do the trick. Meanwhile, just let Sue stew.

CHAPTER 27

The mayor and Ben came to an agreement, in light of the fact that he didn't see ownership of the Golden Door changing hands anytime soon. Ben thought he could sell the coke through the lingerie model he met at the Miners Only Lounge. The mayor cautioned him that, without his protection, it could be dangerous outside his domain.

"Not to worry," Ben assured him. "I'll only deal with her, and then she can sell it to all her friends."

"Sounds simple enough," the mayor agreed.

So he gave Ben one of the bricks and explained that, if he sold them in one-gram packets, it would maximize the profits. He suggested charging eighty dollars a gram to be resold at a hundred dollars a gram, letting the reseller make a handsome profit too. It all sounded good to the mayor: easy money, splitting 80 bucks a gram, all pure profit. No work, no risk for him, and 20 grams in sales a week would give him eight hundred dollars each week till the goods were all gone. He thought, Not bad for taking little risk, and not having to do anything much. It's almost too good to be true.

"Just fold up shop at the first sign of trouble, Ben," he ordered, and then it was agreed.

The mayor considered going with Ben to scope out the joint, but decided against it. "It's your baby," he told him. Besides, John was busy trying to become a new john to a brand-new stripper at the industrial club. This doll needed his full attention. He figured she was just about ready to turn the corner and see things his way.

Ben did some shopping the next day and bought himself an electric scale and a thousand small jewelry baggies. He spent the whole of that night weighing and bagging, weighing and bagging, and sampling the coke as he went along. He hadn't even been to bed yet, and the alarm went off. Time sure flies when you're having fun, he thought.

The reality of it was, his muscles were all sore from such monotonous, tedious tasks, and he was wired to the max. He started grinding his teeth as he put his precious packets and equipment away in his closet.

Ben jumped in the shower and within minutes he was washed, dried, dressed, and ready for patrol duty. It was his dayshift turn, and by noon he had already written six tickets for seatbelt violations. He was so proud of himself for doing a full day's work before lunchtime.

But he was bored. The drugs had worn off, and now he was headed home to recharge his batteries. Just a little snort, he promised himself. There were plenty of bags, he thought, plenty of gram packets. He further justified: What John doesn't know won't hurt him. Soon they'd both be rolling in dough anyway.

He went to the Miners Only Lounge that night and set up his deal. It worked just like he'd planned. He got his blow job from "Linda" and fronted her ten grams of coke. The next night, she gave him another blow job and eight hundred dollars in cash. He fronted her another ten packets and came back the night after that to collect. He and John split the money 50-50. Soon they were happier than pigs wallowing in shit. The loot was just starting to land in their hands.

Ralph Swanson took his position behind the mirror this time, as the matron led Susan Smith back into the interrogation room.

It was decided this time to use reasoning instead of threats, and not a seasoned professional like Ralph either, but a caring type. Cris Minger was selected, barely out of her rookie year. She was chosen for her youth. An unobtrusive approach was desired. Cris was pretty and petite, almost a dead ringer for Susie herself. It was thought that she would have more in common with her, and that this combination might loosen Sue's tongue.

When the matron led Susie into the room, Cris thank her politely and said, "We would like some privacy." After the matron left, she said, "Hi, my name is Cris. I would like to help you out of your little pickle, but for me to do that I need a little help from you. You see, there has been a whole series of murders that you may be able to help us solve. We already know you had nothing to do with them, but it does look bad for you when you leave the state because of one."

Susie opened up. "That was mostly Miranda's doing. She kept seeing perverts lurking in the dark. Then that thing happened to Jennifer, and it just sent her through the roof."

"Exactly. And we already know that you see a man named John Quibly, but what we don't know is who borrowed his cell phone."

"He's *not* my father! He can't be! He can't be!!"

The outburst took Cris completely by surprise.

Susie then stood up and faced the mirror screaming, *"He's not my father!"*

Thinking she might have blown her progress, Cris agreed with her.

"You're right. Of course you're right. Please sit down and relax, OK? I just wanted to ask you about some phone calls."

"I don't know anything about no phone calls!" But then she shot back: "And I only used his cell phone once!"

A breakthrough, Cris thought, and then she asked calmly, "Can you tell me something about the one phone call?"

Susie paused for awhile, thinking, What the hell, he's already dead. She sat back down in her chair.

"Slim Jim," she finally said. "I used his phone to call Slim Jim. He was going to buy me some coke, or something. I was sitting right on his lap! But then Jim got hit. The guys that did it are already in jail."

"All right!" Ralph said to the detectives behind the mirror. "That's a start."

Cris continued, "What guys are in jail?"

"The guys that killed Slim Jim."

"Then who killed Jennifer?"

"I don't know," Susie said. "We were just trying to get jobs at the Golden Door because Johnny wanted to know who was dealing drugs there. He wanted to get the dirt on Jennifer so she would lose her liquor license, and then he could get the bar back. I was supposed to run it. Or, that was the plan anyway."

Now Ralph was all smiles. He told the detectives, "Tell Cris she did a fine job, and we can forget about the assault and battery charges. Release her to her mother on her own recognizance."

He knew his job wasn't over. He had to rethink his strategy. If Susie had given the right information, it let Mickey Swift off the hook and put the mayor right back on it. But that made no sense. Three other people were slaughtered along with Slim Jim, and Ralph figured it couldn't have been the work of only one man. John Quibly wasn't even physically capable of doing it. Something was still missing. Where's that piece of the puzzle? Ralph wondered. Where's the gun?

He thought he'd check with Slim's killers. They claimed they didn't do it, but that's only natural. Ralph thought he'd better go over their story again. He thought and thought. He still had more questions than answers, but he no longer felt empty-handed. As he prepared for his trip back to Indiana, he thought perhaps the mayor needed a visit, too.

Ben and John were whooping it up at John's house, trying to play pool again. Ben had so much money now, he got tired of counting it. The mayor just put his in the safe.

"Don't put so much in the bank at one time," he warned Ben. "The banks report transactions over ten grand to the feds."

"OK, OK already. I know," said Ben. "We gotta get another brick out of the freezer. The first one is almost gone."

"Sure thing." The mayor didn't care anymore, but was carefully staggering the coke's use just the same. He gave Ben one more. "That broad you're dealing with—she doesn't know what you do for a living, does she?"

"Hell no. She doesn't have a clue."

"Good. Keep it that way. You want to play another game?"

"No. I gotta go."

"OK then. Be careful."

"Yeah. See ya."

Ben was on his way to see his new lady, Linda. Quick oral jobs were no longer the norm. Now it was rock 'em – sock 'em ball-busting all-nighters. Ben had a masochistic streak in him. He liked it rough. He loved being spanked, and he loved bending Linda over his knees. *Crack! Crack! Crack!* He's spank her ass. "Now, suck my dick," he'd command.

Then he'd go limp and start his routine all over again. "Spank me! Spank me good and hard!" If that didn't work, they'd do some more lines of coke.

Linda didn't mind his quirks. She loved to play along. He supplied the crank; she supplied the spank. Ben was dipping his nose in the profits more and more all the time. Highly wired, balancing like a tightrope walker, walking that thin line, and not sleeping for days on end, but Ben was doing it all very well.

Nobody could tell at work. Except for his constant runny nose, there were no other indications. He kept nasal spray handy for an excuse, if anyone inquired. At any rate, he was mostly on patrol duty all alone anyway. Whenever boredom set in, he would just do another hit.

That particular night he forgot to bring the packets, but he had the whole brick of coke in his trunk. What little he did have in his personal packet was sucked up quickly. He remembered the brick in his car. He decided he could afford to be daring. He went out and retrieved the brick and brought it into the house in front of his lady Linda. He had pride, and he didn't mind showing off his cache at all. He was in possession of a lot of coke, which translates into a lot of money and power. It was the power he enjoyed the most, and he wanted total control over his ladylove.

"I can get you twenty grand for that," she said.

"Sounds good to me," Ben replied.

He was tired of the tedious chore of making up all those little packets anyway. So the deal was made, with crossed-fingers and a whole lot of kinky spanky sex.

High-wire walker Ben couldn't figure out why the lady Linda didn't show up the next day, nor the day after that. When he crashed, he crashed hard. His pig head started wallowing in the gutter slop, trudging along snoot first. I'll kill her when I find her, he repeated to himself over and over. I'll find her, he thought. She'll never get away with double-crossing me.

The worst, of course, was yet to come. How was he going to explain his fiasco to John? How was he going to get another brick from him? Where would the profits come from selling that brick now? Who could he trust to start selling for them again?

"Shit, shit, shit!" he kept muttering. He was a little more than just pissed off. Sure "I'll get you twenty grand for that brick," he remembered her saying. He might as well start pounding his own head with a real brick, he thought, for all the wretched thoughts that were pounding away on the inside.

He did have some leeway to call himself an asshole, but explaining his blunder to John was going to be a whole 'nother matter. "Shit, shit, shit!" he kept saying.

Ralph pored over the police reports on the Gary massacre before he went to interview the supposed killers in jail. The cops wanted them to point their fingers at each other, to see which one would rat on the other to escape the death penalty in exchange for getting natural life. But it was no dice. The baiting tactics didn't work. Both kept claiming that neither one of them did it. And the one guy swore he saw two white guys leave just before they showed up. No one believed them though, except one guy, Ralph.

Normally, that wouldn't do them any good. They were going to hang for the murder. The judicial system would make sure of that, and the politicians would back this system to the hilt. The preponderance of evidence was overwhelming, with or without the murder weapon. But there was that gun question again. Ralph still wondered, Where was the gun?

He followed some other background checks and found that John Quibly did indeed live in the Cincinnati area before Susan Smith was born. He served in the Ohio National Guard, and his record was clean.

Ralph envisioned himself questioning John Quibly, and leading right off with the question: "How does it feel to be doing your own illegitimate daughter?"

CHAPTER 28

"**A**sshole" was the term the mayor used when Ben finally did tell him what happened. "Fuckin' stupid asshole!" he shouted. "No more! You're shut down. We're back to square one." "Not to worry," Ben assured him. "I'll only deal with her, and then she can sell it to all her friends."

"Get out of my sight!" he bellowed. "I can't think in front of idiots!"

Ben quickly left.

Back to square one, the mayor thought. Back to the Golden Door. Let's just see how much he wants and pay him off. Everybody's got a price. Let's see, he wondered, who can I send in there this time? The Swede? No. If you want to do the job right, he thought, you have to do it yourself. He decided to pay a visit himself to see this slick Mickey.

He finished the pressing paperwork that was in front of him, and then he jumped in his Caddy and proceeded to the Golden Door. The joint looked different to him, almost unrecognizable. It had been so long since he'd actually been inside the place. It was actually clean and painted. The stage seemed different, too. He half-recognized Debbie when he asked at the bar to see the owner.

"He's in the back. I'll get him for you," she said.

Mick returned with Debbie. "Can I help you?" he asked.

"Yeah. Let's sit in the booth. I have some business I would like to discuss in private," said the mayor.

Mick didn't like his attitude from the get-go, and instinctively did not extend his hand in greeting. "All right," he said. They both went and sat down in a corner booth.

"I'm John Quibly," the mayor began. "I used to own this joint and still hold the paper on it. I have a new partner and would like to make you an offer. How much would you want?"

"Well, John, it's like this. I don't want anything."

"What do you mean you don't want anything?"

"Just what I said."

"What kind of businessman are you? I'm prepared to make you a bona fide offer. Let's say, thirty thousand."

"It's not for sale."

"OK, make it forty thousand."

Mick just shook his head.

"Look, uh, Mick, is it? I happen to know you're a convicted felon and the liquor commissioner is a personal friend of mine. You'll never get the liquor license renewed. I'm giving you the chance to get out while the getting's good, with a nice little profit to boot."

Mick countered with, "What part of 'it's not for sale' did you not understand?"

"Look, don't get cute with me. Technically you're not even allowed to be behind a bar, let alone own one."

"I know, John. Thanks for your concern. But, you see, that's why I had the ownership transferred to a corporation. The employees own it now."

Flabbergasted, John got up. "Then I'm wasting my time talking to you."

"Yes, you are."

The mayor made a kind of huffing snort noise and steamrolled his way right out the door.

Debbie came over and met Mick as he was getting up. "So, what did the mayor want?"

"He wants to buy the place."

"What did you tell him?"

"No sale."

"He looked kind of mad."

"So what?"

"I don't think you know all the clout he has."

"Fuck him, Deb. He ain't got no clout over me."

She shrugged her shoulders and walked away to serve a customer.

Ralph had tailed the mayor thinking he was going back to the strip club. "See where the dog wags his tail" was his motto. He didn't know what to think when he saw John Quibly pull into the Golden Door's parking lot.

He got out of his own car and positioned himself by the entrance windows. He cupped the sides of his face to remove the sun's glare. He pressed his nose to the glass and peered in. And a very interesting sight he saw. The mayor and Mickey Swift talking privately in a booth. Damn, he thought, I wish I had a bug in there.

Ralph wanted to know what they were talking about. Business deals, of course, he thought. They're partners in crime, of course! Ralph was especially looking for a cell phone or some envelope stuffed with cash being slipped across—or under—the table. Come on, come on, Ralph was thinking, make a phone call!

A car alarm went off in the parking lot, and Ralph naturally had to turn around and look. It was just some lady goofing up with her remote. He put his face back to the glass, and they were gone. Damn! he thought. He really wanted to know what they were talking about.

Now what? he asked himself. He figured he could follow the mayor, who was probably then going to the strip club. But he could always follow him there. Or, he could try to pull some information out here. Would he be welcome? Ralph figured, after that garage scene during Jennifer's services, Mickey probably wouldn't even talk to him.

But it's a public place, Ralph thought, so maybe I can get in his face and goad him into talking. Let's see how he reacts to questions. Measure the man. Remember, he thought, there were two white men in a van driving away from Slim Jim's. Maybe there were more than two—three or four even?

These guys have got to be mobbed up, Ralph thought. Dope dealers. Juan was killed for his dope. Slim Jim was killed for his dope. That Donald used to work in Jennifer's bar. Jennifer was killed for her bar to sell the dope in. Mickey had the most to gain from her death. Ralph could now see crystal clear how they operate together. But how to prove it? And who's got the gun?

He thought he had it all figured out. After all, he was a professional investigator. So he walked right inside the Golden Door. Mickey was having a beer while watching the ballgame. Ralph went over and sat down right beside him.

"Who's winning?" he asked. He could care less, of course, but he just wanted to start up a conversation.

"The Cubs," Mick replied without looking. But he knew who he was. He had spotted him coming in. Mick always had his eye on the door.

There was a long pause while Debbie got Ralph a screwdriver. Mick still didn't acknowledge his presence. He just stared at the TV, hoping the Cubs' bullpen wouldn't blow the lead again. But Ralph wanted to talk.

"I'm sorry about the other day," he said, "but when I have pot in my pocket, I have to smoke it."

Mick didn't answer. Ignore the fool, he thought, and maybe he'll just go away.

"Maybe you know where I could buy some smoke? I'm all out." His pestering finally paid off.

Mick turned to him and said, "I think you better get out."

Not the kind of response Ralph wanted, but at least he got his attention.

"Sorry, man. I just assumed you were an old hippie from way back like me. You can't tell me you didn't enjoy those swinging '70s and all the love-ins."

"You assumed wrong, mister. I didn't enjoy seeing my government slaughter people in the streets in the '70s, and I've never been to a love-in." Mick was getting pissed, but he turned his attention back to the ballgame.

Ralph was relentless. "Then maybe you know someone else I could score from?"

Mick turned to the pest once more. "The answer's no! And I already know you're a cop, so why don't you just leave me alone?"

Ralph shot right back. "No, I'm not going to leave you alone. I'm investigating a murder, and I think you did it."

Mick didn't answer. He just looked at the TV.

Ralph persisted. "So why did you have Jennifer killed? For the bar? Or, was it because you found out she was pregnant?"

Mick didn't say anything, but he got off his barstool. Debbie was standing within earshot, and she was stunned at the accusation. Ralph thought Mick was going to walk away from him, so he stood up too, ready to follow him with more questions.

"That's right," Ralph continued. "Didn't you read the autopsy report? She was pregnant."

There are certain times in a man's life when his adrenaline makes him strong enough to move mountains. This was one of them.

Mick didn't even have time to see red. His right hand struck faster than a snakebite. His hand clamped around Ralph's throat, right under his chin. Mick's viselike grip started crushing Ralph's larynx. He could no longer talk or breathe. He was back-pedaling on his tiptoes, as Mick's hold was pushing him backwards toward the door. Ralph couldn't even gasp for air, as the grip completely blocked his airway. He could only flay with his arms, trying to break Mick's grip.

Mick's adrenaline was pumping full force as he prepared to push Ralph right through the wooden door. He would have died from crushed windpipes except that, lucky for him, a customer was trying to enter and suddenly opened the door just as Ralph's body came flying out past him. Ralph landed on his back, hitting his head on the sidewalk at impact. He curled up in the fetal position, just glad to be gasping at air. His own hands were now protecting his throat as he whimpered.

Mick stood above him, staring at the pitiful sight. He felt like stomping his foot down on Ralph's exposed ribcage, but that would have punctured his lungs. So he compromised with a swift kick in the ass, followed by, "And stay out!"

That at least left Ralph alive.

Debbie's mouth was still open when Mick returned to his stool. The adrenaline rush still gripped him as he grabbed his beer, and it shook. His hand was trembling nervously. He was lucky to get it all the way to his mouth without spilling. Debbie noticed and did the right thing. She poured him a Chivas on the rocks.

Mick's heart was pounding rapidly. He hadn't felt so much rage—ever. He whiffed down his drink like it was nothing. No language was needed as he put his glass down. Debbie refilled it right away. His chest was expanding and contracting with each breath. His grip on the glass was so tight, it appeared he was going to crush it. He did feel like crushing something. Lucky for Ralph, he was able to make it to his car and leave in one piece.

Reality slowly leaked back into Mick's head. Better get out of here, he thought. That prick might just come back with his cop buddies and press charges. He finished his drink. His breathing finally returned to normal. He said to Deb, "I'm going home. Call me if the cops come around."

"OK, Mick," she said.

With that, he was off.

The cops didn't come because Ralph went to the hospital. He had deep bruises on his neck and swollen glands. He could barely talk above a whisper. He did think of making a police report, but thought better of it. He was in no hurry to mess with Mick again. Also, he felt he made a mistake in character judgment. He was still confused and had more questions than answers, but he had to refocus his investigation. He still felt the Golden Door had something to do with Juan's murder. He wanted to get back to his office and back to the drawing board. Damn, he thought yet again, I'm so tired of coming up empty.

Ben sheepishly gave the mayor an envelope with cash. It was his cash, but he told the mayor he'd found another outlet for the coke, which was another lie. He wanted to soften up the mayor for another brick, and he knew the best way to do that was to slip him cash in an envelope.

Ben justified his little white lie with the thought, Half of it's mine anyway. He just wanted to lift his spirits a little. He figured he could find another lingerie model like Linda easily—if he had the coke. So when he put forth the proposition, John fell for it. Not just because he wanted to go along with him so much—John needed a way to convert coke to cash anyway—but he also knew the Golden Door was slammed in his face.

"You were right, Ben," he said. "That Mick is a tough nut. The motherfucker. I wish he was dead instead of that dyke bitch. He's going to be dead meat anyway, when I put the word out that I want every car driving out of there pulled over and every driver given sobriety tests. I don't care if they're locals or not. I offered the son of a bitch fifty grand for the joint, and he wouldn't take it. So, fuck the motherfucker. And you—you better start being careful."

"I'll be extra careful this time, John."

"You goddamn well better be!" Then he calmed down to give his next instructions. "Stop by the house tonight, and you can pick up the shit."

So it was that Ben stopped by that night and picked up another brick. He went directly home and began the tedious chore of weighing out all those little packets. It took him nearly all night to get a hundred made up before he went to sleep. He felt he had to get a couple hours' rest before starting his shift. He also planned on going out that night, and he wanted to function somewhat refreshed.

This time he went way outside of his jurisdiction, all the way to Valparaiso. He roamed the area, bar-hopping and looking for fashion shows. In the back of his mind, he was also looking for Linda.

He did make two sales that night, one of them in a biker bar. There was a tattoo-laden, bearded white dude that had to borrow money from his buddies to pay for the dope. Ben wasn't about to extend any credit to that motley crew. Then later he found two lingerie models who split a packet between them, but neither one would service him and they didn't know any Linda.

All the joints Ben visited had potential and he could have made more sales, but mostly he just kept a low profile because he didn't want to acquire any undo notoriety nor did he want to step on any other dealer's toes. He was packing his piece just in case, though, but he wasn't looking for any trouble that night.

He did consider though, that if he found another dealer, he might set him up for a robbery at a later date. He didn't even use much coke himself that night. If would have been a different story if he'd found a woman to share some with, but maybe, he thought, he would find someone perhaps the next night. Still in all, he went home with a profit.

CHAPTER 29

Mick had his garage sale. His sofa and chair set sold first. It was practically brand-new, with a Southwestern Indian print pattern. His old waterbed sold next to last. The mattress container had patches on it from the pin pricks left by a spurned female. That seemed so long ago, but regardless of its history, Mick felt he had to keep slashing the price until it sold.

Now with the garage clear of clutter, he could set up his power saws and the like. He was preparing to shop for a new van, but he was in no particular hurry. He still put in his hours at the Golden Door, while trying slowly to wean his way out. At least he'd managed to get out of the office, as Debbie was now the bookkeeper. But that took her away from serving customers, and she was complaining of having to "live there."

"Hire some help then," Mick told her. "You're in charge now."

That wasn't the only problem. Kenny the Crisscross player stopped coming in. There were rumors he was busted for D.U.I. And other regulars seemed to be missing, too. But the daily receipts were only down slightly, which was normal for early fall. Business always picked up as the football season progressed, or when the snow started flying.

Mick himself bowed out as a night customer. When it came to looking for a woman, he started going around to the better lounges and restaurants. He felt funny flirting in the Golden Door. The haunting of a million bug-eyes would always focus on him, if he had even the most casual chat with any available woman. It was just too uncomfortable of a feeling for Mick. Plus he didn't want to deal with any back-stabbing "opinioneers." He knew, unfortunately, that such was part of human nature—garbage collecting. People just have to have something to talk about.

For the most part, the people in-the-know respected Mick to the hilt, and anyone who said otherwise was quickly chastised. Just the same, he tried to keep his private life out of the limelight. There wasn't anything he found interesting enough to chase after anyhow, but he felt that patience would pay dividends, and he was willing to wait before cashing in.

Ralph Swanson had no such patience. He was ready to confront the mayor, either in his office or his favorite strip club. He decided to befriend him at the industrial club first. Even though he'd tailed him there several times, he had never witnessed him use his cell phone.

Ralph knew the oddities of the man full well. He always sat in the same back booth. He always got his lap dance. He always rudely pawed the girls, who rarely complained because he was such a generous tipper. But he hadn't been in the back room in awhile, as far as Ralph knew anyway.

He was sure John didn't know he was doing his own daughter. That didn't matter to Ralph though, but he did want to save his ammo for the most opportune time to yield maximum results. One thing he knew for sure: John Quibly wouldn't be mayor next term.

Ralph still had problems speaking above a whisper. His throat was still swollen. Nevertheless, he approached John in his booth and boldly sat down across from him.

"Is this the action corner?" his voice scratched out.

"Sometimes," John replied. "Who are you?"

"Ralph."

"What's wrong with your voice?"

"Laryngitis."

"Too bad. Listen, uh, Ralph. I sit here in this corner because I like my privacy."

"I was just wondering if I could get laid around here."

"Sometimes. But this crew is stingy, and you're not going to get it for nothing."

"I don't care about money. I've got plenty."

That comment reminded Ralph he was going to have to pad his expense account under a different expenditure. Strip clubs are a no-no to accountants.

"Can I buy you a beer?" he scratchily asked the mayor.

"No. Look, Ralph. You see that guy over there? And that guy over there?" the mayor was pointing out lone men around the club. "They're all sitting all alone because that's the way we like it—private. Understand?"

"Yeah, but I just wanted to find out where I can get laid, or buy some real good shit or something." His voice was scratching along, getting worse with every word.

"What kind of shit are you looking for?"

Ralph thought he was piquing his honor's interest. Bingo, he thought.

"Oh, party stuff," he replied. "You know, coke. Shit that strippers like."

A warning *buzzer* went off in the mayor's head. He knew he'd slipped up by asking that question. He didn't know this guy from Adam, and here he was talking drugs. Warning—*buzz*. Warning—*buzz*. His head started aching, pounding again. He didn't understand the headache. Maybe, he thought, it was more than a headache. A migraine coming on. *Buzz!* He put his hands to his temples to massage them.

Ralph just looked at him. "Are you all right, buddy?"

Buzz! Bing! Bang! Tears were rolling down the mayor's face. "Yeah. I'm all right. I just need a couple aspirins." He got up and left Ralph empty-handed.

Damn! he thought. I almost had him!

The mayor got in his Caddy and drove straight to the nearest drugstore for pain pills. He swore if his headache didn't go away, he'd be at his doctor's first thing in the morning.

Ralph was still sitting in the same booth vacated by the mayor, perplexed by what he'd witnessed and wondering whether he'd lost his touch. His thoughts were interrupted by a young lady.

"You want a lap dance, honey?"

Startled by the toothy smile of a gorgeous stripper, Ralph was at a loss for the moment. He watched her perky nipples just teasing him through the sheerest of brassieres. Then she made her breasts gently sway with a slight twist of her shoulders.

Ralph disliked teasers, but he felt some new urges. He suddenly just blurted out, "No. I want to get fucked."

"That'll cost you a hundred."

He was shocked at the nonchalance of her reply and still at a loss, but he started thinking, It's been a long time for my little buddy, and the company's going to pay for it anyway, so why not?

"What's your name?" he asked.

"They call me Lovely…"

"No, don't tell me! Lovely Linda?"

"That's right! How'd you guess?"

Ralph had always wondered how that back room was set up. After all, he was an insurance investigator—and a man. So, he thought and smiled at the same time, let's investigate. *For insurance purposes*. The fact was, he hadn't actually smiled in an awful long time.

"Show me the way, Lovely Linda!"

"What's wrong with your voice?"

"Laryngitis."

He got up and she took his hand. "Right this way, honey."

They disappeared into the back room. Ralph kept smiling the whole way there.

He never felt he'd actually ever been in love before, but he was later when he walked out the back room door into the parking lot. It had cost him more than a hundred dollars though. There was that packet they used and then the extra one for later. Ralph really didn't have to buy any coke from Linda. He could always get all the drugs he wanted from his boss. All he had to claim was that it's for the operatives. But this was different. He chuckled inside. He'd charge it to the insurance company, and they'd have to raise their premiums. Ralph knew how to cook the books.

Who cares anyway? he thought to himself. The important thing was, he'd never felt so alive before.

Where'd all this adolescent energy come from? he wondered. Wow! This Lovely Linda was good!

He had made a date to see her again. He knew he still had work to do, but now he found a reason to mix work with play—and write off the play on his expense account.

Ben's sales increased slowly, but his popularity grew by leaps and bounds. He became a regular at the biker bar in Valpo. It was a bit of a drive for him, but that didn't matter. He had found a new squeeze. So what, he thought, if she had a few tattoos. She was his biker bitch now. He became attracted to leather the first time he saw her. That ass—in skintight black leather—just wowed him. He wanted to spank it. Plus, he discovered that she liked her sex rough too, just the way he did.

His police training made him love being in command, and that's the way he'd always liked making love as well. He was in charge around her. Whatever way he wanted it, she gave it to him. At first, his short haircut and ivy league looks turned her off, but then she found he had the coke. That made all the difference in the world.

Ben wasn't the kind that liked taking orders, and especially not from the chief—do this, do that, follow the rules but fuck the folks at the Golden Door. To hell with that shit, he thought. He himself dreamed of being the chief of police, so he could give the orders and collect all the kickbacks. Money and power was what Ben Smide wanted. The hell with the fishing lodge. That all seemed too boring to him now. He was an action man. The more action, the better.

So Ben had to make excuses to his biker bitch, when it became his turn to go back on the night shift again. "I have to rendezvous with my suppliers and other customers," he told her.

"Can I go with you?" Vivian asked.

"No."

It would be the end of their relationship if she ever found out he was a cop. He had her fooled, and he wanted to keep it that way. He learned his lesson the last time he gave in to a smile.

John, the forever worry-wart, was always glad to take his share of the profits, but he always warned Ben, "You just be careful."

What the mayor didn't know was that Ben had boosted his selling price to allow skimming an extra twenty off the top, because, as he justified it, he was doing all the work.

I deserve this, Ben was always telling himself. Besides, the coke he and Viv used reduced the bricks' volume which then netted the same dollars for the 50-50 split of the profits. That's your cost of doing business, Ben thought. John never suspected a thing.

Then there was that close call that he would never tell John about either. He'd had a few too many drinks at the biker bar one day, and was higher than a kite flying down the road in a hurry to get home. He needed some sleep before work, but he was pulled over by a state trooper for speeding and weaving. Ben flashed his badge, and that's all it took. Good thing there's such a thing as professional courtesy, Ben thought, because if he'd been arrested and searched, the trooper would have found his pockets stuffed full of packets and cash.

Then there was Viv herself. They were getting it on with fervor one time at her place. It was fantastic lovemaking, Ben thought, but then the inevitable happened.

"Why don't you just move in with me, Benny?" she asked.

"No can do, Viv."

"Why not?"

"I got my business to run."

"You can run it from here."

"I want to buy a bar in Griffith."

"OK, then I'll move in with you!"

For every excuse where he had to say no, Vivian pressed for a yes.

Seeing he was doomed, Ben came up with this off-the-wall lie: "I'm married. But soon to be divorced, Viv. I gotta keep up appearances and stay away from the old lady's lawyer. Otherwise, I'll lose my shirt—and the business. That's why I started coming out this way in the first place."

"Oh," is all she said at first, but then it was, "When is the divorce final?"

"*Ai-yi-yiii!* Can't you leave it alone?" he yelled. Ben was always frustrated with questions he didn't have the answers to. Ultimately, he walked out on her that night, but came back the next.

"Sorry, babe," he apologized. "I just gotta have some space for awhile longer. I'll move in after the deal goes through on that bar I was talking about."

He was thinking about it, too. He had cash stashed away in four different banks now. Things were looking up. John had four bricks left, which he figured should last him quite a while. He also figured Viv would probably dump him anyway as soon as the supply ran out, or he would have to make another score.

He told her he'd ordered a new Harley, which he hadn't. He had the money to buy one, but he didn't like the way she'd become so bossy. Next, he thought, she'd be wanting to get married, or something. His body shuddered at the thought. He knew if he had a bar like the Golden Door, he could have all the bimbos he ever dreamed of. So, if John couldn't get it for him, maybe he should just get it for himself. He figured he could eliminate that one smartass Mickey, and the rest of them would all run.

Ben didn't even like the idea of being partners with the mayor. He thought he was a necessity—his protector. But who needs him though? Ben wondered. The next mayor could be bought, too, he imagined. Actually, Ben feared the mayor—his clout, his friends. The last time the mayor bent down into his deep freeze to retrieve a brick of coke, Ben thought he could easily hit him in the head with a hammer, thrown over the body into the freezer, and taken all the rest of the coke. He thought of that old saying, "He who hesitates is lost."

Ben felt apprehension at not being prepared. He kept overlooking things because they weren't planned. Those thoughts came to him after he saw John bent over. It was lucky for the mayor, though, that Ben didn't have a hammer in his hand.

It could have been all over at an impulse, just like that impulse that made him take Juan out and the impulse that made him take out Slim Jim and friends. That's the way he was trained at the police academy. If they reach for anything and you think your life's in danger, you have the right to use deadly force. What he did to Jennifer, though, was no impulse. That was a plan.

When he saw Susie Q and Miranda take Jennifer inside their apartment, he could only imagine what dyke things were going on in there. What was that dyke bitch teaching his Miranda? She'll be ruined forever, he thought. As he lay in wait there for hours, he stewed and cooked up plan after plan. One of them was: Why don't I just bust on in there and blast away all them fuckin' bitches?

Then, he figured, just eliminate the problem. That's what the mayor would have done. Just eliminate the problem. That's when he hatched the plan. As soon as she comes out, just pull her over like a regular traffic stop and, if nobody's around, plug her. Simple as that. So very, very deadly simple. Then he figured John could get the bar and he could run it. Simple!

After he pulled off his dastardly deed, it occurred to Ben that plans went better when witnesses were eliminated too. There were none that night, but he knew there was one from before that could ruin his plans: the mayor.

John still had a noose around Ben's neck, and he felt like it was getting tighter and tighter all the time. Ben didn't know how John made Donald's murder look like a suicide, but he figured he could do the same thing. But how to come up with a plan slicker than the mayor's? He thought of doing it when John was bending over his open safe. Then he could have all the cash and all the bricks, too. But how to implement such a plan was another matter. Make it look like an accident, he thought. No witnesses, no partners, no noose, and all profits—problem solved.

No, he was only thinking like the mayor. *Bang!* he thought, as he put his finger-pointed hand to his own forehead. He actually thought he felt a little heat, and a pounding as well. He felt a throbbing headache coming on.

Ralph went back to the industrial strip club the next night. He wasn't there to see John, even though he was sitting there in his regular spot. Ralph was there to see the lovely Lovely Linda. He had a change of plans.

Part of his job, he reasoned laughingly, was to let John see him with Linda—show him that he was just a regular john, so the next time he buddies-up next to the mayor, the meeting should produce different results. Play the hard-to-get-next-to routine, Ralph thought, and see what happens. And while playing the waiting game, he might as well get it on with Linda. Perhaps, he figured, she might even be able to help out.

Ralph reasoned that time would tell if Linda herself could qualify to be an operative. She could do a better job on John than me any day of the week, he thought. So when she finally came over and asked, "Hi, Ralphie, you want a ride?"—Ralphie replied, "Yes ma'am!"

"Come with me then, baby."

He followed her right past John and into the back room.

The mayor, taking all this in from his booth, was fuming. He had been hitting on Lovely Linda for two weeks now. All for naught, he figured. He remembered this aggravating little pipsqueak fuck from the other day. This "puke" did say he had lots of cash and that money was no object. Maybe, John thought, the bitch was just holding out for the highest bidder. *Damn! Damn!* He wanted the bitch all to himself. Thump! Thump! He put his hands to his temples again. His headache had returned. He'd passed on going to the doctor's that day because he had felt fine in the morning.

It was that fuckin' pryin' Ralph that aggravated him yesterday, the mayor thought, and now he's aggravating him again. Thump! Thump! Thunder! He reached in his coat pocket for some pain pills. He washed four down with his whiskey.

He couldn't make up his mind if he wanted to stay or go. Not being the type to run from a fight, the mayor decided to stay. He started thinking of ways to fuck up his competition and, like a miracle, he suddenly started feeling better already. So he flagged down a waitress for another round.

Ralph wasn't in the back room long, so John figured all he got was a quickie blow job, but he wondered why she refused him more. He watched Ralph leave with a shit-eating grin, so he decided to proposition the Lovely Linda one more time. When the opportunity arose, he asked her, "How much for a blow job?"

To which she replied, "Those aren't the magic words, and you're not getting anything."

Not giving up so easily, John quickly countered with: "So what's that other guy got that I ain't got?"

Without missing a beat, she said, "Cocaine and manners."

So that's it, he thought, as her info registered and he admired the figure that was walking away from him. Instantly he thought of going home and digging into his stash, but then he thought better of it. He didn't want to get involved with any more druggies, no matter how horny he felt. Might ruin my reputation, he thought. Just find a bitch that wants cash. He was thinking, I got plenty I need to get rid of before the I.R.S. finds it.

Then it was the third straight day of Ralph's little tryst. Again John was watching him from his booth, but this time Ralph didn't look happy. He thought he saw Lovely Linda shake her head no. They were talking about something, but they didn't go into the back room. Aw, too bad, John chuckled to himself. Suddenly he felt like going over to Ralph's table and rubbing it in a little, and he did.

"What happened, buddy? No action today?" John laughed.

Ralph looked at him somewhat surprised. A quick, curt "No" popped out.

"Run out of coke, did ya, Ralphie-boy?"

Actually, it was Lovely Linda who did. Ralph would have bought some more from her, but she claimed she was out. And she does nothing without coke, so she had asked Ralph to get her some instead.

"Yeah, I ran out," he said to the mayor hovering over him.

"Aw, too bad. See ya later!"

John left smiling, and Ralph forgot what he was supposed to be doing. That had been a perfect opportunity to ask John if he knew where he could get some, but Ralph was thinking instead of getting some from his boss. He'd tell him it was for investigative purposes, and he could get all he wanted for free.

Then it dawned on him that he could use the Lovely Linda as an operative, with or without her knowledge or consent. All he would have to do is make sure John sees them carrying on, with the object being: do whatever it takes to get Lovely to service him again. Get her all the coke she wants, and then conveniently dry up until she rebuffs him again. Then, Ralph reasoned, he would have an obvious excuse to go begging the mayor to hook him up with some coke if he had it, or with another dealer. He'd have to put on his best act to fool the mayor, but he just might fall for it this time. One way or another, Ralph was going to find out the extent of John Quibly's knowledge of the drug trade. Meanwhile, he figured, he'd just keep mixing business with pleasure.

Ralph couldn't tell if Linda would be interested in helping catch crooks, or if she was only consumed with her obvious addiction. He didn't fully trust her motivations yet to make her an offer of becoming an operative. He figured he could test her with questions after this case was over. He didn't want to jeopardize his true mission. "Loose lips sink ships," he remembered. It just wasn't worth his taking the risk of being found out.

The next morning Ralph went to his office at the insurance company's corporate headquarters and explained to the C.E.O. what he needed.

"It'll be delivered tonight," he was told. The C.E.O. never touched the stuff himself, but it was always kept at the ready. He knew clandestine operatives were only a phone call away.

Ralph received twenty one-gram packets that night. He thought it was enough to get him started. Then the following night he put his plan into action.

John was in his corner booth, and the Lovely Linda just finished her striptease onstage.

"Hi, Ralphie," she said when she got off the stage and saw him there. "You got anything for me?"

"Yes, ma'am. Sure do!"

"Follow me then, baby."

Knowing John was watching, Ralph flashed him the thumbs-up sign, just to rub it in, just before they disappeared into the back room. The mayor became instantly livid.

"Motherfucker," he cursed under his breath.

The back room was actually four rooms. A narrow short aisle led to four different doors, two adjacent and two across from each other. They were small rooms, only about 8-by-10 foot square. The girls used them whenever they needed to change their outfits, and other things, in a hurry. Inside each room was a single bed and a chair with a night table. A swag lamp was mounted on the ceiling.

Lovely Linda led Ralph to the first room on the right. When she opened the door, Ralph was surprised to see a black girl sitting on the bed in her negligee.

"This is Dee Dee, Ralph. She's a friend of mine," Linda said. "I promised I would get her some coke. She'll pay for it, baby." Linda reached down and started lightly rubbing Ralph's crotch. "And I—I'll make sure Junior here is very, very happy."

"OK," said Ralph. He reached in his jacket pocket and took out two packets of coke. He gave one to Dee Dee, who then gave him a hundred dollar bill and left. Ralph gave the other packet to Linda.

His arousal was complete now. Lovely Linda sat in the chair as Ralph stood. She undid his belt and fly button. She pulled down his zipper and lowered his trousers. Junior was at full attention. She sprinkled his head with the snowy powder and went to town.

Ralph wasn't used to such erotica and was quickly just about to explode, when she paused. She put some coke on a small handheld mirror that was lying on the night table. She made some lines with a credit card and then used a straw to snort one up. Then she handed it all to Ralph, who snorted up the rest. She sprinkled more coke on Junior's head and went crazy on him. Ralph's eyes were rolling into the back of his head. He was ready.

The euphoria of his eruption made his legs shake. His knees were weak as noodles. The smile on his face told a story of pure satisfaction.

Finished then, he slowly pulled up his trousers and thanked Linda for a lovely time. He gave her an extra packet for a tip, and then he waltzed back to his table to gloat. His smile told it all to John, who suddenly had to massage his temples again.

Mick was sitting at the bar watching a ballgame when Jeff Bonds came in and sat next to him. Oh no, Mick thought silently, the last time he was here I had to clean up his vomit.

"Hi, Mick," he said.

"Haven't seen you in awhile, Jeff. Where have you been?"

"Detox."

"I bet that's a lot of fun," Mick said sarcastically.

Debbie came over. "What are you having, Jeff?"

"Nothing. *Er*, wait. How about a glass of water and a cheeseburger?"

Debbie looked puzzled but said, "Coming right up."

When Debbie left, Jeff said, "Sorry I missed Jennifer's funeral. I really liked her."

"That's all right," said Mick. "Don't worry about it."

"Listen, Mick, I came in here to warn you."

"Warn me about what?"

Jeff looked around suspiciously to make sure no one was eavesdropping. Nobody was, but he still lowered his voice to a decibel above a whisper. "When I was in the slammer, I overheard the cops talking about busting every queer and dyke that pulls out of this parking lot, chief's orders."

"Thanks, Jeff, but I already know that. I've got a court date to prove it."

"You wanna know something else?"

"What?"

"Don't tell anybody I told you this, but the night Don committed suicide, he dropped me off at my apartment. He was in good spirits. He was talking about getting the bar back, so it doesn't make sense that he would kill himself. Besides, I could have sworn I saw the mayor following him after I got out. But the thing is, he was in his van. I would have known him for sure if he was in his Caddy. I'm just not sure anymore."

He looked exasperated and worried.

"What were you in jail for, Jeff?" Mick asked.

"Public intoxication. I was just walking home from the bar down the street. They said I was staggering, which I probably was, but what pisses me off is I was busted a long time ago for drinking and driving. Now they won't even let you drink and walk! Anyway, they put me in the interrogation room and start asking me questions about Don. I told 'em I don't know nothing, but they keep hammering away at me, the pricks. Well anyway, they keep me locked up till I sober up, but then I go into seizures from the D.T.'s or something, so they take me to the hospital and all. That's when I get strapped down and hooked up with I.V.'s. I was hurting, man. They wouldn't give me nothing to drink. So I raise a little hell, then they dope me up and all. The next thing I know, I'm in front of some judge and he orders me into the detox center at the jail."

"Wow. I guess it wasn't any fun at all."

"No, it wasn't."

"You want a shot and a beer on me?" Mick wanted to test Jeff to see if he came up with this story just to hustle a drink.

"No. I can't have any more booze. Doc says I've got an enlarged kidney, and I'm well on my way to cirrhosis of the liver. In other words, if I drink I die before my time."

"Then I'll pick up the check for your burger."

"Thanks, Mick, but that ain't necessary."

"Don't worry about it, Jeff. Thanks for the info." Mick figured he was telling the truth, since the mayor himself came in and made him an offer for the bar.

"One more thing, Mick. I think Don was murdered like Jennifer. Don't ever repeat that. If anybody asks me about it, I'll deny it. I don't trust the mob *or* the cops in this town."

Deb came back with the cheeseburger.

"Give me the ticket," Mick said.

"Thanks, Mick," said Jeff.

"No problem. Keep your ears open. If you hear something else, let me know."

"Will do."

Jeff started wolfing down his burger. Mick finished his beer and went to sit in the office. He felt like being alone for awhile. He had some things to think about, like the things Jeff just said. Could it be possible, he wondered, that the mayor wanted the bar back so bad that he would actually kill—or have Jennifer killed—to get it? And would he be next?

CHAPTER 30

Things were moving right along for Ben. He was still seeing Viv, but not as often. He scored with Mary from another rock 'n' roll bar. Now he had two outlets going for his sales and two outlets for his sexual energy. Supplies were getting low and it was time to crack open a new brick, so he called the mayor and made arrangements to meet again at his house that night.

When he got there, he was suddenly more aware of his surroundings. He never did see the wife downstairs, and he didn't have a clue if she was upstairs. The upper garage door was closed, so he couldn't tell if her car was there or not. He gave the mayor his envelope of cash, but he just laid it on the basement bar. Then the mayor made them both drinks—two glasses of whiskey and two bottles of beer for chasers.

Ben was curious enough to ask, "Where's the wife?"

"Don't know and don't care," said the mayor, "as long as she leaves me alone. She might be clubbing with friends. Why?"

"No reason, just wondering. I'm kind of hungry. I thought maybe she could whip us up something."

The mayor started to laugh. "That bitch don't cook for me, and she sure as hell ain't gonna cook for you!"

"Oh, OK. Wanna play some pool?"

"Nah. Let's just get your shit. I'm going to bed early tonight. I haven't been feeling too good lately. You still bein' careful?"

"Yeah, sure."

"Good."

The dastardly deed was still in the back of Ben's mind, but he wasn't ready to implement it yet. He was still trying to figure out a plan. Get him to open the safe first, he thought, then *wham!* Sayonara.

What about blood splatter? Ben wondered. How could he make it look like an accident? Maybe burglary would be better. Can't leave any evidence, he thought. Strangle him then, and hang him from the garage rafters. No, hell. That won't work.

Ben didn't know what to do. Maybe, he thought, it's a bad idea altogether. Maybe try to get the combination to the safe and just burglarize the house while he's at work.

Bang! He stopped in his tracks, thinking of how it could all go wrong.

Ow! Like the mayor, suddenly Ben too felt a headache coming on. He kneaded his temples with the tips of his fingers.

"Yeah," he said. "Let's just get the brick. I'm going to go home, too."

They went to the freezer and John bent down to retrieve a brick. Ben couldn't help but think, bang! Right on the back of his head. Ow! His own head hurt. He wished John would have put that envelope in the safe first, like he did last time. Think of an excuse to stay, Ben thought, then maybe he will put it in there yet.

John handed him the cocaine.

"How about another beer, John?"

"Nah, I'm going to bed."

"OK then. I'll be seeing you."

"You be careful now," the mayor told him as he went out the side door.

On the way home, Ben realized he had to go back and work the night shift. Damn shift schedule, he thought. It was bad for his drug sales. He chuckled to himself, as if he could see it all now: him in his uniform trading coke packets for cash, and seeing the look on his customers' faces.

Or, he thought, he'd just let the girls do it for him again. Maybe just a few packets to satisfy the most desperate druggies. For sure, he would never trust 'em with a whole brick again. He was still kicking himself for that fiasco.

He knew he'd have to make up more excuses to pacify his bimbos, too. Pains in the asses, he thought. Can't live without 'em though. The good thing about the night shift, he thought, is that it's good for spying, or laying in wait. He'd be able to hang by the Golden Door and do his duty with the chief's blessing.

Maybe the opportunity might arise to pop that smartass Mickey fucker, Ben thought. He almost developed a full hard-on just thinking about it. I'll pull him over on a deserted side street this time, Ben imagined, and just see if he mouths off. Then pow! Sayonara, sweetheart. He was smiling as he was driving. *Pow! Pow! Pow!* Simple-simple. Problem solved. To Ben, it almost sounded like a love song.

Ralph knew John didn't come to the club every night. He seemed to switch off nights at random. Sometimes he would even go to his country club and hobnob with the influential mob. Ralph could never gain entrance to the private club anyway. So, because he was now mixing business with pleasure, he was quite satisfied hanging out with Lovely Linda until the mayor came back around. He so enjoyed going into the back room with her—right in front of him. He could imagine steam coming out his ears, like a cartoon character, while he sat in his booth and fumed. Ralph figured once or twice more, and then he would go begging the mayor for coke or a supplier. He felt like he almost had him last time. He was hoping John's greed would make him slip up and offer Ralph a sale—if he had the stuff. Ralph thought of his ace in the hole—his ammo, the picture. But compared with murder and drug charges, it probably wouldn't do much good. The mayor was too savvy to fall apart over a photo. Just the same, Ralph was prepared to push all his buttons. He would do whatever it took to find out all the facts.

What Ralph didn't know was that Susie Q was back in town. She'd had a few tiffs with her mother. The elder Miss Smith kept hounding the younger about what she was doing sitting on her father's lap in her underwear. Susie kept denying it was her father, but her mother knew better. She kept insisting that it was. Nevertheless, Susie just couldn't take it anymore, so she split with the intention of finding out for herself.

CHAPTER 31

Mick went about his business as usual, but he was a bit more leery whenever he pulled out of the parking lot. Jeff's warning had him overly concerned about his own personal safety. He started peering around the parking lot before going to his car.

On this particular day, he leered through his windshield at the seatbelt. That strap is a trap, he thought. The clouds had moved and the sun's glare caused Mick to see a visionary flash of children burning and screaming, trapped in their straps inside a burning vehicle.

He had to step back a moment to think. Who are those murdering mad mother dictators anyway? They're trying to destroy my constitutional rights of self-preservation, Mick thought. He then imagined removing the seatbelt from his car entirely. He felt it was giving him day- and nightmares both. He was sure that just its mere presence alone was affecting his blood pressure and causing these anxiety attacks.

Mick knew he had a lot of house and yard work to do, plus winterize the pool. So he finally jumped in his car and drove home with the intention of accomplishing something.

He started with the pool, draining it a little and then inflating the winter pillow. He threw in the proper chemicals, secured the pillow in the water, and went to the garage for the tarp cover. It was on the shelf with a house brick in the middle, holding it in place. He picked up the brick and held it firmly in his hand. The heft of it flooded his mind with memories as he studied the thing. He tossed it up in the air once and caught it. The heft of the brick—yes, he remembered the feeling of it all. He remembered it rolling off his fingertips. He remembered seeing it twirling through the air and going right through that corporate window.

His head had been bloodied once already by the pigs' billy clubs. For what? He'd asked himself that question over and over through the years, and the answer was always the same: for practicing his constitutional rights and protesting a stupid war. Mick was lucky he escaped the first encounter, but there were so many others who didn't make it. He'd gotten lost in the confusion. The pigs in all their protective gear had a field day busting heads. They hit everything that moved. Then he stumbled upon a construction site. There were so many bricks there, and there were so many corporate windows. He remembered it was a beautiful thing—all those shards of glass sparkling under all the lights.

That's when the pigs got him a second time and beat him even bloodier. They claimed he'd broken every window in a two-block radius. He didn't remember all of it. He was in some kind of a trance at the time. Perhaps that was caused by the first blow to the head he'd suffered at the hands of the pigs.

Of course, that was a long time ago. Mick stood remembering in his garage and tossing and catching the pool-covering weight. The hefty brick in his hand felt comforting to him, but he realized that fighting the Goliath of government was a script for disaster. He might as well commit suicide. He put the brick back on the shelf, and took the tarp out to the pool where he secured it in place.

"Ah," he said aloud when he was finished, "one job done and a hundred more to go." He popped open a beer. By six beers later, he had a finely mowed lawn and a neatly trimmed yard. Satisfied, he went inside and popped a frozen pizza into the oven and settled back to watch a little tube. Mick ate his dinner while watching *The Gladiator* movie on television. It reminded him that some things never change. Men were gambling then over the results of their gladiator sports just like they do now. Football, baseball, basketball—they're all the same gladiator games. Build an arena, he thought, and all the people will come to watch or gamble.

For something as natural as gambling, Mick wondered why it was against the law, partially or completely, in 49 out of the 50 states. Somehow it didn't seem fair to him. Men are going to gamble anyway, he thought. It's impossible to stop it. So, why is it illegal? But as they say, he remembered, life isn't always fair. For sure those gladiators didn't have time to think about being fair, Mick thought. Just look at all those archaic weapons. One mistake, and they're lion's meat.

Mick smiled to himself. He was glad he didn't live in those times. He knew his life now was a lot better, but not necessarily less dangerous. Jeff's warning came again to his mind. He wondered why he was thinking of garbage like this right before bedtime.

He went to the liquor cabinet and made himself a Chivas nightcap. He still had his Moody Blues library in the CD player—soothing music to calm the beast inside. He turned it on, hit the shower, and went to bed.

Dreamy music always calmed him, even though he tossed and turned trying to get comfortable. The last lyric he heard before drifting off to sleep was: "We decide which is right, and which is an illusion."

As he drifted, he saw himself walking barefoot down an ancient Roman cobblestone road. A chariot raced recklessly by, and a glint of horror was in his eyes. Mick kept on walking. He'd been down that same road many times before. He knew every twist and turn. Off in the distance he saw plumes of smoke. Although he wasn't there, the smoke looked like it was coming from the village. Then a family on a hay wagon came barreling at him, and he had to leap out of the way. Before he could get back on the road, another wagon came roaring by, followed by horseback riders.

What's going on here, he wondered. He reached the crest of the hill and saw a column of villagers heading toward him. It looked as if they were deserting the flaming village.

As he stood there gazing at the spectacle, a woman with babe in arms came up to him. "Turn back," she warned.

"Why?" he asked.

"The giant Governor Goliath's loose," she said. "If you don't have silver or gold to pay off the highwaymen, he'll strap man, woman, and child to a hay wagon and burn them alive. Turn back! Save yourself!" With that warning, she was gone down the road.

So, Mick dreamed, the giant Governor Goliath is burning citizens alive again. One would think he'd just get tired of burning people for a little silver and gold. The governor must be gigantic. His appetite is inexhaustible. His peasants run away in fear. He must be stopped, but how?

Mick had no weapons. No spear, armor, or sword. He just had a strap around his robe. The old gladiator saying "nothing to fear but fear itself" came to his mind. He'd seen this Goliath before. He acted invincible, but Mick knew he had a weakness—all dictators do. If he won't let me live in peace, Mick imagined, then he'll have to be destroyed. He felt his gladiator courage ripple his muscles.

He hitched up his robe and felt his waist strap. Then he took a step toward the burning village. Under his foot he felt a loose cobblestone. He picked it up and felt its heft in his hand. Yes, he imagined, this will do the trick. Now Mick felt confident, like a gladiator, ready to do battle for justice.

He started walking again toward the village. As he passed, the fleeing villagers all shouted, "Go back! Turn around!" But he continued on until he found the giant, standing in the middle of the town square. Burning bodies and wagons surrounded him. He was indeed a giant Governor Goliath. He stood two stories tall, monstrously broad in the shoulders with one huge eye in the middle of his ugly forehead.

"Ah-ha!" he roared. "Another victim!" He bellowed at the sight of a man in a robe without silver or gold. But that man had a stone, wrapped in the folded center of a long leather strap and twirling above his head. Then the giant lunged for his victim, but one end of the strap was let go and the stone was flung. It traveled true and hit this Goliath right in his eye. Crystal shards of the eye flew everywhere, and then the giant crashed with a thud—dead as the aim of the stone that hit him.

Although the giant fell on a burning hay wagon full of victims, his body didn't burn. It appeared to vaporize into dust. As the dust settled, it smothered all the fires in the village.

The onlookers high up on the surrounding hills couldn't believe what they witnessed. When the dust finally cleared, the villagers slowly found their way back down to their homes—free men once again.

They tried to reward the gladiator with silver and gold, but he would have none of it. The gladiator did his duty for justice, and he didn't want to carry the extra weight. He was free, light, and limber. He knew that was all he needed, for he had yet another giant to bring down.

Mick was awakened by the cold. He had kicked off his bedcovers during the night. Not only was he cold, his feet were freezing. He looked down at them while he retrieved his blankets. They were all dirty and covered with grass clippings. What the hell? he thought. Then he looked at the floor, and it looked like dirty footprints all over the carpet. He scratched his head, as if that was going to give him the answer to something he couldn't explain. Perhaps he was drunker than he thought and walked out in the yard during the night? His body shuddered, partly because he was cold and partly because he thought maybe he was sleepwalking. He didn't think it was possible, but he couldn't explain the bathrobe he was wearing or why his feet were dirty. He thought surely he'd taken a shower the night before—*didn't he?*

Anyway, he knew for sure it was time for another one. He got up and started the water running. He jumped right in and the heat from the shower warmed him up fast. He felt refreshed, light, and limber.

He started the coffeepot brewing and got out the vacuum to clean up his tracks. He figured he might as well do the den and the rec room carpets, too, while he was at it.

Mick had a good coffee buzz going by the time he finished cleaning the downstairs. He was still reluctant to go upstairs. He would always pause at the bottom of the stairs, as if he were expecting Jennifer to walk down magically from her upstairs bedroom.

He felt her spirit everywhere, but he couldn't explain it to himself nor dare to try explaining it to anyone else. And not just for fear of receiving "you're crazy" comments; no, it was actually a very personal thing. Jennifer had a special energy and it still radiated out from her room. It floated around the house. Mick felt it out in the yard. It was a free energy, much like a young mother's watching over her babe. Mick made no mistake about it, he could *feel* that energy.

With his chores all finished, he figured he'd over to the Golden Door. When he walked into the garage, he paused before getting in his car. Something was missing. He didn't know that for a fact, but it was an eerie feeling just the same. He looked around, and everything seemed to be in its proper place. He shrugged his shoulders and opened the driver's door. There he stood frozen. His seatbelt was gone.

He looked around the garage until he came to the shelf where the pool tarp had been. The brick was gone!

He inspected his car seat again. Yes, it had been professionally removed. No seatbelt? Good! he thought privately. But how could that be? He closed the car door again and went back to inspect the shelf still closer. That's when he noticed footprints on the concrete floor.

He was sleepwalking! Oh my God, he thought. Then it's true. I do!

But then he thought, What did I do with the seatbelt? What did I do with that brick? He started to get worried. He looked in the garbage cans—nothing. He searched around briefly outside. Nada. What happened to them? he mused. He questioned himself, and he worried. Then he started questioning his own sanity. Was he really walking in his sleep? Or, was he walking with *Jennifer?*

CHAPTER 32

There mayor was on the phone in an instant. First, he called big Jake, the chief of police.

"What the fuck is going on with your department?" he roared. "Do I need to remind you that city hall is right next door to your station, and you let some vandal throw a brick *right through my fucking window!?* And you put the word out right now. I want every officer on notice to arrest anybody whose car is missing a seatbelt!"

"What?" Jake was astonished.

"Some motherfucker tied a fucking brick to a seatbelt and fucking flung it through my office window—that's fucking what!!" Click! The mayor was pissed off to say the least. He was "fucking this" and "fucking that" and "motherfucking everybody else." He cursed the janitor for not cleaning up the glass fast enough. He cursed the city's insurance agent for not being able to get a glazier to come to his office that day. He cursed the emergency board-up crew for tracking sawdust on his carpet. And now he had to call back the motherfucking janitor to vacuum again, and then big Jake for not arresting the *motherfucker* yet.

He was fit to be tied all right. The brick had landed on his mahogany desk, making all sorts of nasty dents and scratch marks that he was going to have to look at every day.

He was glad to see the laborers finally leave. He needed a drink. He pulled out his hideaway bar and poured himself a real stiff one, which went down quickly. Then he poured another one for sipping. He was a bundle of nerves and the whiskey seemed to soothe his tormented soul. But he knew he needed more than whiskey to do the job right. He needed sex.

Immediately the mayor planned on doing whatever it took to make sure that happened. He was going out to his club that night.

Ralph was already there when John walked in. He was a regular customer now. Then the mayor spotted Lovely Linda shaking her head no at Ralph's table. It all was happening just as Ralph planned. Now it was do or die time.

He walked over to the mayor's booth, sat down uninvited, and said, "Hey, John. You know where I can score me some cocaine?"

"Nope."

"Aw, come on, man! I can't get any fuckin' without more coke!"

"Too bad then, ain't it."

Damn it all to hell, Ralph thought. Maybe he really doesn't have any then.

"OK, thanks anyway, buddy," he said, and got out of the seat across from the mayor and went back to his own table.

Now what? Ralph thought. The picture! Confront him head-on. What other options do I have? he asked himself.

John, on the other hand, had only one thing on his mind. He'd driven home earlier to get some coke before he came to the club. If this is what that bitch wants, he told himself, then she's gonna have to get it from me. John wasn't about to sell any to Ralph. Ralph was the competition. The mayor just scraped a couple spoonfuls off a brick and put it all in a baggie. Ben would never know, he figured. His scrapings barely made a dent in the brick.

When John got Lovely's attention, he flagged her over.

"I've got some cocaine," he whispered to her.

"You got some coke?" she whispered back.

"Yeah, and I'll give it all to you for a blow job."

"Why, you are a bad boy, aren't you? But those aren't the magic words."

"What magic words?"

"I want to get fucked."

"Oh, yeah sure. OK. I want to get fucked then."

She gave him a big smile. "Then follow me, baby."

John got up and followed Lovely into the back room.

He was so excited, he forgot to give Ralph the thumbs-up—just to rub it in. But Ralph did notice. Why, that son of a bitch does have some coke, he thought.

That's right! Ralph thought again, beginning to get the picture. He slapped himself upside the head. Why would he sell me the stuff so I could bust a nut? He wants it himself!

Now it was Ralph's turn to fume. He felt like leaving, but he knew he had to stay. He thought of a line of questions for "his honor" whenever he finally came out of the back room. Maybe, he thought, I can catch him in a weak moment of gloating.

The Lovely Linda led John to the first room on the right. John was surprised when he saw a black girl there in her negligee.

"This is Dee Dee, John. I promised her I would get her some cocaine. She's a friend of mine. She'll pay for it of course."

"I don't sell the shit," said John. "But there's plenty here for the both of you. You can split it if you like, but I only want to have sex with you. She's gotta take a hike."

"OK," Lovely said.

John took out his baggie and parceled out half to Dee Dee, who happened to have her own empty little baggie. Then she left, saying, "Thank you, Johnny."

Then the Lovely Linda gave the mayor all the satisfaction he could handle.

Well worth the price of admission, John thought. On his way back to his booth, he flashed Ralph the thumbs-up sign that he forgot to give earlier. That insult gave Ralph all the impetus he needed to get right up and follow the mayor to his booth.

"Lovely sure has a way of making a man feel good, *eh*, John?"

"Yeah. She sure does."

"She goes wild over that cocaine, doesn't she?"

"I think you better go sit at your own table now." John didn't like Ralph intruding on his privacy at all. But Ralph wasn't about to be put off so easily this time.

"You can't fool me, John. I know you've got the stuff. I just want to buy some for Lovely."

What he really wanted to do was make a buy, so he could turn the evidence over to the proper authorities in order to get a search warrant for drugs and guns. At this point in time, Ralph was even willing to lie to a grand jury to get his desired result: an indictment.

"Take a hike, Ralph," the mayor said.

"I know you want to keep Lovely for yourself," Ralph countered. "So, OK, I'll make you a deal. You can keep her. I've got another girl on the line."

"I don't give a fuck how many broads you got on the line. I don't sell no shit!" John was feeling another headache coming on, caused by the aggravating little fuck in front of him. He was just about ready to walk out himself, when his ears latched on to a familiar tune.

Ta-dum, ta-dum, ta-dum. "There was a crack in the mirror and a bloodstain on my bed."

John recognized the song immediately, and he shot his gaze unbelievingly at the dance stage. There she was in all her nearly naked glory: his long lost Susie Q.

Ralph wasn't that enthralled and kept right on hammering at deaf ears.

"Aw, come on, John. Let's make a deal. Who can I make a buy from?"

The mayor paid him no mind. Susie Q was back. He fixed his gawk on her every shimmy.

Ta-dum, ta-dum, ta-dum-ditty-dum. "The ways and means to New Orleans. Going down by the river where it's warm and green." Ta-dum, ta-dum. Ralph was getting nowhere fast, except frustrated.

"Come on, John! I've got lots of money. I need *cocaine!*"

Ta-dum, ta-dum-ditty-dum.

"I'm gonna have a drink and walk around," John finally said. "I got lots to think about. Oh, *yeah!*"

The song was over and John was all bug-eyed, as Susie Q came off the stage and started walking over to his booth.

Ralph was preparing to ask another question when his head did a double-take of the approaching figure. Oh no! he thought.

He didn't know what to do. It was suddenly too late to run and hide.

Susie Q was upon them. "Hi, big daddy. What are you doing talking to the cops?"

"What cops? Who? *Him?*" He whirled around to face Ralph. "*You???* Why you dirty motherfucker! I told your ass before—take a *hike!!!*"

John came to his senses immediately. But his fantasy of having sex twice that day just went poof!

"I ain't going anywhere," Ralph snapped back, "until you tell me where you got the coke from!"

"You got some blow, big daddy?"

"No! I don't have nothing!" He gave Ralph the evil eye, and practically spat in his face. "Now you get the fuck otta here!"

"Why? You want to fuck your daughter again?"

Ralph sure knew how to push some buttons. So, he shouldn't have been surprised when John shoved the table right into his chest. The drinks went flying, but otherwise he was unscathed. He did get the message, though, and finally got up out of the booth. He noticed other customers were now staring at them because of the ruckus. Not wanting to attract any more unwanted attention, he left.

"Come, sit on my lap, Susie. I've missed you!"

Susie just stood there staring down at him until finally she said, "Do you know Naomi Smith?"

He didn't answer, but he didn't have to. His facial expression told it all.

Susie reached back and slapped his face as hard as she could.

He barely flinched. He was in a total state of shock. He did indeed know Naomi Smith. His life flashed back to him in an instant.

She was the one that ruined his life with his wife. Naomi refused to get an abortion, when he wanted to further his political career using his wife's clout. The resulting near-scandal forced them both to leave his home town.

Fuckin' bitches—all of 'em, was all the mayor could think about, until his headache returned and started pounding again. *Ow!*

Susie Q walked away. John sat there motionless in his booth. He was trying to recover from the shock. The skeleton in his closet had finally come out to strangle him. He suddenly felt a noose around his neck, and it started to tighten. His head was pounding, pounding, pounding. "Goddamn it!" he cursed out loud.

His hands went to his head to massage his temples. He finally got up from the booth on wobbly legs and managed to stagger outside to his Caddy and drove home. He hoped some rest might help him recover. Ralph, being a naturally vindictive person, went straight to the Gary Times with his photos and story. Not that he thought it would help him solve his case, he just wanted some credulity before going to court to procure his warrant. He wanted drugs or guns and felt positive that the mayor had both in his possession. So what, he thought, if he had to lie about the mayor selling him cocaine. He figured the end would justify the means. The important thing was, the mayor's reputation and credibility would be in ruins because of just one picture.

And the next day, there it was: front page news. "Incestuous Mayor Caught in Scandal." As if the picture of a nearly naked young woman sitting on the lap of a town's chief executive wasn't bad enough, the caption beneath it read: "Mayor John Quibly is shown groping a stripper known as Susie Q, alleged to be his own illegitimate daughter."

The story made Susie an instant star. She was suddenly in demand beyond her wildest dreams. No longer did she have to scrounge for work. Offers came pouring in from every direction.

The mayor's office phone was ringing off the hook. Naturally, he left the office very early, claiming he had a headache. He needed a little sympathy, so he finally did go see his doctor in hopes of getting a strong prescription for both the pain in his head and the jitters in his nerves. It seemed he also needed medicine for all his excuses, such as: "I was ill and not responsible for my actions" or "It was a total invasion of my personal privacy" or "I'm being victimized by blackmail fraud!"

The mayor felt all he needed was to play on sympathy for awhile, until this new news became old news, and then everything would get back to normal in no time. If worse came to worst, he figured he'd just retire at the end of his term. No harm, no foul. He assured himself that it would all blow over soon enough.

He was delirious of course. His wife, for one, wasn't about to let this one blow over. She was at her lawyer's office that very same day.

"Divorce," she told her attorney. "I want a divorce A.S.A.P.! I'll never be able to socialize in this town ever again. I'll be ostracized at the country club. My friends won't talk to me. I want you to press for everything. Take that filthy bastard straight to hell!"

It didn't look good for John on the home front. He had to beg and plead just to sleep in the basement that night. "Fuckin' bitches—all of 'em," he kept mumbling all night long. His wife gave him exactly one week to find another place and move all of his shit out of her house.

And he should have called Ben to pick up the cocaine, but he was too busy.

Ben had gotten the edict the day before to arrest anyone whose car was missing a seatbelt. He had a sneaking suspicion whose that might be, too.

He staked out the Golden Door. Mick's house was just outside the city limits, but he drove by there anyway. He found Mick's car parked at the Golden Door the same day the mayor's picture hit the newspaper.

Ben got out of his cruiser and sneaked up on the parked car. Sure enough, no seatbelt on the driver's side at all. Now all he had to do was wait for the smartass to come out of the bar.

That Ben did, but not near the parking lot this time. He knew the route Mick had to take to drive home, so we waited a couple of blocks down and around the corner. He figured the longer he waited, the better, because that way he'd have more time to drink and less of a chance to pass the breathalyzer test—if he was lucky enough to get one.

So Ben waited in a prime location, between some parked cars at the beginning of what turned into a long, tree-lined road. He snorted his coke as he waited. After a while, bingo! Sure enough, here came Mick's T-bird zipping past his unmarked cruiser and roar off down the road.

Ben was all pumped up and ready for action. He flipped on his flashing lights immediately and ran Mick's car down about a quarter mile into the rural countryside. He pulled Mick over at a perfect spot for an ambush.

He even broke protocol on purpose by not radioing his stop in to the dispatcher.

Mick had seen that unmarked squad before and, as the officer approached his vehicle, he knew he was watching a very familiar figure in his left rearview mirror. The officer carried no ticket book with him, but then suddenly pulled his service revolver out of its holster.

Time to split, Mick figured in a millisecond. He gassed it and spun his tires. He knew instinctively this was no time to fool around. He briefly checked his mirrors to see the cop rushing back to his squad.

Mick knew he couldn't go home, so he made a sharp right and raced toward the expressway.

Ben called into the dispatcher. "In pursuit of speeding Ford Thunderbird, late model, north on Burr." It only took a moment for dispatch to respond: "Calling Gary P.D. End pursuit at I-94."

Mick had a good two-block head-start, and he was flying. He wasn't flying nearly as high as Ben was, but his car was racing at a very high speed. No stopping now, he thought, as he cautiously looked and then blew through his first red light. Other drivers who had seen the squad's emergency lights were pulling over, which gave Mick extra room to maneuver. He had to slam on his brakes to make a quick left onto the freeway. He gunned the engine for all it was worth, and up the ramp he went.

The radio is faster than your car, Mick reminded himself. When he checked his mirrors again, it looked like the cruiser was gaining ground. Then he thought, State troopers have to be around here somewhere. When they join the chase, give up. It might mean a ticket, he thought, but that's better than being executed on a country road.

He was doing about 95 miles per hour now and catching up to a line of trucks. The passing lane was full of other traffic. He flew around the trucks on the right-hand shoulder, but then another truck ahead was exiting on the off ramp. Mick went with the flow. He had no choice. As he slammed on the brakes to avoid the truck, his car fishtailed violently for a second until he regained control.

"Whew!" he breathed. He knew he was lucky to escape hitting the truck. His heart pounded in his chest. He knew he was pumping high octane adrenaline now. His tires screeched again as he spun a real sharp right going onto the frontage road. It was a nearly impossible turn at that speed, but he made it. For a moment he thought he lost the cruiser. No such luck. He was still a block back, but Mick almost expected to be swarmed with troopers by now. Not so.

What Mick didn't know was that dispatch had called off pursuit. But Ben was flying high and he wanted to be a hero. He was racing on a different kind of adrenaline, so he ignored the dispatch calls.

Mick made it back to the expressway at the next interchange. He was hitting on all eight cylinders and pushing a hundred miles per hour. The exits came up fast, and he wanted to get off again. He knew one mistake at that speed spelled *curtains.*

He hit the Indianapolis Boulevard exit like a NASCAR driver. He was going so fast around the curve that his car was scraping the concrete barrier. All kinds of hideous sparks flew from the side of his car, but he made it. His survival skills were at their best.

The cruiser was still behind him. Damn, he thought to himself. Where are the state troopers when you need them? He was headed toward a more heavily traveled area and had to slow down a little. His plan was to make a few more quick right turns and head back to the expressway. The cruiser was gaining ground, but the inevitable happened. Cars were trying to get out of the way of the speeding squad, and Ben had to zig and zag like crazy through all the people driving cautiously. He was afraid of losing Mick, who suddenly made another screeching right turn that Ben tried to copy. His lights were still flashing as he lost control. The squad car bounced and bounded, bottoming out on the concrete curb before slamming into a well-rooted utility pole.

Pow! went the airbag. The explosion knocked him out temporarily. Ben's firm grip on the steering wheel caused his thumbs to break. The seatbelt went taut and the impact pushed the steering column right up against his chest.

The pain in both of his hands is what roused him. Most people don't realize how important the thumb is to a functioning hand, but it was the airbag and seatbelt that saved Ben's life.

People had already begun to gather. The emergency number 911 was called many times on cell phones.

"Get an ambulance!" one caller said.

The newspaper photographer was listening to that emergency band on his radio. He was right down the block. He rushed right over to get pictures of the accident.

The squad car's gas tank had ruptured when it bottomed on the concrete curb. There was a steady drip of gas on the ground where the grass was burning.

The people that were trying to open the car door didn't see it. The door was buckled in such a way that it would take a Jaws Of Life to open it. The window had shattered and a would-be rescuer was leaning in, reaching for the door handle. Ben told him, "I think my thumbs are broken," as he looked at his useless limbs.

Ben was trapped. He tried to unbuckle the seatbelt , but he couldn't. It was too taut. He repeatedly jabbed at it with his fingers, but with every jab came severe pain.

Then the rescuer screamed and backed away from the squad. His pant leg was on fire. A look of horror lit Ben's face when he saw him run away, swatting at his pants.

Now there was a sense of real urgency. Ben tried to jab at the safety belt buckle with his fingers. Pain, pain, pain! He tried to apply just constant pressure against the buckle with body gyrations, but the belt was too taut. He felt the heat of the fire creeping in through the floor jam opening made by the buckled driver's door.

Then Ben saw flames shoot out at him from the air vents on the dashboard. His eyelids singed from the lick of flames. He let out a peculiarly hellish scream mixed with the crackling of fire.

He had to close his eyes as his nostrils filled with the stench of his own hair burning. The top of his head was literally aflame from the hairspray he used. The tops of both ears burned. *Crack, crackle.* He was listening to his hair burn in stereo. The hairs on his arms were singed and in their place he saw boiling blisters. Ben frantically tried to undo the buckle on his safety belt.

His polyester shirt melted on his skin. He felt all the burning, blistering pain. He felt like he was being splashed with boiling oil. The fire was so hot, it started to melt the nylon straps that held him tight in his seat. He screamed and screamed while poking at the buckle.

The plastic air bag which had earlier saved his life was now burning in his face. His eyes were closed from the heat. In between his screams he would suck in the flames that blistered and burned his lungs. As he roasted alive, the last thing he heard on his police radio was, "End the pursuit."

The newspaper photographer was taking pictures of all the action. The fire department had just pulled up when the gas tank exploded. The whole car was engulfed in fire. Flames flickered and danced upon the roof. Other flames seemingly climbed the utility pole. The crowd screamed as the policeman's blackened corpse started to shrink into a hellish-looking skeleton.

The photographer snapped away as the flames reached the transformer atop the pole, and it exploded in a flurry of eerie sparks and buzzes. The crowd retreated in fear, screaming, as the firemen readied their hoses to douse the flames. All the action was caught on film.

As for Mick, he had doubled back to the freeway and was taking the long way home. He thought he saw the squad car leave the road in his rearview mirror. Whatever ended the chase was fine by him, except he didn't want anyone getting hurt. He didn't have time to worry about innocent bystanders during the chase—it was more of an afterthought. At any rate, he was very glad to finally arrive home and pull his car in the garage.

He didn't even think to inspect the damage on the passenger side. He went right inside for the fridge and got himself a beer. He felt like his nerves were still on a knife-edge, and he had to calm them down. For sure, Mick had no idea how truly lucky he was to be alive.

CHAPTER 33

There it was, right there in the picture of Ben's flaming squad car on the front page of the Times. Mick saw it, the mayor saw it, the photographer who took the picture noticed it, and everyone else who had a keen eye also saw it—the image in the photograph. Right there in the flames were two devils dancing on the roof of the squad car.

"Patrolman Dead in Fiery Crash" is how the headline read. The photo caption was headed with: "Public servant dies in the line of duty." Farther down, the accompanying story said, "Officer Smide will be missed. Anyone with information relating to the accident is asked to contact the Griffith Police Department."

Perhaps as a disclaimer, pending litigation, the newspaper had added in to the story: "It was alleged that the officer may have broken police rules or departmental procedures."

Mick, for one, was not going to contact the police department. Somehow, he felt, the cops would twist the truth and hide the facts. He reasoned, If those people truly believed in the Constitution and the freedom it guarantees, all of this could have been avoided.

He actually started to wonder if he should leave the country. The police might trump up some bogus charges, he thought, if they didn't have any evidence to bring other charges in this case. The blue shirts always cover their own, Mick reasoned, and the government is going to want to hang somebody—anybody. The cops don't care as long as their own asses are covered.

Mick was half-expecting the police to come knocking at his door already. Did they get his license number? Maybe not. Did the cop have a video camera? Did the tape burn up in the fire? Had the cop radioed in a description of the car? How accurate could that be? Would it hold up in court? *Court!* That reminded him: his traffic case was coming up in a couple of weeks. He thought it was time to call the lawyer and check on its status.

What Mick didn't know was that Ben never called in his plate number, and the dispatcher instructed him repeatedly to "end the pursuit." The descriptions that were called in left the police with no viable evidence whatsoever. Some of Ben's descriptions were even counterproductive. The police couldn't decide if he was chasing a Ford or a Sunbird, which is a

Pontiac. What was the color? Ben never said. He only stated that it was a late model, which could be anything. One witness said, "They were going so fast, it was all a blur." So actually Mick was off the hook. The police had no leads to go on.

The mayor was a different matter. He was popping pain pills for his headaches and other pills for his anxieties. His fortified walls seemed to be closing in on him. He took the fiery crash news in stride, but now he had to deal with Ben's death. The newspaper from the day before, showing him with Susie Q, lay crumpled up in his wastebasket. But this new picture haunted him. He had it right on his desk.

He saw himself dancing on the roof of Ben's car. He couldn't make out the face of the other devil, but it seemed to be chasing him, prancing after him while poking him with a pitchfork as they went. The photo was not moving, so John kept wondering why they were moving when he looked at it. He shook his head and rubbed his eyes with his hands. Must be they're bloodshot, he thought. He got up and made himself a drink, even though it was still well before noon.

After the first drink, he started to laugh out loud. He looked at the brick and the seatbelt that were on his file cabinet. He started to laugh again. He was thinking, Pretty clever how he tied that slipknot to the brick. He laughed again and make another drink. Back at his desk, he lit a cigar and looked out his new window at the flag pole. He thought, That flag should be flying at half mast for the fallen officer. Then he thought that he really shouldn't be caring that Ben was dead.

"That stupid fuck," he mumbled under his breath. He laughed again. He'd told him to be careful. Ha! Now he knew he had all that cocaine for himself. *Whoopie!* He laughed. So now what was he going to do with it, save it for his retirement in the Cayman Islands?

The mayor started to think again, and bang! His headache came right back. Damn thing! he thought and then laughed it off. He was actually getting used to them. Now he was thinking up a plan, a different plan. After all, he reasoned, he was a professional lying, thieving politician. Surely he could come up with something to milk out a little sympathy.

Sitting in his oversized office chair, he started to look at the flaming squad car picture again. It was a color photo, and he could swear he could feel the heat of the flames lapping at his face. He started sweating a little on his brow. He felt the heat all right. It was so hot he had to turn away and look at the flag flapping in the wind. For some reason, it made him think of the way Susie Q had slapped him. Who cares if I done my daughter? he asked himself, laughing. That comes with the government job—fuck everybody! He started to laugh again. He was laughing at his every thought, like a giddy schoolgirl.

He was slightly disoriented. Wherever he looked, things would pop into his mind that would either give him a headache or make him laugh. Mostly they were things that he didn't want to think about—like that haunting picture. He went back to his bar and fixed himself another drink. Whiskey straight up, he thought. That'll cure me. It always has in the past.

Wanting to get some good thoughts going again, he tried looking out his new window at the flag again. Then he realized why it wasn't flying at half mast. When he had first taken office, he charged the city ten grand for a hundred dollars worth of unneeded machinery. The new mayor pushed for a brand-new state-of-the-art heavy-duty automatic flag raiser.

"Waste of money!" his critics clamored. So, he and his police chief collected garbage on his critics, until they were all forced to leave town. The mayor started to laugh again. He made five grand in kickbacks from that flag-raiser deal alone. But the thing was never programmed to only go halfway up the pole. It either moved the flag all the way up or all the way down. He reasoned now that one would have to kill the power switch to get it to stop at half mast. Well, he thought, since I engineered the project in the first place, I'm just the man to show that fucking janitor how to do the job.

Yes, he'd pocketed a lot of cash off that swindle. He started to laugh again. And now the mayor had to fix the flag, too. Fix the flag to mourn his fallen star, he thought, that's the politically correct thing to do! He was laughing so hard now that he doubled over and had to hold his Goliath belly in place.

He wasn't always such a porker. After his stint in the National Guard, his gut just kept getting fatter and fatter. Then his greed also got bigger and bigger, but that picture in the paper had always haunted him. He was bound and determined not to let this one haunt him too.

Sacrificial lambs must be sacrificed, he reasoned, that's the government's job. Always has been, always will be. That's why he didn't crumple up this particular newspaper picture. This one, he told himself, is going to be stared down no matter how much it moves. He thought he might even frame it. He started to look for places on the wall where he could hang it. He found a spot right over his file cabinet. The brick and seatbelt will have to go, he thought. They belong in the evidence room at the police station anyway.

That's it, he decided. He would fix the flag at half mast, and then give the chief this safety strap evidence and then bitch him out for not catching the motherfucker yet. Bitching out the chief always made the mayor feel better.

He loosened the brick from its seatbelt noose and flung the safety strap over his shoulder. Then he took down the brick. This is damn heavy, he thought, a lot heavier than a normal brick. What'd it take, some kind of Hercules to sling this up here? He immediately resolved, when he would later bitch out the chief, to make sure his people understood they were looking for a very strong man. It took the mayor both hands just to lift it. In fact, it was so heavy he decided not to take it down to the chief at all—just the seatbelt. He struggled mightily to hoist it back on top of the file cabinet.

Find the motherfucker that's missing this safety belt, he imagined telling Jake, and we have our man.

With those thoughts in mind, the mayor went downstairs and outdoors to attend to the flag. Opening the control box on the mechanism, he pushed the *down* button. As soon as the flag was lowered all the way, a cool breeze kicked up and the flag slapped him in the face, knocking the seatbelt off his shoulder. He picked it up and draped it over the same shoulder, only this time putting both his head and arm through the belt so it couldn't fall off again. Then, gathering up the flag in his arms, he saw that the bottom snap-hook was twisted on the hoist cable. He reached over and unhooked it from the bottom eyehole of the flag.

That's when he thought he heard a voice calling for him.

"Come on, big daddy, come on…"

He looked up at the top of the flagpole. The voice seemed to be coming from the eagle at the top. It half sounded to him like Susie Q was calling him from the sky.

Then suddenly an ice-cold gust of wind slapped his face. It slapped him harder than Susie did. He let the flag unfurl and pushed the up button. That flag was now giving him the creeps. He turned to go but was suddenly, violently yanked back. The back of his head thumped against the pole. The hoist's motor, under the added strain, started humming, *"Come on, Johnnnn, Johnnnnnnnn…"*

He felt like he was being choked and pulled upward. Before he realized what was going on, he was standing on his tippy-toes reaching for the control box—but it was now out of reach. He felt a slipknot tighten around his neck and shoulder. It was the safety strap getting tighter and tighter. He had unwittingly reattached the cable snap-hook to the end of the strap and the flag both.

The mayor was choking. He quickly turned around and grabbed the pole. Then he started to shimmy upwards as the automatic raiser pulled his head higher and higher. He kept trying to relieve the tension on the strap. With one arm around the pole and the other one grappling for the snap-hook, he struggled against the strap that was stretching his neck. Farther and farther he had to shimmy up the flagpole, and this was not easy to do for a fat man.

The strap kept pulling him up and the hoist motor kept humming, "Come onnnn, Johnnnnn. Come onnnnnnn Johnnnnnnnnnn…"

He was halfway up the mast before he passed out and lost his grip. Then the fuse blew on the motor and the humming stopped. That didn't stop the icy hand of the wind from slapping his face about. The flag fluttered in the wind as well, occasionally slapping the fat man's face for itself.

The mayor hung there, like a politician's open jaw flapping in the breeze, until the fire department came and got him down.

The news photographer showed up again, snapping away. One fireman said, "Some politicians will do anything to get their picture in the paper." That may have been true, but it wasn't quoted in the printed story.

The reporter wrote it this way: "Under apparent extreme stress, Mayor John Quibly committed suicide yesterday in front of city hall." Farther down, the story read: "Quibly was under investigation for alleged drug sales and for possibly being an accessory to the recent murder of Jennifer Tuttle. It is unknown why he had apparently decided to commit suicide by using an automobile's safety belt. No suicide note has been found, according to police."

Nobody could have been more disappointed than the mayor's wife. She had wanted to make him suffer. She wanted to take his home, his cash, Cadillac, *everything*. Especially because, while he was hanging from the flag pole, the F.B.I. was ransacking her house looking for drugs and guns.

They had the almighty search warrant, but even after they found what they were looking for, they still tore up the house—for practice. It was all possible because the mayor had traded cocaine to F.B.I. agent Dee Dee McCall in return for sex from F.B.I. agent "Lovely" Linda Walker.

Their testimony in front of the standing judge in circuit court sealed John Quibly's fate.

The female agents were originally called in to investigate the drug overdose of a senator's son. That led them to Juan Beamer, a.k.a. the dead drug dealer, and his supplier, Ralph Swanson, who was arrested and charged with illegal delivery of a controlled substance.

Ralph made a phone call to his boss, who made another phone call to a senator. It didn't go around too far before the F.B.I. conveniently lost all the evidence. The tapes, computer files, the dope—everything just seemed to disappear like magic. Ralph was out of jail before bond court even convened.

"Sorry for any inconvenience," the F.B.I. said to him.

Ralph even hooked up again with Lovely to discuss a possible career in the insurance industry. "Pay's triple what you can make as an F.B.I. agent," he told her. "Guaranteed. Plus all the cocaine you want." She jumped on board—and on him, too.

Ralph did have a question for her. "What's with the magic words?"

Linda just said, "There's more than one way to fuck a person, and trading sex for drugs is the same as cash. That's where the mayor fucked up. To top it all off, he *asked* to get fucked!"

"And you were going to do the same thing to me," he smiled.

"That's before I found out who you were. You know, it turns me on when men ask me to fuck them."

"Well," said Ralph, "if that's the case, then I want to get fucked again."

"Then follow me, Ralphie-baby."

Meanwhile, the two black guys pled guilty to a crime they didn't commit in order to escape the death penalty that the prosecutors were pushing for. The F.B.I. knew those guys were innocent of that crime, but they weren't about to share that information with the local cops without a subpoena. Besides, the politicians wanted to close the books on that case for political reasons. They had them dead to rights on possession-with-intent-to-deliver charges anyway. One way or another, those two were going to do hard time.

Mick had his D.U.I. case thrown out of court because the arresting officer was no longer available to testify against him. Of course, that made Mick madder than all get out. He wanted to expose the profiling, the frauds, the lies on the police report. He wanted to protest the legality of the seatbelt law under the Second Amendment, using the argument that there really is only one person in charge of anyone's personal safety—and that is the person him- or herself. He wanted to argue, "No matter how some Jewish Nazi forked-tongue lawyer or judge interprets it, this is the purpose of the Bill of Rights and the United States Constitution. As James Madison once said, 'Protecting freedom takes eternal vigilance.'"

But Mick was denied his glory. He knew he would win his case. No matter how expensive it proved to be, he knew it'd be worth it. He was willing to take his case all the way to the Supreme Court.

A week after Mick's case was thrown out of court, Jeff Bonds came back to the Golden Door. He sat down next to Mick.

"Hey, what's going on, Jeff? You still on the wagon?"

"Nah. I cut out the booze though. I just drink beer now and again. I figure if I can't enjoy my life, I might as well be dead. Listen, the word on the street is that the cops know Smide was chasing you when he wrecked, but the chief called off the hounds. They won't be bothering anybody here no more."

"Thanks for the info, Jeff."

"Hey, whoever did the body work on your car did a nice job. Who painted it?"

"My car was never wrecked, Jeff. I sold it to Debbie a couple weeks ago."

"Oh." Jeff scratched the top of his head, bewildered. "Then I guess I got it wrong."

"Yes, you did," Mick said. "Can I buy you a beer then?"

"No, not today. I gotta run. See ya!"

With that, Jeff left and got into Ralph Swanson's waiting van. "Give me my money, and take this wire off me."

Ralph turned off his recording equipment and said, "He sure is a tough nut to crack."

Jeff agreed.

Without a taped confession, the cops had nothing to go on, and the lawsuit Mick had going against the Town of Griffith was compounding. The pending litigation could take years to settle. Mick felt the best thing for his own personal safety was to take an extended vacation.

As it happened, he was looking through his wallet for his own attorney's business card and came across one he'd received from an interesting woman in Las Vegas. He decided to dare, and placed a call to California.

"Hello, Marie?"

"Yes."

"This is the 'cad' you met in Las Vegas. I promised you I would call if I ever had an interesting story for you. If you can give me a minute of your time, I would like to explain a little of what happened."

As it happened, they talked for half an hour or so before Mick got confirmation that Marie wasn't seeing anybody seriously, and so his question just popped out, "Do you have anything against the idea of adopting a child?"

"No," she answered. "Of course not."

So Mick's idea of taking a California vacation was set in motion. Their conversation was going so smoothly, that he didn't want to have to cut it short; but after an hour he developed hand cramps from holding the phone. He promised to call again tomorrow to resume the chat.

With that settled, the very next day Mick went out and bought himself an R.V. He was planning a long road trip, and the best part was, it isn't against the law not to wear a suicide strap in a recreational vehicle.